G000164732

Edith Courtney, the daughter of a Romany gypsy and a Lancashire woman, has had a varied career, having sold insurance, worked in hotel catering, and been a sub postmistress. Yet writing has always been her main interest. She has had many short stories printed, was on the staff of a Swansea newspaper for some years, has broadcast and had three volumes of autobiography published.

Edith Courtney founded the Swansea & District Writers' Circle of which she is president, and is also a vice-president of the South and Mid Wales Association of Writers. She and her husband live on the border between Swansea and the Gower Peninsula. They have three grown up children and one granddaughter.

Also by Edith Courtney
THE PRICE OF LOVING
and published by Corgi Books

Edith Courtney

Over the Bridge

CORGI BOOKS

OVER THE BRIDGE
A CORGI BOOK 0 552 13204 7

First publication in Great Britain

PRINTING HISTORY
Corgi edition published 1987

Copyright © Edith Courtney 1987

This book is set in 10/11 Mallard

Corgi Books are published by Transworld Publishers
Ltd., 61–63 Uxbridge Road, Ealing, London W5 5SA, in
Australia by Transworld Publishers (Aust.) Pty. Ltd.,
15–23 Helles Avenue, Moorebank, NSW 2170, and in New
Zealand by Transworld Publishers (N.Z.) Ltd., Cnr. Moselle
and Waipareira Avenues, Henderson, Auckland.

Printed and bound in Great Britain by
Cox & Wyman Ltd., Reading, Berks.

To Cecil Trevor Lionel Harding de Courtney

Over the Bridge

CHAPTER ONE

A black cat lay, stretched out, belly down, against the wall, its yellow eyes watching him without interest, and Bertie Hemsworthy thought he had never seen anything so mangy. He hissed at the animal because he had no one else to hiss at, and the early April air was so warm it presaged a hot summer. He dreaded it, along with the foot-slogging his job entailed.

The sudden longing for Elsie Buckley eased and he pushed his trilby to the back of his head. He drew his cigarette case from the inside pocket of his dark jacket and took his time over choosing a cigarette; cork-tipped or plain? He took even longer over lighting up. He cursed his high starched collar, and he cursed Kit for sending the damn things to the Chinese laundry; they came back with edges like tin and were never clean. He wished he could remove his tie and jacket.

The smoke filled his lungs, tangy, and his self-pity fled. The beach was there, in front of him, over the road. Get in there, into the sea and paddle. Roll up your trouser legs, man. Forget insurance. Indulge yourself. Think of Elsie. Go on, think of her, wallow in the past, the happiness, the loving.

He grinned at the cat and clicked his tongue at a mongrel flecking frantically in the middle of the road. The one diseased, the other lousy.

He strode fast but the guilt didn't go away, it stayed with the pining for Elsie. A married man aching for his dead lover, and when he crossed the railway lines and stood on the slipway looking at the Bristol Channel, he

9

knew he wouldn't suddenly become uninhibited, free. He hadn't paddled with Elsie. She had gone alone, laughing, filled with youth and mischief. He certainly wouldn't paddle without her.

He leaned on the rail and watched the crowds, the kiosks, the swings, the bathing-huts, all ready for Easter, and he felt alien to it all. No matter how severe the guilt, no matter the difficulty he had facing himself in the mirror, he still needed Elsie.

He left the slipway quickly, jealous of those able to enjoy life, and ran across the road, swerving around the Bay View Hotel as if he had forgotten something and was rushing back to get it, and there was the yellow shop window, the sun catching it at an angle.

The masses of flowers were reflected in the backdrop of mirrors. A sudden glory of gold. Freesias in a red bucket near the doorway, pots of yellow chrysanthemums against the red tiling of the wall beneath the window.

Bertie stopped running and stood panting, his face glossy with the beginnings of perspiration. He had given Elsie flowers for her eighteenth birthday.

Now he went into the shop where the gold of the sun didn't reach and the smell was like that of Elsie's funeral.

'Yes sir?' The woman was grey-haired, grey-faced.

'Flowers,' Bertie said, not quite sure why he was in there. 'A bouquet. All yellow and gold.'

He was glad Kit wasn't grey. Grey wouldn't suit her; her eyes were too dark, like amber beads.

Thoughts of his wife made him want Elsie more. God forgive him, he needed Elsie. Had needed her for hours. Days. Weeks.

'With fern, sir?'

'No. Just yellow and gold.'

He came from the shop with the flowers cradled against him like a baby, not sure what he planned to do, yet already ashamed of doing it. She had been dead over a month and he still wanted to cry. He walked back to the junction and knew he was going to catch the electric train. He stood in the queue with a little smile on his high cheek boned face. It was a sort of happiness, deciding to take flowers to Elsie, a temporary transcending into a world of no-concern.

Then it came, crashing into his consciousness. 'Daddy! Daddy!'

The cries were unmistakable and his senses awakened to it. No other Daddy could answer that particular call. 'Mind the road!' he yelled, and a Morris Cowley, resplendent in black and chrome with the hood back, tooted vulgarly at his daughters as they charged towards him, bare feet thumping like sand-smothered pistons, arms waving, mouths agape with laughter and the anxiety to claim his attention.

They unslung their shoes from around their necks, fiddling with the laces that tied them, then Emma gripped his hand, almost swinging on it, beaming up at him, her dark brown fringe on end where salt-wet fingers had forced it. 'Where're you going, Dad?'

'To Timbuctoo.' He was vexed they had appeared, spoiling his self-indulgent moments.

Both girls giggled. Linda, at fourteen, more shy of him. 'We were down the beach.'

'Oh aye.' As if they could have been anywhere else in that state.

'We saw you and we ran to catch you. Can we come too? Can we?'

He lowered the bouquet, holding it as one holds a bucket, and Linda said in sober judgement, 'You're going to the cemetery.'

'Yes,' he agreed, and his gaze dared her to run home and tell Kit. 'No one has been there since the funeral.' His voice became that of a father, not a lover; glad his need of Elsie had suddenly become less.

Emma tugged his arm. 'We can come too.'

Your mother will be expecting you.'

'Nup,' said Emma, and her eyes gleamed up at him with seven-year-old cunning. 'She's gone to town. Shopping.'

'If you don't mind,' Bertie said tolerantly, 'I would prefer to go alone,' and he became aware of other people's smiles, the amusement his daughters were giving the rest of the queue.

Linda snuggled to him like a cat needing a scratch and murmured, 'We won't tell,' and looked at his shoulder, not at him.

Others joined the queue, laughing, ready for this early summer, buckets and spades, babies, celluloid windmills. The electric train rattled along the rails that ran parallel with the main line, its antenna hissing on the overhead wires, and Linda rubbed her brow against his lapel. She was going to be as tall as Kit. And as thin. Then she went ahead of him, onto the train, finding her own seat, unconsciously independent. He and Emma scrambled to be near her and he struggled with the mass of flowers, feeling a bit of an ass now as he dug his hand into his trouser pocket, seeking money.

The two girls quickly put on their shoes and socks, swaying with the movement of the train, concentrating, gasping, flicking wet sand everywhere, then Linda leaned across the aisle. 'Shall I hold them?' She took the bouquet and held it against her face, smelling into it. 'Whooff!' she exclaimed, and jerked the flowers away. 'They pong!' Bertie turned from her, smiling down at the expectant face of Emma. She was uncritical, eager for the day, and he told himself he didn't care whether Linda liked the flowers or not; they weren't for her, they were for Elsie, who was buried under six feet of reddish clay-like earth.

The train clattered and rocked, seemingly too near the grey stone wall that sheltered it from the curving beach and, when the wall came to an end, he could see the lace edging of the shallow waves. It was like the trimming on Elsie's satin French knickers, and his longing for her came sweeping back in a swirl that caught from spine to groin. He thought he could smell Phul-Nana, her musk-like perfume, see the gentle curve of her cheek

12

with its covering of pink powder, its rose-coloured rouge and its heart-shaped mouth that laughed and teased and seduced . . .

He thrust a hand across his lips, stifling a groan, and Linda shot a look at him, her eyes large, luminous, the same amber as her mother's.

She leaned to him, the flowers clasped on her lap, hiding her bare knees beneath the hem of her grey pleated skirt. 'Dad.' It was a whisper; they were confederates. 'Loving isn't nice, is it?'

'How would you know?' He laughed sideways at her, and she blushed and moved back.

The train stopped and he idly watched people get off and others get on, then it rumbled away again, picking up speed that seemed too fast for it, swaying and swerving on the single track, racing.

He and the girls left it at Oystermouth, an uphill walk before them, and Bertie wished he hadn't come, hadn't bought the flowers in the first place.

Emma skipped happily. 'I can smell it! The ozone!' and Linda glanced at her father, wanting to be the adult, on his side.

Seaweed lay in dark blobs all along the tidemark and Bertie said, 'A healthy smell. Breathe in deeply. There's a good kid. It'll cure anything,' but his mind was saying, 'It didn't cure Elsie.'

The climb was steep, the ruins of the castle on their right, then the pavement eased and they were on the crest of the hill, too warm, glad of the breeze that fluttered about them. They turned into the cemetery grounds, silent now, up the long, gently sloping drive, where trees sheltered peace with sorrow, and Bertie slowed at the foot of the flight of white stone steps. They were surrounded by marble slabs, marble and granite crosses, marble angels, and he was painfully aware that Elsie was at the top, waiting for him. He could sense her anticipation. Plump knees in glossy art silk stockings. Brazen, adorable hussy.

Then he was following the girls, seeking the mound that was Elsie.

When they found it he sat on the kerbstone of someone else's black marble surround, his shoulders slumped. So that was Elsie. That oblong of earth lumps where grass was already showing through, and the lot was beginning to sink.

Linda sat beside him, still clutching the bouquet, her gaze on the blue vastness of sky, then turning to look down, at the view below them; the sea, the Devon hills. She took a deep fill of air and made a little sad sound. 'It's nice up here. But awfully lonely.'

Bertie bestirred himself enough to nod. Nice up here. But lonely. Cold in winter. Bitter when the wind howled from the sea.

Emma began galloping around the grave, slapping her knees as they rose to her waist, and Bertie didn't stop her. A large crow cackled echoingly in the budding branches of a whitebeam, and Linda said confidentially, 'Daddy?'

'Yes?'

She went pink, averted her eyes and stuttered slightly. 'If a boy kisses you - ' then it came with a rush, an anxiety to be reassured. 'Does it mean he loves you?'

'Could be?' Bertie waited, wishing he wasn't so edgy. His hackles rose easily. What the hell was a school kid asking questions like this for?

She stretched out her legs and pulled up her white socks. 'And, Daddy?'

'Yes?'

'If a boy loves you. Does it mean you get married and have babies?'

'Usually.' Bertie tried to smile, to stop his mouth going tight, to look as if he wasn't ready to scold, but Linda knew he didn't understand. She sighed deeply and stood up, handing him the flowers. 'I'll get some pots to put them in. The tap is over there. I saw it. Emma? You coming to help?'

They ran, gangling schoolgirls with all their lives

14

before them, and he wondered if they would make the same mistake; marry the wrong person. Believe any mate was better than no mate at all?

They came back laughing, Emma's fingers dripping water before her. 'I lost my hanky!'

'Jam-jars,' Linda said, matter of fact. 'They were up there. I pinched them.' She bent carefully, lowering the water-filled jam-jars to the earth, and Bertie said, 'Don't bend like that, Linda. You're showing all your bottom.'

'I know,' she returned, quietly rebellious, and bent still further. 'Tommy likes it.'

There was silence, as if the breeze had died and the crow had fallen from its branch, then Bertie said deliberately, 'It would be better if you didn't see him.'

She grunted, poking stems into jars, finding them too long and snapping them, then inserting them again. 'Pardon?'

'You heard.'

She tore the lower leaves off a chrysanthemum and flicked them away. 'If I understood you, Daddy, I would not have said pardon?'

'Don't play silly fellers with me, Linda. You know damn well what I told you.'

She stood up, staring down at him. 'But Daddy! He lives with us!'

'Not any more, he doesn't. He's in the army now. That is where he lives and that is where he can stay. The Buckleys have nothing more to do with us. Compris?'

For a moment Linda's eyes sparked red flecks like her mother's, then she lowered the lids to hide the answering fury in them. 'Why are we here then? At Elsie Buckley's graveside, if they're nothing to do with us any more?'

Bertie wagged a long forefinger, controlling his anger and guilt. 'I am warning you, young woman. If I catch you and Tommy together, there'll be one hell of a row.' He gazed up at her as she stood against the sky, her nostrils slightly distended.

'Daddy.' Her fists were clenched at her sides. 'I am

fourteen. I will be leaving school in July. I am old enough to run my own life.'

'It's because you are fourteen, and not old enough to run your own life that I am warning you to keep away from Tommy Buckley.'

'I love him!' It was a frantic squeal. 'I'm going to marry him!'

Bertie jerked to his feet and Linda recoiled as if she expected a blow. Emma put her hands against her ears and screamed, 'Don't fight! Please don't fight again!'

Bertie walked away, hating himself for the morass, hurt because it was necessary to deny Tommy while his sister lay beneath the soil, listening. His head was drumming. The tension was in his stomach again.

'Daddy! The flowers!' Linda was in despair.

'You see to them.' Why in hell had he bought them?

'Daddy!' she yelled, as he strode on, winding between the angels and marble open books. 'I hate you! Hate you!' She stood, legs apart, stolid, the yellow and gold of the chrysanthemums spread about her feet. 'Just like Mummy hates you!'

He looked back, demoralised, but having to prove his authority. 'Linda. Put those flowers down and come here.'

'No!'

'Linda?'

'No. Not until I've done the flowers. They're for Elsie. I want her to have them.' Emma hurried to her, scrambling, and took her hand; they were a picture of solidarity against their father. Linda's voice became more steady. It carried on the consecrated air. 'You didn't think of me, did you? Nor of Emma. You didn't think we loved her too? You only think of yourself –'

He stood at the top of the steps and waited for them. Linda didn't bend now, she crouched, arranging the flowers, obviously crying, sending darting looks towards him, and the hurt in him grew worse. She was right. He hadn't thought of her and Emma – of anyone but himself – loving Elsie.

16

He leaned his hip against the rail at the top of the steps and stared at his daughters, realising he had never truly desired their mother. Kit had been handy. He had married and assumed nature would do the rest.

And nature hadn't.

The two girls came to him, distrusting but obeying, and Bertie wondered if any man hated himself as much as he did. Maybe it was as well Elsie had sold his son to Maggie and John. Maybe the boy would be happier halfway up a mountain in Port Talbot with such people.

And, while Bertie went down the steps with his daughters, Maggie Davies was singing lustily as she pegged nappies on the line. 'Wonderful world. Wonderful world. Wonderful world of lu-u-uv,' and John, digging a hole for the new lavatory, laughed as he sweated and panted and echoed, 'Wonderful world of lu-u-uv.'

They stopped work for a few moments, singing at each other over the fifty yards of cabbages, beansticks and potatoes. Below them the tiny town of Port Talbot sighed in the early warmth, while the Bristol Channel curled and rolled about its bay.

When the clothes line was laden Maggie propped its centre with the long forked pole, put her hands on her splendid hips and watched John's Welsh flannel shirt and her voluminous white nightie billow out against the sky.

She lifted the empty basket and carried it against her, as she carried her wares around the houses on other days. She strolled to the baby in the high black pram, and readjusted the beige canopy with its long silk fringe. 'Mamgi's cariad,' she breathed over him, and the three-month-old kicked with delight. Maggie bent lower, sniffing the scent of Johnson's baby powder, of Lux soap, and the most expensive silks and satins she could buy without breaking too far into her cache of gold sovereigns. She tweaked the baby's chin, murmuring her endearments so low she was almost growling, adoring. She put the tip of her little finger through the bubbles of the soft pink lips and felt along the lower gum. 'Oh

17

darro, boyo.' She enjoyed the teasing. 'No teeth yet! No peggies!'

The baby grimaced, tasting the residue of ammonia on her skin, and she frowned. 'It's only Mamgi's finger.' She stood up straight, her body uncorseted here on the mountainside, soft, preparing to ooze when she grew older.

She sauntered down the cinder path, her long black skirt full, approved by the chapel, and protected by a white apron. She spoke to John in Welsh. 'Thought you'd be done by now.' He was still digging, bent low so the shovel hit the bottom of the hole.

'This'll do,' he replied. 'Help me bring it over? Will you?'

She put the basket down and he stood the shovel against the garden wall, then they wandered to the small shack ten yards away. They knew the drill. There was no spare breath to talk.

On opposite sides they each caught the jutting wooden arms, then they carried the whole lavatory in the same manner as a sedan chair.

'I like to sit facing the sun,' John said.

'No, not this time of year,' Maggie gasped. 'Be too hot, I think.' They planted their burden and surveyed it. 'Turn it round,' Maggie said, so we can sit with the door open. Get a bit more air in. Those looking up from town can't see us round the other way.'

So they turned the lavatory around, their feet plodding around the hole, and they visualised the next sessions of sitting there, which patterns they would see in the stars at night, and which way the wind would come to douse the candle in its glass-sided lantern.

They took their time, the washing blowing, the baby gurgling.

'There,' Maggie breathed, and pushed back a strand of her dyed black hair. The lavatory was resited. Neatly cut squares of newspaper dangled from new white string on a hook inside the door. 'You know –' she said

18

thoughtfully, as John took up the spade and filled in the old hole, 'it can't be healthy. That sort of lavatory,' and the heavy brown earth fell on the lime-smothered used newspaper squares.

'Gives us good veg.'

'I'd like a proper lavatory. With a cistern and a chain to pull. I don't want the baby using this.'

John trod the earth down, his long booted feet stomping. 'Won't be long now, I should think. Once the new chairman's in and the Old Man's retired. Carruthers knows, and he said they'll shift Bertie. Be an opening for me then.' He leaned on the shovel. 'Did you tell Bertie we're having the christening in the Church of England special for him?' and when she nodded, 'He can't be Welsh, mind. Not with a name like Bertie Hemsworthy.'

Maggies' fleshy shoulders in the black cotton blouse seemed to fold in half as she hugged his words. 'Ooo John. Imagine me a manager's wife.'

He bent, his earth-stained fingers removing a stone, flinging it over the wall so it rolled downhill. 'Imagine me.' He laughed deeply. 'A manager. Buy the house off them, I think, Mag. You and me and Buck behind that brass plate they got. Our address. Three hundred Prince Edward Road. Posh, heh?'

He stood tall, loose-jointed, with heavy, clumsy hands and feet, screwing up his eyes to look at her, then over the township, to the sea and the Devon hills. 'We've earned it, Mag. He's been foolish, but we've earned it.'

They stood together, her arms about his waist, and Maggie whispered, 'There's lucky we are, John.'

They came up the path together, he with the shovel on his shoulder, she with the clothes basket at her hip, and they stopped at the pram to admire.

Maggie said, 'I do feel sorry for Bertie, mind. To lose Elsie Buckley like that, and then for us to take the baby.'

'Bought,' John retorted. 'Not take. Bought. Straight-forward and honest. With a solicitor. If Bertie had been as honest, put his name on the birth certificate, it

19

couldn't have happened, now could it? Best to be God-fearing, Mag.'

'Yes,' said Maggie, and put her finger in the baby's grasp. 'Soon have a name now,' she cooed at her purchased son. 'Tomorrow God will give you a name. Take you into his keeping then, cariad. Watch over you all your life. But in Church of England, mind.' She shook her finger gently so the tiny fist shook with it, and the baby legs threshed with renewed interest. 'I am happy, John, to be given everything like this. Everything.'

John turned on the tap at the base of the water butt on the bench beside the lean-to, and let the water run over the shovel. 'John!' Maggie yelped. 'Don't you use that! If there's a heat wave this summer we'll need every drop,' and he turned the tap off instantly.

'Thought it better,' he said quietly, 'than using a patch of grass, now we've got a baby,' and Maggie agreed quickly, repentant.

The following day the new lavatory stood, whitewashed and smelling of Lysol, awaiting the influx of guests.

They met at the edge of Port Talbot, on the steps of the church, its aged and ornate frontage looking softly golden in the sunlight.

Bertie grumbled as he travelled. 'Damn silly day. No blasted trains. Must think we're made of money. Taxi all this way.'

'You needn't pay for it,' Kit said calmly, holding the skirt of her cream-coloured coat closer to her. 'Maggie has savings.'

'She knows damn well what she can do with her savings.'

'Come to think of it, they must be doing all right. You built his round up for him. It's one of our biggest now –'

'Yes, yes. Heard it all before. And there's us scrimping along on tuppence ha'penny, and it's all my fault.'

'I didn't say that. Stop being nasty. The driver will hear. Emma. Put your face straight. It'll stick like that one day.'

'I've got a loose tooth.'

20

'Emma! Don't answer your mother back, and you, Linda, stop sulking.'

The taxi stopped and they got out. Kit smiled, waved to those already on the steps, and shepherded the girls before her, the ribbons on their straw boaters wafting. Bertie saluted politely, found his wallet and passed a note to the driver with great cordiality. 'It's all right.' He was the manager, the man in charge, 'Keep the change,' then he was sprinting across the pavement, up the steps, into the mixture of Sunday best navy blue suits and special occasion pastel-coloured dresses and hats.

Maggie was in the new brown shot-silk costume she had bought in Lewis Lewis; its neck so low her great bosom had room to breathe, to peep out for the sly delighted glances of men. Her thick hair was redyed black, given the texture of wool, but her eyes sparkled and the baby, dripping with white lace and white satin, lay in her right arm, its face squashed against that soft breast.

'Ooo Kit, there's nice you look. So slim. Makes me feel all fat and ugly.'

John's left arm slid about her corseted waist and squeezed a warning. He whispered, 'You're as good as she is, if not better,' while his mouth gave its crooked smile around its long misshapen teeth, and his great right hand took Bertie's in a grasp of welcome.

'Nice to see you, guv'nor. Glad you could come.'

'Nice to be able to join you, John.' But it wasn't. He hated it. His baby. His son. The only son he would ever have, and they had him. He tried to blank his mind to the past, to concentrate on his employee standing there like he owned the bloody town, not just a glorified shepherd's hut halfway up the mountain. And he hated himself more. Wondered where the real Bertie had gone, and whether he would ever come back.

They filed into the church, the children awed by the atmosphere of it, the aisle's dark red carpeting, the sun streaming brilliant colours through the stained-glass

21

windows, the minister in snow-white surplice, soft clean hands clasped before him.

Bertie was a godfather.

It sickened him. He stood with the service printed on a card in his right hand, his left in his trouser pocket, casual, charming, interested in everyone, tall and good-looking, waiting for the service to begin. When it did he wanted to weep again, and the dreadful familiar feeling swept through him. Elsie should be here. This was Elsie's child. She had been Catholic. The child should be Catholic. He had betrayed her again.

'. . . Grant that this child, now to be baptised therein, may receive the fulness of thy grace, and ever remain in the number of thy faithful and elect children; through Jesus Christ our Lord. Amen . . . Name this child.'

'Buck.' A whisper.

The minister making sure. 'Buck? Just Buck?'

'Just Buck,' a lot of nodding, silent smiling, agreeing.

Just Buck, Bertie thought, he should be grateful to John and Maggie; they'll love the child. Love him enough to call him Buck; short for Buckley.

He wanted to get out of here, escape. Everyone must know it's his kid. Must know. Gossip. Kit said they gossip, and Maggie more than most.

'Our Father, which art in heaven . . .' He felt Kit touching him, her fingers light on his back, and he smiled at her, disliking the pity in her eyes, so she sensed it and took her hand away, her face tensing.

She looked at the baby in the minister's arms, the Buckley forehead wet with holy water, and she tried to understand, while her inside lurched with renewed disgust. How could he? How could any man behave as Bertie had done? With a young girl? But there, she had been a tart.

Everyone was smiling when they returned to the street, to the fresh air of a silent day. The minister stood in the doorway shaking everyone's hand as they passed him, murmuring words people instantly forgot.

Maggie had the baby, surrounded by cooing females, tweaking the little cheeks, pressing the tiny nose, laughing because the face began to screw up, ready to scream. 'Bertie.' She came to him. 'Would you like to hold your godchild?'

'No!' He was brusque, suffocating the urge to clutch his son and escape, run with him, keep him for always. 'He's nothing to do with me now. He's yours.'

Maggie's smile whipped away, her eyes glaring an insult, then she smiled at everyone else, seeking someone to coo over her baby.

Linda and Emma stood together beside their mother, serious faces, clean white socks held up with new white elastic garters, and best black patent leather ankle-strap shoes.

People strolled away in groups, talking more avidly as the church was left behind, and Bertie said quietly, 'Kit, let's get out of this. Let's get home. I need a cup of tea.'

'Sssh,' Kit said, and walked tall, coldly beautifully elegant, a chocolate-brown straw hat with a wide brim straight on top of her head, the knob of the gilt pin shining in the sunlight. 'They'll think it funny if we go now.'

'Why should they? I'm John's boss, not –' but he couldn't say it because, for ever and ever, he would remain Buck's father.

'You have to be there,' Kit said, and, when the track began at the foot of the mountain, he glanced back to make sure the girls were following. Then he gripped Kit's elbow and, together, they climbed with the other guests to where the christening cake stood, with three bottles of Maggie's home-made parsnip wine in the centre of the white-clothed kitchen table; where the fat black cat sat on the windowsill beside the orange Busy Lizzie.

Maggie handed the baby to a cooing matron in frilled front and cameo brooch, and Kit tried to quell the jealousy she was experiencing. That child was Bertie's;

23

a bastard maybe, but still Bertie's, and she, Kit, had been there, at the birth in her own back bedroom; she had nursed him, bathed him, cuddled him, come to love him, considered keeping him. She had even been with Elsie when they bought that pram. Bertie paid for it with new pound notes.

Bertie paid for everything. Retribution.

'And so –' Maggie was telling everyone, '– my great-grandfather built this house. Brought every slate and every stone, he did, from the quarry himself.'

'Must have been a road up in them days,' said Sion's mother from the shop.

'No. The track was wider,' Maggie said. 'But it wasn't a road. Never been a road. Just wide enough for the pony and trap.'

'Horse and cart,' said John, and poured Maggie another glass of parsnip wine.

Bertie said, 'You could do with a road there now,' and stopped because he was going to say, 'for the baby's sake' and that wouldn't be wise, not with so many people ready to put two and two together.

'All right,' Maggie snapped, 'I suppose we are out of the way up here, but the air is fresh and healthy. We don't want old cars and things coming up, do we John?'

'No,' said John, because he wasn't expecting to stay there much longer.

'I can tell you this,' Maggie insisted. 'Another sandwich, Kit? Ham, mind. He did it all himself. It was only a shepherd's hut. In the beginning.'

People laughed or agreed, or looked awed and impressed; others wandered in or wandered out, gazing at the view, exclaiming at the texture of the air, while Bertie remained elegantly charming, with them, yet separate.

When he and his family took their leave a crowd gathered at the gate to wave them away, and they walked slowly so none would guess they were uncomfortable, unhappy and anxious to go.

That night Bertie stretched in bed, yawned and said,

'Tomorrow starts another week,' and wondered how he kept surviving the days.

'Yes,' Kit said, and stood near the basket chair to undress, her hair loosened from its plaits, shining under the pink-shaded electric bulb.

'Wonder if there'll be a letter,' he said, watching her, noticing the length of her legs, the slight swell of her belly.

She nodded 'It's over a month now since Carruthers was here, and he seemed to be in the know when he said they'd shove us off to Merseyside.'

Bertie didn't answer, and Kit slammed on, 'All because you gave Miss Buckley a job.'

Bertie's lips twitched, his thoughts back to Elsie. 'She was a blighter, wasn't she?'

'She landed us in this mess. She was a thief.' Kit lifted her dress over her head.

'Not a thief.' He felt uncomfortable now, talking of Elsie, wanting to make love, seeing Kit get undressed. 'More sinned against than sinning.'

'Tripe!' said Kit. 'All I know is that the waiting is wearing me out. Will we be here for Christmas or won't we? Will you have a job much longer or won't you? They know quite well they have you over a barrel.'

As she talked she became more cross and the colour rose in her cheeks. Bertie saw the light flicker to and fro on the glossiness of her white satin petticoat. She was lithe, sensuous, and, at the back of his mind, he told himself it was true he would never be unfaithful again. He was too old, and there would never be another Elsie.

Kit hung her dress in the wardrobe, then lifted off her petticoat so it made little frou-frouing sounds, causing goosepimples on his shins. She stood in shimmering white silk bloomers that bagged above her knees, and a white knitted silk vest that had long ribbon straps, barely hiding her small flattened breasts.

She said, 'We'll just have to wait and see, I suppose,' and shook out her lilac-coloured chiffon nightie. She dropped it over her head and took the vest off under it, then the bloomers, shy of him, aware of his attention. She said, 'I don't like you looking at me like that.'

'Like what?' He felt a sort of power, as if he was holding a torch, mesmerising a rabbit. He said, 'Do you realise I have never seen you naked?'

'You have. In bed.'

'In the dark. Take your nightie off now.'

She blushed.

'Go on,' he said. 'I dare you. I'm your husband and you promised to obey.'

'Stop it.'

'Stop what?'

'Being filthy.'

He laughed wryly, concentrating on her, wondering how she could be married to him, give birth to his daughters, yet never stand naked before him.

She said, to ease her own embarrassment, 'When Henderson-Hobbs becomes chairman things will begin to move. Our feet might not touch the ground.'

'Are you losing weight?'

'No. Why?'

'You look all bones and no flesh.'

She turned her back to him and saw herself in the dressing-table mirror. She was skinny, straight up and down, no matter which way she stood, but it didn't matter, she didn't want to be attractive, didn't want to be desired. There were prostitutes for that. Let them get on with it.

She delayed getting into bed, not wanting the close-ness of his body yet in need of his warmth, his life energy. She flitted to her underclothes, folding them, rearranging the hair brush on the dressing-table.

Bertie said, 'Are you coming into bed or not?'

'Or not,' she replied, then was sorry because she had nagged him too much and today had been a bitter day. She ran to the switch near the door and put out the light. In the darkness, she paused, like a diver before heading into cold water, then she ran and sprang into bed, laughing in an effort to dispel the look she had seen in his eyes, and the mixture of wanting and not wanting within her. Her feet reached down, clamping on his, and her head flopped to the pillow. 'Aaah,' she sighed, and Bertie rearranged the bedclothes about her.

'You're like a flaming elephant.'

'Praise. Praise,' Kit scorned and knew her heart was leaden, still cut and bruised and unforgiving, so she cuddled up to him so he wouldn't know, and she put her hand on his chest inside his pyjama jacket, and played with the few dark hairs that curled there.

He put one hand behind his head, looking into the shock of blackness, watching it ease to grey as his eyes became accustomed to it.

A faint throbbing started in his groin, and a sickness in his throat. He wanted Elsie, the feel of her flesh beneath his hands, the musky, hungry passion of her.

Kit was talking softly, and, all the time, her fingers played, while her breath against his shoulder scorched through the striped cloth of his jacket and into his skin.

'Kit –' He didn't want Kit, but he needed succour, forgiveness. 'Kit –'

'Oh no! Not tonight, Bertie,' and she drew her fingers away from his chest, her body tightening.

'For God's sake!' He wished the words hadn't gasped from him; he mustn't quarrel with her. 'It's human nature.'

'I know.'

She clenched her hands across her, as if to guard herself, and she closed her eyes, hoping he would let her sleep. He turned to face her and she couldn't keep the wobble from her voice.

'Bertie, leave me alone.'

His hand moved to her.

'Bertie.' It was an agonised whisper. 'I want to sleep.'

The sound of his breathing filled the room and Kit bit her lip.

27

He leaned up on his elbow, over her, his mouth reaching for hers. She pouted and accepted his kiss, but gave nothing in return. 'Bertie. I'm tired.'

'So am I, Kit. Tired of having a wife who acts like a housekeeper. In fact a housekeeper might be more accommodating.'

'You got yourself a secretary against my wishes, so get yourself a housekeeper. I don't care.'

'I can't afford one. I'm keeping you and two grown girls. Did you know Linda is on the verge of having an affair with Tommy Buckley?'

She gasped, astounded at his thinking. 'Go to sleep. It'll do you more good than the other thing.'

'What do you know about the other thing? It's so long since you tried it you must be healed up.'

'You disgust me!'

'It's your duty to say yes.' His voice hardened. 'I am your husband, Kit, not some bloke who has picked up a stray piece.'

She wriggled from him, the edge of the bed dangerously near. 'You're deliberately trying to cause a row, to wake the girls.'

His hand caught her chin and pulled her to him. His mouth closed on hers and he held her there, forcing her, his hatred of himself mingled with a hatred of her, with anger at being continually repulsed, being found wanting.

Kit lay still, frightened. He had never insisted this way before. She murmured against his pressure, 'You feeling all right?'

'Why?' He drew away.

'Nothing. I just wondered.'

She removed his loosened hand from her jaw. 'You were hurting me,' and his hand strayed to the angle of her hip, sliding on the chiffon, ruffling it up, sensing her flesh tightening beneath his touch, her thighs coming together like clamps.

'Kit. I want to fondle you,' and when she didn't answer, 'I'm going to have you.'

'No.'

His fingers came back up, hesitated so there was a little time of waiting, of no movement, of tension, and then there was decision, they went to her breast.

'Bertie. I hate you.'

'I know. Linda told me,' and the need for revenge on someone, on her, for all his hurts, caused a rasping in his throat.

Kit lay still, waiting. He would pinion her and do as he wished. She was his chattel.

When he finally moved from her she waited for him to rise and go to the bathroom, then she lay and the tears slowly crawled down her face. She pushed them away with the back of her hand, and wondered what was wrong with her.

Her body often felt starved and hungered, yet the moment Bertie turned to her something inside went cold, froze up and refused to awaken. 'Dirty swine,' she whispered in misery. 'Oh you dirty swine.'

She shammed sleep when he returned, but he tried to talk to her, explain the inexplicable. 'Kit. You're inhibited. That's your trouble. Your goddamned mother filled your head with nonsense.'

'Go to sleep. If you want to keep your job you need all your energy.'

'I need more help in the office.'

'I help.'

'I mean proper help. A secretary. Someone in there all the time when I have to be out.'

'Go to sleep.'

He turned his back on her. She was unapproachable in so many ways. When he awakened it was gone nine o'clock.

He sprang from bed in near panic and ran to the bathroom. He could smell bacon, toast, but wanted none. He washed and dressed then went straight into the office. He didn't want to face Kit yet.

The morning's mail was on his desk and he glanced

through it, flicking the envelopes, recognising the contents, the work continually piling up.

The room seemed laden with the aura of Kit, and he knew it was because her silent struggles of last night were still with him, the writhing of her thighs in their attempt to avoid his, the moisture of her silent tears as his face moved on hers.

His mind cursed him: Bertie, you're a skunk. None of the letters interested him; people moaning, had a fire, someone's dead. Trouble. Trouble. He couldn't cope with his own. How could he help others with theirs? Millions starving, pop-eyed children with big bellies, bare arses, bare feet, consumption, fevers. Unemployment.

His head hurt as pictures flashed through it, became grotesque and noisy.

Kit had already been cleaning in here. There was no dust and his blotter was clean. The inkwells had been replenished and she had spilled some of the red. Looked as if she had dabbed it up then tried to rub out the stain. Blasted woman. Elsie was laughing. Christ, Elsie, get out of my mind. Leave me in peace before I lose my wits.

He couldn't stay in here today. He would have to get out. Escape. Go canvassing.

The telephone jangled and he reached for it so sharply he almost knocked it over. It tottered and he caught it. Kit was in the open doorway.

'It's probably Mother,' she said.

It was. The highfaluting voice came over the wires, 'Albert, dear boy! How nice to hear your dulcet tones once more. How are you? Feeling better? Kit was telling me . . .'

He handed the phone to his wife without comment, and his gaze caught the square white envelope propped beside the wooden clock on the mantelpiece. His feet became heavy. An envelope of that quality came from one place. Head Office.

He glanced at Kit, hoping she would make it unnecessary for him to enquire. She said, over the top of the mouthpiece, 'It's not a letter. It's a card. An invitation. A banquet.'

He frowned and crossed to the mantelpiece, lifting the square of white card out of the envelope. He read the gilt lettering. There was no R.S.V.P. 'This isn't an invitation,' he said quietly. 'It's a summons.'

'Sssh,' Kit mouthed, and Bertie re-read the card, then stood tapping it against his knuckles. Lorraine Nolan's voice came clearly through the telephone. 'Kit darling! Are you still there?'

'Yes, Mother.'

'What's the matter, dear? Has he been upsetting you again?'

'Mother, I'm all right.'

'Yes dear, of course you are, but it is a cross we all have to bear, the price we pay for our children's sakes. When you were born –'

Bertie flung a scowl of disgust at the telephone. 'Tell her to jump in the dock. You're a grown woman now.'

'Shut up,' Kit hissed, and the voice of her mother kept going.

Bertie said, 'Is the kettle boiling?'

'Isn't it always?' She moved her head from the mouthpiece, then back again. 'Yes, Mother. No, Mother.'

'What is Albert on about now? I can hear him in the room with you. Has he heard from Head Office yet? You'll never be happy on Merseyside, you know, dear. The riots up there didn't stop the rot. The poverty is the worst in the country –'

Kit put in quickly, 'We've been invited to a banquet.'

There was a sudden silence, then Lorraine echoed softly, 'A banquet?' and Kit could sense her mother's surprise, then the preening, the immaculately waved silver hair being patted with renewed calculation, then, 'Oh darling. From Head Office? From the new chairman?'

'Yes.'

'How lovely! You will accept, of course. One can't be churlish in these matters.'

'Yes Mother,' and Kit managed a small smile as Bertie strode away.

'Do be nice to the new chairman.' Her mother was oozing satisfaction. 'Use your wiles, darling. I'm sure you can save the day.'

'Mother. Please.'

'Oh, come now, Kit. I'm not being facetious. It's women who make men successful. The fools would never get anywhere otherwise. I was always charming to your father's superior officers. It's a knack, you know, dear, and you have it. If only you'd come out of your shell. What are you going to wear?'

'I haven't thought about it.'

'Then the problem is solved. Your father and I will treat you. You and I can go up to town. Oh, what a splendid idea. I haven't been around London for ages. Get something truly devastating. Give you confidence.'

'Mother –'

'When is it? The banquet, I mean.'

'In two weeks or so.'

There was a moment's beautiful silence, then Lorraine had it all planned. 'What about this Saturday? You could manage Saturday. Get an early train. Surely there's one before nine. I shall meet you at Paddington. Spend Sunday here. We can walk on the hills. Have a little chat. You can travel back to Swansea on Monday. Leave here early.'

'I can buy a dress here, in Swansea. Or in Cardiff.'

'A dress!' Lorraine almost squealed with shock and dismay. 'A dress? To go to a banquet? Oh no, darling. No child of mine will appear before a man of influence – at a banquet – in a dress. You need a gown. Something slinky but not vulgar, emphasise that wonderful style you have when you saunter.'

Kit reached for the chair, drew it to her, and sat, while Lorraine broke into tinkling laughter. 'Darling, you have cheered me enormously. I was feeling so utterly wretched. Worcester seems to be still asleep at this time of year. A few days in London will be lovely. I'll pop up on Thursday and take a peep around. Would you like to come on Thursday?'

'No, Mother.' Kit sighed and looked up at the sepia portrait of old Claud Hobbs that hung over the filing cabinet. His white Vandyke beard and silver-topped cane all spoke of success and, at the moment, he seemed to look down on her with more disapproval than ever before. She wondered what he would say to her and Bertie when they met again. At the banquet.

CHAPTER TWO

One of the things John Davies loved above all else was his wife's backside. On that Tuesday morning he felt it move from him, taking most of the warmth of the bed with it, and he lifted his eyelids just a glimmer to watch.

Believing he was still asleep Maggie slid from the sheets, not unlike a two-ton sealion, and John watched her with a shiver of delight. Her white nightie hung from her shoulders in such folds he thought fleetingly of a draped clock tower. She tiptoed on the bare polished wooden floor to the still sleeping baby, paused there beside the cot with her eyes soft and her hands clasped, then went to the open latticed window and, leaning on the sill, stuck out her head with its tangled mass of dyed black hair.

She saw sheep grazing, pale spots on the rugged face of the mountain below, then Port Talbot, rows of houses extending to the sand dunes.

The air was newly washed, mixed with the perfume of bracken and wild wet earth. Maggie looked down at her half-acre of garden where the colours seemed deeper, more glossy; dark green cabbages, rose leaves, fading yellow daffodils, while the chickens clucked anxiously in the hen house.

Maggie hunched her shoulders with glee. All those vegetables to be sold by her, carried in two big baskets, one or two days a week. And God had sent rain onto it, feeding it, during the night.

Oh duw annwyl. Life was good.

She wriggled her body and felt the calico of her nightie

rasp against her skin while, with a little smile about his lips, John waited and, sure enough, Maggie's hands caught the sides of her nightie and, gradually, she pleated it up from her chubby feet, her knees, then her thighs, and John, seeing only the still drooping fullness at the back, thought of ruched curtains on secret windows.

Maggie wriggled her shoulders, slowly drawing the nightie higher until it was like a heavy scarf about the small of her back, then she tugged it from side to side. To and fro. The room filled with the gentle rasping sound, and Maggie's face, still shining with the residue of last night's cold cream, creased into delight. John watched and, as Maggie's pleasure grew, so she bent forward, wriggling with the roughing of the calico against her flesh, her backside rolling from side to side in gratification.

John knew she was unaware of him, convinced he was fast asleep, so he opened his eyes, the bedding up past his nose, giving him the luxurious feeling of peeping at the not-to-be-seen, and Maggie's backside was dimpled and fulsome, the skin pure and white. Here, before John's feasting eyes, was the eighth wonder of the world. He wanted to touch it, smooth it, place his hands under it so he felt the weight and warmth of it, and his longing made him sigh.

Maggie turned, a full-sized sculpture. She saw his nose jutting over the folded edge of the blue checked sheet, saw his untidy thinning head of hair on the night-dented pillow, and she laughed at him, softly. 'John Davies! I thought you were dead—oh.'

'With a view like that?'

She let the hem of the nightie drop, and patted her stomach. 'It's a lovely day,' she whispered, remembering the baby. 'Sun shining like it was summer.'

'Get back in here for a minute.'

'A minute?' She blinked; a mock effort to flutter her eyelashes, the sunlight behind her. Then she took the nightie off and climbed in beside him, ample and naughty.

His hands reached for her and pulled her close, sucking in the relief of pressing against her softness. 'Ooo Mag. I couldn't stand it if you were skinny.'

'Of course you could.'

'No. Indeed. I wouldn't be able to squash you into all my odd corners.'

She laughed against his neck, feeling his Adam's apple jump as he talked, and her hands caught his hips and pulled him even closer. 'Ooooo,' she whispered in mock agony. 'It's cold out there.'

'I'll warm you.'

'I bet you will.'

They laughed, snuggled together. Maggie murmured, 'Aren't we lucky, cariad?'

The baby lay in the wooden cot in the corner of the room undisturbed, while Maggie and John giggled like children, explored each other's bodies, found excitement and made love.

Then they both lay, grinning, his hairy chest filmed with sweat, her arms outspread as if wishing the bed was ten times bigger, and the grandfather clock downstairs chimed the half-hour.

Maggie jerked up, sitting, those wonderful breasts a few inches from John's face. She hissed, 'We're late.'

'Aye,' John smirked, all crooked mouth in a long crooked face. 'Nice though, isn't it?'

She ran to her clothes piled on the small chair, and beamed, 'I'll get dressed downstairs. Be warmer.'

He reached out an arm as if to grab her, but she dodged, glanced towards the cot, and ran down the stairs, hoping the postman wouldn't come at that moment; she had caught him, before now, opening the letterbox and peering in.

The letter was on the coconut mat and Maggie dived for it, knowing the quality of the paper. 'John!' It was a stage whisper. 'There's a letter. From London.' She checked the date stamp again. 'Yes, it is. I'll open it.'

She went into the kitchen and sat beside the big

black range. Her short pointed fingers prised open the envelope and her eyes widened in surprise.

John appeared in the doorway, long and gangling, tying the cord on his pyjama trousers.

'A banquet,' Maggie breathed. 'Oooh John. A banquet. I'll need a gown. Something special. Let them see you got a lady for a wife. What colour? What colour d'you think?'

'Red, Mag.' He took the envelope and card, his face expressionless.

Maggie rummaged in the clothes barely balanced on her lap, and found her brassiere. She began wrapping it about her. 'I wonder if everybody in Swansea's been invited. Or only us.'

'Everyone. Bound to be.'

'Maybe this is it.' She gazed up at him, clipping hooks and eyes. 'Maybe Henderson-Hobbs will tell us then.'

She laughed and hugged herself and lifted the long brass poker. She dug it into the dead-looking fire and a wisp of smoke escaped. 'There now,' she breathed. 'It's still in. Get the blower, bach, and I'll finish getting dressed. I'll write to Carruthers,' she added. 'See what he knows.'

'I shouldn't,' John warned, and went for the great oblong of tin, then fitted it against the fire, provoking a greater draught, causing flames to flicker and a roaring up the flue. 'Don't write,' he said. 'Better not.'

'What then?'

'We don't want any more upsets.'

Maggie frowned as she dressed. 'It's at the Hotel Splendide,' she said pensively. 'I bet it'll be lovely. All glamorous and expensive.'

*   *   *

The Hotel Splendide was baroque. Curves and scrolls were everywhere. Maggie loved it. She stood in the large foyer, amid the date palms and bougainvillea, and raised her arms like a variety queen accepting a standing

37

ovation. 'Look John, oh just look.' John obliged by looking, and saw the gilt scrolls entwined in the ironwork banisters of the wide staircase. He nodded, unimpressed.

Maggie wore her best hat: a large straw with a brim that held anything she cared to pile on it. Today it carried cherries and grapes that were glossed as if with sea mist, and everyone in Port Talbot knew Maggie decorated it herself. Maggie knew it looked lovely. She allowed John to wander to the reception desk while she beamed around, her lipstick the deep scarlet she wore whenever she escaped the Welsh-Welsh confines of the mountainside, and there was no ordinary coat for her today, but a cape of olive green velvet, with an emerald green lining.

John signed them in, accepted the key, and made for the stairs. Maggie swanned after him, glorying in the polite, if slightly amazed attention she was receiving from all around.

From the curve of the top landing she paused to gaze down. 'Here,' she sent the silent message, 'is the future manager of all South Wales. With his wife'. Her eyes searched unsuccessfully for a man with a white Vandyke beard, and a younger man who might be his son, Henderson-Hobbs, the chairman elect. Then she and John sauntered along to room 317 while, in room 318, Kit was thinking how good-looking Bertie was. She said, as she poured a cup of weak tea from the china pot supplied by the hotel, 'You look a lot better.'

'This might be it,' Bertie smiled, and the pink of his lips made his teeth glisten even more whitely. 'It's like preparing to go over the top.' He took the porcelain cup and saucer she offered. 'You know that within a couple of hours it'll be all over.'

Kit sat in a new mauve negligee, her silk-clad knees crossed. She was, he thought, like an advertisement in a glossy magazine. Unreal.

He said, 'We ought to get downstairs. See Carruthers. Find out if he knows anything?' and Kit accepted this as a veiled request to get ready.

38

She said while she dressed, 'Have you any idea why young Robert calls himself Henderson-Hobbs? Is he too grand to be called just Hobbs, like his father?'

Bertie sat watching her. 'His mother never dropped her single name, and he incorporated it in his.'

'Nice fellow,' Kit responded. 'Backs his mother all the way.'

Bertie grimaced. 'More likely a mummy's boy.'

'Maybe he's like his father. Gentle on the outside and tough on the inside. The Old Man has always been nice to me whenever we've met.'

'How often has that been?' Bertie was quietly derisive.

Kit smiled sideways at him. 'I have been to one or two annual dinners. He always makes a point of speaking to me.'

'You had better watch out,' Bertie warned facetiously. 'He might have his eye on you.'

Kit humphed and, when they left their room, they met Maggie and John in the corridor.

A gleeful Maggie pirouetted, her soft full lips painted scarlet, a black beauty spot stuck beside her right eye, her dyed hair brushed loose to her comely bare shoulders, her body wrapped in scarlet taffeta.

Bertie put his hand on John's shoulder, and the four went down the stairs together.

Maggie loved the sensation of gradually merging with the melee below, but Kit's heart tightened and her inhibitions made pleasure impossible. She clutched her white evening purse to her, and wondered if she looked like a candle in the gown her mother had paid the earth for. It was of white silk jersey, not tight-fitting, yet emphasising every tiny movement of her body. The neck was high at the throat, but swooped to a deep U at the back.

Bertie touched her there, but she was cold and didn't react.

All four strolled to the lounge and Carruthers came towards them as if he had been watching for them. He seemed to roll his enormous bulk through the crowd, his dimpled right hand extended, and Kit unwittingly moved faster to greet him. 'Carruthers! You are here!'

'Of course I'm here, dear lady. Where else would I be on a night like this?' He gasped slightly, his asthmatic lungs tight in the smoke-filled room.

'Carruthers,' Kit whispered quickly. 'Is tonight the night?'

But there was no time for his reply. Maggie was there with her confident voice. 'Isn't it wonderful? D'you think Robert will tell us what he plans to do?'

'My dear Margaret,' Carruthers replied, 'how do you expect me to know?'

'Oh go on, Carruthers.' Maggie became playful. 'You know everything.'

His soft warm hand stayed on Kit's wrist, and she made no attempt to move it.

'Right then,' Bertie said, and stretched his neck in an effort to see the lie of the land. 'What is everyone drinking?'

Maggie beamed, 'Port and lemon for me.'

Carruthers turned to Bertie. 'I'll come with you. John? Will you be so kind as to escort the ladies? Over there. Dave and Celia Morris are at a table holding places for you. They're from Liverpool.'

Bertie glanced at Kit, his message clear: a diplomatic introduction to Merseyside?

She smiled in return and Maggie cried, 'Liverpool? Never been there, have we John?'

'There is still time,' Kit returned calmly, and Bertie winked, 'Chin up, old girl,' then, aloud, 'What for you, Kit?'

Maggie's eyes popped in distrust. 'What did Kit mean by that?' but John's hand caught her and drew her away.

Bertie laughed and went after Carruthers. He saw the football-like head with the grey fringing of hair, and pushed towards it. Carruthers had already ordered, booming, but puffing now as his lungs struggled to survive. 'God, Albert, I endeavour to keep pace with this job because it means being out, in the fresh air, but witness the depravity to which it has brought me. Beer and bull.'

Bertie laughed, greeting others, and a tray of drinks slid between his hands. Carruthers was handing money to the barman, a fiver, and Bertie lifted his brows in question. 'Prices steep?'

'Phenomenal,' answered the fat man. 'That's why you can carry the damn things. I'll carry them next time. When you pay.'

Bertie nodded, turning, calling, 'Gangway please. Gangway. Unless you want a whisky down your back!'

At the edge of the crowd he paused, and Carruthers came beside him, his breathing audible now, his stomach thrust forward. 'Carruthers,' Bertie said, 'what's going to happen? Have you any idea?'

Carruthers rubbed his many chins and viewed the room while people acknowledged him, smiling, saluting. 'This is not the best place for discussion of such matters, Albert.'

'You must help. It was you told us I was not to get the push. I'm living on a knife-edge!'

Carruthers raised a fat hand placatingly. 'I carried out the Old Man's orders, Albert. I was instructed to tell you you would be transferred to somewhere uncomfortable for your sins.'

'That was weeks ago. Is this young Robert likely to listen to his father?'

Carruthers pouted, noncommittal. 'To me, the Old Man is an open book, Albert, but his son is, as yet, an unknown factor. We all need the utmost patience.'

The tray in Bertie's hands shuddered, the drinks in the glasses quivering. 'Do you have any idea how it's likely to happen? A letter one morning? An invitation to some private sanctum tonight? An open announcement like they did to poor Johnson a few years back?'

'Johnson?'

41

'You know damn well who I mean, Carruthers. The Old Man announced in his after-dinner speech the poor devil was presented with a tremendous challenge. And the next we heard he'd gone to the Isle of Skye or some silly place.'

Carruthers drew himself up. 'Would you accept such an offer, Albert?'

'You know damn well I would have no option. What I want to know is how and when?'

Carruthers sniffed and stared around and Bertie snapped, 'Carruthers! Are you saying now that you honestly don't know what is going to happen to me?'

'I am not saying anything,' the fat man returned, and the great football of a head shook slowly, and his short legs carried him away.

Bertie went after him, eyeing the drinks on the tray, and when they reached the table in the corner everyone was laughing except Kit. She was faintly flushed, her eyes too bright as they sought Bertie's, and the question was there in the little movement of her head.

'No,' he mouthed, and shrugged.

She gazed up at him as hands were taking the drinks, spreading them about, and the air seemed full of fug, tension, expectation, laughter, and dread.

Carruthers sensed it all and saw Kit's face. He leaned over her. 'Mañana, dear lady. Mañana.'

'Carruthers.' Her hand reached for him but touched nothing. 'The waiting is terrible. Old Claud did say we would be transferred. Didn't he?'

'That was what I was commanded to tell you.'

'By the Old Man?' she persisted.

'By Mr Claud Hobbs himself.'

Kit saw Maggie watching, lip-reading, and she turned her head away slightly. 'Could you find out? Please.' She stared up at Carruthers. 'Could you? Could you ask him?'

For a few moments Carruthers remained looking down at her, his full lips pouting into greater softness. Finally he stood up, touched the single link button of his jacket and murmured to Bertie, 'I am about to go walkabout, Albert. I shall endeavour to return before the meal begins, but if I am delayed, you can be assured it is not for want of trying.'

Bertie nodded, his glance going from the fat man to Kit and back again.

Casually, slowly, Carruthers moved away, his drink left on the table. He was searching for Henderson-Hobbs.

* * *

That young man had just hurried from his car without waiting for the niceties of the chauffeur's duties, slammed the door behind him, called, 'Right ho, George. Off you go,' and buttoned the jacket of his evening suit as if making a last-minute effort to look tidy. He ran up the wide steps, past the commissionaire who saluted in all his scarlet and gilt glory, and strode expectantly into the foyer.

His shoulders jerked as he rubbed his hands rapidly in anticipation. He was ready and eager to go. As from tonight he would be the acknowledged, official, signed and sealed Chairman of the Unicorn Insurance Company. Hi ho world, here we come!

A pause, a glance, told him he was probably the last to arrive, and he grinned as a pageboy approached him. 'Mr Henderson-Hobbs, sir?' and, on seeing Robert's agreeing nod, 'That way, sir, in the blue room.'

His father was already waiting with five other members of the board. Claud Hobbs' white Vandyke beard and sparse white hair were superbly groomed, his expression almost fierce with vitality. He looked up from his blue plush chair and lifted his forefinger, beckoning, and Robert strode to him, agile, anticipating.

'Evening Father!' and the old man smiled, proud. He gestured to the small table behind them, 'Help yourself, son,' and Robert moved to the decanters that were arrayed there.

43

The walls were festooned with large mirrors and Robert liked what he saw in them. He felt good. His hair was, as near as dammit, golden, and that light tan did things for him. He paused without true vanity to admire himself, smiling, his green eyes approving, smiling back. The white dickie didn't look too bad after all, and the black bow was straight. He tweaked the pink satin handkerchief that jutted perfectly from his breast pocket, then lifted it slightly, naughtily, watching the miniature silk-clad leg appear. If the Old Man knew he was carrying the thing tonight he'd have forty fits, but it was lucky, by jingo, it was lucky, and he couldn't leave it home. Not tonight, Josephine. Oh no, not tonight.

His father called dryly across the expensively cushioned softness of the room, 'You won't get any better-looking by admiring yourself!'

Robert laughed and addressed his reflection, 'How d'you do, Robert old pal?' and watched his image laugh back. He refrained from the temptation to vault over the back of the chair that had been reserved for him, and sat, lips apart with anticipation, beside his father.

'Cigar?' Claud Hobbs offered, and Robert accepted and lit up, enjoying this moment as he enjoyed every moment. He felt superior to his colleagues, these old men with their pale eyes and tissue paper complexions.

Claud said humorously as he studied the ash on his own cigar, 'Have you decided which, of the hundred speeches you have practised, you intend using tonight, Robert?'

Robert took a deep breath, aware that these men thought him a young pup needing a collar and lead. He began, 'I have said it before and I will say it again.' His smile encompassed all six wise men. 'This company needs young blood, and I mean young. Great Britain is easing out of the Depression. America is coming back into her own. We are ready for expansion greater than ever before –'

'Hm,' said one old gent.

'– we need young men with boundless energy, men who can resurrect –' Robert paused, regretting that last word, but went on quickly, '– who can carry the Unicorn into an even better, more prosperous future.'

His hand moved as if scratching his cheek, though his fingers didn't touch his face, and the Old Man knew it was a gesture of nervousness. Claud followed his son's glance and saw the great hulk of his Chief Inspector coming from the foyer; Carruthers, carrying his protruding belly with pride before him. Carruthers, unfamiliar in evening dress, but intent on divining if any conclusions were likely to be reached this night.

Robert drew an impatient breath through tight lips, wanting to dismiss the fat man, deny him access to this unofficial meeting. He stared at his father, waiting for Claud to understand, to beckon Carruthers away, but the Old Man nodded gently. 'It's all right,' he said quietly. 'He, too, is a necessary part of the business,' and Carruthers sank into a chair and stretched out his legs, crossing his ankles comfortably.

Robert's lips jammed together and, for a moment, it seemed he would not continue his discourse, but then his impatience changed to an air of deferment and, with an adjustment of his legs, he went on, 'You all know damn well what I want to do tonight. I want the men to know I need a new policy, a forward-looking policy, and tonight's as good a time as any to tell them.'

'Hear, hear!' said Carruthers lazily, and prickles of irritation ran up Robert's spine.

'I want to know how much I don't know,' he said, 'and as soon as I get the chance I shall visit every office. I can't know the managers as well as you people do. I haven't had the time to meet them. But I will.'

The oldest board member, who looked ninety, leaned forward and tapped Robert's knee benignly. 'You know about the Hemsworthy situation, do you, lad?'

'Naturally,' Robert returned, resenting the feeling that these men underestimated him. 'And I have every intention of attending to the matter as soon as possible.'

The ancient one leaned nearer. 'Aye, as long as you go slow on this. You remember your father and us, we built up this firm from nothing but courage –'

Robert nodded forcefully, 'I agree. You worked miracles, but you aren't young any more.' He jabbed a finger in the air. 'You are out of touch with the new commerce. We're into the thirties, gentlemen. The twenties have gone. Kaput!'

'Shall we stick to the point?' another suggested. 'The Hemsworthy fellow.'

Robert looked into the speaker's face and saw firm resolution, so he relaxed slightly, humouring his audience. 'I shall arrange to meet Hemsworthy,' he said. 'Privately. Explain the situation.'

Carruthers said ponderously, 'What situation?'

Henderson-Hobbs turned to him, the invisible hackles soaring. 'That we cannot have people pilfering funds and putting eighteen-year-old girls –' He broke off and the others sat watching him, silent for a moment.

Carruthers said lazily, 'Sack Hemsworthy for any reason at all and you bring a holocaust on your head.'

'Nonsense!' returned Henderson-Hobbs. 'We're grown men –'

'Tch tch!' his father put in. 'Take the advice of we old ones, Robert. Take your time.'

Robert gazed around at the faces of wisdom and wondered if they were silently laughing at him. 'I shall play it as it comes,' he said. 'But I would like to think you have the courage to accept young ideas, new ideas.' He jabbed a forefinger at his knee. 'I won't sabotage all your work. If any one of you would like to say, right now, Robert, stick to our ways or get out, then you are free to say it.' He smiled at each man in turn, looking into their eyes, threatening, persuasive. 'And I will know what to do.'

The old man sat back, needing him as chairman.

Carruthers' voice came up from the realms of fat, his

expression sleepy. 'You are referring to some particular action you are prepared to take.'

'I, too, can leave the firm,' Robert answered. 'There is a new world across the water. I can try my chances there,' and the silence became such that outside there seemed to be a hubbub of voices.

Claud Hobbs said, 'I rather think I would like another brandy, son.'

Robert smiled more widely and got to his feet. 'Any more orders, gentlemen?' He crossed to the decanters, his ears stretched for any comment that might follow him, but the silence remained. He looked in the mirror to watch the old men, and saw a tall svelte figure in white glide past the open double doors.

Robert whistled soundlessly. Who the heck was she? Not of the insurance world. Not in that outfit. Mannequin material. Definitely. Up his street. What ho?

The men began talking again, discussing Robert, but Robert took them their drinks, mentally assuring himself that if he didn't win today, he would win tomorrow.

In the meantime: who was she?

He held out a glass to Carruthers, and Carruthers said heavily, 'Being an inferior appendage to the Unicorn, I work in close proximity to the men who came in on the ground floor, men who were in the trenches offering their lives for this bright new future when you, Robert, were hardly out of knickerbockers. I am fully conversant with the Albert Hemsworthys of this world.'

'He's dispensable, Carruthers! The man's a fool!'

'He's an honest fool. In your world a man hides his bit of fluff under the carpet, discards and pays off. Albert's crime was that he stuck to the girl. Cared about her.'

Robert felt the flush rise to his neck and head, felt his eyes become hard, even threatening. He was aware of his father, of the other men waiting and watching, and of the fact that the woman with the long sleek body and elegant poise had strolled past the open doors again.

He shrugged. What the hell. Keep business for the

office. Another board meeting. He said, 'Excuse me, gentlemen, please.' He smiled more widely, his eyes without animosity. 'I have just espied an old friend.'

Carruthers continued to stare at him, the toad at the edge of the pond, and in his mind was the thought, 'Posturing idiot,' while the other men sipped their drinks and said nothing.

Robert inclined his head towards his father. 'If you'll excuse me?'

'Certainly. The night is yours. Make the most of it,' and the Old Man watched his son march away, his blue eyes twinkling with amusement. He laid the stub of his cigar carefully in the onyx ashtray beside him, then turned and lifted his brows to Carruthers. 'You still don't approve of him.'

'He does not approve of me.'

'Nonsense, the boy is afraid of you. You know your job and he needs you. Young men never enjoy needing an older man.'

'Why are none of you stopping him?' Carruthers pulled his jacket about himself, stretching his upper half as if to ease his back.

'He has been given our views,' Claud replied. 'Now we wait and watch him learn.'

'If you let him sack Hemsworthy,' Carruthers warned, 'the others will smell a rat. They'll conclude the man is to be crucified because he's too old. At forty-nine. While the rest of you touch eighty!' His chins flattened against the top of his barrel-like chest and his heavy brows came down in a rare scowl.

Claud Hobbs laughed. 'The firm is stronger than my son, Carruthers. There might be fireworks before he's much older, but he won't go too far.'

One of the old men, his walking stick by his chair, said dryly, 'I still maintain we should put Hemsworthy up north. Purge the firm's name in South Wales and keep a good man on his toes.'

Carruthers' fat lips smacked together in disgust. He

heaved himself out of his chair. He, too, had seen Kit, and now sought a way of avoiding her.

* * *

She had sat in the main lounge while the noise rose; drinks, bright lights, like-minded company, but Kit could not wait. She tasted the sherry and her throat refused it. She groped for the small white handkerchief in her purse and coughed into it.

Maggie slapped her on the back, a psychological thumping of jealousy. 'There!' Maggie's red mouth was wide in her happy face. 'Better now?' But Kit wasn't. Her attention had gone with Carruthers and her body wanted to follow. She spluttered, went scarlet and looked appealingly across the table at Bertie. He raised his glass to her, sober-eyed, knowing what was troubling her. 'Take another sip of your drink,' he said. 'It might help.'

She managed a self-conscious laugh, and realised that here was the excuse to get away. She mouthed back, 'Powder room,' then hurriedly left.

She told herself for the millionth time it didn't matter what decision the doyens of commerce came to; it could be for the best. Meryseyside still fed those like Bertie. She and he would settle in and be taking extra men on before they knew where they were and, if the worst came to the worst, there were other firms, bigger firms, firms that might overlook Bertie's great age in preference for his experience. She walked faster as her thoughts became feverish.

She couldn't find Carruthers. She eyed the narrow corridor between the pink and white cupid sculptures. A strange man smiled at her, still patting the buttons on his flies, and Kit hurried away, embarrassed.

Then there came the special room, an almost empty smokey blue room. She strolled past, her face forward and calm, held high, but a flitting sideways glance had seen the white Vandyke beard.

49

They were there! Kit shuddered with discovery. A group of affluent-looking old men sitting like Red Indians holding a pow-wow, their pipes of peace individually wrapped leaves called cigars.

Kit scented money, position. The men at the top.

Even now they could be discussing the plan to dismiss Bertie. The knowledge that some men had such power, to cripple with a word, made her want to retch. Her helplessness was infuriating. If it had been her job, her employers, she could have gone in there, cornered the lot of them; but it was Bertie's job, Bertie's employer.

She stood, controlling indignation and frustration, then she lifted her head in decision and sauntered past the room once more, her eyeballs sliding to the side, looking in, then she looked away again, fast.

Henderson-Hobbs had noticed her.

It was an intangible thing. How can gazes meet like that? How could she feel so sure he shared her sudden lurch of recognition? Yet she believed he had; it was so easy to know instinctively who he was.

Her heart was swinging, banging, and she told herself it was trepidation, not excitement, that caused it. She looked for somewhere to escape, without going too far away, and she strolled in an easy I-don't-need-any-of-you attitude, then kept going forward to anywhere. There appeared a tiny room behind a trailing mass of pink bougainvillea, a small but well cushioned settee, and an atmosphere of stillness, peace.

With a sigh of resignation Kit went into it. She sank to the settee and sat back, her knees crossed beneath the elegance of the silk jersey gown, one forearm resting across the deep blue of the large cushion beside her. She didn't know how beautiful, how cool and distant she looked, and she surveyed the foyer through the carefully arranged tangle of foliage. Small groups of people were thinning, wandering away, and she wondered how she would know when it was time to enter the banqueting hall.

Then Henderson-Hobbs emerged from that special room. She watched him. He was slim-faced, not unlike a younger, fairer Bertie, his right hand in his trouser pocket, casual, his left hand raised in acknowledgement to others. With keen narrowed eyes he appraised the foyer, then saw the bougainvillea and, as if he understood her already, came to her.

She could see the half smile that might be of gentle derision, and she deliberately turned her head, pretending to ignore him. Her gaze fell on a row of buttons on a narrow slit of wall, and realisation hit her. She was sitting in a lift!

Quelling her panic emphasised her show of serenity. She looked even more aloof, and Henderson-Hobbs stood no more than six feet from her, his legs astride as if to block her escape, his expression whimsical, intent on her.

He said, 'Good evening,' and Kit languidly focused her attention on him while a jumble of accusing words clamoured to burst from her.

'Good evening.' Her voice was low, lacking any accent, while her mind tried to accept the idea that this arrogant-looking male, with the appearance of a blonde pirate attempting to be respectable, could give John Davies all she and Bertie had worked for.

His voice was deep, musical, as if he had trained it. 'Haven't we met before?'

Kit wanted to laugh at his assuredness. Here was a man who was used to women.

He smiled charmingly. 'Correct me if I am wrong, but you are not of the insurance world.' He tweaked the pink satin handkerchief jutting brazenly from his breast pocket, then rammed it down again hurriedly.

Kit's shaped brows rose without welcome. 'Are there others in the hotel tonight?'

His smile widened a little as he realised his faux pas, then he duelled, 'The hotel staff.'

She gazed over his left shoulder. 'Then surely,' she

51

returned, 'I am the kitchen maid.' She smiled patiently and let her gaze return to his.

He nodded slightly, accepting the rebuke, and reached inside his jacket pocket, bringing out a silver cigarette case. He flicked it open and held it out to her, but he didn't enter the lift. Kit shook her head, hoping the lift wouldn't shudder, the doors slide closed and the lot take her floatingly out of sight. Her brows stayed up, her crossed knees emphasising the length of her thighs and narrowness of her waist.

He inclined his head in question, 'D'you mind if I smoke?' and her disinterested gesture of "you carry on" set his mouth twitching with amusement.

He took a Turkish cigarette and lit it with a lighter that fitted snugly into the palm of his hand. A wisp of smoke filtered from his wide bow lips and his head lifted in appreciation and speculation.

Kit became aware that the foyer behind him was completely empty. There was an odd silence, but if she got up she would have to walk past him so closely he could touch her. She didn't want that. Already his nearness was making her tingle.

She hesitated, undecided, then relaxed as the familiar Welsh voice cut the air. Maggie Davies and the rustling of her scarlet taffeta. Maggie strutted around the foyer, peeping into side rooms, down a passage and up again, as if she were at home seeking a stray hen.

Kit watched, slightly mesmerised by Maggie's attitude, and wondering what Maggie would make of this little tableau when she found it. Then Maggie turned, glanced at the bougainvillea, then through it, and couldn't believe her eyes.

The message hammered home with such volume Maggie blinked and her soft double chin dropped. Then she recovered and advanced, her right hand held out as if calming millions. 'I am so sorry to interrupt your little tête-à-tête, Kit –' She rustled around the bourgainvillea, vying with it for colour, and her open-mouthed smile went to the man. 'Oooh, Mr Henderson-Hobbs! There's an honour it is to meet you.'

His eyes twinkled, always ready to acknowledge accolades. 'You are from Welsh Wales,' he said, and Maggie's great bust lifted with pride and pleasure.

She said sincerely, 'How did you guess? I'm Margaret Davies.'

'Of course.' He took her hand, then let it slide away, his gaze on her face as he tried to remember. Davies? Davies?

'Port Talbot!' Maggie laughed, rescinding any ideas of being posh. 'Halfway up the mountain. Can see right over the town from where we are.'

Henderson-Hobbs nodded, agreeing, but not having a clue where Port Talbot was, and Maggie went on, 'But what are you both doing out here, then?' and Kit strolled from the lift.

She moved into the well of the foyer while Maggie looked after her and said apologetically. 'I promised to be quick. They're all going in, you see, but it's lovely meeting you. Lovely.' Her hands flayed a little as her desire to stay with Henderson-Hobbs fought with her need to return to the crowd. Then, on the other side of the bougainvillea appeared Claud Hobbs, his voice a loud exclamation as he saw Kit.

'My dear! How beautiful you look,' and Kit crossed to him, letting him kiss her cheek, admiring his faultless memory, liking him in spite of the rude words she often flung at his portrait in the office.

He took her hand and held on to it. 'How long is it? Four years since we last had a little chat?'

She nodded and he went on, 'You should come to the annual dinners more often, Kit. Accompany that errant husband of yours.'

His old eyes took in the faint pink of her cheeks, the long slinky lines of her body, and he nodded sagely. 'What did Albert see in that Buckley girl?'

'Youth,' Kit said softly, both hands in his.

'Ach!' he retorted. 'He felt old age coming on and tried to kick against it,' then he let her hands drop and gazed about. 'I'm looking for Robert.'

Kit jerked her head towards the lift. 'He's in conversation with Maggie Davies. Her husband, John, is our Port Talbot agent.'

She looked at the Old Man's profile as he turned from her, and wondered if she ought to ask now, 'Are you going to sack my husband?' but she smiled, remained outwardly composed, and said nothing.

Robert heard his father's voice and came through the fronds and flowers, allowing a still radiant Maggie to precede him. 'Oh Mr Claud!' she glowed. 'An honour indeed,' and Claud took her outstretched hands in both his and laughed, as if meeting her had been his prime consideration.

Kit watched and distrust waxed strong. These men, who exuded such bonhomie, whose well-bred faces were alive with goodwill, could return to their office, dictate a letter, and put Bertie – and John – in the gutter.

Kit jabbed the heel of her left sandal into the thickness of grey carpet then swung herself away. She felt repulsed by the hypocrisy; surely even Maggie was being two-faced; if those men had been tramps no one would shake hands with them. Money, power, influence, each demanded and invariably got. She, Kitty Hemsworthy, wanted, at this moment, to distance herself from it.

'Hi, I say!' Robert strode beside her, stopping her from walking on. 'Are you in the habit of leaving friends so abruptly?'

'Friends?' Kit was surprised, and looked back to where the Old Man listened to Maggie prattling on. The strong Welsh accent came with urgency. 'Wonderful managerial material he is, and speaks Welsh fluent.'

Kit wondered if Maggie was doing the heavy accent deliberately, impressing her Welsh birthright on Claud Hobbs.

Robert laughed. 'I wasn't referring to the ravishing creature in red, but to myself.'

Kit gazed up at him, finding he was one of the rare men who was taller than she, then remembered it was his use of the word 'friends' that had made her look at Maggie. She smiled, a little ashamed of the way her mind often worked, and Robert liked the softening. He said, 'Are you the wife of an agent too?'

'No.' Kit walked on easily. He excited her and she was nervous of it. She had expected Robert Henderson-Hobbs to be the chinless wonder Carruthers often called him, but this man was not chinless; his face was classic, more chiselled than Bertie's, with a finer, healthier complexion.

She liked him: he and his father. Likeable hypocrites.

As together they reached the doorway of the banqueting hall, she forgave all such men, and flashed a smile at him that made his brows leap and a new interest rush across his face.

He said, 'Father called you Kit.'

'Did he?' She was being coquettish, and Maggie was approaching with Old Claud. Kit held out her hand. 'It has been nice meeting you, Mr Henderson-Hobbs.'

He touched her hand, but only in a gesture of moving it away. 'You'll have a drink with me later?'

'Thank you, but no –'

Maggie was laughing. 'Ooo, everybody's sitting down. Waiting.'

The two men nodded au revoir and Maggie's face was hot with pleasure.

She and Kit walked up the hall, seeking the South Wales table. Bertie and John were raised half out of their chairs, waving, askance at seeing their wives with the nobs, their anxious faces silently beseeching, 'Any news? Anyone said anything?'

'Sssh,' both women mouthed, and the men exchanged glances, while Bertie felt shudders up his spine, and wished he had paid more attention to Henderson-Hobbs

55

in former years. Then he reassured himself. He could not be expected to have done so; Robert had always sat well away from his father, apparently disinterested in anything commercial.

Nevertheless, Bertie wanted to kick himself. He should have foreseen this situation, realised young Henderson-Hobbs was insidious, had been watching and waiting to take over.

Kit sat, then smiled at him. 'Do we have a choice? Soup? Melon?'

He reached for a menu and handed it to her, his voice utterly casual as he asked, 'Did the Old Man have much to say?'

'Only hello.'

'And the chinless wonder?'

'He's not so chinless.' Her voice carried the hint of a warning and Bertie caught it. He smiled ruefully and decided it was unwise to ask more questions where so many people could overhear. He gazed across the tables and faces to where Robert Henderson-Hobbs sat, and wondered if Kit had found the man attractive. If the man was about to become his nemesis.

The ceiling was high, crystal chandeliers hung, white and silver, emphasising the electric lighting, while the walls held large oil paintings of war scenes; puttied, helmeted men with cannons, frenzied horses rearing, frenzied riders lashing swords. Bertie tried not to look at them; he could hear them, smell them, and this was supposed to be a festive night. There were bunches of balloons waiting to fall, and a Union Jack festooned a platform at the end of the hall, presaging a concert.

Maggie struggled to follow Kit between the chairs. 'Excuse me, can I squash through here?' and to herself, 'Oh duw duw, I'll have to lose weight, I will indeed,' but, when she prepared to sit between John and another agent, John put his hand against her bottom and gave a gentle tap. He grinned at her, looking ungainly in his

56

dinner suit. 'Lovely Mag,' he whispered. 'Lovely bum you got.'

She sat hurriedly, whispering, 'Fancy us being with Old Claud and Robert. Got on well, we did.'

'Did he say anything? Any hint?'

Maggie shook her head, sending frantic eye signals, while she flicked her table napkin and arranged it across her knees. She touched her décolletage nervously then concentrated on the top table, ready to twiddle her fingers in greeting at Claud Hobbs and his eldest son, longing to show the whole room that she was 'in', but neither man looked at her. They seemed to be holding a little conference of their own.

Kit sat quietly. She felt unnerved, as if she had made an exhibition of herself. In so many ways Henderson-Hobbs wasn't what she expected. He was no post-graduate playboy. He was shrewd. She had seen it in the lines beside his eyes, and his brows could furrow in concentration or exasperation. She dabbed her lips with her handkerchief, as if he had already tasted them, then she tucked the handkerchief away quickly, perplexed by her own inner quivering.

She noticed a fixed expression on Bertie's face. He was staring at the men of power. She nudged his thigh and smiled, trying to ease his tension.

Then the toastmaster came into prominence, embellished in scarlet and gilt: 'Ladies and gentlemen. Please rise for the first toast of the evening. The Unicorn Insurance Company!'

Everyone stood and there came the rallying cry, 'The Unicorn!' as glasses were raised and lips were allowed to sip.

'God bless it,' came the usual solemn muttered additions, then everyone sat and the meal began to be served.

It progressed with Bertie having only Kit to talk to; the empty end of the top table on his right and, although Maggie kept eyeing the Hobbs men, Bertie and Kit avoided looking that way.

It was when the sucking pigs arrived that the enormous room fell silent, and Bertie swore later he could hear the gentle scuffing of the young chefs' shoes on the carpet as the laden silver salvers were carried shoulder high; the pigs' eyes glazed, their mouths stuffed open with apples.

Bertie heard Kit give a little gasp and he turned to her. She was watching Henderson-Hobbs, her lips apart, very pink, and Bertie was certain she was panting. He observed her carefully; she was like one of the sculptures in the hotel, beautiful, unmoving, yet there was this sensation of panting.

Bertie felt his guts twist and twirl. For God's sake, did she think making goo-goo eyes at Henderson-Hobbs would save the day? What had the man said to her and Maggie?

He snapped, 'Kit!' and her attention sprang to him. 'You're staring,' he said, and she flushed guiltily; she had caught the gleam of satisfaction in Henderson-Hobbs' eyes as she had turned in surprise to him from the sucking pigs, and now he was leaning forward and sideways against the table, as if subconsciously he wanted to come to her.

Kit sipped from her glass, the red wine swaying, her face taking on its usual calm detached look, and Bertie tried to relax, but his nerves were stretched and the room was airless. His head was buzzing. He didn't want the strain of so many people, the need to keep a pleasant expression on his face. He wanted to be home, in his chair or, better still, in his bed, and he wondered how his daughters were. They had been left alone, big girls now, they had said, and quite safe for one night without Mum and Dad.

As the pigs slid to a prepared table people began clapping, men called complimentary things and women laughed, the chefs made a ceremony of sharpening great knives, and Robert leaned towards his father, murmuring, 'That is Hemsworthy, isn't it?' while a toss of his head indicated Bertie.

Claud Hobbs didn't smile. He had known the question was coming. 'Are you interested in the man? Or the lady in white beside him?'

'All right,' Robert returned testily. 'Who are they?' but he knew. If the buxom one in noisy scarlet was from Welsh Wales, then the siren had to be too, and there they were, at the top of the Swansea table. Hemsworthy. The man who had risked all for a tart.

Robert rubbed his chin, undecided. It was, as Conan Doyle would say, elementary, my dear Watson.

His father sat back and folded his arms. 'I was under the impression you already knew her.'

'No. I was trying to rectify the matter when her companion came to the rescue.'

'Do you still believe I am wrong when I advocate transfer, not his dismissal?'

Robert made the nervous movement of his hand towards his face. 'I'm not sure. He doesn't look a lecher, or an idiot, but damn it all, we can't let men pull the name of the firm into the gutter and get away with it!'

'Fascinating, isn't she?'

'You advise shifting him and leaving it at that?'

'At a push, I advise leaving it.'

Henderson-Hobbs jerked his jacket impatiently and eased his neck as if the high stiff collar irked him. 'We'll have to see,' he said.

His father nodded shortly while Robert reached inside his jacket and drew out the typewritten sheets of his speech.

Claud Hobbs smiled and nodded. He had not been wrong. His son was willing to learn. Particularly when a beautiful woman was willing to teach.

He smiled across at Kit, and she sent a sidelong glance that became a reciprocal smile, but her attention drifted to the new chairman, her mind pleading with him not to sack Bertie.

He was very handsome, clean-cut, assured in a relaxed

easy way, the fingers about the wine glass firm, masculine, and ringless. He felt her attention and turned to it. He nodded slightly and she smiled, but her mind was still pleading. Not only with him, but also with God.

Robert lowered his head, his jacket open as if he had eaten well and was now at peace. Then he looked up again, quickly, straight at her, and he examined her boldly before he smiled, and the unspoken language was more effective than words.

Maggie coughed on a cigarette in a long tortoiseshell holder and leaned forward to see more; she couldn't believe it; Kitty Hemsworthy playing the same game as herself – keep in with the bosses. She took another sip of her now cold coffee, and everyone waited for the next stage of this function.

The toastmaster called, 'Pray silence for Mr Claud Hobbs!'

There came a listening hush as Claud got to his feet and surveyed the faces before him. Clapping broke out until the Old Man held up a quietening hand, and Claud's voice fell on the smoke-hazed room. He looked small, but distinguished, glistening clean with silver-streaked white hair and immaculate Vandyke beard. Nothing moved. Claud paused, then began, 'My dear friends –' and Bertie thought he would choke with disbelief.

Kit clasped her hands in her lap. This could be leading up to it. Old Claud could address you as dear friends today and, tomorrow, see you turned into paupers.

Her gaze searched frantically for Carruthers. It suddenly seemed vital for the fat man to be near, a support, a guide, but he was lost in the sea of heads, and Kit's hand enveloped Bertie's. She smiled wanly at him and he winked back. He bent his head, whispering, 'We'll be all right,' and she gave an answering whisper, 'Of course,' but neither knew who was reassuring whom.

Bertie gazed at the ceiling, finding flaws, listening to the Old Man. Before the night was over the old boy would probably be paralytic. He usually was at the end of the annual dinners. Tonight was his retirement night. He might be even worse. Damn good luck to him, Bertie thought, he wouldn't mind the chance to be in the same state himself.

'. . . And so,' the Old Man went on, 'I thank you with deepest affection for your toil on the firm's behalf, for your loyalty in the darkest hours . . .'

Stuff and nonsense, Bertie thought, but nodded sagely, in case the Old Man should look his way.

'. . . and there comes a time when we all have to retire . . .'

Bertie's ears pricked up. Retire? Was the Old Man hinting that next week, tomorrow, one of his managers in South Wales would be retiring?

'. . . and so I settle for becoming a non-executive president.' The Old Man laughed, his fingers playing with a fork that had not been cleared away. '. . . This means I can spend my time in my garden. Unless my son gets into difficulty and calls upon me. I won't even have to attend board meetings unless I feel inclined.' He waited for audience reaction, and it came in the form of polite laughter. 'And so now . . .' He lifted a square tangerine-coloured cushion and tipped it so everyone could see the embroidered insignia on it: the unicorn. '. . . I hand over a symbolic key of office to my son, Robert, knowing he will carry on the fine traditions of this company. He will care for each of you as I have done, and I ask that you back him and work for him, as you have done for me.'

There was a poignant pause, then the Old Man bent his head and, for a few moments, utter silence reigned. Kit frowned, convinced Claud was shedding tears, and she craned to see more.

Claud Hobbs placed a golden key on the cushion, then passed it ceremoniously to Robert who got to his feet beside his father.

The applause was deafening. Kit clapped. Bertie held his cigar between his teeth and clapped. Maggie and John clapped loudly and called ' 'ear 'ear!'

It was an emotional ovation, an emotional adieu. Someone stood. They all stood. Someone began singing, 'For he's a jolly good fellow . . .' and Robert put an arm about his father's shoulders, the cushion on the table before them.

Claud smiled, holding up both arms, nodding his thanks, then he was seated.

Robert coughed into his hand, looked at his notes, then at his men. Here was no chinless wonder. Here was authority. A man who could wear different cloaks, all successfully.

'. . . I have discussed with members of the board certain changes I wish to make within the company. I am after a more progressive image. We are up against stiff competition and it will get stiffer . . .'

He told them what they already knew, but he told them with more conviction. He talked for about twenty minutes and, all that time, Bertie and Kit held hands, Maggie and John held hands. Then Robert Henderson-Hobbs stopped talking and smiled. He lifted his glass. 'To the founder and lifeblood of the Unicorn. To the man whose genius has given us all jobs in a world where the unemployed sit on doorsteps and starve. I give you Mr Claud Hobbs!'

Everyone stood to echo the toast, sombre now, then Henderson-Hobbs also sat. Bertie glance at Kit, and found John watching him. He winked at both of them, expressing relief. No hint had been given that changes were imminent.

The room buzzed and scraped as people became reseated and the toastmaster was calling, 'Ladies and gentlemen! There will now be an interval of fifteen minutes, after which there will be a programme of light entertainment.'

Bertie heaved in breath and drew back his shoulders, the manager in charge again. 'Come on, you lot,' he commanded. 'Let's get to the bar. You can each order one on me.'

There was general laughter, but John came to him. 'Fine speech,' he said quietly.

'Aye,' Bertie returned cryptically, wanting to thrust John out of his way.

Maggie pushed her head close, laughing softly, secretly. 'See Henderson-Hobbs watching us?'

'No,' said Kit. 'We didn't.'

The other Swansea agents were grinning, talking, smoking. They knew what Bertie had done, they knew what Elsie had done but, good lor', he seemed to be getting away with it. In groups, they dawdled towards the main lounge and the bar.

'So here we are,' Maggie said, as the men went to order and the women found a table.

Kit laid her head back against the dark green velvet of the chair, spread her hands on the wide arms and sighed.

John and Bertie returned with drinks and took their seats, staring around. Then, unexpectedly, the directors sauntered into the room, greeting people, and Old Claud approached Bertie and the group.

'Albert!'

'Good evening, sir.' Bertie got to his feet.

'Enjoying yourself?'

'Thank you, sir.'

'Splendid. Splendid.' Claud Hobbs shook hands all round, John on his feet smiling awkwardly. Claud gripped Bertie's shoulder. 'Robert will probably have a private chat with you. Later on.'

'Yes sir,' and the Old Man was strolling away.

Bertie's hands were shaking and he stuffed them in his jacket pockets. It irritated him, this ague that gripped when he least expected it, this weakness that threatened to sink him. He had been scared before; every serving man was, but why this? God, he thought derisively, I'm like a woman on the change.

He excused himself from the group, laughing, 'Nature calls,' and he was away.

Kit watched him go, sad for him and sad for herself,

63

wishing she could return to the children now.

Restless, she too excused herself and worked her way through the throng to the comparatively refreshing foyer. Henderson-Hobbs saw her go and followed.

'Good evening,' he said, as if this was their first meeting, and Kit was flattered and nervous, wishing he didn't stand so close.

'Do you come up to London often?' he asked, watching her face.

'No. Not at all.'

'But I understand you have a special trip arranged for the morning, to Windsor. Isn't there a coach picking you up here?' He was at his most attentive, green eyes concentrating. 'I live out that way,' he said. 'Wouldn't it be more interesting if I offer you and your friends a lift? Possibly lunch before you return to Wales?'

Kit moved from him, smiling now because he was the boss. She said, 'I'll ask the others, but I doubt we'll be able to accept. Thank you. You are most kind,' and her voice became husky as his nearness swamped her in a strange awareness.

He laughed quietly, as if he knew what was happening inside her. 'Splendid idea. I'll ask them with you,' and he strolled, nonchalantly, at her side.

Bertie was already back at the table, and he and John stood as they saw Kit and Robert approach. John murmured, 'Hi hup, here it comes,' but Bertie took the cigar from his mouth and went to meet his wife.

'Good evening,' Henderson-Hobbs said, no smile now.

'Good evening,' Bertie returned. 'You made a fine speech.'

'I'm glad you approved.'

For a few seconds the two men stared at each other, both so alike in build and features, though Robert was the taller.

Kit said quickly, 'Mr Henderson-Hobbs has suggested he takes us to Windsor in the morning –' and her words drained away as the steeliness crept into Bertie's blue gaze.

'How unfortunate,' he said charmingly, and clicked his thumb and forefinger together. 'If I had known a few minutes earlier we could have accepted, but as it is I have just telephoned home to say we're taking an earlier train. They'll be expecting us for lunch.' He drew Kit away, smiling, leaving Robert smiling back, but far from pleased.

Kit was furious, but waited until they were near the table before she hissed, 'You snubbed him. Ridiculously.'

Bertie kept hold of her hand. 'I was extremely courteous.'

'He was trying to be friendly. He needs to talk to you.'

'He can talk to me another time. The world will not come to an end during the next twenty-four hours.'

They reached Maggie's side and Bertie said pleasantly, 'Kit has a bit of a headache, so we're turning in early.'

'Ooo!' Maggie was dismayed. 'Why didn't Robert come over?'

'Probably because he has other things to do. Good night both.'

'Night,' said John. 'See you in the morning.'

'I doubt it,' Bertie returned. 'Kit wants to get back to the girls,' and he persuaded Kit away and up to their room.

He sat on the bed and watched her at the dressing-table, taking off the diamanté earrings, examining her face in the brightly lit mirror, her body tense with anger.

He said, 'I was high-handed, wasn't I?' and she didn't reply. He relaxed back, then lay on the bed. 'I was thinking you and I could go off on our own in the morning. Maybe visit the zoo or the Tower. If either are open.' He waited for her reply, and she sighed, then laughed, easing.

'You are an old fox, Mr Hemsworthy, but yes, I will come to the zoo with you.'

CHAPTER THREE

Those who went to Windsor met those who didn't as the London train puffed into Slough station. Bertie leaned through his carriage window grinning and waving, and Maggie and John were the first to join him, laughing, scrambling for seats.

The snack trolley trundled along the platform and Bertie carolled, 'What are you all having?'

'Pies. Pasties. Sandwiches,' called the fresh-faced youth propelling the trolley. 'Tea? Coffee?'

'Pasties all round,' Bertie cried, and dug into his inside pocket for his wallet. It was as if the weekend had been a success after all.

Once outside High Street station in Swansea, Kit and Bertie waved everyone off in their taxis or on their bikes. 'Out early tomorrow. Get new business in.' Then came the comparative hush, the anti-climax after hours crammed with people. The Swansea sky was shaded from black to purple, the street lights sending golden glows of welcome.

Bertie said, 'Thank God Maggie and John got off at Port Talbot. They were beinning to get on my nerves.'

'Beginning?' Kit's face flashed with impatience. 'I used to like Maggie Davies, but she was practically panting after Henderson-Hobbs.'

Bertie thought fleetingly of his impression that Kit, too, had been panting during the dinner. He said, 'You don't get friends in business. They're probably nice to me for the same reason that we're nice to Old Claud.'

'They're making no secret about wanting Swansea.'

'Our John Davies thinks he's a better man than I,

Gunga Din.' Bertie watched a taxi return to the yard and beckoned it. 'He told Henderson-Hobbs. With me standing there. I heard because he wanted me to. An old army game. Beat the enemy by telling him he's already lost.'

Kit lifted her suitcase, ready to board the advancing taxi, her heart heavy, the laughter and bright faces wiped from her mind.

'It was Maggie doing the pushing,' Bertie said. 'There's no doubt about that, but John wasn't slow in telling how he increased his debit over the last –'

'He did nothing of the kind!' Kit blurted. 'You spent weeks there. You. And Carruthers.' The taxi stopped before them. 'Did Henderson-Hobbs swallow it?'

'Wouldn't you?' Bertie asked. 'In his position.'

The taxi driver hurried to open the rear door, then stowed their luggage.

'Prince Edward Road,' Bertie instructed absently, and Kit got into the back seat.

'If I had my way,' she said quietly, her face a blur in the gloom, the cream-coloured coat drawn closely about her, 'I'd sack him. Now. Before he does any real harm.'

Bertie got in beside her. 'What reason do I give Head Office? I don't trust the man so I sacked him? There was enough trouble after Maggie's Christmas card to Carruthers. Imagine the hoo-ha she could cause with a phone call to –' he paused, then said caustically, '– Robert.' He turned from her, looking at Alexander Road stretching before them.

And when they got to the house, Tommy Buckley was there.

Linda heard them coming as if her antennae had been waving more anxiously than Emma's, and her eyes were wide with defiance and guilt as she greeted them at the hallstand with a breathless, 'Tommy's here! Tommy's come home.'

Bertie plonked his hat on the hook and ignored his reflection in the small mirror. 'Linda! I told you –'

'Sssh,' Kit hissed. Tommy Buckley was coming from the kitchen. After six weeks army training, eighteen years old, he filled the rough-clothed khaki uniform with new patriotic confidence.

'Mr Hemsworthy, sir.' The youth's hand was extended as he strode forward, and Bertie had an instant in which to ignore or accept it. He saw Linda's face, the big eyes so like her mother's, the expression appealing, drawn with anxiety. He had the sensation of time passing, of wishing Tommy had saluted him and not had the effrontery to assume friendship by offering his hand. Distance was needed between him and the boy. He said finally, 'Hello soldier,' and felt Tommy's fingers in his own, strong, hard, a fighter's clasp.

But it was the face above the thickness of neck that brought a great shuddering to Bertie. In so many ways here was Elsie, risen from the dead. Six foot, built like a young bull, with a barrel of a chest and not an inch of fat but, for those first dreadful moments, he had been his sister.

Bertie's tired, stunned brain momentarily reacted to a renewed sensation of drowning in sorrow. Slowly he released the boy's hand.

Linda hopped, her smile a brilliant crescent almost from ear to ear, and she moved closer to Tommy.

Emma pranced beyond, anxious to be in on the welcome. 'Shall I pour a cup of tea, Mummy? Daddy? Shall I pour a cup of tea?' They all moved to the kitchen and Emma scrambled for the tea cosy, her mouth moving in excitement and agitation. 'Cups! I put them ready. Didn't I, Linda?' She was prepared to fall over herself, as if she, too, had feared their homecoming, but was now released.

'No rush!' Kit cried. 'Just let your dad and me get in.'

Bertie stood behind his battered chair for a moment, watching. His family. His responsibility. He couldn't let the boy know how unnerving he found him. He said conversationally. 'When did you get in, soldier?'

'Last night.'

'Eleven o'clock,' Linda volunteered, and couldn't refrain from wriggling with barely controlled excitement. 'We couldn't think who it was. We got up from bed, didn't we, Emma? I ran and looked out of your bedroom window, and there he was, waving.'

Tommy grinned down at her, his shoulders consciously stiff in his effort to impress. Bertie remembered once doing the same thing, so he kept smiling, though his mouth tasted rancid; his fourteen-year-old daughter, in her nightie, warm from bed, and this young buck – a soldier. He lifted a forefinger while his mouth began to frame a warning, a lecture, but Kit clapped her hands sharply. 'Look Daddy! Look at your younger daughter. She's poured you a cup of tea.'

'Fine,' Bertie said, but that odd jumble of voices was in his head again, all coming from a distance, the room fading, dimming.

'Daddy? Are you ill?' That was Linda.

'Sit down. You're tired.' Kit was years away. He felt his legs propelled, hands and arms supporting him, then there was the lowering that became a flop, a fall, and the familiarity of cushions, his chair. He put his face in his hands as if preparing to wash it, rubbing his fingers across his cheeks, and the aberration passed. 'I'm tired,' he said, and felt Kit's hand smoothing his temple; gentle, tender.

'We'll have a nice cup of tea,' she said. 'Then we can all get to bed early. It must be nearly ten.'

'Mum?' It was Linda, anxious again. 'Can I stay home from school tomorrow?'

'Yes, Linda, yes.' Anything to avoid more bother now, and Kit caught the almost empty teapot as Emma fumbled with the cosy. 'You kids carry on with your supper. Dad and I will see to ourselves. You have all been very good.'

'Did you enjoy yourself, Mummy?'

'Yes. It was lovely. All lovely.'

She watched Bertie. He was yellow, ill. 'Shall I telephone the doctor?'

'No. I'll be all right tomorrow.'

Tomorrow, her mind screeched. Tomorrow. Then she felt calmer, though her mind groped desperately. Maybe he was right. Tomorrow would be better.

Her thoughts rambled on, a crease between her brows as she fretted, giving Bertie his cup of tea, talking gently, wishing she had asked Robert straight out, told him about the strain of waiting, and a little smile softened her mouth. Robert would have understood. He was rather nice. His touch was delicate, warm even – and she drew a quick breath while she caressed her husband's hair.

Next morning Bertie awakened and tried to muster resolution. The world was still out there, waiting to be conquered and, if he didn't conquer it, John Davies would; then he knew he was tired, shattered. The world was waiting all right, but he was too weary to join it. He remembered Kit's murmured good night. 'See the doctor, Bertie. Maybe he can help.'

'Maybe,' Bertie thought, and his mind darted back to the short conversation which he had not related to Kit.

'Fifty percent,' Henderson-Hobbs had said. 'Albert,' as if they were friends, 'we want the Swansea District densified. Too few houses booked up in too many streets means agents wasting time, and shoe leather. A good manager would watch things like that.'

Now Bertie moved his legs restlessly against the heat of the bedding. It had been a warning, he knew it, and he couldn't be ill; he had to get the old stamina going. There was Kit to think about. And the girls. Linda! And that boy.

He got cleaned up and dressed, then ran down the stairs. Where was the soldier?

He was sitting in Bertie's chair.

'Tommy!'

'Sir!' Tommy stood, instinctively the private soldier responding to that particular tone in an officer's voice.

'It isn't wise for you to stay in this house any longer. My daughter is too vulnerable.'

'Mr Hemsworthy –'

'Mr Hemsworthy nothing. It's about time you found your father?'

'He's in Dagenham. We know where he is.'

'Fine. Your place is with him.'

Kit came from the scullery, her lips tight. 'Good morning, Bertie. Nice to hear you're in such good spirits. Tommy. Here are the sandwiches. Put them in the carrier bag with the flask. You and Linda go on your way. Enjoy yourselves. You'll just get the bus if you hurry.'

Bertie gasped, straightening his wide shoulders, ready for battle, but Linda came running from the passage. 'Tara, Dad. Did you have a good sleep?' Her lips pecked his chin. He saw her brilliant happiness and knew more fear.

'Linda!'

'Tara, Dad. Tara, Mum.' She had Tommy's hand, pulling him after her.

The porch door slammed behind them and Bertie stared accusingly at Kit. 'Where are they going?'

'Caswell Bay.'

'Am I master in my own house or am I not? I do not want him here.'

Kit brushed crumbs from the white-clothed table and said quietly, 'I didn't want his sister here. I know how you feel.'

Bertie frowned, not appreciating insubordination, while Kit smiled and wondered why she had never before considered him pompous.

Out in the sunshine of this early May morning Linda and Tommy ran, he in a mixture of freedom and caution, wary of her father's warning.

'There's the bus!' Linda cried. 'It's going! Hi! Wait for us! Wait!' But it didn't and, gasping, Linda stood in the middle of the road she had been trying to cross, and watched the bus grinding away. Horses, carts, cars, bikes milled about her.

'It's gone.' Indignation and disappointment made her head jerk about. 'It went without us.'

Tommy's arm squeezed her shoulders while a pony whinnied in his ear, and he smelled the animal's heated breath and sweat. 'Never mind. Let's go to Singleton.'

'The park?' She felt let down.

'Better than nowhere.' He didn't want to return to Bertie.

A car horn blasted in vexation, a male voice bellowed, 'Out the way, soldier,' and Tommy laughed, his gap-toothed grin embracing everyone, then he guided Linda to the pavement and safety. 'D'you want to wait for the next bus?'

'It's not for ages. Hours, I think.'

And Singleton was only half a mile away. So they walked, and Bertie's command sank into the past. The acres of parkland enveloped them in another world, a land where magnolia trees had finished flowering, but cherry trees held pink and white trusses, and Linda was prepared to be in love with everything.

On the path between soft green tree-fringed meadows she became more aware of the warmth and strength of Tommy's fingers, the nearness of him, while he exclaimed, 'Cor, the place is empty!' and the brilliant black and white flicker of a magpie sped across the grasses into the woods. 'We come 'ere once,' he said happily. 'For the Whitsun treat.'

'Whitsun treat?' Linda said airily. 'Our Sunday School had those. When I was young,' and she kept walking, smiling, as if she had proved Whitsun treats were for babies.

The next field was smooth, part of it a cricket pitch, and a copse of trees beckoned from beside the lily pond. Tommy made for it. Without turning to Linda he chose a spot, took off his jacket and lowered himself to the grass. He jerked his head in satisfaction, 'This is the life,' then he leaned up on an elbow, watching Linda decide to come beside him. She did so self-consciously, sitting, drawing up her knees, then thrusting them down again, remembering young ladies never sit like that in a public place.

She glanced at Tommy and he was chewing a blade of grass, his grey eyes narrowed as they peered up at her. 'Come on, Linda. Lie down. This time next week I'll be back in barracks.'

A sense of drama engulfed her. She saw herself irresistibly, passionately, enslaved by a man prepared to give his life for King and Country, and her heart was weeping. 'I may never see you again.'

'Gerraway!' Her old man was right. He ought to scarper, vamoose.

'They might send you abroad. To China.'

'Yeh. Getta good time out there –' He decided she was not going to lie down, so he rolled on his back, fingers linked behind his head. 'And they'll tell us first. Give us special leave.'

'Honest?'

'Honest injun.'

The air was warm, unmoving. Linda stretched her arms above her head, pointed her toes, and slowly, luxuriously, lay back.

'Oooh Tommy. Isn't this lovely?'

'Scrumptious,' he agreed, and used a blade of grass to tickle her ear. She squealed, exaggerating the fun, and jerked her head to one side, but when he paused in his tickling she brought her head near again, and they laughed together, quietly.

Carefully, gently, he bent over her and let his lips touch hers. Linda looked at the sky, her body tense. 'There,' he whispered, 'nothing wrong in that, is there?' and Linda shook her head doubtfully.

'Shall I do it again?'

'Somebody might see.'

Tommy laughed, but he was thoughtful, and he went back to moving the blade of grass about her ear, across her mouth, down her throat, to the base of the V neck on the voile dress, as if the grass was doing what his fingers mustn't.

They were content with each other and their secret dreams. They ate their picnic and went to the pond, quacking back at the ducks, seeking tadpoles or newts.

'They turn in to frogs,' Tommy said, airing his knowledge.

Linda glanced sideways at him. He had kissed her before, on the station as his train prepared to puff away. Today he had kissed her again. That meant they were lovers.

She said. 'Let's go and look for squirrels.'

'Where?'

'In the rose garden.'

She ran and he chased, and the hours scudded past.

A little breeze arose as the sun slid to the west and strands of Linda's thick brown hair lifted and floated against her head, so the lights in it glittered like miniature rainbows. Tommy wanted to fondle her, breathe into those lights, feel their silkiness against his face.

He swung the carrier bag with the empty flask, and grinned, thinking of the fellows in barracks, the laughter when they talked of girls, and wondered why he could never talk of Linda like that. Maybe he was daft.

Linda led him towards the stream that gushed and ran in a belt of woods and rhododendrons. There, in a dappled world of closeness, they walked without speaking, each terribly aware of the other.

They stopped to watch a black labrador gallop into the stream, splashing, yapping, then lapping noisily and wading out. Linda laughed, then took off her shoes and the art silk stockings, hopping on one leg, giggling, her fingers unused to suspenders, and Tommy stood with the carrier bag dangling beside him, his uniform too warm and heavy, his cap on the side of his almost shorn head. 'What're you doing?'

'Going for a paddle.'

He groaned, raised his eyebrows. 'Girls!'

'My feet are hot. Hot. Hot.'

He watched her move down the shallow bank, then

slip her white toes into the skidding water. 'Oooh,' she squealed, and lifted her face in delighted horror, the unaccustomed powder worn off her nose, but clinging to her cheeks. He watched her tuck the wide fluttering transparent skirt of the blue voile dress up, into the elastic legs of her thick navy knickers, and while her innocence took over, Tommy's manhood brought desire. He looked away from Linda's joy while she trod carefully across the pebbled bottom of the stream until she reached its centre. She kept laughing, gazing down at the twigs swimming in black and silver flashes past her ankles.

Tommy scowled. She was childish. Showing him up. And him in uniform. Hell, he had nothing else to wear. He turned to the oak tree and placed his feet amid its gnarled spreading roots. Linda's stockings lay there, crumpled, as she had flung them, and he wanted to lift them, put them in his pocket and keep them. For ever. He leaned against the bole of the tree and looked nonchalant, indulging the silly kid, but the heat was upon him and he didn't know what to do about it.

'Tommy! Look! Someone's made a boat!' Linda demanded his attention, and pointed with her big toe to the folded paper bobbing past her. 'It's going to wreck!' she cried. 'Oh! The poor sailors'll drown!' and the vitality in her voice made Tommy's nape prickle, made him want to bed her. Over and over.

He was sweating, burning. 'Linda! Come on out of there! Yer acting daft!' There was malice in his voice, his eyes glaring. Linda looked up at him, startled.

'I was only playing. It's fun.'

'It's not fun at all. It's childish.' His face was red with self-shame, his body bent in an effort to ease the craving she had awakened.

Linda considered, then acquiesced. She came from the stream. 'All right. It is cold anyway. My feet are all pink.'

Tommy looked at her feet as they came on to the bank, moving softly on the sparse grass, and he wanted to kneel beside them, take them to him and kiss them. Kiss all the way up.

Jesus! He would have to get away from here! And not come back. Ever. Bertie Hemsworthy would hang him.

'I'm going, Linda.' He swung away from the tree, towards the field, no longer following the stream.

Linda watched, disbelieving, then 'Pig!' she yelled, and tears made her eyes red and sore, but didn't fall. 'Pig,' she muttered again to herself. 'Pig. Pig.'

She slipped her bare feet awkwardly into her shoes, their wetness making them stick, having to be pushed and forced. She grabbed the stockings from the ground and screwed them to a ball in her hand, then, her ankle straps flapping, she ran after Tommy. 'I'm sorry, I didn't mean anything. I'm quite grown up. I am. Tommy! I am.'

Tommy marched on, his shoulders tense.

Linda caught him up but didn't walk beside him. She paused long enough to crouch and fasten the button of one shoe strap, but Tommy was moving fast and she hurried after him again, getting to within a yard of him before she stopped to button the other.

They were nearing town when she finally had the courage to draw abreast of him.

'Tommy!' She clutched his arm. 'If you treat me like this, you'll never stay in our house again!'

He stopped marching, the heat gone from him now, but the anxiety remained. 'That's just the way I want it!'

Linda let him walk on. She couldn't think what she had done that was so terrible, 'Bums to you,' she whispered scowlingly, but when she got home and Tommy wasn't there, she thought it the end of the world.

Bertie looked at her flushed ill-tempered face, at the way she flopped her body around and he said, with satisfaction, 'The tyke's probably gone off to get drunk. Squaddies always do.'

'Shut up!' Linda squealed, and saw his hand tighten as if to avoid slapping her. 'It's your fault!' she cried. 'You did it! You told him!'

'Sssh!' Kit stood, shocked. 'Linda! Don't speak to your father like that!'

'I'm leaving school soon. I'll go away. Have my own life.' She glared, tearful, at her father. 'I hate you. I told you before. You ruined us. All our happiness.' She ran from the room, sprinting up the stairs. Kit went to follow her but Bertie caught her arm. 'Tell her to come back here. I want to talk to her. Pronto.'

'No, Bertie. It is partly your fault.

'Tell her I want her.'

Kit's body wavered, her mind undecided. Emma was curled in her mother's chair, knees to her chin, eyes wide as she listened. 'No,' Kit said. 'There have been too many upsets in this house already. Every one of them caused by a Buckley. I don't want any more.'

Bertie marched past her, shouting 'Lindah! Get down here at once.'

The house became silent and Bertie went back to the kitchen. 'If you give in to her now, Kit, you might as well say goodbye to her. She'll follow that boy over St Thomas, and when he goes back to camp she'll be left there. With that crew. God knows who she'll get in with. Slave-traders. You know the dangers. You see the newspapers.'

'Don't be ridiculous, Bertie. Nothing could happen. Not in Swansea.'

'The ships are there. The docks. The Arabs.'

'They're ordinary sailors!'

'How do we know? If girls can disappear on Paddington station what can happen near dock gates?'

Kit shuddered, her voice rueful. 'She wouldn't talk to seamen, coloured men. Not our daughter. She must know there are wicked people about. Bad people!'

'Have you told her so?' Kit didn't reply and he went on, 'Go and get her.'

Kit hurried up the stairs, her hand to her mouth. 'Linda? Darling?' She tapped the bedroom door. 'Do try and understand. A bad man could get you. Carry you away.'

She went in and Linda was on the bed, her head turned to Kit. 'Come on,' Kit urged, 'listen to your father.'

'I've heard him before,' Linda said, and pulled the pillow over her head.

Kit went down to Bertie. 'Let's forget it. Tommy has gone and I'll explain the dangers to her later.'

Emma came to her father and put her arms about his thighs. 'I don't like bad people,' she said, and Bertie reluctantly left Linda upstairs while he sat and cuddled Emma.

On Wednesday morning he felt no better. He left the bed and drew back the curtains to find the world wet and grey.

By eleven o'clock all eight agents were waiting in the middle room, drinking tea and eating biscuits. Kit flurried about, removing trays, returning ledgers and, at half-past twelve, she stood before Bertie's desk and said, 'We're ready for your pep talk.'

'So am I,' he replied, and then the postman came, whistling, his yellow cape about his shoulders glistening and running with rain.

'Mornin',' he grinned at Kit and handed her a small but heavy package while the wet ran off the peak of his cap.

She watched him cock his leg over his bicycle and enter the swirl of traffic. She would have liked to have been him, out there, away from the sombre atmosphere of the house.

She went back to the office. 'A London date stamp,' she said.

Bertie was going through the claim receipts, making notes on strips of paper.

'Shall I open it?' Kit asked.

'Somebody has to.'

She shot an impatient glance at him. 'You might have decided it should be you.'

He stared up at her. 'Why should I decide it should be me?'

She put the parcel on the desk. 'I am not one of your

employees, Bertie. I'm your wife and partner and I would appreciate being treated as such.'

She used the ivory paper knife to jab the wrapping off the parcel, her movements vicious. 'It's from London,' she repeated. 'Must be Head Office.'

Bertie sat back, his expression softening. 'Obviously a box,' and he smiled at her.

She hesitated a moment in her paper-slicing and said reassuringly, 'We're both worrying too much. If H.-H. intended sacking you he really would have done it by now.'

Bertie went broody again, his attention on the purple cardboard showing from the parcel. 'Looks like chocolates. Good God!'

His head shot up, his eyes widening, accusing. 'You even damn well told him what your favourite chocolates were!'

'I did nothing of the sort, and I'll thank you not to bawl at me. I don't like it.'

He lowered his voice. 'I haven't known you ever like anything, Kit. That's the trouble.'

Kit's hands began to shake as they pulled the last of the brown paper away, and two boxes sat on the desk. One contained her favourite chocolates, the other was plain brown cardboard. 'I imagine,' Kit said patiently, 'this one is for you,' and she lifted it onto the stack of papers by his elbow.

'I've made all those notes!' he said sharply, 'and you can't wait for the blasted ink to dry before you stick a damned box on them.'

'It is from Henderson-Hobbs,' Kit retorted, reading a small card attached to the chocolates, and waited.

Male laughter came muffled from the next room and a tram driver stamped on his bell outside the window. Bertie drew his hand across his chin hard, then removed the lid of the box.

'What the hell . . .' he breathed, and his face was furrowed as he lifted out a wooden base on which stood a miniature Rolls-Royce; it had a fountain pen standing in a tube-like compartment at the back. 'That's gold! I'll swear it!' He stared at Kit. 'Gold plating.'

'Is it stamped?' Kit, disbelieving, reached over and took the Rolls-Royce from him, then she gave a sigh of awe. 'He can't possibly be planning to sack you.' There was a hint of hysterical laughter in her voice. 'He wouldn't sent you a gift like that if he was.'

'Could be a farewell gift,' Bertie said, and poked his tongue into his cheek. 'A Rolls-Royce,' he said grimly. 'I suppose you told the man you would like a Rolls-Royce and your husband couldn't supply one.'

'I hardly spoke to him!'

'Liar!'

'Bertie! Don't you dare – I have stuck to you through thick and thin –'

He sat forward again, holding up a hand. 'I'm sorry. Whatever you told him you were trying to help.'

'I told him nothing.'

Bertie glanced at the papers beside him, then blew on them as if trying to make sure the ink was dry. 'Somebody told him what chocolates you like.'

Kit leaned forward, gripping the edge of his desk. 'Then send the bloody lot back.'

Bertie nodded slowly. He was getting reaction from her and he liked it. 'It would be arrant bad manners to return it, but I don't want it anywhere near me. If Henderson-Hobbs wants to buy you he'll find you exceptionally expensive.'

'You're rotten!'

He dabbed his mouth with the clean white handkerchief still folded from his breast pocket. 'Shall we get on with the job? Are you coming into the other room?'

'Go to hell, Bertie Hemsworthy, and tell the devil why you're at his door. I'm going to clean the vegetables.'

He straightened his shoulders and eased his neck in the stiff collar, dismissing the sensation of slowly choking. He left his chair and marched to the middle room, singing quietly, keeping up a front. He rapped loudly on the door – let them finish swopping their dirty jokes – then he went in, full of authority and confidence. 'Enjoyed yourselves in London, lads? Splendid. Now you are expected to pay for it.'

He took up position before the white fireplace, the back of his dark head reflected in the large mirror on the mantelpiece. 'The new man at the top doesn't think much of Swansea. You John, he thinks you're a drip and your wife a creep.' John's mouth dropped open, his hands fisting on his spread knees. 'But you can keep your shirt on. The great man has offered salvation.' Bertie leaned a forearm along the mantelpiece beside the black marble rearing horses. He smiled around at his audience. He had talked men into mass murder, he could talk these into sweated labour.

'Unless your debits – every one of you – are up fifty percent in the next twelve months, you're out. The lot of you. Me and all. There is no sacking me and sitting one of you in my chair. Compris?'

He waited, watching them, listening as a little sigh of concern floated from every man. They exchanged quick glances and shifted their legs and arms in discomfort.

'That on the level, guv?'

'On the level.'

They all filled their lungs, and John's hands dropped between his knees. 'When did he tell you that?' His tone was dubious.

'When d'you suppose he told me, John? You surprised he didn't tell you and Maggie first?'

John's face coloured, but he said nothing.

'Right then,' Bertie went on. 'The fact is he did tell me. He doesn't want the district extended. Not yet anyway. He wants more houses per street. And he wants them pronto. I'm in full accord with him. It's high time we had a younger man at the top. Somebody who'll put his foot down and get rid of the slackers.'

Bertie waited for someone to speak, but there was

silence. 'Right,' he smiled, easing now, the charm coming through. 'This week all do your damnedest. An extra hour every day on the knocker.'

'We don't finish till dark on Fridays as it is,' a low voice said. 'It's the night we get a lot of the money in.'

'Simple answer,' Bertie replied. 'Put extra hours in on Saturday.'

'That's our busiest day!' John exclaimed. 'Be fair, guv'nor. You know people get their money on Friday and we got to be there Saturday, or they pay it to someone else.'

'Don't blame me,' Bertie said. 'You blame Henderson-Hobbs. He wants blood, and if we want our jobs we have to give it to him. I've been making out lists of each man's claims this year, and if you want to keep paying out you've got to start bringing in. We're in business, lads, not running a charity.'

They nodded slowly, accepting. It was logic.

Bertie stood away from the mantelpiece. 'You'll find Henderson-Hobbs all right. Kit and I had a couple of gifts from him this morning. John, he sent Kit chocolates but she doesn't like them. You can give them to Maggie with our good wishes.' He smiled around, knowing he had them where he wanted. He strode from the room, then returned with the purple box. 'Here you are, old chap. Give her my regards and teach her to keep her mouth shut. Stop her sticking her foot in it.'

Seven agents laughed self-consciously while John took the chocolates and lifted his briefcase. He stood and stared eye to eye with Bertie, and Bertie gripped his shoulder. 'Cheer up, John. We're not dead yet.'

John turned from him, and the men filed out.

When Bertie went to the kitchen he was grinning broadly. 'I gave the chocolates to John for Maggie.'

'Fine,' Kit retorted. 'I'll give your Rolls-Royce to the school fete,' and Bertie went back to the office, stood looking at the Rolls-Royce and the pen jutting up at him. 'Bloody phallus symbol,' he muttered, and wondered what Henderson-Hobbs was up to. The man couldn't seriously want Kit. She was too skinny by half.

* * *

In St Hilda's School for Young Ladies Emma pulled up her navy knickers, whipped her white pleated skirt into place, stood on the lavatory seat, and took the stub of blue chalk off the tiny stone windowsill that was almost out of reach. She wrote on the whitewashed wall MISS GRIFFITHS GOT A BIG NOES. Then, smirking happily, Emma dived out from the centre of the line of lavatories, and ran like mad across the grass, into the main building.

She joined the end of a crocodile of girls processing into the hall, the piano banging out the Double Eagle march under the spidery fingers of Miss Griffiths herself.

Miss Griffiths saw the seven-year-old Emma attach herself to the line of fourteen-year-olds and, as Emma came abreast of her, Miss Griffiths whipped out her right hand while her left kept vamping. She caught Emma by the shoulder of her blouse and yanked her to the piano. 'Where have you been, Emma Hemsworthy?' Miss Griffiths glowered while her right hand went back to the keys and her voice cried, 'Left right. Left right. Hold your heads up, girls!' and Emma stood with her blue eyes popping beneath her dark brown fringe.

'Come on, girls!' Miss Griffiths shouted. 'Swing those arms. We're all British, you know. Hold your heads up. Be proud!' Linda was doing what Emma had done. She came through the big door at the end of the corridor and ran to the fast-receding crocodile as it wound into the hall.

Emma hissed 'Linda!' and Linda instinctively heard her through all other sounds. She left the tail of the column and came, walking, as if rightfully proud to be British, head up, tummy in, and stood beside Emma.

The corridor emptied of marching feet, the noise from the hall became muted as someone demanded silence, but there were chairs bumping, feet shuffling, echoing through the building. Miss Griffiths took her right foot off the loud pedal and her hands from the keys.

'Please Miss,' Linda smiled. 'I've come to collect my sister. My father says I have to stay with her as much as I can because she's got a cold in her bladder.'

Miss Griffiths stared into Linda's face, suspecting Father had said nothing of the kind. Emma's brows were high, stretched, her mouth open, showing that another of her top front teeth had gone. Miss Griffiths said patiently, 'Emma, where have you been?'

'Across the lawn, Miss. I couldn't find you so I went on my own. It is the cold in my bladder.' Emma ran short of air and her chest rose as she filled it again.

Miss Griffiths tightened her lips. 'You must remember, your parents pay for you to come here, so I have the responsibility of seeing you are safe at all times. If you had fallen, been hurt, I wouldn't have known where to look for you.' She returned her gaze to Linda. 'Go along the two of you, and for heaven's sake be more considerate in future.'

The two girls laughed with relief and nodded agreement, then they caught hands and walked quickly to the hall, taking their places on the end of a choral horseshoe.

Miss Griffiths strode in and took up position before them, her baton raised. Another piano became ill-treated and fifty young mouths were urged to bellow. 'Oh let the prayer re-echo, God bless the Prince of Wales . . .'

Emma sang with fervour, wondered why the prairie should echo, then paused to pull a face at Bunty Morris who stood opposite.

Bunty swung her long yellow plaits with their end bows of black velvet and rolled her eyes at Linda. Linda elbowed Emma surreptitiously and hissed threateningly from the corner of her mouth, 'She's my best friend,' then exchanged martyrd looks with Bunty.

Emma sang loudly then muttered disparagingly, 'Finishing School will finish her off,' and Linda didn't elbow her; she understood the jealousy. It seemed as if everyone was going to Finishing School but herself.

The piano went silent for a while and Miss Griffiths chastised, praised and urged all onto greater effort. The pianist bent to her task and again the voices rose in accord. '. . . our emblem dear. The Maple leaf for ever . . .'

Linda bent a little to one side, hoping to get nearer Emma's ear. 'I just saved you from doing lines, didn't I?'

Emma's eyes swivelled towards her sister, knowing there was now a price to pay.

Linda went on, 'Tell Mummy I had to stay in to swot.'

'She knows you don't any more. You're leaving –'

'Tell her it's for French, and I want to learn before I leave here for ever.'

Emma nodded, aware of drama enfolding her. 'Where're you really going?'

'To find Tommy before he goes back to camp.'

Emma's mouth made an O and her shoulders wriggled in fear and pleasure. It was agonisingly wonderful to be involved in Linda's passionate love affair. 'If you go over St Thomas,' she warned hissingly, 'a bad man might get you and take you away in a boat.'

'Don't be silly,' Linda returned, but she found the information unnerving.

So, at half-past four, Emma ran all the way home, her panama bobbing behind her, held on by the white elastic about her neck, while Linda ran along the lanes to the centre of town, dreading being seen by someone who would tell Daddy.

Down through the narrowness of Wind Street where the buildings were ornate, blackened by age, under the railway bridge and into another world. A world that smelled of sea, of fish, with seamen wandering aimlessly, some already drunk, and girls with wary eyes posing on corners.

Linda didn't run so fast now. She wanted to absorb it all, this forbidden land, and she wanted to find Tommy while her face was cool and calm, not hot and red and ugly.

A massive negro loped along the iron swing bridge towards her, loose-limbed, arms dangling with pale-palmed hands, and Linda knew a delicious feeling of danger. She watched him surreptitiously; was he a slave-trader?

She edged to the side of the bridge and linked her arms through the ironwork, gripping tightly, hardly breathing. If the negro grabbed her now she would cling. Scream. Kick. People would understand she was being kidnapped. They would rescue her.

The negro kept loping, his stomach sunken in baggy grey flannels, his eyes looking nowhere but ahead, and Linda didn't breathe at all as he passed, silent-footed, alien.

The traffic rumbled on the wood base of the bridge, a ship moaned, the thick-looking green waters lapped, and Linda ran, into St Thomas, the land of little shops and terraced houses.

She made for Salubrious Terrace, the first of many rows siding Kilvey Hill, and there was the Buckley house, cracked, placed high above the road, supported by a tall stone wall.

There were three boys sitting on the steps leading up to Salubrious Terrace, scruffy boys, and they knew which way she wanted to go. They looked at her, snuffling, scratching their behinds through ragged short trousers.

Linda stared at them and the youngest boy shot out his tongue to clean his nose. Linda turned away in horror, her stomach heaving. The boys laughed uproariously, slapping each other, pushing their feet out to make sure the steps were truly blocked.

Linda slowly approached. 'Excuse me,' she said primly. 'I wish to pass.' The boys stared at her, not moving, their complexions so clear they were almost transparent, colourless.

'Where yer goying, love?' the youngest sniggered.

'Up those steps.'

'You gotta pay.'

All three boys wore bland expressions, their eyes too big.

'I shall call the police.'

The boys leaned together, giving hoots of derisive laughter, clearing their throats and spitting on the pavement.

Linda's nose wrinkled. She had to decide. Go home and not see Tommy, or brave these common people. She stepped forward, her chin stubborn. 'If you don't mind,' she said. 'I wish to climb those steps.'

'You gotta pay,' they replied, and settled for long hard bargaining.

Linda stamped her foot. 'I'll punch you!'

The laughter became immense, necks stretched as heads rolled back, and Linda wanted to squeal with frustration. A dark brown hand landed on her shoulder, and a velvety voice said, 'This way with Ali, love. Ali take you where you want to go.'

Linda's gaze travelled from the hand so near her ear, up to the triangular face above her. He looked like a brown hawk, beaked nose, black jutting brows and sunken cheeks. 'Hi you kids!' he cried, and shook his fist. 'You want me to do the punch on the nose?'

The boys hesitated, their eyelids drooping in dislike. 'We wuz only fooling,' and they sidled away.

'So'm I,' said the Arab, and his hand on Linda's shoulder propelled her forward. She climbed the steps self-consciously, aware of the coloured face so near her own, and, at the top of the steps, she paused to smile diffidently.

'Thank you,' she said, but had no idea what to do next. To walk away would be terribly rude, yet to stay and talk – goosepimples of fear rose all over her.

He said with a gold-toothed smile, 'You're looking for someone, sweetheart?' and his black eyes missed nothing of her, the private school uniform, the real leather shoes, the expensive panama and blazer.

'Yes. Tommy Buckley.'

'Tommeee!' He drew his thin shoulders in their black shirt up to his ears. 'Tommeee lives in my house. You come with Ali. We are friends.'

'In your house?' It didn't sound right.

'Same house as me. Maud Jeffries' house, but Tommeee been with us since Monday.' Again there was the ear-touching shrug, the sideways movement of powerful arms. 'Tommeee had no home, nowhere to sleep, so I was kind to him. I am kind to everybody. I told Maud Jeffries now give that boy a bed.' He put both brown hands to his chest. 'I love Tommeee. I love everybody. No trouble with Ali anywhere.'

Linda smiled and the boys sat on the steps again, craning to stare upwards.

Ali put an arm about Linda's shoulders and led her to an open doorway.

The narrow passage floor was subsiding beneath frayed oilcloth. There was the smell of damp and too many people. The stairs rose without covering, their bare wood scrubbed white.

'Tommeee!' Ali yelled, and the kitchen door opened. Faces peered out.

'Come by 'ere, love,' an old crone called. 'I knows you. You're the insurance man's daughter.'

Linda nodded, not sure of anything.

The crone looked at Ali. 'Best send her off 'ome!' she called. 'Get rid of her.'

'She wants to see Tommeee,' Ali said.

'Huh,' said the crone, still in the kitchen, and a tall blonde appeared beside her, long diamanté earrings swinging, dabs of rouge the size of half-crowns on her full wide cheeks, her lips disguised by an accentuated bow.

Linda stared. She had never seen anything as garish.

The blonde moved forward and leaned against the door jamb, popping a white pellet of Wrigley's gum into her mouth. She leaned and chewed, one hand on a jutting hip while the earrings glittered. 'Look a bit longer love,' she sneered, without malice, 'and yer'll know me.'

Linda jerked from her stupor and said, 'I'm sorry.'

'That's Stella,' said Ali. 'She is my best sweetheart.'

Stella heaved herself upright and shot him a disparaging glance. 'I better be your only sweetheart, boyo,' then she gazed back at Linda. 'Go home, love. You get all sorts round this place.'

'She wants to see Tommeee,' Ali repeated.

The crone pulled her black shawl closer about her narrow shoulders. 'Does yer father know you're here?' she addressed Linda, and Linda shook her head.

The old woman hesitated, sniffed, then said, 'He's upstairs. Give him a yell,' and Stella sauntered, hips first, towards Ali, still chewing, still sparkling. 'All together,' she said. 'One! Two! Three!' and she and Ali yelled, 'Tommeee!'

He came to the top of the stairs in grey flannel trousers held up with cord like, Linda thought, the old days, when he had a pony and sold firewood around the doors.

His voice was churlish as he demanded, 'What are you doing here?'

Ali called, 'She was looking for you,' and his brown hand pushed Linda forward. 'She was very afraid of those boys on the steps out there, so I help her.'

'Tommy!' the old crone ordered without coming to look up at him. 'You bring yer friend inter the kitchen for a cuppa tea, then she better go again before her father finds out.'

Tommy came down the stairs, clattering, his army boots too big for the narrow depth of the stairs.

Gloom swallowed Linda's heart. This public, tawdry meeting was not what she had expected.

'C'mon,' Tommy said, and yanked her from Ali, then to the kitchen where it seemed a multitude sat. A ginger cat washed itself on the table, its tail against an open tin of condensed milk.

'Get another cup,' the crone said, and hobbled to a

wooden chair that wobbled as she sat. 'Annie! You wash the one you got there. Make sure you get the lipstick off of it.' Linda felt an oddity. There were so many curious pairs of eyes concentrating on her.

Annie ran to the scullery and Linda saw her swish the cup in a bowl of standing water, shake it and bring it back. 'There,' she beamed, and Tommy stuffed his hands in his trouser pockets and said, 'Your dad'll hang me,' but he was grinning, pleased now the initial surprise had worn off.

Linda watched stewed tea spurting from the spout of the teapot into the wet cup. Two huge teaspoon loads of condensed milk were ladled into it. Annie stirred it then held it out to Linda. Linda took it, seeing the grease spots floating on top, and wondered how to avoid drinking it.

'Cliff!' ordered the crone. 'You get up, let the young lady sit by there.'

Linda sat on the wooden chair that had no back, and Tommy came and stood beside her. She said tentatively, 'Do you all live here? In this house?'

'Not me,' said Stella casually. 'I got my own room. To myself. Up the next but one road.'

'The rest of us do,' said Tommy quietly, watching Linda to see how she took the information.

She asked, awed, 'But where d'you all sleep? There are only two bedrooms, aren't there?'

Ali smiled easily and poured himself tea into a cracked cup that no one bothered to wash. 'We share,' he said. 'Take it in turns in beds on the floor.'

The crone wagged a warning finger at him. 'Don't you start any complaining or you can find a bed somewhere else m'boy,' and everyone murmured, 'True. True,' and rolled their eyeballs to emphasise the foolishness of Ali's words.

Linda managed a small smile, the cup hot between her hands. The cat finished its grooming and stared at her. She stood up and handed Tommy the untouched tea. 'As long as you're all right, I won't stay.'

He hunched his shoulders. 'I'll walk along with you,' and the crone looked at the filled cup as he put it on the table. 'What's a matter with that?' She glared at Linda. 'Not good enough for you?'

'Thank you,' Linda smiled nervously. 'I mustn't wait for it to cool. My father will be home.'

She went out, and the three boys moved from the steps as the massive negro she had seen on the swing bridge came up them. 'Hi folks.'

He wasn't ignoring anyone now, and Linda stared in fascination at the shiny black face.

'Hi!' everyone replied, and it was evident he lived there too. He flapped a hand at Linda and wobbled his eyebrows flirtatiously.

Tommy grinned, 'Keep orf! She's not from around here,' then to Linda, 'His name's Ebony,' and Linda nodded and hurried down to the pavement, ashamed of her fear and snobbishness.

Tommy said, as they walked quickly along the pavement, 'What d'you want to come here for? You got no business here.'

'I wanted us to be friends again.'

'We are friends. You don't have ter run after me. Make me look soft in front of everybody.'

Linda watched her feet and wanted to run hard, and maybe cry, because nothing was right, and her father would surely know where she had been.

'I don't like you coming over here. Seeing all the muck and that. Now they'll make fun behind my back, saying you're all la-di-da.'

'Well I'm not la-di-da! I just want to be with you, and if my dad loses his job we might have to live in a house like yours.'

'It isn't mine. The landlord let it to Ma Jeffries after my ma died and my pa went to England.'

Linda said nothing and he asked, 'Why's your dad going ter lose his job then?'

His tone was slightly belligerent, as if he didn't believe

91

her and, piqued, she answered, 'Because your sister swindled the Unicorn and my dad gets the blame.'

'Your dad deserves the blame. She was only eighteen when he put her in the club. My family had the shame. It killed my mother.'

'Consumption killed your mother. And my father paid for her to be in Malvern!'

They stopped to stare at each other, and gradually the animosity waned from each young face. Linda stood on her toes and pressed her nose to his cheek. 'Tommy. Please don't be angry. Everybody's angry with me. It was all terrible. And my dad still loves your sister. He takes flowers to her grave.'

Tommy wanted to wrap her to him, console her, but said, 'Better get home, Linda. Quick. Your father'll be after me –'

'Tommy.' Her lips were offered, ready, anxious.

He stepped back. 'Go on home. Go on. Quick.' He turned from her, his boots clomping, the studs striking sparks against the pavement as he walked away. 'I'll send you a postcard,' he called over his shoulder. 'I'll try and write to you.'

For a moment she watched him striding down the street, then she turned and ran, her cheeks flaming with humiliation. 'I hate him,' she sobbed. 'I hate him, hate him.'

Her father was waiting at the gate of three hundred, his eyes narrowed as they watched the long road. She saw his white sleeves jutting from his navy waistcoat more easily than she saw his face from way down the corner, and his head didn't move as he began to recognise her.

Linda clasped her fist to her chest, her breathing difficult. Never had her father hit her, but now his stance was a threat.

'Lindah!'

Her inside cringed.

She ran to him, then tried to swerve around him.

'To bed. And stay there!'

'Yes Daddy.' She crashed the porch door wide open and stampeded into the house. He came after her, relief that she was safe only fuel for his anger.

'Turn your sister into a liar again and I'll thrash both of you!'

'Yes Daddy.' She pounded up the stairs. She could hear Emma screaming, 'I didn't tell, Linda. I didn't!'

'Quiet,' Kit's voice instructed, and she came to the bedroom, her voice also cross. 'Don't you dare go over there again. It isn't nice.'

Emma sidled in, her face stained with tears. 'Daddy telephoned the school, Linda, because Miss Griffiths mustn't keep you in, and it was shut. The caretaker said so.'

Downstairs Bertie went into the office and closed the door after him, blotting the world and all its responsibilities out. The smell of ink, of paper, the enclosure of privacy, was manna.

He sat at his desk and opened and closed drawers. The brown cardboard box was there, containing the gold Rolls-Royce pen stand; it reminded him that Henderson-Hobbs had the power to blast him – and his kids.

The headache shot into place and he went to the hallstand, plonking the homburg on his head, putting his coat over his arm.

'Bertie?' It was Kit coming down the stairs.

'I'm going for a walk. Along the beach.'

She followed him to the gate and watched him go. He didn't look back, didn't see the expression on her face as he strode down the road that led to town, and not to the beach.

Kit ran back into the house, called, 'Linda! Keep an eye on things. D'you hear me?' She took her coat and scarf off the hallstand. 'Emma! Tell Linda I have to go out for a while. Be good. Love you,' then Kit was running on the balls of her feet, making hardly any sound, already furtive. Bertie was going to row with Tommy. She could not allow that, yet couldn't think how to stop it.

Never once did he hesitate or look back, although it was a long way. She kept behind Bertie and had no need to be careful.

As they hurried over the bridge the lights came on, and Kit glanced up at them quickly. The sky was streaked with darkness overtaking day, and the waters of the dock lapped and bobbed flotsam in a disturbing way.

Bertie stopped on the pavement opposite the terraced houses above their supporting wall, his hat pulled down, the top of his face in shadow, and Kit stood in an alcove beside a shop window and watched him through the glass.

Men walked passed, laughing, smoking, then came young couples, and Kit shivered. She missed her hat and gloves. The cold seeped up through her rubber-soled flat house shoes.

The houses opposite remained unlit. No door opened or closed, but still Bertie stood, a cigarette burning between his fingers.

As darkness fell and the street became silent, Kit held her collar about her mouth, glad of its protection, but Bertie seemed unaware of night or cold.

Kit sighed over him, glared at the back of him and knew he had not come to confront Tommy. He had come to moon over the memory of Elsie. She stamped her feet and rubbed her hands, exasperated, then suddenly turned and marched home, dissatisfied and exhausted.

As she walked she told herself she had tried to forgive his love and lust for Elsie Buckley, but now she felt betrayed all over again. She could not forgive his chasing shadows.

Tomorrow she would write to Henderson-Hobbs, enjoy the distant acquaintanceship of a man. After all, it was 1933; time women stopped being owned by their husbands, doormats for the unfaithful.

As she hurried, her head high now with resolve, she

became aware of being a respectable woman out alone after dark, and a shudder like impending death ran through her. What if Bertie never came back to her? What if the rest of her life was spent in limbo, a wife, yet not a wife?

Divorce didn't enter her mind. The shame, the scandal, the expense, the subsequent ostracism; such a trauma could never be remotely considered.

CHAPTER FOUR

John Davies sang quietly as his big narrow feet pounded the pavement, 'Feed me till I want no more . . .' His lips framed the words while his mind echoed the next 'want no more . . .' Half a day's tramping had brought in only threepence worth of new business. He paused to sit on the low wall surrounding someone's ragged garden.

To go on, or not to go on; that was the question.

It was Thursday, the day he usually did a bit in the garden, squeezed Maggie's bottom when she brought out the parsnip wine, and talked baby talk to young Buck.

The street wound on, so clean it looked lonely, the handkerchief gardens made of starved grass and, up there, the mountain loomed. There was no sign of life about the farmhouse, no white nightie fluttering like a tent fighting the guy ropes. Maggie must be out. Taken the baby somewhere.

No sense in going home yet.

Might as well canvass a bit more.

He examined the street again. There was a Mr and Mrs Capriolli living down there somewhere. They made ice cream; in their scullery, so folk said, and it was nice too. John had seen Mr Capriolli pedalling a white cart full of the stuff, a wide banner saying STOP ME AND BUY ONE.

John wondered if Mr Capriolli would buy one off him; an insurance policy. Preferably a big one.

He left the wall, dusted the shiny seat of his navy blue trousers, yawned loudly and plodded on. He found the house easily enough. It had red painted windows and looked more prosperous than all the others. John rapped his knuckles where a knocker ought to be.

Mrs Capriolli appeared with a flourish, in a hurry, her fingers wiping on a tea towel.

'Money,' thought John; that towel. Linen. Not cotton. He smiled and leaned one hand on the wall as if to stop Mrs Capriolli running out and away.

'Good afternoon,' he said.

'Good afternoon,' returned Mrs Capriolli with a strong Italian accent.

'So you do speak English,' said John doubtfully.

'Oh yea yea,' beamed Mrs Capriolli, her black eyes sparkling at him, and she flung the towel over her shoulder. 'You want something of me, heh? You wanta the ice cream cornet or the wafer? Special cornet today. With the raspberry on. You come inside to look, heh?'

She turned, happy, and moved busily down the passage.

So they did make ice cream in the scullery. He was lucky, she said, Mr Capriolli had just taken it all away to sell, except this, here, the scrapings, you understand? And that would be twopence, because there were a lot of scrapings and a lot of raspberry.

'Just you look at it!' she exclaimed delightedly. 'Heh heh. It is running down the biscuit. You will have to lick very fast. Fast! Fast!'

John licked and relished and wanted to put his hat somewhere, because he couldn't hold that, lick raspberry and talk insurance at the same time.

'Now.' Mrs Capriolli made sure her sleeves were rolled above her beefy biceps. 'While I clean, you talk, heh? Tell me how you come to call on Mrs Capriolli when Mr Capriolli is out.'

'To sell you accident cover,' he said casually. 'For your husband when he's on his rounds. You see now –'

'Oh no,' interrupted Mrs Capriolli, as she turned on the tap and watched water gush into a noisy galvanised bucket. 'I have the insurance. Plenty of it. With the Widows and Orphans.'

'Oh darro,' said John, between spasms of stretching his tongue to catch drips of ice cream. 'There's a name to turn anybody off. We're the ones you want to be with. Even sound more solid, we do. The Unicorn. Sturdy, climbing animal, the Unicorn.'

Mrs Capriolli worked as if he wasn't there, swishing a cloth under the tap and wiping the bucket out, upending it on the top of the copper.

'How much will you get if Mr Capriolli breaks a leg when he's pedalling that trike? What will happen then? Will you go and pedal for him?'

Still she said nothing, her back to him.

'Silly you'd look,' he said, 'pedalling, admitting to the world he hadn't provided for you properly.'

Mrs Capriolli turned, one fist tucked into her hip. 'And what is for me if Mr Capriolli broke a leg, heh?'

'As much as you like,' said John, looking at the cornet, then his tongue thrusting in, after the ice cream.

'How much then, heh?'

'Ten pounds. Twenty pounds. Any pounds you like.'

She hesitated long enough to turn and swish the remaining blocks of ice down the plug hole in the big earthenware sink, then she turned back to him, her eyes sparkling again. 'You come into the parlour. That's the best place to do the business.'

John followed her, but the front door stayed open, as if Mrs Capriolli visualised throwing him out. John went to it and closed it slowly, grinning, the cornet finished, his sticky hands wiping on his big white handkerchief.

It took twenty minutes of sitting at the lace-covered parlour table, talking, laughing, before the proposal form was signed and sealed, then a young man in a yellow open-necked shirt and white flannels leaned into the room.

'Hi Ma!'

'Why you hi Ma me, heh? You got no respect for your elders?'

He laughed at John, his eyes as black as his mother's. 'You've just sold her something?'

'Insurance.'

Mrs Capriolli took her purse from the table and popped it into the sideboard drawer, carefully turning the key in the lock before replacing it in her overall pocket. 'He is my son, Antonio,' she said, and Antonio was curly-haired, keyed up.

'Anthony,' he said, and one stride brought him beside John. 'Any jobs going in your office?'

John scooped Mrs Capriolli's half-crown off the table and folded the relevant papers into a long buff-coloured envelope. 'Why?' he grinned.

'Because I'm out of work a long time.'

John pouted negatively and looked down at the young man's tennis-shoed feet. 'You look like you got plenty of energy.'

'Enough to sell insurance.'

Mrs Capriolli clapped her hands together in castigation. 'You can be selling the ice-cream with your papa.'

Anthony whipped an arm about her and squeezed while she went red-faced with pleasure and tried to push him away.

John stood up, grinning again. 'Indeed,' he said, 'I wish I could help, that I do, but I'm only an agent, you see, not a manager,' and his mind added, not yet boyo, not yet. He made for the street, replacing his hat, touching it respectfully. 'I thank you both. Very much indeed.'

When he got to the corner, where he had propped his bicycle, he mopped his forehead and looked up the mountain. Smoke was coming from the old chimney. Maggie had disturbed the banked-up fire. Maggie was home. The kettle was on. Young Buck was ready for his dad's attention.

John got on his bike and pedalled strongly towards the track up the mountainside.

Maggie, up in her eyrie, watched for him sporadically, saw him coming and put the knives and forks in place on the table, then she lifted the baby and took him out

99

to the top of the track to wait, his mouth still puckered from his feed of Cow and Gate.

After a splashing, gasping wash, under the cold tap out the back, John and Maggie shared a dish of cawl and slices of bread cut like doorsteps, then they sat in basket chairs at the bottom of the garden and watched the town of Port Talbot carry on without them, smoke rising lazily from red chimneys, children skipping, hopscotching, the orange-streaked evening bringing day to a close, and John told Maggie about Mrs Capriolli and Antonio.

'Think, Mag. If I'd been a manager. Taken that kid on, I would. Given him a job. Just like that.' John jerked his head in quick regret. 'Selling comes natural to him. Got loads of energy. Bristling with it. Nice, friendly energy. Not the fighting stuff.'

Maggie nursed the baby to her. 'You know, cariad, our son is noticing everything. Knows your voice, he does. He'll be a good salesman one day.'

John jerked his head again, grinning with contentment. 'He'll be anything we want him to be Mag. Money he'll be needing. And education. The time is coming when you can't get anywhere if you aren't educated. Money. And position. You know that, don't you?'

Maggie did know and, on Tuesday morning, she was in the garden again by seven, her big black-handled scissors going snip-snip as she gathered narcissi and golden forsythia, bits of this and bits of that, and laid them in the old zinc bath that was full of rainwater near the lean-to.

She brought an earthenware bowl of laverbread from the cold slate shelf in the pantry, and swedes, carrots, onions and other things from the shed. She placed them all in the two big baskets on the kitchen table.

At half-past nine she saw John off on his bike, then she wrapped the baby in the great fringed wool shawl, Welsh fashion, about her, and carried him down to the little general shop on the corner of the first street past the bottom of the mountain. She went in to the smell of cheese and sawdust, and hot bread and lamp oil. She was panting but laughing. 'You'll watch him for me now, cariad.'

'Of course, of course.' The diminutive Mrs Roberts held out her arms. 'Give him here. I'll put him by there. In our Sion's pram. Old it is, but still good. You go and put the napkins on the line by the fire. Keep them warm for his little botty.'

Maggie went through the bamboo curtain that rattled and swung about her, to the great black range, and hung the napkins on the string line. She came back to the shop, her hands rubbing her thighs as if they longed to lift the baby again.

'Just you look at him,' she cried. 'Bright as a button. And he's got teeth coming through. He has. I can feel them. In the front.'

'Isn't it lovely to have a baby?' said Mrs Roberts, and Maggie had to remind herself that Sion Roberts was not all there, so it wasn't kind of her to preen about the super-intelligence of young Buck.

'I hope he'll be good for you,' she said, matter of fact now. 'I'll be as quick as I can, but I've got to go. You do understand, don't you?'

'Of course, of course,' said Mrs Roberts. 'We all got to work. Look at me, here in the shop all day,' and Maggie left her and climbed the mountain again, hurrying now because there was so much to be done.

Once more in her kitchen, flush-faced and gasping, her hair already breezed awry, she put the smaller Welsh shawl about her shoulders, caught it on her bosom with a large cameo brooch, and put John's flat cap on her head.

Then she slipped an arm through each of the two large baskets, glanced at the fire to make sure it was safely damped down, at the cauldron of perpetual cawl above it, and went out.

Maggie had her regular customers and rarely spent time seeking others. 'Good morning, m'dear.' Maggie could be as obeisant as the next. 'Pulled a lovely swede for you this morning. Still had the dew on it. Pulled you a couple of early carrots, too. You can have those. For nothing.'

The vegetables were all ordered, the flowers were impulse buying, and Maggie shared many a good belly laugh with people as they handed over their money.

When one basket was empty, she balanced it on her head and she walked more purposefully, her rounded hips swaying in the long black cotton skirt. Maggie's heart sang with contentment while the breeze wafted silvery speckles of sand about.

It was close on lunchtime when she decided to call on Mrs Capriolli, and she had left just half a dozen eggs and one bunch of highly scented bluebells that she had picked at the foot of the mountain yesterday.

Mrs Capriolli gazed hard at Maggie and said, 'Noh speak English in this house. Me Italiano.'

Maggie put up one hand to support the basket on her head and said, 'I could help your Antonio, Mrs Capriolli.'

The black eyes flickered interest but the mouth said nothing.

'My husband is John Davies. The insurance man.'

'Insurance man? Oh noh noh.' Mrs Capriolli feigned ignorance.

'You do have a son called Antonio?'

'What if I do have a son, heh?'

'If he is willing to work for commission only, and can canvass, my husband will help him.'

'Your husband say he is not the manager. Pah! He can do nothing.'

Maggie shrugged and lifted the edge of her skirt a little as if in disdain. 'Please yourself, Mrs Capriolli, but if I had a son out of work I would try to help him. I would tell him to see my husband. Up there. In the farmhouse on the mountain.'

'Huh,' said Mrs Capriolli, while she gazed thoughtfully up the mountainside. 'There is no need for my Antonio to work. We have the money.'

Maggie smiled and half turned away, straight-backed and confident, her face scrubbed shiny. 'Up to your son it would be, whether he makes anything of it or not.'

'What you mean, make anything of it? Of course my boy make anything of it. He is a good boy.'

Maggie swung the basket on her arm forward. 'Eggs?' she said. 'From my own hens they are. Cheap to you, Mrs Capriolli, because we're both businesswomen. The bluebells you can have free, to perfume the parlour.'

'Huh,' said Mrs Capriolli, but went back to the hall-stand and took a ten-shilling note from the glove drawer. 'If the eggs are not fresh. You have them back. Si?'

'Si,' agreed Maggie and took the money, then gave change from the pocket heavy with cash beneath her white apron.

She left Mrs Capriolli, still smiling, confident Antonio would present himself at the farmhouse, that he would bring in a lot of new business, that Henderson-Hobbs would be so impressed he would immediately transfer Bertie, and instate John.

Maggie had the Davies family's future mapped out, but she knew nothing about Kit, at Prince Edward Road, planning her letter to Henderson-Hobbs to express her appreciation for the gifts.

It had taken some days to decide what to say, then Kit bought a pad of best blue watermarked paper, and wrote in it with the fine-nibbed pen from the golden Rolls-Royce. 'Dear Mr Henderson-Hobbs,

How considerate of you to send such a splendid memento of our meeting. As you probably perceive, I find the pen a delight to use –'

Kit told herself that thoughts of Henderson-Hobbs kept her calm, made her a better wife and mother and could never harm anyone.

She sealed the envelope with orange-coloured sealing wax, almost burning her fingers as the match flamed to its end, then she admired the businesslike way she had typed, in the top left-hand corner, in red capital letters, STRICTLY CONFIDENTIAL.

She had another cup of tea then went out to the small garden.

The roses were budding and she fingered one while the word soppy came to mind. She liked feeling soppy; it was nice to have something to be soppy about. But she did wish Bertie hadn't given the chocolates to John.

Thoughts of Bertie led to wondering if she had ever loved him in the way a wife should love her husband. Then she laughed at herself. Bertie was all she had. Of course she loved him. All she had to do was stop disliking him.

She went back into the house, sighing at the dirty dishes awaiting her attention, and she heard him come in, heard Emma charging down the stairs to greet him. 'Daddy! Daddy!'

She heard the laughter, felt the fresh air blast in from the street, then the draught was cut off as doors closed, and the familiar smells took over. Linda was screaming down the stairs. 'Emma! I'll pulverise you. Don't you tell! Don't you!' There were tears and anger in her voice and Kit's heart lurched. There had been no news from Tommy, no letter, and Linda was beginning to look ill and sallow.

Kit hurried to them all and Emma had sprung to Bertie, her arms about his neck, her legs about his waist, as she laughed wickedly, 'Bunty Morris said her father got a dirty book in his shop. Heh heh heh.'

Kit cried, 'All the books in Mr Morris' shop are dirty. The man never dusts them! Bertie! Stop favouring the child.'

'What the hell are you talking about?' he retorted. 'Can't you stand a bit of fun?'

In the dull light of the hall his eyes seemed even deeper set, his straight dark brows drawn together in readiness for anger.

Kit backed away. She looked up the stairs and Linda

was still there, her skirt too short again, her bare thighs visible from here. 'Come on down,' Kit told her. 'Help me set the table.' She heard Emma slip from her father's body, heard her whisper to Bertie, 'It is true. Bunty told Linda —'

'Emma!' Kit turned. 'If you're so interested in books, study one on good manners,' and she marched both scowling girls to the kitchen.

Linda murmured, 'I'll pinch you,' to Emma, and Kit caught sight of her younger daughter squinting her eyes towards her nose. 'Emma!' she cried. 'Stop it. Or I'll smack you!'

Bertie laughed. Kit glared, 'Is this what we struggled to send them to private school for?' and the day wore into night.

Bertie lay in bed beside Kit, staring into the darkness and said, 'Linda's becoming something of a problem.'

'It's her age,' Kit murmured. 'She's like me. At a funny time of life.'

'I suppose there's no chance we could send her to that finishing school. It's up near your mother.'

'And what happens if you have no job next week?'

Bertie turned his head on the pillow, inwardly groaning. He said defensively, 'She should have tried for a scholarship.'

'You told her she needn't. You were going to see she got much more than a scholarship out of life. The chance to meet the right sort of man —' Kit bounced irritably as she turned over.

Bertie let the minutes tick by but, finally, he whispered, 'Kit. Would you like a cuddle?'

She thought about it, sighed, then snuggled closer to him, lower in the bed than he was, and he put his arms about her.

Her black hair was loose, smelling faintly of Lux soap, soft and tickly about his nose, and he wanted to catch a strand of it with his tongue, let it become a caress to the gentle curves of her throat. He sensed her stiffen and released her, then felt admonished when she wriggled away.

She said peevishly, 'You always want to take advantage.'

He lay on his back, his hands to his chest where they couldn't be accused of touching anything. He heard the YMCA clock chime one through the silence of the streets, and he wondered if clouds were scudding over the full moon.

He fell asleep, unhappy, guilty, lonely and insecure.

He awakened later drenched in sweat. He was still on his back, his hands on his chest, like a corpse, and he had to force himself to draw breath.

He had been dreaming, sinking, dying. Now he was gasping, terrorised. Kit was still curled away from him.

He moved slightly, trying to ease the stickiness of his pyjamas from his body, rid the blackness from his mind. He could smell himself, the stench of acrid perspiration, and he slowly moved his legs, trying to get cool. He stretched the back of his neck where he felt stuck to the pillow, and extended his nostrils in a greater effort to breathe. He had to tell himself he wasn't dying, that it, whatever it was, had passed.

He slid, sluggish, so one foot, then that leg went out from under the sheet into the cold of the room. Kit didn't move. Bertie turned slightly so his hips came out, then his torso, and he almost crouched on the floor in his efforts not to disturb her.

She mustn't see him like this: the sweat beaded on his face. He could feel it dripping, running, his upper lip, his brows, under his chin. God, he was in hell.

He stood up, groping for his dressing-gown off the chair, then put it over his arm and crept from the room, the sweat turning to icy drops on his skin.

He went down the stairs, the soles of his feet cold, and in the kitchen he switched on the light, closed his eyes against the glare and leaned against the wall, ashamed of his palpitations. He wanted to get a spade.

Rush to the cemetery. Dig Elsie up, hear her whisper, 'Oh darling. Oh Bertie.'

He moved like an old man, bent, supporting himself by touching furniture, the back of a chair, the table, and he longed for Kit to appear in the doorway, to say she understood and forgave. He went to the scullery where there was no electricity and he lit a candle, the shaking of his hand making it difficult to hold match to wick.

For a few seconds he held the candlestick up, staring into the flickering shadows of the flagstoned room with its shelved walls, assuring himself this was the right place. This was not a tomb. He had not come down for Elsie. He felt sick with himself, disgusted with his terror and longings, then he put the candlestick back on the low cupboard and half filled the small tin kettle at the tap. He lit the gas with another match, concentrating. There was the faint popping sound as the jets shot flames, and he sighed heavily, the banging of his heart easing.

He went back to the kitchen and put on his dressing-gown, then sat in Kit's chair, trying to absorb the strength of her aura.

The kettle in the scullery began to sing, then to throb, and he went to it, making tea, knowing that if Kit came down she would complain because he had put too much tea in the pot. Wasting it.

He went back to bed just before dawn, when the air was beginning to grow cold, as if the sun objected to rising, and Kit had turned towards his place, one arm outflung.

Gratefully he climbed in beside her, knowing now she had missed him, even in her sleep. He lay still and his thoughts went yet again to Linda, her moods, her heartache. He turned slowly on to his side, away from Kit, feeling her warmth behind him, and he wished he could love her the way he had loved Elsie Buckley.

*　　*　　*

On Wednesday Bertie jerked his head up from the account sheet before him and exclaimed, 'God almighty!' then he leaned forward again and re-examined the figures set out so neatly in their columns. When he finally stood up his face was blank with shock.

He went to the passage, then marched down it in his usual manner, whistling, passed the middle room, the hair on the back of his neck tingling as if picking up the expectant signals from the men in there.

'Kit!' He closed the kitchen door behind him, leaning against it as if subconsciously preventing anyone bursting in.

'Yes?' She came from the scullery, and he strode to meet her.

'John's been up to some monkey business.'

'John?' There was a second of thinking, then, 'What?'

'Brought in five and tuppence worth of new business.'

'How much?' She put the knife she had been holding on the table and her chin lifted a little so that, even wearing an apron, she looked elegant.

'Five and tuppence.'

For seconds more they stared at each other, instinct silencing them, and the middle room door clicked as it closed; someone had come out, then gone back in. The deep hum of men's voices drummed through the walls, then someone passed the kitchen window, having come out through the French doors. Kit waved to him. 'Smile,' she instructed Bertie through the corner of her mouth. 'Don't let them see we're worried.'

Bertie merely nodded to the agent who grinned back. 'They're all in cahoots,' he murmured. 'They're just waiting for my reaction.'

'I'll come and see,' Kit said. 'Maybe there's a mistake.'

'That's what I hoped,' Bertie agreed, and whistled as he went back up the passage. He stopped at the middle room door, opened it and stuck his head inside. 'Won't be long, boys. Sorry to keep you waiting.'

'That's all right guv.' John was on the settee, gangling legs stretched out.

Bertie withdrew and made sure the door was closed properly, the knob turned and clicked.

Kit came in a few minutes later carrying a tray. 'Here, have a cup of tea. Where's his sheet?'

Bertie pushed it across his desk and Kit stood examining it. 'He can't have done this on his own,' she said thoughtfully. 'There are about twenty new cases. And last week he did all right. He brought in half a crown from just one person.'

She replaced the sheet on the desk. 'Do you know what you ought to do? Pull out all the stops. Beat him any way you can.' She held the box of cigars out and Bertie took one, then bit the tip away. Kit went on, 'Employ a canvasser. Someone who does nothing else. Put him on the road.'

'How do I pay him?'

'Commission only. You and I did it when we first came here, and we'll have to do it again when we're moved.'

'That's the flaw, Kit. When we move. I can't go plunging into new schemes until I know where I am and, anyway –' he changed his mind about the cigar and laid it aside, 'he would have to be officially trained, and that would need Head Office clearance. All the usual red tape.'

Kit looked out of the window. 'Blast the man,' she whispered, and Bertie misunderstood. He said, 'I bet Maggie's got a finger in it. John's a worker, but she's the schemer.'

'I wasn't thinking of John. I mean Robert.'

'Robert?' His head jerked.

'Henderson-Hobbs.'

'Since when have you been calling him Robert?'

'It just happened.'

Bertie sat tapping the blotter with the end of his pencil. 'Yes,' he agreed quietly, 'these things do.'

A burst of laughter came from the next room, and

Kit said quickly, 'How have the other men done?'

'They've all made an effort, but nothing like John's.'

'What are you going to say?'

'The usual. Hold him up as a shining example. If one can do it, they all can.'

Kit laughed. 'That sounds more like my man,' and Bertie laughed with her, his worry far less.

On Friday the completed district accounts were in the mail and, about ten o'clock on Monday morning, Miss Lilian Gibbs, private secretary to Mr R. Henderson-Hobbs, took herself into his office and said, 'There is something I think you ought to see.'

Henderson-Hobbs laughed at her in a low growling tone, knowing she considered every man a wolf and him the most dangerous of all. She kept well to the furthest side of his desk, her face frozen, and she handed the account sheet over as if afraid he would suddenly grab her and bite. 'It's Mr Davies,' she said. 'The man you were considering promoting in South Wales.'

'Ha,' breathed Henderson-Hobbs, and his gold tie-pin, his gold watch, glistened as he took the sheet and perused it.

Two minutes later Robert was making that little nervous gesture of putting his fingers to his face without touching it. 'Funny goings-on among the Welsh, Lilian, what what?'

'Ambition, Mr Henderson-Hobbs.'

'So how do we assess the situation?' He didn't expect a reply so went on, 'Is Mr Davies so anxious to usurp his master that he should not be trusted? Or is he such a good agent he should be encouraged?' He smiled at her, pleased with his astute comprehension.

Miss Gibbs smiled back cautiously. 'I'm sure you will make the right decision, Mr Henderson-Hobbs.'

'Yes,' he said slowly, and a little excitement was growing in the pit of his stomach, then he asked, 'will you get the Swansea office on the line, please? I think I'll have a chat with our Mr Hemsworthy.'

'Personally, Mr Henderson-Hobbs?' Her surprise was unveiled.

'Personally,' he said sharply, and she hurried from the room, dumpy legs in flat black shoes.

A few minutes later Kit turned from the pigeon holes on the wall as the telephone rang.

Impatiently she crossed to the desk and lifted the black candle-shaped instrument. 'Hello?' She tried to keep the harassment from her voice. 'Unicorn Insurance Company.'

'Mrs Hemsworthy?'

'Speaking.'

'Will you call your husband to the phone please? Mr Henderson-Hobbs wishes to speak to him.'

'Oh, does he?' said Kit, and Lilian Gibbs went off the line. Robert's voice came clearly.

'Mr Hemsworthy? Albert?'

'No!' blurted Kit, surprise making her voice wobble. 'My husband is out. Canvassing.'

Henderson-Hobbs slid down in the cushioned softness of his leather armchair. 'Well, well, hello Mrs Hemsworthy,' and the low, provocative tone came instinctively.

'Good morning, Mr Henderson-Hobbs. I'm afraid you are unlucky. You have missed my husband,' and she wished her hands didn't quiver with this unexpected shock, the telephone almost rattling before her mouth.

'Not unlucky at all, Mrs Hemsworthy. Most fortunate. Though I did want to have a chat with Albert.'

'Maybe I can help.' Her lips were dry.

'Do you have much to do with the business?'

'I am head cook and bottle-washer. My husband's salary does not stretch to secretaries.'

He accepted the edge to her voice; it went with his memory of her. He said, tentatively, 'This man – er – John Davies.'

Kit made no sound.

'It would appear he is doing extremely well. Bringing in new business.'

'It looks that way.'

'How does he account for it? Has Port Talbot suddenly become a boom town?'

'We did ask him.' Kit clipped her words in an effort to keep her voice steady. 'He said it was hard work, and accepted all our compliments.'

'But a trifle unusual. Two weeks running. After months of mediocre results.'

'I shall tell my husband you phoned.' Her voice was low, tinged with a Welsh accent, and he wanted to see her again, watch that svelte walk.

'Mrs Hemsworthy?'

'Yes, Mr Henderson-Hobbs?'

'Um . . .' then, 'is your husband always out at this time of day?'

'On a Monday. Very probably.' She wanted him off the line, to leave her alone, yet she wanted him closer, here in the room with her. 'Especially now he has such competition.' She managed a polite laugh. 'He has no desire to go to Merseyside.' How easy it would be to expound their labours to a disembodied voice on the phone, but he cut in, 'None of us enjoy being rerouted, Mrs Hemsworthy,' then, as if to make amends, 'Thank you for your letter,' and Kit blushed furiously because his tone had become familiar, here again was the blond pirate who had not entered the lift.

'It was nothing,' she averred quickly. 'It was kind of you to send the gifts.'

'Did you enjoy the chocolates?'

'Thank you. They were my favourite.'

'I must send you more.'

'I would prefer you didn't, Mr Henderson-Hobbs.'

'Why ever not, Mrs Hemsworthy?' He was laughing at her, teasing, and she became icy-voiced. 'No reason, Mr Henderson-Hobbs. None at all, other than my particular preference for not receiving gifts.'

'Mrs Hemsworthy.' His voice went very low.

'Yes?' She could hardly breathe.

'I think you would like to sleep with me.'

Kit's jaw dropped, her eyes blinked. How could he know such a thing? 'If you will excuse me,' she said curtly. 'I have work to do.'

'Of course,' he was laughing openly, twitching the pink satin in his breast pocket. 'And I shall leave you to get on with it. Cooking something special?'

'I am busy in the office, Mr Henderson-Hobbs. Both my husband and myself are dedicated workers on behalf of the Unicorn.'

'I shall remember, Mrs Hemsworthy. I shall remember. Au revoir,' and he had gone.

Kit moved to the straight-backed chair and flopped into it. Stupid. Stupid. She was forty-two. Almost forty-three, and going goo-ga over a man. She felt horrified because, yes, this morning, she had wanted to sleep with him.

*   *   *

Next morning Linda ran to the front door when she heard the gate clang, then stood watching the mail pour through the large wide letterbox, and there was still nothing for her. She picked up all the white and buff envelopes and arranged them in their sizes, then took them to the office and placed them on her father's desk, then she went to the window and watched the postman go next door, his uniform pressed and neat, his loaded bag on his back, then she returned to the kitchen, sat at the table and tried to eat breakfast.

When the time came to escape to school she got ready quickly. She and Emma dutifully kissed their parents, then hurried from the house.

In the street there was the tumult of a Tuesday at almost nine a.m. as the town got into its stride, and the voice calling was almost lost amid it all. 'Miss Hemsworthy! I say there! Young lady!' The major, next door, rapped his step with his walking stick, and called again, his monocle already swinging from around his neck. 'I say there. Oh I say!' He hurried down the path and to the pavement and Emma turned, saw and gripped Linda's arm, shaking it.

'He wants you!' she cried.

Linda turned and the major lifted his left hand. In it was an envelope that looked the right shape, the right size, and Linda's laugh smashed into the morning. 'Oh Major!' and she ran to him.

They met almost outside number 300 and Linda gasped, 'For me, Major?'

'There's no one else I'm having to expend energy on, young woman,' he retorted testily. 'That dratted postman not thinking of what he's doing. Left this in our place.' The precious letter came down from the heights of being waved, and Linda held out her hand politely, not giving in to the urge to snatch.

'Kindly tell that young man of yours to learn to write properly. The damn thing is practically illegible.'

'Yes, I will. Thank you. Thank you.' She was breathless, and already Bertie was coming from the house.

'Emma!' he called sharply. 'You'll be late. Where's Linda?'

In the shelter of the privet hedge Linda panicked. The letter needed a secret place. She swept it up the leg of her knickers. 'Coming, Daddy. Coming!'

She ran, and the corners of the envelope scratched and hurt, but Daddy was at the gate. 'Where've you been?' Then he saw the major and greeted him, while the major nodded, chomped a bit, then stamped back into his own house.

Bertie said, 'What did the old coot want?'

'The time,' Linda said quickly. 'Their clock stopped.'

'All of them?' Bertie stared at the next house and Linda ran.

She bore the discomfort of a four-cornered envelope against her tuppence onto the tram and into school assembly, and all the time there was that other agony, of waiting. What words were hidden so close

114

to her? Had Tommy said nice things? Or nasty?

The letter stayed in the warmth of her knickers until Break, then she walked painfully to the row of lavatories and, with excitement and relief, she stood and opened the envelope, but already others were banging on the door, hopping up and down in the anguish of waiting, so she made for the wooden bench in the furthest corner of the grounds. She peered about to make sure no one was comtemplating joining her, and then opened the sheet of paper frantically, her gaze scanning for the end. Did he finish it with the wonderful word 'Love' or with 'Goodbye for ever?' Like her mother, her determination to look unruffled took over and she sat sedately, sideways into the corner of the bench, and read: 'Dear Linda, Your father said my pa was back in Swansea but nobody seen him. I asked Stella to write to me if he does come back and Maud Jeffries is sending letters to some address she knew in Dagenham where he might be. It was alright seeing you but you are just a kid.

Your friend,
Tommy.'

Linda took out her handkerchief and had a little cry. The letter had come, but held no comfort, and Bunty Morris heard her from behind the hedge.

The girl crept out. 'Linda. You crying?'

'No.'

'You are.'

Bunty sat beside her, her yellow plaits thick down her back. 'It's your boy,' she breathed. 'He said something horrid in that letter.'

'No!' Linda snapped. 'Oh no,' and her fingers were tearing the letter into tiny pieces so no one else would ever be able to read them.

Bunty whispered, 'I got that book,' and Linda's face brightened with naughty curiosity.

'What book?'

'I told you. My father had it in his shop.' Their heads

115

came together, linked by secrets. 'He put it in the rubbish and I saw it.'

'You stole it?' A shocked whisper.

'I can always put it back.'

'Is it the one about the lovers?'

Bunty gave a series of nods, her face intent. 'They stay together till death. Nothing ever mars their love.'

'Honestly? And it's got the word bum in it?'

Giggles burst from both girls, hands across mouths, eyes watering.

'What else is in it?' Linda bit her lower lip, loving this sense of discovery.

'I'll lend it to you.'

There were moments of awe, of thinking. 'It is about lovers,' Bunty encouraged, and Miss Griffiths blew hard on her whistle near the school doors. 'Come along girls.' Her feet were in white tennis shoes, her legs in white lisle stockings.

She chanted loudly as the girls marched into school, 'Left. Right. Left. Right.' Her gaze settled on the last two. Poor dear Linda Hemsworthy; her dreadful parents changing their mind about her going to finishing school like the Morris girl. She decided to have a chat with Mr Hemsworthy, and Bertie received the call next morning, his busy morning. Wednesday.

'Mr Hemsworthy?'

'That's right. What can I do for you?' An agent sat opposite him, the man's collections on the desk, the ledger open, the sheet checked.

'Miss Griffiths here.' She tried to sound friendly and failed. 'St Hilda's School for Young Ladies.'

'Oh! Ah!' His mind swerved from insurance to daughters. 'What is it, Miss Griffiths?' and his stomach tipped with apprehension.

'We are most concerned about Linda. She has been crying a great deal lately.'

He waited for her to come to the point.

'You have noticed, of course, Mr Hemsworthy.'

116

'It's probably someone in school upsetting her.'

'Certainly not, Mr Hemsworthy, and I am phoning in the hope something can be done to help the child. She really should go on to finishing school, you know. Build her self-confidence –'

'Thank you for calling, Miss Griffiths. I shall certainly reconsider the matter, but now I am terribly busy, so if you'll excuse me –'

'I do pride myself on my interest in all our girls.'

He heard the wounded note in her voice and relented. 'Of course you do. If you weren't interested you would not have taken the trouble to telephone, and I do thank you.'

'Yes, but she does cry a lot –'

'Thank you, Miss Griffiths. We can have a chat another time. Bye –' He put the receiver down, his heart aching. He didn't want Linda crying, didn't want her experiencing that sort of hurt so early in life.

He rubbed his eyes. Nothing was on course, his blasted job, Linda, Kit. He stared at the man before him. 'Now,' he smiled. 'Where were we?'

Towards the end of the day, when the rooms were left with the smell of agents and their tobacco, and the cloth bags in his desk were filled with money, he stretched and went to the window, his jacket open, creased from a day of sitting. He watched a tram come up the street and thought of Linda and he thought of Kit, then he strode to the kitchen where the fire warmed and the clock ticked, and Kit greeted him with a smile. 'Cup of tea now?' she asked, and he said abruptly, 'How about you and me going to a dance?'

'A dance?' She put the teapot back on the hob and stared at him. 'We haven't been for years. I've forgotten how.'

'What about Whit Monday?'

'Oh no. I've promised to take the kids to Porthcawl.'

'Without me?'

'I didn't think you'd notice.'

He stood with his feet slightly astride, vexed they

could make plans that didn't include him, then he said, 'Are they to have new dresses for Whitsun?'

'They always do.'

'I had St Hilda's on the phone this morning. Apparently Linda cries a lot in school.'

'She cries quite a bit here at home.'

'D'you know what dress she'd like? I could treat her.'

'Be far better if you stopped interfering between her and Tommy. This really is a case of ignore it and it will go away.'

They laughed derisively at each other, knowing neither would change.

'Anyway,' he said. 'You choose a night out for us.'

'A new dress for me too?'

'You've just had a new dress. The white slinky thing that makes Henderson-Hobbs go weak at the knees.'

She turned from him. 'My mother bought that. I'd like one you buy for me.'

'All right,' then, thoughtfully, 'Kit, if you were going to sack a man, would you keep him waiting all this time?'

She looked back at him and saw the blue in his eyes and the grey splintering his hair. She said, 'If we haven't heard by the end of August we'll know we're safe.'

'Why the end of August?'

'H.-H. will want to start his reign in earnest in September. The holiday season will be over and he'll really be in power.'

CHAPTER FIVE

At the end of the Whitsun bank holiday the London pavements scorched, and Mr Carruthers, the Chief Office Inspector, strutted along on his little fat legs, ignoring the glittering shop windows.

At the entrance to the Unicorn Insurance Building he paused, put his briefcase between his knees, and took off his bowler to mop his head. He replaced the bowler, brought the briefcase up under his arm, and climbed the three wide stone steps. There he paused again, this time to tap the wooden plaque beside the scarred doors; it bore the insignia of a unicorn on its hind legs, grasping a shield.

Carruthers gave a perfunctory nod to the porter in the glass den, and ignored the inner stone steps with their iron bannisters. He made for the lift. A few seconds later he entered a corridor lined with potted plants and regularly placed frosted glass doors. On the wall opposite him a notice board directed you to STAFF ONLY.

Carruthers hoisted his scuffed case further under his right arm and marched on. He had a premonition: something of interest was about to come up. After two monotonous weeks in Birmingham, discovering the man there had committed no sin, his report had not taken long to write.

Now the mottled green fountain pen, in the breast pocket of his dusty-looking beige suit, was filled with blue ink and ready for the next assignment. He pursed his soft red lips and held his head high, so the back of his neck bulged in rolls of flesh, and still he marched on.

Henderson-Hobbs marched along the same corridor in the opposite direction.

The two men passed each other. 'Morning, H.-H.' It was a formality, and Robert gave a dismissive nod, then he frowned, thought quickly and stopped.

'Mr Carruthers!' he called, as he turned, and Carruthers not only turned, he strolled back, corpulently, expansively. 'Mr Carruthers. You know the Swansea man pretty well, don't you?'

'I know them all pretty well.'

'Him particularly.'

'No. Not him particularly.'

Robert smiled, understanding the politics of inspectors. 'What is your general opinion of the man?'

'I was under the impression I had voiced that on a previous occasion.'

'Then voice it again.'

'Sound. Loyal to a fault.'

'You still think it would be a mistake to dispense with his services?'

'Mr Claud Hobbs gave me the express instruction, some months ago, that Mr Hemsworthy was to be relieved of any fear of unemployment. I took it upon myself to pass on the assurance. The worst that could happen would be a transfer to Merseyside.'

Robert scratched his upper lip speculatively. 'You would approve of that, Inspector?'

'Not at all. Such a move would damage the goodwill Mr Hemsworthy has built in the Swansea area. It would be a matter of the Unicorn seeming to pass judgement on his private life.'

Robert laughed shortly. 'His private life! The girl chiselled the firm, Carruthers. This firm.'

'The policy-holders in that area are not aware of that, sir. They would consider it right to assume you persecuted a man because he loved the wrong woman.'

Robert stared at him, loath to question further. 'I'd like you to take a trip down that way. There's no rush if you have other things on hand. Give Mr and Mrs Hemsworthy my regards and take a stroll through the round of one of their agents.' Carruthers' brows lifted in question. 'You know him, of course, a chap called Davies. Of Port Talbot?'

Carruthers' bulbous eyes half closed. Here was the answer to his premonition. 'Something in the wind down there?' he asked.

'Not necessarily,' smiled Henderson-Hobbs, 'but wasn't the trouble in that area before? Bogey business, and that sort of thing?'

'Yes, but not Davies.'

'Get me a run-down on the present situation, there's a good fellow. I'm looking for promotional material. You know the sort of thing. Someone capable of working on their own initiative, being a credit to the firm.'

He clicked his fingers at his sides impatiently; the fat man irked him. 'You'll keep me informed, won't you?' He turned as if to leave, but added, 'It would be preferable if South Wales knew nothing of the reason for your visit.'

The marble like eyes became momentarily hidden in a toad-like blink. 'I shall endeavour to arrive there completely invisible,' said Carruthers, and his voice was quite even.

The fingers stopped clicking. 'I mean, man, that you do not notify them beforehand.'

Carruthers gave a big smile and hugged the leather case higher. 'The handle fell off,' he explained, and Henderson-Hobbs marched from him, up the corridor, while Carruthers marched down it.

*   *   *

Each morning for a week Kit rivalled Linda for the front door as the mail shot through. 'Darling,' she would say to her daughter as she lifted the letters, 'I'll leave you to open the front door and fix the mat in front of it. All

121

right?' And, while Linda tried to see an envelope of a particular shape and colour in her mother's hands, Kit hurried to the office, disappointed. The miracle had not happened.

She knew it wouldn't. She hoped it wouldn't. What would a respectable married woman want from a liaison with another man?

On the Monday morning she arranged the letters in a small pile, patting them, tapping them, knowing she was wasting time. She heard Bertie go upstairs and come down again. He didn't come in to her, didn't stick his head around the door and wink. He didn't even pause at the foot of the stairs. It seemed the gap between them was getting wider.

She heard Linda and Emma at the hallstand, heard them putting on blazers, heaving on satchels, gasping, groaning, then, 'Mummy? We're going now.'

Kit hurried to them, two pairs of round eyes that had become perpetually apprehensive. 'Have you both got clean handkerchiefs?'

They nodded.

'Tram fare?'

More nods.

Kit went to the gate with them, then the pavement; the traffic was already busy at this crossroads and she stood watching them, sad, even bereft at the knowledge they would grow up to a world filled with disillusionment.

They waved as the tram came and she waved back. 'Be careful darlings. I love you,' then they were gone, and all Kit could do was go back to Bertie.

He was standing at his desk. 'You didn't open the letters,' he said, and she took it as an accusation.

'I have only one pair of hands.'

'Yes,' he said, and smiled, regretting the stress between them. 'I do understand.'

She wanted to shout, 'You don't. You damn well don't!' but couldn't remember ever shouting like that, so she went to the kitchen and cleared the breakfast table.

A few minutes later Bertie called, 'I'm going now, Kit.'

She went to see him off, even blowing the customary kiss for the benefit of the neighbours.

Then she went upstairs to make the beds, and saw herself enter her bedroom in the dressing-table's tilted mirror. She told herself she knew well what she saw, she was plain, and remembered her mother saying, sixteen years ago, 'In the circumstances, dear, you must consider yourself fortunate. Captain Hemsworthy isn't such a bad catch.'

The war had killed millions of men. Those who were left were prized possessions.

She had won a prize. And look at her.

She raised the hem of her grey thin wool dress and assessed her legs; how pale they looked where stockings ended and suspenders stretched.

She strode to the window and drew the curtains. She switched on the light and went again to her reflection.

What did other women look like naked? She didn't even see Linda naked any more. It wouldn't be nice.

She walked a little towards the mirror. Her mother had said something about the way she sauntered. Wasn't that why Lorraine had bought the white gown?

Kit shuddered. Her mother must be a liar, trying to boost her daughter's morale.

She took the dress off. Her shoulders, above the cream lace of her petticoat, were bony, square, her arms angular, and she hesitated, not eager to see more of herself, yet anxious to see what a lover might see.

She stared in the mirror for a long time, stunned by her own rude, vanity-ridden behaviour, and she had to draw breath before going on. This must surely be a harlot's procedure.

Then she was naked. And horrified.

She was ugly. Bony. Sallow, with small drooping breasts and a hollow back. She tucked her bottom in and tried to control the swell of her belly, then she put her hands to her face and knew it was no good. She was

123

not the sort any man with a choice would care to ravish. No wonder Bertie preferred Elsie Buckley.

She dressed quickly, fumbling, shivering with the shock of the thoughts she had been nursing, the realisation that the world of romance and excitement would always be closed to her. She made the beds in near frenzy, the longing to get away from large mirrors overwhelming, and she ran, hot-faced, down the stairs.

At eleven o'clock the telephone rang.

'Hello. Unicorn Insurance Company.'

'Good morning, Mrs Hemsworthy,' he said, and prickles ran up and down her spine.

'Good morning, Mr Henderson-Hobbs.' She sounded breathless.

'Is your husband available this morning?'

'I'm afraid not. He really does have an awful lot of work to do.'

'Such a pity I keep missing him. Did you tell him I called last Monday?'

'No, Mr Henderson-Hobbs. You left no message.'

'I didn't?' His tone was filled with teasing.

'You didn't,' she said firmly.

'Will you tell him I phoned this morning?'

'If you care to leave a message. Of course.'

'And why not if I don't leave a message?'

'Because there would be no reason, Mr Henderson-Hobbs,' and she wanted to be cross with him, because he was flirting, and because it might lead to something – and she was ugly.

He said soothingly, 'I see Mr Davies sent in a lot of new business again this week. He's consolidating well.'

'If you wish to give Mr Davies my husband's job I suggest you do so, and stop playing cat and mouse.'

The silence seemed abrupt and, for a moment, she worried.

Then he said calmly, 'When I wish to give your husband's position to another, Mrs Hemsworthy, I shall tell your husband. Not you.'

More silence.

She said quietly, 'Is that why you phone? To catch him in for that?'

'Did I say so?'

She licked her lower lip, undecided, then, 'Good day Mr Henderson-Hobbs.'

She wondered whether to hang up, but he was laughing, softly, deep in his throat, and she didn't hear much laughter these days.

'Mr Henderson-Hobbs,' she began, then became defiant again. 'I have no intention of pandering to you. My husband is having to live on a knife-edge, awaiting your pleasure, and I do not appreciate it.'

'My pleasure, Mrs Hemsworthy?'

'Yours.' She heard him draw breath and sensed his mood had gone thoughtful, then he said, 'I am a new boy in a new seat, Mrs Hemsworthy, and I have not dismissed your husband as yet for misappropriation of funds, simply because it would mean countermanding Mr Claud's wishes. I am also giving your husband ample time in which to pull his socks up, to prove worthy of the responsibility entrusted to him by the firm.'

Kit felt herself grow smaller as his voice became more definite, and her voice was thin as she said, 'I understand.'

'Splendid.'

'And Merseyside?'

'That is still under consideration.'

'Yes,' she said, and felt very bleak.

He waited a while, then reverted to his former tone, the hint of laughter in his voice, the man who was pleased with his speech and her reaction.

'I shall telephone about the same time next Monday. You will be there?'

'Probably Mr Henderson-Hobbs.'

'Au revoir.'

'Goodbye.'

She sat for a while, excited, ashamed of that excitement,

and giggling in a way Bertie would never believe. So there was hope. No final decision had been made. Bertie had a chance. She stood up and flung out her arms, enveloping the whole room, and looked at the portrait of the stern-faced, Vandyke-bearded Claud Hobbs, now non-executive president of the firm. Long may the old boy live. And please God let Bertie pull himself together.

In the meantime, there was Bertie's invitation to the dance. Glorious thought. And a new dress?

When she bought it, it reflected her new outlook. It was shorter than she usually wore and, although the top was plain and sleeveless, the straight skirt boasted three deep frills. She revolved before the dressing-table and felt thrilled because the dress gave her shape.

'Like it?' She stood, a beautiful, sophisticated-looking woman in a girl's flippant dress, and Bertie nodded obligingly.

She crossed to him, eager to hug, but his fingers fumbled with his back collar stud, and the Chinese laundry starched white collar sprang out, flicking his ear as it went. He swore loudly. For him the night was already ruined. Didn't she have the intelligence to see that a purple dress was a nonsense, a bloody farce?

For both him and her the evening called for a supreme effort, and they left the house arm in arm, laughing, having made sure the girls had chocolates, comics, and the fire was neatly banked.

They walked to the Assembly rooms, and some of the conscious effort to be patient waned, because there was no need of it. He enjoyed being dressed up. His black patent pointed shoes were so shiny they glinted as he strolled, and the white silk scarf about his neck made him feel prosperous and carefree. He gripped Kit's arm through his, their hands clasped, and he grinned into her face. 'Hi! We're courting again.'

She gave a little tripping step, the skirt of her coat not meeting in front because of the bulge of frills, and she absorbed his attention, relishing it.

126

He smiled. 'I hope I've remembered how to dance.'

'Of course you have,' she laughed. 'It will all be perfect.'

In the ballroom there were the once familiar smells of resin, perfume, cheap cigarettes, even the odd waft of body odour. The small band played and Bertie took her into his arms, the lights dimmed and he was humming in her ear, 'One night of love . . .' He heard her sigh and felt her relax against him. The music seeped into them both and he popped a kiss into the hollow of her ear. She was willowy, giving to him, swaying into him because he was her husband and she was used to him.

He moved smoothly, long-legged, gliding, and he whispered against her smooth coiled hair, 'Hello Kit.' It was as if they were lovers who had just met again.

He kept her to the outside edge of the stream of dancers, moving rhythmically anti-clockwise around the floor, and when the waltz finished they found chairs and sat and stared around, nosey, to see who else was there and what the women were wearing.

'Like a drink?' he asked.

'No thank you.' She smiled over-brightly, because she had been wondering if Henderson-Hobbs danced well.

'Ladies and gentlemen!' called the M.C. 'Take your partners for the two-step,' and Kit stood up, anxious to begin.

'You haven't forgotten how to dance at all,' she told him. 'You're perfect.'

'That is what the ideal partner does for me.' He flexed his shoulders, ready for the releasing of tension in the long swinging strides to come.

'Flatterer,' she said, and her body went to his.

The evening flew.

'Ladies and gentlemen. Take your parteners for the tango!'

'Good Lor'! I haven't done this for ages.'

'We'll follow the others. Bet we'll ache tomorrow. All over.'

They laughed into each other's eyes now, singing together, "Twas on the Isle of Capri that I found her – boom boom.' The music, the tango, ended, but Bertie went on, swirling her, his face young and gleeful.

'Oh Bertie. You are a fool!'

It was bliss, a haven of forgetting.

Until Linda appeared.

Kit saw her first, a girl not yet ready to be a woman. 'Bertie! There's Linda.'

'Where? Good Lord!'

They held hands as they ran and skated across the floor, dodging other couples, waving, trying to attract the attention of the frantic-faced Linda.

'Darling. What is it? Why are you here?' Kit was ashen with fright. 'Where's Emma?'

Linda was panting, hatless, her coat unbuttoned. 'Mr Carruthers telephoned. He's on his way.'

'Carruthers!' Bertie exclaimed. 'What the deuce is Head Office playing at?'

Kit thought of the phone calls each Monday morning, and of her stupidity in caring about her naked body.

The insecurity was back. Henderson-Hobbs was a man of finance, not to be trusted in her little world. 'Let's get home quickly,' she said. 'Did he say what time he'll be here?'

'Only that he's in Bristol waiting for a connection,' Linda told them. 'There's been a hold-up with the train or something.'

'Bristol?' Bertie anticipated the worst. 'It's late. We ought to get a taxi,' and he hurried away. 'Get your coat, Kit. See you at the door.'

'Daddy – ' Linda said.

'Leave him alone now, dear.'

'But Mummy – '

'Go and wait at the door for Daddy. I won't be a minute.'

'No – '

'Go on, dear. I'll be as fast as I can.'

It was when they got into the house that Linda's frantic

face really registered with them. Her eyes glittered with defiance, and Tommy's khaki cap was on the hallstand.

Bertie stormed into the kitchen, Kit and Linda gasping behind him. The youth sat in Kit's chair, his wide grey eyes bloodshot, his hands gripping the arms.

'What are you doing here?'

'I had a twenty-four-hour pass – '

'Stand when you speak to me.'

Tommy sprang to his feet, his boots clomping.

'Now tell me. Fast.'

'I had a twenty-four-hour pass but the trains are all wrong because there's been an accident the other side of Bristol, and I haven't been here long.'

'When are you due back?'

'Six o'clock in the morning.'

'You chose a hell of a time to reach this house!'

'Maud Jeffries wrote to me. She said my father might be home, so I been over to St Thomas and waited. I been calling people too, looking fer him.'

'How are you going to get back to camp by six? Intend to sprout wings?'

'No sir. I'll be AWOL.'

'To hell you will. Not while you're using my address.'

Tommy shrugged as if the open neck of his jacket was chafing him.

Linda stepped beside him. 'He wanted to see me.'

Bertie stared at her, saw the lack of knowledge in her eyes, and turned to Kit, silently appealing for help. She said briskly, 'Well, let's not dwell on problems too long tonight. Tommy. Get into the office and telephone the barracks. Tell them the position, and I'll find some blankets. You'll have to sleep on the settee in the middle room again. We'll have to get a bigger house or something, the way people keep popping in. Linda, shift your things out of that back room. Carruthers will have to go in there.'

'I'm always having to shift. Let Carruthers go up the attic on the floor.'

'If you don't share with Emma, you go up the attic on the floor.'

'It's awful up there. All spooky.'

'Right then. In with Emma.' Emma sat in her father's chair, glassy-eyed with tiredness, another front tooth missing, her smile the most courageous. 'I know I'm all ugly now, but the fairies owe me a shilling.'

'They'll leave it for you,' Bertie said hurriedly. 'Maybe even two shillings.'

Kit's hands seemed to be everywhere, patting Emma, persuading Linda, heaving blankets off the top shelf of the airing cupboard in the bathroom. Bertie found himself in the office with Tommy. 'Let me ring High Street station first, soldier. Find out what time the Head Office man is likely to descend on us, then you ring camp. Right?'

Tommy nodded and Bertie rattled the receiver arm, impatient for his connection. When it came he said quickly, 'I'm expecting a friend from Bristol – '

'Oh aye,' came the yawning reply. 'There's been delays all along the line. Ought to be in in about half an hour.'

Bertie waited for no more. He rang off. 'Come on, soldier. Do your stuff. Remember you're a man, not a half-baked kid any more,' and all the time the overhead bulb was playing tricks, sending light and shadows on Tommy's face, turning him into Elsie.

Tommy took the phone, pouting a little in his effort to look tough, but then he said hoarsely, 'I dunno the number.'

Bertie wondered if Tommy had ever used a telephone before. 'D'you know what you're going to say when you are connected?'

The youth looked back, startled, and shook his head.

'Right, soldier.' Bertie developed his instructor's tone. 'The operator will attend to the number, but you make up your mind what you are going to say. Develop clear thinking. It'll lead to promotion.'

'It'll only be the duty clerk.'

'Practise on him. Dazzle him with your brilliance,' and for a fleeting moment Bertie wished again he had a son to be proud of, not a son whose name was now Davies. 'Get a move on!' he snapped. 'Then get some kip. Tell them there's no train. The line is up,' and he squinted, because odd things were occurring in his head, a tight, heavy sensation, like a mud wall, with happenings behind it, trying to break through.

He tried blinking the problem away and, a few minutes later, he was striding to the other end of town and the station, the faint buzzing in his ears and the captive activity in his brain still threatening to explode and take over.

The roads were empty, silent, and his footsteps echoed hollowly between shops and houses. He tried not to think, but the thoughts kept coming, Carruthers wheezing, fat, gasping. Carruthers snooping, seeking flaws.

He tripped and lunged against a wall, scraping his hand on the roughcast, and part of his mind instructed, 'Don't mark your suit. It's the only decent one you have.' There was blood and dirt on his shirt cuff!

He hurried to a lamp, seeking light, fumbling for his handkerchief. What the hell would Carruthers think, seeing him like this? Blast the man!

He examined his pocket watch, then began running. The voices in his head began drumming with the thudding of his feet. He was being followed.

A robber!

Don't be a fool, man. Stop sweating. Should have got a taxi. Who in hell can afford two taxis in one night?

He looked back and the road glittered greyly, the tramlines double. He called breathlessly, 'Who's there?' and listened to the indistinct humming that comes with passing midnight, felt the inexplicable terror, like waiting for gunfire, the sniper, end of life. Alone. In the dark.

The white handkerchief with its smears of blood and dirt mopped his forehead and wiped his eyes. He didn't like what was happening to him, as if a cog was slipping in his mind. He tried to reason with himself. Elsie had defrauded the firm. He was carrying the can. That was all. Hundreds of men had suffered that. God almighty! The memories crashed in his head like an agony of bayonets. Hundreds of men . . . Thousands of men . . .

His weary, frightened brain tangled the responsibilities of past and present. Pictures stabbed, intermingled. British boys. Like Tommy Buckley. Hundreds. Thousands. In khaki. Falling. Ninepins. Shocked baby faces gibbering. Elsie and Tommy screaming.

He gripped his ears, bent, commanding himself to regain control, his nerves screeching for easement.

The seconds passed. The blackness in his head turned to grey. He was shuddering, feeling sick, not knowing what was happening to him. Dreading insanity.

He listened, hearing his blood pounding, then his heart turned. There WAS someone behind him. Get him. Before he gets you.

Bertie ran back and dodged, then peered around the corner. His panting deafened him, threatened to choke him. Bloody fool! Bloody fool!

He stayed near a lamp and lit a cigarette, drawing on it deeply, forcing himself to be calm. Can't crack. Wife. Kids. Chin up, man, where're your guts?

He felt better, even amused, a cat called, orange eyes glittering a moment as it slunk into a lane.

Bertie looked up and there were stars. It seemed he hadn't seen stars for years, had forgotten they existed. He swung away from the glow of the lamp and marched into the shadows. The world was left to him and a cat.

The station seemed huge, cold, almost dark, but a sanctuary from the suffocating fears inside him; he strode through the open gate, then sat on the first bench to wait. The thoughts, the tiredness and dejection continued. He tried to think of Kit, but she was in that awful frilled purple dress.

Elsie was in white. A shroud. White satin all around

her. Linda was yelling. Not going to finishing school. A misfit among the rich and the poor.

He drooped his aching head into his hands. For God's sake stop thinking, but 'they' were there with bloody great bayonets at the ready, and he was carrying a sixty-pound pack, a pick and blankets, ammunition and bombs. Christ! Strike a match and it would be over.

He tried to duck, there on the station, and a coffee cup was on the end of the bench. White with a green band. He sat up to stare at it, fix his attention on it, bring himself back to High Street station. The cup was dirty, drip marks down the side, the saucer scarred by chipping. Someone should be hauled over the coals for leaving that there.

The train whistled on the night air, and the platform vibrated slightly with its thundering approach, bringing the end of all he and Kit had worked for, struggled for, its buffers clamping, clanging, hitting each other in its effort to stop. There was steam, the stench of sulphur, a great cloud hiding the fireman on the footplate. There was the banging of a carriage door swinging open, and the coffee cup was making the place untidy, dirty.

Carruthers stepped from the train in his usual ridiculous ballerina way, his small foot pointed to the sliding platform, poised and waiting for the train to stop, then Bertie stood up and the cup was still there, on the end of the bench. Bertie saw a man, just like himself, quite calmly pick it up, then turn and aim it at the hissing, steaming engine. Bertie heard it smash, saw it splinter in the way he wanted and, as it fell between engine and platform into nothing, he laughed. He laughed until the tears ran down his cheeks, and Carruthers held the cigar away from his fat face and stared with worried bulbous eyes.

'Albert! What the hell, man?'

It was then Bertie realised there had been no other man. A dawning spread through him. He had thrown that cup. He had gone off his rocker!

He found his handkerchief again and blew his nose, not caring that Carruthers saw the blood and dust. Terribly, sickeningly weary. He wanted to lie down and breathe no more.

The engine driver and fireman stared down to where the fragments had disappeared, and up again, their hands still rubbing on oily cloths, the blue caps on the back of their heads.

'Jeezus!' Bertie gasped. 'They must think I'm bonkers!'

'They'd be bloody right,' Carruthers snorted, and took Bertie's elbow. 'Come on, man. Away from here before they arrest us. We both need a stiff drink.'

'Pubs are shut. Gone midnight.'

'None in your house?' Carruthers was bronchial again, wheezing.

Bertie kept shaking his head, blinking, wishing the stabbing behind his eyes would go; then, out on the pavement, the sudden silence was eerie.

Carruthers' teeth jammed on his cigar and his thumb and forefinger dug into Bertie's arm. 'We'll find a taxi.'

'Around the corner. There's an all-night place.' Bertie was sweating, trying not to acknowledge he was afraid of Carruthers' presence. He said gingerly, 'I'm sorry. I have no idea why . . .'

'Mental aberration, dear boy. Temporary, but disquieting. Quite temporary.'

They found a taxi and both climbed in gratefully. Carruthers stuck his cigar between his teeth, his fat hands between his fat knees and humphed, 'How long have you been like this? Propelling cups at engines?'

'It's the first time. I had a rough period following the battle on the Somme, but I thought I was all right.'

'You probably are, old chap,' and Carruthers patted Bertie's knee.

The taxi rumbled along the centre of the road, and neither man spoke again until Carruthers finished the cigar and opened the window to throw the butt out. He said then, 'I assume by your attire that you have been on the town tonight.'

'If you are asking have I drunk something I shouldn't, the answer is no, but I did take Kit to a dance.'

Bertie undid his dickie bow and pulled it from his neck, then yanked his collar open.

'Splendid idea,' Carruthers said dryly, and Bertie didn't know whether he was approving the dancing or the removal of the dickie bow.

Carruthers sat back. 'There are periods when I would like to release the tension within. Golfers do it all the time. And cricketers. Liberate the aggressive instincts by bashing the ball.'

Bertie didn't answer; he felt annihilated and couldn't understand his loss of control.

Carruthers said, 'How are your girls?' and had to repeat it. 'Albert? The girls?'

Bertie jerked to the command, and stuttered a little. 'Linda is due to leave school shortly.'

'I thought she was going on,' Carruthers said calmly.

'Change of plan,' Bertie returned.

'Girls don't need education,' Carruthers said, staring blandly at the back of the driver's neck.

'If my job goes – ' Bertie left the sentence in the air, hoping Carruthers would pick it up and reassure him.

Carruthers didn't. He said softly, 'He's a tyke.'

'Henderson-Hobbs?'

'The same.'

'I think he's sucking up to Kit. To put it crudely.'

'A beautiful woman.'

'And cold.'

Carruthers nodded shortly. 'Our chairman will find that a new experience.'

Bertie's hands clasped tightly on his knees. 'Has he sent you to fire me?'

Carruthers wiggled his squat nose as if it itched. 'You won't be fired. Transferred. Keep the company name clean.'

'Then why are you here? Why the surprise visit?'

'John. This time you're a by the way.'

'Thank you,' Bertie sighed, and felt quite ill with relief.

Carruthers opened his waistcoat and relaxed back as if he, too, was glad that bit of dialogue was finished. 'I suggest, Albert, that you inform me of the complexities of the case. Set me on the road to understanding.'

'Regarding?'

'All this new business. It has the same pattern as last time.'

'It's all good stuff.'

'Then he's a good man.'

'Good man, my Aunt Fanny.' Bertie's courage was back. 'He wants my job. He'll go to any ends to get it.'

'Honest ends, Albert. Surely you mean honest ends.'

'I mean any damn ends.'

The taxi was careering towards the corner of Prince Edward Road when Carruthers said, 'Have you tried doing the same?'

Bertie's reply was irritable. 'I'm working all the hours God sends. I can't equal what he brings in. Not on top of my own work. I can't think how he's doing it.'

Carruthers' lips released a long low gust of air, and Bertie went on, 'There's a lot at stake. Who wants to be uprooted at my age?'

'It occurs to me, Albert,' Carruthers wheezed, 'that if you were to be turfed out you would have been informed before this. I would go so far as to say the future looks optimistic. Especially with the new chairman approving of your wife. In the meantime we must endeavour to increase your canvassing ability.'

'How?'

'A new man.'

'Can't afford it. Last year left us with debts that are crippling us.'

The taxi stopped and Carruthers offered splendidly, 'I shall remunerate the driver, Albert. On this occasion. I shall also take Kit under my wing.'

'Kit?' Bertie followed Carruthers out of the taxi. 'Did you say Kit?' He was quietly fuming. Henderson-Hobbs and now this fat man after Kit?

'We shall place the good lady upon the knocker, Albert.'

'You're talking through the back of your red neck! She's got a big house to run. She helps in the office. She has two daughters – '

'Precisely. Two daughters. I imagine Linda is becoming as lovely as her mother.'

Bertie's hackles rose with suspicion. 'What does that have to do with Kit?'

'It could leave the lady free to canvass, Albert. Canvass.'

It took Bertie a few moments to understand, then he said adamantly, 'Kit is not going out to work again.' He stood before Carruthers, subconsciously blocking the fat man's path. 'I am her husband. It is my place to support her.'

'She works in your office,' Carruthers commented dryly.

'That is different. I do as much as I can in there. Out on the road she'd be a drudge, getting soaked, taking insults – '

'Dear dear!' The marble-like eyes blinked slowly.

'When we first came here, I had to allow her to do it. That or watch her die of starvation. Now the position is different.'

'The position is a damn sight more precarious, Albert. You are an experienced man. In default. You are not proving you are worthy of the job. You are fighting to preserve it!'

Bertie stopped ranting and stared into the flabby face. Carruthers was irritated and Carruthers had power in influential quarters. Bertie glanced around at the upper windows of his neighbours and gave a short laugh. 'We'll be disturbing those who wish to sleep. We can talk about this tomorrow.'

He moved to open the gate but the taxi hadn't gone, and Carruthers had an arm out to it. 'I have no intention of arguing, Albert. I can find other accommodation.'

Bertie looked from the fat outstretched hand to the taxi driver's face, then to Carruthers who confronted him, the stiff curled brim of his black bowler pushed slightly back. 'Is this why you are really here?' Bertie asked slowly. 'To send my wife out to work?'

'To guide you, Albert. Endeavour to fulfil my obligations to the firm, and assist you in your efforts.'

Bertie opened the gate, his head on one side, defeated. 'I seem to have no choice.'

Carruthers paid the taxi driver then waved him away. 'Linda will make you an excellent assistant, and you will make an excellent tutor for her. I shall take it upon myself to train your wife.'

'My wife needs no training. We worked side by side.'

'And you shall do so again. I shall merely polish her style, so to speak.'

Carruthers went into the house laughing. He hung his hat on the hallstand and Kit came up the passage. 'Hello Carruthers.'

'Hello Kit.' They openly surveyed each other, like old friends.

'This is a surprise,' she said, but the question, the suspicion was in her voice.

Carruthers eased his back which sent his belly forward. 'You need fear not, dear lady. Not at this juncture. Albert will explain.'

'You need to lose weight, Carruthers.'

The fat man swung around to face Bertie. 'You note, the lady takes it upon herself to mother me.'

'As long as that is all the lady does to you, old chap, you, too, have nothing to fear.' Bertie didn't look at Kit.

Carruthers' chest rumbled with goodwill. 'Any other endeavours would be completely fruitless. I have been immune to the artful wiles of females for years.' He dropped his bald-topped head and gazed archly into Kit's amused face. 'That explains why the ladies are

138

so often kind to me. The mothering instinct. The only instinct I am capable of awakening.'

Bertie laughed politely. 'Well, dump your briefcase in the office. We'll have a cup of tea,' then he went to the kitchen, gesturing a bewildered Kit before him. He whispered, 'It's John he has come to see, and he's got the damn cheek to order you out to work. On the knocker.'

'Oh lovely!' Kit grimaced. 'When do I work in the office?'

'Apparently you don't. Linda does.'

'Linda?'

'It won't last. Once winter comes you'll have to be inside. I can't allow – '

'Sssh, he'll hear,' Kit smiled and, in the office, Carruthers was examining the golden Rolls-Royce.

He came to the kitchen, almost filling the doorway, tired, smelling of trains and cigars. He said, 'Nice automobile on your desk, Albert. Starting a collection?'

Bertie shook his head, but Kit whispered, 'The new chairman sent it – with a box of chocolates,' and, while Carruthers' brows rose, she moved behind and closed the door. 'The girls are asleep,' she explained, and Curruthers sagged into her chair, wondering how she would deal with Henderson-Hobbs.

CHAPTER SIX

Although baby Buck had been christened at the Church of England Maggie and John rarely went there for Sunday morning service. They preferred the old Welsh mission hall and, on that glorious Sunday morning after Whitsun, Maggie stood beside John, with the baby sitting on her arm, and sang lustily, 'On a hill far away . . .'

The service ended, people began whispering to each other, and John replaced his hymn book on the back ledge of the chair before him. 'Good it is to be emptying our lungs like that, Mag.'

'You've gone all Welshy again,' she admonished quietly. 'You become a manager and you'll have to talk English all the time.' His great knuckly hand stole to the small of her back, threatening to pat that much-loved backside, and she swung away from him and into the aisle, sending back laughing glances, humping the baby more safely to her. 'I'll show you up,' she threatened softly. 'Scream out loud, I will.'

The pastor was on the doorstep, 'Good morning John. In fine voice this morning, boy. Fine indeed,' and a man prodded John's arm. 'Someone going up your way. You expecting visitors today?'

'Us? No!' said Maggie, and hurried to the pavement.

'Hope you locked up, then,' said the man, and Maggie returned, 'Nothing there to pinch.'

But there was. Sovereigns in the wardrobe and John's collections in the basin in the pantry. And she never locked up.

She smiled around. 'But we'd better go and see. Say

ta-ta,' she encouraged the baby, and held one tiny hand and wagged it up and down. 'Ta-ta everybody,' then she and John were hurrying along the pavement, her long black skirt as full and flowing as a nun's habit, while John strode easily beside her.

'Must be Sion the shop,' he said. 'Come for more eggs.'

'No,' Maggie argued. 'He knows I'm in chapel this morning.'

They turned a corner then stood in the middle of the Sunday-silent road. They screwed up their eyes against the sunlight and gazed up the mountain.

'Carruthers!' John gasped. 'On the path. Look there. Just going up. Near the house.'

Maggie blinked as if to make the fat man disappear. 'No one said he was coming!' and the rest of the congregation came trailing to see.

'D'you know him, Maggie?'

'Yes, oh yes!' she cried. 'He's a friend of ours. Lovely to see him. Oh yes, lovely it is.'

They all saw Chief Inspector Carruthers go into the farmhouse the front way, then come out the back way carrying a deck chair.

As if on a hill not so far away, Carruthers plonked his seat beside the rows of beansticks, took off his jacket, hung it on the side of the lavatory, then sat and flicked his bowler forward over his face.

The pastor said as he rubbed his hands, 'No doubt waiting for you, so no need to rush,' but Maggie and John exchanged glances, shook hands again, praised the sermon, smiled as if they were not wondering what the Chief Inspector wanted, and hurried away.

'Oh John, if only we had a proper road up, I could have fetched the pram. We'd have been quicker then.'

'Give him to me. He's getting heavy now. There. Better?' He took the baby, but watched the recumbent figure in his back garden. 'What d'you think he's up to, Mag?'

'Sly old devil. Coming like this. No warning.'

141

'Any rhubarb tart left? He likes rhubarb tart.'

'Yes. And you give him stuff from the garden. Sweeten him. I'll give him dinner. Hope it chokes him. Coming like this.'

John laughed shortly, the initial shock wearing off. 'Maybe it's good news, Mag. Maybe I'm in.'

'You'd get a letter. Bertie'd know.'

'Not if it's his district I'm having.'

Maggie stopped to digest the idea, her great breasts stifled beneath pleated black blouse and cameo brooch. 'It'd be lovely. But it'd be terrible too. Poor Bertie and Kit. Everything they ever had. Gone.'

'You want Buck to be rich, don't you? Have a nice house with a proper bathroom and a toilet?'

'Only for the baby's sake, John. Only for the baby. I'm not greedy otherwise.'

He nodded, resolving to be her strength and guide. 'This is business, Mag. Them or us,' and he pressed a forefinger against the baby's button nose. The baby laughed and dribbled so the blue ribbon about his bonnet got stuck to his chin.

Maggie said inconsequently, 'It's his teeth,' and John stuck a finger into the baby's mouth and slid it about. 'Aye,' he said, and Maggie slapped his hand away.

'You can't feel a thing! Daft! You are!'

'Mag!'

It was the closest they had been to a quarrel in months, and they stopped walking to stare at each other.

The baby watched, felt ignored, gurgled, screamed, and jerked both arms stiffly.

John snapped 'Shurrup!' in Welsh, and Maggie took the baby from him, crooning and soothing.

For a second, John seemed to be seething, then he said, 'I'll go on up. See what Carruthers wants.'

'Don't you go looking all anxious. Let him wait.'

So they continued to travel together, John's hand on Maggie's waist in a gesture of assistance.

Carruthers saw them appear then disappear as the

track wound. He righted his bowler and put on his jacket. He folded the chair and took it back into the house, then he went to their front gate, closed it after him, and stood waiting.

'Beautiful morning, Margaret. And you reside so close to God.' He looked at the sky meaningfully.

'We didn't expect you, Mr Carruthers. We wouldn't have gone to chapel if we'd known.'

'No inconvenience. None whatever. Good morning, John. All well with you?'

'I hope so, Mr Carruthers. Indeed I do.'

All three went into the house, all three smiling. Maggie put Buck into the high black pram and took off his bonnet and coatee, his mittens and bootees, then she lifted off her hat, stuck the pin back in it and excused herself.'I'll go upstairs and change.'

By the time she came back down in her usual black dress and white apron, John had brewed tea in the big blue pot.

'You'll stay for dinner, Mr Carruthers,' she said, and he ponderously took his watch from his waistcoat pocket and checked it against the grandfather clock in the darkest corner.

'Of course he will,' John said quickly, and Maggie didn't wait.

'It is all ready. In the oven. I'll put it out while John shows you the garden.'

John thought of Antonio Capriolli and tried to ease the skipping of his heart. He said, 'Come and choose a lettuce, Mr Carruthers.'

'You grow them up here as early as this?'

'In the greenhouse. Round the other side.' John led the fat man through the lean-to where the smell of carbolic soap fought with the smell of roasting beef. 'You'll have to taste our parsnip wine, too, Mr Carruthers. We were lucky with this lot. Cleared lovely.'

Carruthers carried his enormous belly forward like a bulldozer forcing a rock. He enjoyed detective work, but he enjoyed Maggie and John too and, at the moment, at this Sunday lunchtime, he felt nasty, a snooper, so he tried to make up for it by smiling and chuckling, while his attention missed nothing and his eyeballs slithered fast in their effort to see all.

'You like beetroot, Mr Carruthers, don't you? I'll let you have some before you go. Sweet it is. Nice.' John kept talking, longing to know why Carruthers was here, but not daring to ask. The meal was finished, the plates, smeared with the residue of dark brown gravy, stacked on the wooden draining board beside the sink. Carruthers burped, wiped his lips on the paper serviette, and John and Maggie tried not to look intense or glance at each other too often.

Maggie changed the baby's napkin then bumped the child about on her lap. 'This is the way the lady rides, nimby nimby nimbo.' The golden light streamed in through the front window as the sun worked its way around to the west, and the Busy Lizzie on the sill took on a new glossy green and tangerine brilliance.

'Well,' said Carruthers, from the hardness of John's wooden armchair, and the baby-bumping stopped. The bottle of milk that had been heating in the pan of hot water was taken up quickly and the teat stuck in the baby's mouth. Maggie and John awaited the important man's announcement, and he said, 'Margaret, you are an expert in culinary matters. I have never before partaken of such rhubarb tart.'

Maggie inclined her head, wishing he would get on with an explanation of his visit. She asked, 'Are you staying with the Hemsworthys?'

'Yes,' said Carruthers, and gazed up at the black beams, the salted side of bacon in its white cheesecloth hanging beside the clock in the corner. 'In the little town below us,' Carruthers went on, 'people are starving, but up here, Maggie and John, we are apart from it.' The word contentment came into Carruthers' mind, then was replaced by smugness, and he decided that was

144

it; John and Maggie were smug. He said slowly, 'Mr Henderson-Hobbs knew I intended visiting you, and he sent his regards.'

The half lie worked. He saw both Maggie and John relax. So they did have guilty consciences. 'He is interested in the quantity or new business you have been acquiring lately.' Carruthers' fleshy mouth opened in a wide scarlet-tongued grin, and his chins flattened and turned purply red. 'He used the terminology, working on his own initiative,' and Carruthers watched John blatantly.

'Ah yes,' said John, still wondering what was coming next.

Maggie put in quickly. 'We've both been working flat out. Haven't we, John?'

Carruthers nodded as if satisfied. 'That is what the man at the top enjoys. Get the people booked up, safeguard themselves from any dire consequences of the future,' and silence fell; Carruthers waiting for the great confession and John and Maggie hoping not to give it.

'Well,' said Carruthers, at last. 'I regret the need to get on my way. Leave you good people to recover from your erstwhile toil,' and he stood.

'Are you in Swansea long?' It was John, anxious, but not awaiting a reply. 'I'll get the beetroot for you.'

'A few days.' Carruthers wiggled his fingers at the baby who tried to stare him out. 'A few days should be sufficient' and, as Carruthers trod carefully back down the mountainside laden with brown paper carriers holding vegetables, eggs and wine, he turned and nodded a couple of times, his arms too weighted down to wave.

He would have to report that John was, indisputably, good promotional material, if only because he had a damn good wife.

That Sunday evening Carruthers sat at Bertie's desk, hearing the church bells tolling over the town, and the echoing footsteps of people hurrying to worship. He carefully considered his report for Head Office.

Eventually he wrote it. Short and to the point. As far as he was able to ascertain, Mr John Davies, of Port Talbot, did have certain attributes conducive to a successful managership, but it might be sagacious to delay any decision.

He knew Henderson-Hobbs would want the report explained, but perhaps by then there would be nothing requiring explanation.

Next morning Carruthers emerged from the bathroom oddly munificent in his dusty-looking beige suit, but with a blue shirt instead of the eternal white or cream and, with a shock, Kit noticed how very blue his eyes were. It embarrassed her and he smiled as if he knew something had unsettled her. She rushed to the scullery and concentrated on preparing breakfast. As she forked over slices of bacon, turned sausages and cracked eggs, she marvelled over Carruthers' eyes. For years she had been aware of their bulbousness, their marble-looking texture, but the depth of their colour had gone unnoticed.

Now she heard him sit gaspingly at the table between the two girls, his deep fat voice talking, questioning, flattering.

She passed the filled plates to Bertie and he took them to the kitchen, making light remarks. 'Here Emma. Get your gums into that,' and there was laughter. When the meal was finished, Carruthers spent almost a quarter of an hour wandering up and down the small back garden, commenting on the honeysuckle, the mint, and the miracle of so much growing in such a salt sea air.

At nine-thirty he said, 'Well, Albert, we had better make a start,' and Kit stifled a sigh of relief. The house had to be empty, but for herself, by eleven.

Bertie said, 'I'm afraid you are on your own today, old chap. I have claims to investigate and there's a backlog of paperwork in the office.'

Carruthers pressed his hands into his trouser pockets and looked across the room, through the window to the whitewashed wall of next door. He wobbled his fat mouth in thought and announced, 'I have decided to look around Port Talbot.'

There was a surprised silence. Kit looked at the cleared table and Bertie wondered what the fat brain was working on.

'All right,' he said. 'Five minutes,' and in that time he and Carruthers were marching from the house, trouser turnups flapping with each stride. Kit watched from the office window and, as they turned to salute her, she blew them a kiss, then laughed as both men returned it.

Carruthers said sonorously, his shoulders back, his jacket pockets bulging with papers, 'You have a splendid family, Albert.'

'Agreed,' laughed Bertie, and felt like his old self, ready for the knocker, a new week, a new challenge.

In Port Talbot Carruthers produced a list, and he stood in the middle of an almost empty street to read it. 'Sandhill Road,' he ruminated. 'Where, Albert, are we likely to find Sandhill Road?'

Bertie jerked his head in the right direction. Things were beginning to click into place. He said, 'Is that the list of John's new business?'

'How perceptive of you,' Carruthers returned, 'but I would prefer not to be aware you have rumbled it. Keep the dirty business to myself, if you understand.'

They tramped for an hour and got no lead. 'Channel View Road,' Carruthers said heavily, and Bertie led him to the other side of town, then out towards Margam.

They began with number one, and neither man commented that Channel View Road seemed to stretch endlessly to the hills in the east.

'Good morning, madam.' Carruthers assessed the woman who opened the dog-scratched door. She was tired, probably starved, bent and bony. He gestured with the hand now holding a roll of papers. 'I'm from the Unicorn Insurance Company.'

'Oh aye,' said the woman, and looked as if the yellow gold of the sand had got into the whites of her eyes. 'I

147

don't need no more insurance. I got – ' She screeched as a tall greyhound galloped from behind and hit the backs of her knees. 'George! Keep the bloody dog in!' but the bloody dog knew the signs and how to avoid them; its high-bellied body shot out, between Carruthers and Bertie, its gazelle-like gaze reflecting light and determination.

'Jeezuz!' screamed the woman, waving her arms about. 'He's bloody gorn!' and a man came running, his braces dangling, one hand clutching the top of his trousers.

'Hi up mate!' he ordered Carruthers. 'He's gotter race ternight.' He placed two fingers between his teeth and sent a piercing whistle past Carruthers' ear. Carruthers jumped, his face screwing up against the horror of the sound.

The woman shrugged at Bertie. 'We got no time to bother now,' and the passage was filled with people who were anxious to get out and chase the dog. 'Outer the way, chum. I got a bob on him fer tonight.'

Carruthers and Bertie backed further towards the pavement, still slightly off balance, but Carruthers called, 'My dear woman. Does a Mr Davies call upon you?'

'Sometimes,' she called back, between rushing bodies, 'but I likes the other one best.' She put a hand to her mouth, laughing as the sweep of chasers threatened to knock her off her ragged-slippered feet. 'Handsome boys, them Italians.'

Carruthers nodded, raised his bowler in salute, and marched on. Bertie marched with him while the whistles in every note seared up and down Channel View Road.

'You notice, Albert.' Carruthers came to a puffing halt around the corner. 'Instinct assured me we were on the right track,' and he took the puce pencil from his breast pocket and ticked another name on the list.

Bertie laughed at him, admiring. Mad dogs and Englishmen, he thought, still concentrate on insurance. So he asked, 'Where do we go from here?'

'A coffee, dear boy. I find that sort of hullabaloo

disturbing.' He patted his stomach with both hands and looked complacent. Bertie didn't believe he was disturbed at all.

In the cafe carruthers stirred sugar into his coffee, gazed at the empty tables about them and said laboriously, 'Where do we find a young handsome Italian? Preferably in the immediate vicinity.'

'Shouldn't be too difficult,' Bertie said, and vaguely remembered two and sixpence in John's account. It was against an Italian name.

'Any ice cream merchants?' Carruthers prodded.

'Ice cream!' Bertie echoed, still thinking of that half a crown.

Carruthers' bulbous little nose twitched and he gave a thoughtful sniff. 'Ever known an Italian who does not sell ice cream?'

'I know of a family,' Bertie said.

'Admirable,' gasped Carruthers. 'You are henceforth in charge of directions. Lead on Macduff.'

Bertie would have gone straight to Mrs Capriolli's front door, but Carruthers' fingers, lightly touching his arm, stopped him. 'Caution, Albert. Caution.'

Carruthers shoved his papers into his pockets until he looked bulgy and bumpy all over, then he took off his bowler, mopped his forehead with a large white handkerchief, and wiped the leather lining band of the hat clear of sweat. 'I think I shall partake of a cigar,' he said, and Bertie took the hint and offered him one, the gilt paper band still about its centre.

They stood, like detectives, at the corner of the street and waited.

Mr Capriolli pedalled from the lane running behind the row of houses, and touched his brow in salute as he and his ice cream cart picked up speed.

Carruthers watched, but his eyes were half closed as if without interest.

Antonio Capriolli came home a short while later,

almost dancing along the opposite pavement, his black curls as shining as his eyes.

'Helloh to you!' he called merrily.

Carruthers nodded, Bertie grinned and called back, 'Helloh to yourself.'

Antonio stopped, undecided but ever optimistic. 'You are waiting for someone?'

'The insurance man,' said Carruthers, and his eyes opened slowly.

'Ah yes,' came the youthful reply. 'I am the insurance man.'

'No,' said Carruthers. 'You are the wrong one. We are looking for the tall fellow, gingery hair, thin – '

'Aaaah,' Antonio strode across the empty road to them. 'You mean Mr Davies. My boss. Do you want to do business? Accident? Endowment? I can do them all for you. Pronto.'

'A car,' said Carruthers, and the young man's face dropped.

'Noh,' he said, apparently in deep disappointment. 'We don't touch cars. Not yet. Maybe one day soon.' His optimism returned. 'You give me your names and addresses, yes? And as soon as our new chairman brings in his new policies I, personally, will contact you.'

'How kind,' Carruthers said, and placed his small feet a little apart. 'But I believe it will be more convenient if we conduct our business with this – er – Mr Davies ourselves.'

'As you would wish,' Antonio agreed. 'You might find him in his house right now. It's a farmhouse. If you will come down the road a little way. Come. I'll show you.'

Carruthers nodded and obeyed, his fat face without expression, and Bertie didn't know whether to respect his aplomb or be ashamed of his deceit.

Up on the mountainside Maggie didn't see Capriolli but, as she hung out more napkins and towels, she paused to admire the grey-blue of the channel beneath a blue-grey haze, and there, below, was the figure she

150

could never mistake: the roly poly Carruthers. And Bertie Hemsworthy too.

She rushed to tidy the kitchen and remove a bib from young Buck. By the time the visitors arrived the parsnip wine and seed cake were in the centre of the clean-clothed table. The baby, in the pram, was on clean white lace pillows, ready to receive all the attention bestowed on him.

For a while Carruthers remained the senior, Head Office man and spy, receiving the news that John rarely came home for midday meal on Mondays, but then the wine mellowed, and the seed cake was preceded by poached fresh eggs on toast with home-made tomato chutney.

The baby lifted his head, chuckled at Bertie, and held out his arms to him. Without thought Bertie strode to the pram and laughed with the child, then lifted him. His heart began singing, this is my son, this is my son. He held the boy close, he tickled the wet chin, he cuddled and loved and smelled and longed. Then came a sort of anger, a need to possess, to carry away, and Maggie sensed it and hurried to him, buxom and worried. 'I'll take him, Bertie. Let me put him back in the pram while you have a slice of cake. Made it myself, I did.'

'Maggie,' he whispered steadily, and held the baby to his chest, 'I want him back. He's my flesh and blood.'

He was fully aware of Carruthers pretending not to listen, of the sudden pallor on Maggie's face, the horror and dispute in her eyes. 'You took him without my knowledge. I want him back.'

'Never!' breathed Maggie. Her hands reached for the baby and, for a moment, Bertie resisted, The child felt the antagonism and wrinkled its face, ready for the great scream. Bertie saw it and let Maggie take him. Even his child, not old enough to know anything, disliked him.

Maggie replaced the baby in the pram, buckling harness ties about him, then she turned to Bertie. 'Get one thing straight, Mr Hemsworthy. He was never yours. You never admitted a thing. Elsie Buckley's man died in China. We swallowed that story. So now you swallow this. I'll sell my soul to keep that baby. He's mine. You keep your hands off him.'

The black cat streched beside the brass fender, then sprang to the old leather couch and onto the windowsill. Carruthers stood up, flicking white cigar ash off the corrugations of his waistcoat. 'Well, Margaret, thank you for a welcome repast, but now we must endeavour to do more on behalf of the great gods in London. If you will excuse us.'

She turned to him in panic. 'But you haven't told me why you came?'

'Not serious, dear lady. Not serious at all. I shall be in the office when your husband pays in on Wednesday.' He plucked his hat from the sideboard. 'In the meantime, kindly give him my best wishes, will you?' His eyes were warning Bertie not to defy him and, as the two men left, Bertie was hot with fury.

'What in hell made you do that?' he muttered as they met the top of the track.

'Paternal instinct,' Carruthers returned.

'I want the child back.'

'Give your wife one like him,' Carruthers retorted. 'Do you both good.'

When they got back to Prince Edward Road Kit looked blooming. Her amber eyes shone, her black hair was loose about her shoulders as if she wanted to be unrestrained. She wore a plain dandelion-coloured dress with a wide chocolate-coloured belt, and Carruthers said expansively, 'Tomorrow, beautiful lady, I shall dedicate myself entirely to you,' and his smile was brilliant.

Bertie kissed Kit's cheek, but neither he nor Carruthers associated her transformation with another telephone call from Henderson-Hobbs.

By ten o'clock next morning Carruthers and Kit were in the train to Llanelly. Kit laughed a lot. She felt ridiculously free. Today the work in the office could pile up, the house could look after itself; to her, this was a day off, six hours of fresh air and new faces. 'You take that street, Carruthers. I'll take this. All right?'

He paused, not used to being given menial instructions, but silently accepting that the female species, once married, became overbearing. 'I think not, dear lady. I wish to ascertain you are still fully competent as a representative of the firm.'

She laughed at him. 'Of course I'm competent. Do you suppose Bertie built the whole district on his own? It was I who tramped around Port Talbot in the beginning. I canvassed and collected until it was big enough to give to an agent.'

'Our Mr Davies?'

'Certainly not. He's only been with us three or four years. The first man there was – '

'Out of the way, Kitty!' Carruthers' arm whipped about her as a go-cart, made from an apple box, carrying two harum-scarum boys careered down the slope towards them. The driver steered erratically, a rope tied to the front wheels. 'Whoops! Sorry!' he yelled and careered on, shrieking with laughter and fear.

'My word!' Carruthers gasped indignantly. 'Even the pavements are unsafe these days.'

Kit leaned against him, held tightly, and the go-cart toppled its contents into the gutter. A horse reared, heavily blinkered and leather-shafted.

'Imbeciles!' Carruthers exploded, and the boys looked sheepish as they righted themselves. Kit said, 'Very well then, Carruthers. You are the boss, so we'll do alternative houses. That suit you?'

Carruthers gazed at the drayman shaking his fist and yelling rude things, then at Kit, resigned. 'As you say, dear lady. As you say.'

He took his arm from about her casually, but Kit didn't look into his face. It was the first time she had been that close to a man other than Bertie. Carruthers moved from

153

her and strode on his little legs to the first house, his face impersonal, and Kit called after him, 'Carruthers! Shall I come with you?'

He half turned then, his brows lifted. 'You are under the impression it is I who need training?' and Kit was dismayed.

'No. Oh no. I'm sorry.' Her hands fluttered in her effort to explain she had meant no harm. 'I was trying to please you – '

Over the untidy green of a privet hedge they stared into each other's eyes and Kit remembered he was wearing something scented. Soap? Hair cream? She could no longer smell it but it had been strong when he hugged her to him.

So many thoughts flashed through her mind at once. Carruthers not being a snooper any more, but a man with blue eyes and a wife who, as he put it, found her pleasure elsewhere. Carruthers helping her and Bertie in so many ways. Carruthers the Head Office lap dog, the lonesome fat man.

She shrugged dismissively. She had liked that hug, the unexpected sensation of being saved from danger, held close by a big-bodied, gentle-armed man.

Yet look at him!

She laughed, unaware it was a flirtatious laugh. 'I'll go next door.'

She tried to pretend he had given the instruction, but he knew he hadn't and, in resignation, he turned and lifted the knocker.

As she worked, talked insurance, took refusals, and called Carruthers for the odd acceptances, a small cell at the back of her mind savoured the day and considered the foolishness of her past; she had been wrong to marry Bertie, unfair to him and herself. She supposed there was a perfect man somewhere for every woman, but Bertie wasn't hers.

She swung her arms as she crossed the road, as near to striding as a woman dared, and warned herself to stop thinking. A woman should never think. She was born to obey.

They lunched in a fish and chip shop. It was small, empty but for themelves. The man wiping the counter with a wet cloth said, 'Rum do. This chap Hitler in Germany. Think we'll have ter have another bash at them soon,' and Kit turned away in distaste.

Carruthers ate as if he was famished, and Kit stopped worrying about the Germans and spread her proposal forms across the table. 'Look how much I've done,' she laughed. She pointed a finger to the figures, and there was a long ragged red scratch on her wrist.

'My dear lady, where have you been?' Carruthers murmured. 'Caught against a rose bush?'

'No-o-o.' She tried to remember.

The tip of his finger lightly smoothed along the speckled scarlet line, and Kit's flesh rose in goose-pimples.

She snatched her arm from him. 'It's nothing. Nothing at all!' Her voice shook and she felt foolishly sixteen.

He too jerked from her. Both knew it had been an oddly intimate moment, and neither was happy about it.

Carruthers drank his coffee in a few gulps, then belched, patting his stomach and gazing, toad-eyed, as if to tell her this uncouth creature was his real self, not the concerned man with the tenderly caressing finger. The familiarity of the moment gave Kit courage to blurt, 'Carruthers. Why haven't you divorced your wife?'

There was a long heavy silence, then Carruthers picked up her papers from the table and shuffled them together. He said quietly, not looking at her, 'And with exactly how many people in that uncomfortable state of being are you acquainted?'

'None,' she said, a little surprised.

'Precisely. Divorce is for film stars. Maurice Chevalier and Mademoiselle Vallee.' He handed her the rolled papers. 'Have you not noticed, Kit, that divorce proceedings are invariably hidden in the inner pages of a newspaper? Barely reported. Not even for those who can afford them. I perceived in the *News of the World* some time ago that titles figure conspicuously, and of three baronets named in matrimonial suits one week, one was a defended suit by a wife for a judicial separation.'

Kit took the papers, stunned by the idea of Carruthers reading the *News of the World*, then she smiled waveringly. 'You are adept at not answering a question. I genuinely want to know.'

Carruthers stood and tidied his jacket about him, his mouth pouting in thought. 'There are two important ties between men and women, dear lady. Pure love and desire. It is unfortunate they rarely come together.'

He went to the counter and paid the bill, then Kit followed him to the pavement. Pure love, she thought, and desire.

Carruthers' stomach swelled before him and, at the corner, he said, 'You may work unsupervised for the next hour or two,' and they separated without another word.

The afternoon passed with neither contacting the other. The sun was still glorious as they caught the train home. Carruthers sat in one corner of the carriage, silent, his attention never wavering from the countryside rushing past. Kit sat amid the other passengers, her eyes closed, and in number 300 Prince Edward Road, Bertie cooked a meal.

The thick blue fog of it met the opened porch door and surged to the street as if the house was on fire.

Kit smiled at Carruthers. 'Chops,' she said, while wondering how much they had cost. She knew Bertie would wave grandly at the butcher and say, 'We had better have a couple each, that makes ten so we'll have the round dozen.'

There were obviously onions too, probably fried black. While Kit smiled she charged into the scullery, and there Bertie sweated. She pecked his red-hot cheek, took back the pinny and whispered, 'Get Carruthers a drink. He needs it.' Bertie rolled down his sleeves, adjusted his cuff-links, and Kit was left amid the stench of boiled-over potatoes and a pan of peas that were like bullets.

Linda hovered around her. 'Shall I wave a towel, Mummy? Let the fug out?'

'Please darling. The heat in here is killing.'

Linda opened the back door and swung a teatowel. The blueness rushed into the clear air of the garden and the frying pan stopped spitting. Kit cleaned the fat off the red tiled floor, and Linda said, 'Mummy. I would like to do what Carruthers says and work in the office.'

'Oh yes, darling.' Kit turned off the grill that was turning the 'warming' plates beneath it dark brown, and Linda went on, 'I did go to the Labour Exchange after school, but they only want skivvies. You have to sleep in. Get up in the morning and light fires. Look after children, scrub floors, and you only get two and sixpence a week. And that was in London. I wouldn't like to be in London.'

'Poor darling.'

'I can't light fires. Nor scrub floors.'

'No, dear.'

'Will Daddy pay me?'

'You'll have to ask him.'

'Can I start in two weeks?'

'Two weeks?' Kit took the pan of potatoes to the sink and strained them. 'These are mashed already. Bash them with a big fork, will you?'

'Can I, Mummy?'

'Can you what?'

'Start in two weeks when I leave school?'

'Two weeks!' Kit stood with the scalding pan in her hand, the sink still steaming beside her, and stared at her daughter. Two weeks and, officially, Linda would be a woman; out of school, another on the list of millions unemployed.

*   *   *

That same Tuesday evening John came home to the farmhouse, emptied his pockets of papers and money, and asked, 'Where's Antonio's stuff for this week? He's been, I suppose?'

'On the sideboard. He was early.' Maggie nursed the baby against her shoulder. 'Gone selling ice cream with his father tonight. The fair's in at Neath.'

John went to the sideboard and read notes and counted money, then he scratched his thin gingery hair and said, 'I'm going back down. Get rid of him. Be safer.'

'Oooh, now John, don't go doing anything silly,' but John put the Italian's commission in his trouser pocket, strode out to his bike, and went freewheeling down the track, standing on the pedals, his rear held up, away from the thudding of the hard leather saddle.

Next morning he lay in bed and watched the wonder of Maggie getting dressed. It had not been a good night, the baby had been wanting attention, and John would have liked the same.

'Maggie?'

'What then?' She was tired.

'Why did you marry me?'

She paused before answering, examining the fit of her brassiere. 'So you could ask dull questions.'

He flung himself off the bed. 'I married you because you were made of good wife stuff.' He waited. Would she say he was good husband stuff?

She didn't. She laughed at him. 'Oh duwch, feeling sorry for yourself this morning. You go into that office now, and don't take any nonsense.'

John reached for his vest off the top of the washing stand. 'I bet you Carruthers knows about Antonio. Bound to. Got a nose like a bloodhound. Give me hell, they will. Him and Bertie.'

'Your clean shirt's on the line in the kitchen. A white one. Look as good as they do.'

'Better,' he grinned, in an effort to please her, and rubbed his stubbly chin.

When he got to Prince Edward Road he was sweating again, but he glided off his bike before the wheels stopped singing. He strode into the house whistling and was met by utter silence.

He put his head down and strode on, past the closed office door and the laden hallstand, his inside tight. He rapped, pseudo playful, on the ajar door of the middle room, then he grinned, outwardly a cocky bighead, and strode in. 'Morning, boys.'

'Morning.' The response was lazy.

His fellow agents sprawled on the blue damask chairs and settee, their faces concentrated into the serious task of waiting.

'Anybody been in yet?'

Five heads turned and nodded shortly towards the sixth. 'George has.'

George said, through a walrus moustache, 'The great man himself holdeth court,' and John went to a leather pouffe beside the white fireplace and sat, low, his bony knees as high as his bony shoulders. 'It's Henderson-Hobbs,' he said, 'sending his lap dog to sniff around.'

George said, 'He told me they're expecting big changes all round the country. New policies coming in. Expansion.'

'Bound to,' someone else agreed, and John groped in his jacket pocket for his battered packet of ten Woodbines; he lit one, waving the dead match until six pairs of feet manoeuvred the waste paper basket to him like footballers dribbling the ball.

Linda came in, wearing her art silk stockings and lipstick, a navy skirt and white blouse. 'Any more books?' She laughed at the men, loving being with them.

John handed her his. 'No school today?'

'Nup.' She shook her head, still laughing. 'I'm learning the business.'

'Thought you were going to Malvern,' John said.

'Nup,' she repeated. 'New plans now.'

John nodded, but his expression said he would never

159

do that to his kid, and Linda hesitated, sensing his displeasure.

George called lazily, 'How long, sweetheart, before I can go?'

'Not long,' she smiled. 'I have done yours. It's all correct,' and he laughed teasingly at the girl of fourteen who was given the job of checking his work. He said, 'You'll be boss around here one day. The first woman manager, heh?'

'Poof!' She flicked a foot up behind her, then went, calling, 'Who wants to be boss of a place like this?' and John winced, because he did.

He stubbed out the Woodbine and put it back in the packet. He could smoke the rest when he came in next week.

It was another hour before Linda beckoned him into the office, and only one man was left to go in after him.

He entered the room, and thought yet again that Carruthers looked like a fat spider behind Bertie's desk; eyes protruding, assessing the poor bloody fly as it heard the door close behind it.

'*Shw mai*, John.' So Carruthers was being chummy. A bad sign.

'*Shw mai*,' John returned, and sat with his clumsy-looking hands dangling between his spread knees, his attitude unconsciously insolent.

Carruthers passed the ledger back to him. 'As always, this is right,' he smiled and his chins were flattened, white against the top of his chest. 'I thought Maggie looked well.'

'Blooming.' John felt suspicion crawling through him and awaited the evil moment.

Carruthers gave a few little nods, then sat back and poked in his waistcoat pocket with his forefinger, but wanted nothing from it. 'The beetroot was excellent. We had it for supper that day, didn't we, Albert?'

Albert's chair creaked as he half turned from the small desk to agree.

Carruthers said ponderously, 'You would make a highly efficient farmer, John. Ever considered the possibility?'

The sick feeling in John made his Adam's apple plop, but he stood up and brought his wallet from his inside pocket.

'More new business, John?'

John concentrated on emptying his wallet.

'You have surpassed yourself these last weeks, John. Maggie preparing to wear mink this winter?'

Bertie listened and cringed for John.

Carruthers sat back, his global eyes concentrating on the helpless agent. 'Are you acquainted with a young fellow by the name of Capriolli?'

John tipped change from his pockets on to the desk. 'Everybody round our way knows the Capriollis.'

'You employ this Antonio in some capacity?'

'No.'

Bertie stiffened, and Linda, sitting at a small table between her father and the filing cabinet, kept her head down.

Carruthers said comfortably, 'I happened to come across the young man. He tried to book me up.'

John stared down at Carruthers, his face set in its long crooked lines. 'He doesn't canvass. Or collect. Any more.'

Carruthers sat forward, patting his jacket pockets as if he could now get on with the day. 'I am gratified to hear you say so, John,' and the fat man's voice had regained some of its usual timbre.

John said aggressively, 'It's not against the law to give a man a chance!' and Carruthers' reply came sharply. 'A man who is not employed by the Unicorn Insurance Company, who is not responsible to Head Office, has no business handling monies in the firm's name.' John looked at the inkwells, and Carruthers said more gently, 'You get my meaning, John,' and he beckoned Linda. 'You can count the money, little lady, then Mr Davies can be on his way.'

Bertie's chair creaked more loudly as he raised

161

himself from it. 'Linda,' he said with a sigh. 'You go and see to cups of tea all round. Tell Mummy we're ready. I'll count John's collections.' He and John exchanged glances that excluded the Chief Inspector, while Linda looked at Carruthers and received a nod of agreement.

* * *

On Saturday morning Linda charged up the stairs, collided with Emma on the landing and crowed, 'Dad gave me two and six. Look!' She opened her hand to expose the silver coin and laughed at Emma's lofty disdain, then she dived into the bathroom. She washed, smeared cold cream, wiped it off, parted her hair on the side, put it back to the middle and, when she finally arrived on the landing, she looked just like Linda Hemsworthy wearing pink powder and red lipstick.

Bertie didn't shudder when he saw her, but he had to control his tongue. 'Where are you off to?'

'I'm meeting Bunty Morris.'

He helped her slip into her blazer, then watched her leave the house. He felt permanently uncomfortable about her, and she kept running as though she was late.

The clock in Woolworths' said she was on time.

But Bunty Morris wasn't.

Linda waited half an hour, not believing Bunty could let her down.

She stopped waiting at the kerb and went into Woolworths' doorway, ignoring the words NOTHING OVER SIXPENCE, her eyes searching the moving sea of faces on both sides of the road.

She saw Ali almost at the same moment as he saw her, and Linda thought Stella, beside him, more garish than ever. Like a blonde doll dressed as a fairy.

Ali waved then nudged the fairy, and they both dodged the traffic to come across the road.

'Hello there!' Stella was chewing gum with relish, aglitter with sequined combs and earrings.

'Where you off to?' Ali's arm was about Stella's waist.

'Nowhere now.' Linda shuffled her feet awkwardly. Everyone seemed to have a friend, except her.

'You come with us,' Ali said. 'We are to buy Stella a leetle present.'

'In the jewellers' further up,' the chomping jaws said.

Linda thought of the glitter of jewellery. 'I've never been in one.'

The fairy laughed compassionately. 'Come on, kid, maybe we'll let Ali buy you a present too.' She winked and Linda was, unexpectedly, very happy.

They walked together, blocking the pavement for others, and Linda asked, 'Have you heard from Tommy?'

Ali shook his head like a hawk that had just finished eating. 'No, but Maud Jeffries, she found his father and sent him a letter. Maybe he will come home again, heh?' He turned to the fairy. 'You heard anything, Stella?' but Stella shook her blonde head and walked easily on silver sandals with high thin heels.

Linda hesitated as they reached the window of the jewellers'. It was big, the inside gaping like a cavern, with a dark carpet on the floor.

Stella nudged closer to Ali, and he squeezed her a little as they exchanged a secretive laugh. Linda thought it all a bit scaring, but exciting, and wonderful too. She said admiringly, 'Are you going to get engaged?' and both Stella and Ali laughed aloud, as if Linda had cracked a joke.

Ali put his free arm about her, and his touch was so light it was creepy. The jeweller looked up from a watch he was winding and said, 'Good morning, Mr Naggee. A nice morning?'

As if he already knew, he brought out strings of pearls in black velvet-lined boxes, and Stella bent to gaze at them. Linda watched, her eyes moving slowly as more boxes appeared and were arranged on top of the glass counter.

Prices were breathed and, when fifty pounds was

mentioned, Linda shuddered. Ali must be very rich. She gazed at him, wondering why he didn't look it, or speak as Mummy said all wealthy people spoke.

She turned from the couple, captivated by the sparkle about her, and caught sight of the pair of snake bracelets in the bottom of the glass case on the far wall. Linda went closer to gaze at them, to see red stone eyes and silvery scales as the bodies curved sensually. She wanted to touch them. Try one on. Flaunt it before Bunty Morris.

She was vaguely aware of Ali standing beside her, opening a fat black wallet, of Stella laughing and saying, 'And me, my precious one. And me. I like it too.'

Ali paused, then grinned. 'Two,' he said, to the man. 'We will make it two, so both girls are happy. I like girls who are happy.'

The jeweller handed Stella the pearls in a packet tied with gold string, and his assistant took the snakes from the glass case. Ali paid and was given a receipt on crinkly paper, then a silvery snake was put about Linda's wrist. She moved her arm slowly so the red eyes shone at her. She was Ali's friend. He had one arm about her and the other about Stella.

Stella kept chewing. She said, 'D'yer fancy some ice cream, kid?' and Linda nodded, almost ecstatic. She looked at Ali's triangular face with the funny curved nose, and thought how kind he was.

By the time she returned home she was humming contentedly to herself, the silvery scales still about her wrist. She went into the house and ran up the stairs and into the bathroom. Seriously she filled the basin and christened the bracelet. 'In the name of the Father, and of the Son, you are now called Cedric, and you are mine.' Then she hid him at the back of the low dark cupboard in the washing stand.

CHAPTER SEVEN

Carruthers left amid much bonhomie on Thursday morning. Emma laughed, he had given her a necklace. Linda laughed, he had saved her from skivvying. Kit laughed, he had given her freedom from the house, and Bertie laughed because he considered the old coot meant well.

They all laughed because Carruthers was leaving at last.

The fat man strutted down the street and chuckled all the way around the first corner; he had enjoyed the embroilment in family life, and he had found nothing criminal, only people anxious to remain with the firm.

Kit waved him off, then hurried back into the house. 'Linda! Be a darling. Strip Carruthers' bed. The laundry van will be here in the morning. Get the dirty sheets ready for it.'

Linda charged up the stairs, and Kit knew the bed-changing would mean great shakes of the bedding and fluff flying everywhere.

She hurried to the scullery, to prepare labels for the washing and, when Linda came, she looked up to see the girl grinning. 'Mummy!' Linda lifted the end of a white sheet before her face and put her nose through a tear. 'Mr Carruthers stuck his toe through it.' She was laughing, grimacing.

Kit stared and said, 'Damn. I didn't think it was that thin.' She took the sheet, examined it, and said, 'I can't send it to the laundry like that. Get the sewing machine out. We'll patch it,' then she was running up the stairs, making for the dark cupboard in the washing stand. In there lay the ragged remains of other sheets. Kit gave one a tug and they all fell out.

She gave a sigh of satisfaction as one proved the right colour and texture, then she knelt and started to bundle the unwanted remnants back in the cupboard.

It was then she saw Cedric. He was shining, bright-red-eyed, right at the back, and Kit peered, paused, then reached in for him. She sat back on her heels, turning him in her fingers and screwing up her face; he was vile, gruesome, and she made a sound of distaste then flung him away into the darkness.

She closed the doors on him, got to her feet and went downstairs to sew.

It was at dinner-time that she thought of him again, and said casually, 'I found a bracelet this morning. In the washing stand cupboard. I can't think where it came from.'

'Oh?' said Bertie. 'Maybe it's one you mislaid.'

Kit shook her head quickly. 'No. Definitely not one of mine. It's gaudy. Nasty – '

She stopped talking, aware of the silence about the table, and she gazed intently at her daughters while Bertie stopped eating. He laid down his knife and fork and said, 'What does this bracelet look like, Mummy?'

Kit hesitated, aware now she might be causing distress. 'It's a well – a rather unusual design. A serpent. With red eyes watching you.'

Bertie rested an elbow on the table, contemplating Linda and Emma. 'Which one of you owns this bracelet? And why are you so loath to admit it?'

Emma kept her head down but watched Linda sideways.

Linda cringed, afraid to say 'a coloured man gave it to me.'

Bertie recognised the signs and his voice rapped out. 'Linda!'

Kit said hastily, 'Sssh dear. It probably isn't anything important,' and regretted mentioning the serpent. 'Maybe it was borrowed off Bunty Morris.'

'No!' Linda said quickly, as she looked up, her face defiant again. 'Tommy gave it to me,' and Kit smiled, telling herself how precious the vicious-looking serpent must be.

Bertie scowled. 'Kit, get the bracelet. Let's have a look at it.' Kit paused, not wishing for a scene. 'Go on,' he ordered. 'Get the thing. Let's see it.'

When the bracelet lay glinting in the centre of the white tablecloth Bertie said, 'Phew . . .' then, 'one thing is certain, Tommy Buckley could never afford to buy that on his pay.'

'He did!' Linda cried. 'He did. Really he did!'

'Why?' demanded her father.

'Bertie!' cried Kit. 'What are you insinuating?'

'Why?' he demanded again, and his face was going hot and red, with the big vein throbbing purple in his forehead.

Linda's lips trembled and her shoulders hunched in misery. Emma became inspired, her head shot up, her voice piped in defence of her sister. 'Because she let him be her lover. That's why!'

Bertie blinked, unable to decide where to look, at the daughter who spoke up, the daughter who sat guiltily, or his wife who should have trained his daughters into respectability. Slowly he turned his head and looked at Kit, his eyes bleak. Good God, he was silently saying. Fourteen years of age, and has a lover!

Kit said sharply, 'Stop being so silly all of you. Linda does not have a lover. She had a friend. Now Linda. Get upstairs to your room. You do seem to insist on behaving foolishly.'

'I haven't done anything!'

Bertie barked, 'You must have, to look so guilty.'

'Stop it! Stop it!' Kit tried to gain command, and Linda barged from the room and up the passage. 'For heaven's sake Bertie, stop playing the heavy father, and imagining every male does what you took pleasure in doing.'

167

'Don't turn on me, Kit. You've let that youth in here, at night, when we've been away – '

'I didn't know he was coming any more than you did, and I certainly don't think Emma's version of a lover is the same as yours.'

Husband and wife glared at each other, both desperately worried and unhappy. Kit said, 'I'm going up to see Linda. You and Emma finish your food.'

'Kit!' She paused on her way out. 'If that girl lands in the family way, the blame is at your door. Remember that.'

'Hypocrite!' The word grated. 'You and your big boss performance. Me very pure big chief. Do as I say, not as I do.' She strode from the room, and Bertie pushed his plate away.

Emma sat wide-eyed and shaking. Linda would kill her for making things worse, and she had only been trying to help.

Bertie heard her gulp and so remembered her. He left the table and collapsed into his chair, then beckoned her. She scrambled from the table to get to him fast, her mouth open so the gap between her teeth looked even bigger than it was, and she fell onto his lap. He drew her up and held her head against his shoulder.

'Daddy. Is it naughty to have a lover?'

Bertie nodded against her hair. 'Until after you get married,' and Emma snuffled against his white starched collar, but frowned hard in the secrecy of his neck. Not understanding.

Upstairs Linda mopped her eyes and Kit nursed her. 'Daddy's in a state of nerves,' she excused him. 'He used to be so patient with you. Playing games. Marching up and down the passage. Being soldiers . . .'

'I hate him!'

'Nonsense. He doesn't hate you. He loves you.'

'He doesn't love anybody except Elsie. Not even baby Buck.'

'Don't say such awful things,' Kit retorted. 'He loves you and Emma and Buck.'

'No. The war stopped him. They told us in school. The war stopped people loving and made them all hate and kill and be nasty.'

'Linda! That is all wrong!'

Linda looked down at her sopping handkerchief and Kit said more gently, 'You must understand, men don't give presents for nothing. Tommy must love you. Why else would he spend so much on you?'

'Mr Henderson-Hobbs must love you too then. He sent you presents.' It was said sourly, accusingly.

'That's different,' her mother retorted, but the suspicion was planted in Kit's mind. Was Tommy Buckley another of the same? Trying to buy something or, God forbid, could Bertie be right, and Tommy was paying for something he had already received?

Yet, on Monday morning, Kit sent Linda shopping, making sure she had the place to herself by eleven o'clock.

As usual, Henderson-Hobbs was on time.

'Good morning,' she said into the mouthpiece. 'Unicorn Insurance Company.'

'Good morning, Mrs Hemsworthy. Could I have a word with Mr Hemsworthy?' His voice was an aphrodisiac, and Kit wondered if the delicious secret excitement within her was an overture to something infinitely beautiful.

'Oh hello Mr Henderson-Hobbs. I regret my husband isn't available this morning.'

'How unfortunate. I understand Mr Carruthers enjoyed your hospitality during last week.'

'He is always most helpful.'

'That is precisely what I expect of him.' Then came a change of tone. 'And how is Kitten this lovely morning?'

'Quite well, thank you,' and, as a sense of intimacy came along the wires, she crossed her knees without realising she had done so. 'Though it isn't a lovely morning here. It's drizzling.'

The minutes sped by, their talk went through insurance to gossip, then to banter. He laughed, 'With a leg like Carruthers' one would expect the escaping dog to take a lump out of it. Special piece of beef there, what!'

'Bertie said much the same thing. He thought it funny, in retrospect.'

Henderson-Hobbs said, 'Bertie?' as if he had forgotten him. 'I shall be inviting him to Windsor shortly. I shall expect him to bring you. In America there is an idea that wives should be – er – interviewed in the same way as the men.'

'Interviewed? Or vetted?'

He laughed again. 'Same thing, one supposes.'

'I regret I would have to refuse any invitation. It's necessary for someone to be here in the office.'

'I would arrange it for the weekend.'

'No!' She didn't like the way the word shot from her, and hurried to ease it. 'Really. It is kind of you, but we do hate leaving the children alone.'

'Kitten – '

'No! Thank you and all that, but no. Really.' She stopped, aware of how panic had taken hold of her.

'Other wives will be there.'

:'No. If you insist it will ruin our friendship.'

'Very well,' he said. 'I shall see the invitation is addressed to your husband only.'

'Thank you,' she breathed.

'Good day,' he said, and the line went dead. Her heart was pounding. He might never telephone again.

But he did. The following Monday, and the one after that. Then the letter came.

Linda had it with the rest of the mail, and Kit called from the middle room as she dusted, plumped up cushions and swept crumbs of soot from the grate. 'Linda! Anything interesting?'

'No,' Linda said, coming to her, disappointed again. 'Unless this one is. It's from Head Office.'

'Give it to your father,' Kit instructed, and kept her

170

voice steady, wishing she had the courage to go to Windsor.

She followed Linda to the office and watched Bertie turn the envelope between his fingers, while Linda used the ivory paper knife on the rest.

'This man,' Linda said, as she read a scrap of paper, 'says no one has collected his premiums because he's never in. He's working down the docks.'

Bertie looked at her and at the letter in her hand. 'Blast it!' he said. 'I did tell George to get down there. The man will be writing to Head Office next.'

'George is a good agent,' Kit soothed. 'I'll put a note in his pigeon hole. What's the letter from London about?' As if she didn't know, and Bertie apparently didn't want to open it.

He sat there, at his desk with the clean pink blotter in its leather binder, and stared at the envelope. She said, 'It can't be the transfer.'

'It would be a relief if it was.'

Kit nodded, the blue and white checked duster in her fist.

'Even executions don't take this long.'

'Linda. Hand Daddy the knife, please.'

Linda did so, desultory now, not interested, then stood ripping up the empty envelopes, clipping the letters into a bundle and dropping them into the 'In' tray.

Bertie put on his spectacles, slit the letter open, then took the spectacles off and looked up at Kit. 'It's another invitation.'

'To what?'

'You read the damn thing,' he snapped, and flicked it across the desk.

'You're getting irritable again. You really should see the doctor. Get a tonic.'

Linda moved away and began using the typewriter. Kit lifted the invitation.

It was short and to the point. The time had come to discuss future policies within the company. Mr Henderson-

171

Hobbs requested his presence at Coombe House, Windsor, where, he hoped, the assembled managers and their wives would enjoy the delights of the area, while putting forward their own ideas for the firm's advancement. Such ideas would be considered at a conference to be convened later in the year. Possibly at Bournemouth.

Kit said, slightly scathing, 'A weekend AND a conference at Bournemouth? The firm IS coming out.'

Linda swivelled around in her chair, 'Does that mean you're both going away again?'

Bertie returned, 'Get on with what you are doing, And remember, Linda, everything said or done in this office is highly confidential. Compris?'

'Yes, Daddy.' She hunched her shoulders, scolded again, and Kit said quickly, 'Have you heard from Tommy lately?'

'No Mummy,' and there was anguish in the words. 'But Stella said he must be all right or somebody would have heard.'

'Stella?' Kit was mildly interested, still staring at Henderson-Hobbs' letter.

'My friend.'

'Oh,' said Kit, and flicked the letter back to Bertie.

He said, 'I suggest you wear your costume when we go, Kit. The nights are already drawing in, and a woman's costume seems to typify autumn. And you look nice in it.'

'I shan't be coming.'

'Of course you will. The letter distinctly says the assembled managers and their wives.'

'Look at the envelope. It's addressed to you. And look at the beginning of the letter. It's not Dear Mr and Mrs. Neither do the contents include me.'

'Of course they include you.'

She leaned across the desk towards him. 'You forget. As far as Henderson-Hobbs is concerned I am no longer your wife. I am merely another agent. Building up a new book.'

172

Bertie gazed into the amber eyes and couldn't understand why he thought he saw triumph there. 'All right,' he said conclusively. 'I shall go on my own.'

And, once the decision was made, he liked the idea.

When the day came he wore his lovat tweed suit and his lovat flat cap. He flung his Burberry over his arm, lifted the new tan weekend case, and set forth.

He was going into the lion's den.

He grinned at everybody and touched his cap to many.

At Windsor station, Miss Lilian Gibbs met him and the couple from Bristol. With her was an imposing white Bentley. There was also a green-clad chauffeur, impartial and polite.

Bertie wished Kit had come, been more supportive. Blast the whims of women. Miss Gibbs was like a smartly dressed plank of wood, and his headache was coming on.

Claude Hobbs greeted them at Coombe House. The Old Man stood on the wide curving steps beneath the pseudo marble portico, and shook hands with everyone.

Inside, the house was not as big as Bertie had anticipated. A hall with a gallery and faint murmuring echo. Large oil paintings on the wall rising beside the curved staircase, and an old chap in a dusty-looking penguin suit receiving hats and coats.

'Thank you, Lewis,' Henderson-Hobbs said, as he approached from across the hall, and Lewis tottered to a corridor then dissolved into its narrow gloom. Bertie wondered if there were any more staff.

There were. A housekeeper and a flabby chef who kept bobbing out of his kitchen to discuss the menu.

Bertie found the socialising amicable, and the stroll around the grounds and through the woods a chance to kid himself he was landed gentry.

The meeting around the long polished table, in what was the dining-room turned into boardroom, was less pleasurable.

'Now gentlemen,' said Henderson-Hobbs. 'Ideas

please? You people are on the ground floor, so to speak.' He tweaked the pink satin in the breast pocket of his light grey striped suit and looked, blank-faced, at Albert Hemsworthy, then he went on, 'You are down there, among the policy-holders; the folk that count.' And Bertie's face was just as blank, watching the new chairman with his damn silly notion of bringing in the boys, then telling them they were less important than the policy-holders. Bertie sat back on the highly polished leather-seated chair and folded his arms.

Henderson-Hobbs was probably right, but it was sheer one-upmanship to rub it in.

He listened to the 'ideas' and became irritated and tired. Inside him grew a mixture of needing to stand up and take charge, or go to sleep.

Someone suggested, 'I think the premium books could do with more detail inside the covers.'

Miss Gibbs made Pitman notes in her pad.

Another said, 'The fire report claims are too short, y'know. Hang it all, I had a member recently – ' He went on and Miss Gibbs kept making notes.

Bertie sighed and turned his head to the big velvet-draped window. He saw a bird had dropped a message on it. Splurged. He gave a bland smile and began to feel better.

Henderson-Hobbs said, 'And what of Swansea? I assume they are still on the map.'

Bertie drew in breath and said in a take it or leave it manner, 'Why don't we sell car insurance, or horse cover, extend our interests?' and no one moved. Miss Gibbs' pencil stayed poised, then Henderson-Hobbs recovered from his surprise and said, 'I doubt that's a workable proposition. Not for a firm like ours. We do specialise in life insurance.'

Bertie looked at Henderson-Hobbs and thought him an idiot.

For seconds the two men stared into each other's eyes, a silent duel of minds, then Claud Hobbs said, 'I anticipated that, you know, Albert, but wondered how best to promote the idea.'

He clicked his finger and thumb and Miss Gibbs produced a folder of papers and placed it before him. 'Work already done on the idea,' he smiled at Bertie. 'But no one would back me. Considered me too senile to be original, you know.'

Everyone but Bertie leaned forward with desperately eager approving faces.

That evening the dinner was good. The wine was good. The brandy was excellent. Bertie and Henderson-Hobbs shook hands and had a cigar each.

The Cardiff manager told a risqué joke while the ladies were in the powder room and, when Bertie got on to the train to come home on Sunday, he felt it was forty-eight hours well spent.

The Cardiff man grabbed one corner seat near the window and his wife sagged into the other. Bertie got one next to the door, and wondered if the others realised they had all been experimented upon; guinea-pigs put into a position by commercial scientists, questioned, fed and watched. He flung his suitcase up onto the net rack and his cap on top of it. Right now, he told himself, the Hobbs men were probably discussing them, and the great shuffle being prepared.

He eased himself into his seat and smiled at the Bristol manager beside him.

The train gathered speed, began to rumble, whistle and rock. The Bristol man talked to the Cardiff man, and Bertie told himself that if the Unicorn gave him the push it would be better than a transfer. That way he could set up on his own: be a packie; canvass people with small domestic needs, kettles, buckets: buy the commodities, then sell them to those same people on credit. Shilling in the pound. The first shilling, plus profit on the goods, to be his.

And Kit's.

She would help him.

The ladies in the carriage stopped talking as if with plums in their mouths and began to laugh together.

Bertie knew they looked a fairly prosperous crowd, a decent, hard-working crowd, and everyone seemed to approve of Henderson-Hobbs.

'Fine upstanding young fellow, y'know, old pal,' said the chap from Newport. 'This firm will go from strength to strength.'

Bertie nodded and agreed with everything, but he didn't want to smile, or listen, or talk. He wanted to be home. With Kit.

Why the devil hadn't she come this weekend? It was the first time they had been apart overnight in fifteen years.

He leaned forward and slid the carriage door open, let some of the smoke and strength of perfume out, and a big man lurched past. Bertie saw him. Knew him. Yet it didn't register.

Then the big man came back, the stump of his right wrist extended to the wall, as if he still tried to use it like a hand. He caught sight of Bertie and stopped lurching with the swaying of the train. He lowered his wide balding head, and his swollen red-veined nose looked worse than ever.

Bertie stared, not wanting to believe, and felt his flesh tighten with apprehension.

Big Tom Buckley was drunk again. Not falling over drunk, but the drunk of a man who was rarely anything else. He leaned against the edge of the doorway, and his leer was that of an all-in wrestler who breaks his opponent's arm. 'You,' he said, loud enough for all to hear. 'Took my wife. Let 'er die. Alone. In a strange bed. You took my daughter. Ruined her. Killed her. And now you thinks yer got my son.' His handless arm rose beside his head as if holding an invisible fist. 'I'm on my way 'ome, Mr High'n Mighty. And I'll 'ave my own back. I'll get yer daughter made a Buckley. Bring 'er down ter my level. How d'yer fancy that, heh?' He leered low and sniggered, slightly drooling, and the Cardiff manager

176

left his corner, stepping over his wife's legs. 'Here, I say, old fellow. Drat it all – '

Big Tom's bull-like shoulders swivelled and his only hand pointed. 'Keep out pansy boy, or I land yer one right on yer pretty kisser!'

Pansy boy's smooth-skinned face went blank and his light-coloured eyes flickered. His wife caught his arm. 'Sit down, dear. I'm sure there must be some mistake.'

Bertie smiled at her. It was odd, but his adrenaline was running again, as if months of frustration wanted to give way to aggression. To fight. Even though it was no longer for King and country.

'Hello Tom,' he said evenly. 'I haven't seen your son for weeks. I warned him off my daughter, so there isn't much chance of her becoming a Buckley.' Bewilderment crossed the ex-steelman's scorched face. 'I did,' Bertie assured him, and languidly brought his wallet from his inside jacket pocket. 'Here, get some flowers for Gwen's grave. If I knew where she was resting I would have done so myself – the same as I do for Elsie.'

The big man stared at the proffered five-pound note. He took it, grinning, then he spat, a great phlegm-filled globule, so it landed, phut, between Bertie's new brown brogues.

The Cardiff man jerked forward again, waving a rolled copy of The Sunday Times, while his wife piped, 'No dear, no. Better to call the guard.'

Bertie stared up into Tom Buckley's face and his gaze didn't waver. For so long he had dreaded this moment, yet now it had happened he was glad. He had met greater threats in trenches, controlled greater feeling among defiant men.

Big Tom knew it, saw it in the granite of Bertie's blue eyes, and retreated in the only way he knew how. 'Yah!' he jeered, and screwed up his big square face in a leer that he focused on each member of the Unicorn in turn. No one spoke or moved, then Tom Buckley lurched away.

The Cardiff man sprang to his feet and dragged the

door closed with a snap that could have been born of terror. 'Filthy swine,' he grunted, and his wife lifted the leather strap beside her and let down the window. Black spots flew in on all of them, but the fresh air was good too. Bertie's lungs filled with it and a nervous reaction took over. His hands quivered as he replaced his wallet and smiled around, his eyes showing relief. Flashes of lightning shot through his brain and he knew another hellish headache was on the way.

He sat stiffly, not scared of Tom Buckley, but scared of becoming soft, old, unable to cope completely, being ill. Cracking up again. Panic came and was quelled. He wanted to move his feet, but didn't. They might touch that blob of phlegm, and he couldn't tolerate that.

By the time the train steamed into Swansea Bertie was alone in the carriage, his cap on his head, his case on his lap as if that would speed his journey home, and in the back of his mind was the knowledge that Big Tom Buckley would also be leaving the train here. Big Tom might accost him on the station. Create a ghastly scene.

He watched the platform slide past, then it stopped and Bertie sprang into action. He strode towards the exit, not looking back, while sunlight filtered through the ill-fitting roof and a pigeon cooed contentedly.

Bertie gave up his ticket and strode to the courtyard. A small group of people stood on the corner watching him, their attention making him stare back, wondering if they were policy-holders, due to be acknowledged with charm. There was a hawk-faced Arab with a body too short for his legs, a monstrous negro with tight woolly hair, an old crone who might be eighty, but could be fifty, and a tall slim blonde with insolent challenging eyes. She gave a sidelong smile as if to entice, and raised a hand to her peroxided hair; on her wrist a silver bracelet sparkled.

Bertie watched that sparkle for a moment, thinking it familiar, then he touched his cap to the group, and each of them nodded, the crone smiling with worn teeth.

Bertie forgot them as easily as he had seen them and gestured to a taxi. He climbed in and said, 'Three hundred Prince Edward Road, please, driver,' while wondering why he hadn't told Kit what time he was arriving. He mused vaguely that some part of him hoped he wouldn't come home at all. Yet he needed the place.

He strolled into number 300, and it was empty. He went from room to room, calling, knowing his rising ill temper was unreasonable. He plonked himself into his chair, cursing the way the seat had collapsed, cursing that he lacked the energy needed to repair the damn thing, and it was teatime, gone five o'clock, when his family came home.

He was standing on the front doorstep, telling himself he was admiring the end of a late autumn day, and he heard Kit's laughter. the sort of laughter that first attracted him to her: young, clear and innocent. He couldn't believe it. She hadn't laughed like that since – when?

But his head turned in the right direction, and there they were; Kit with silvery sand on her bare ankles, her feet in ancient-looking flat sandals. Where the hell had she dug those up from? Emma was hopping, carrying her wooden spade and red tin sand bucket. Linda was behind them.

Linda was – Christ! With Tommy Buckley.

Bertie glared, remembering the phut of phlegm landing between his feet.

He left the front of the house to storm forward, get rid of the youth, but they had seen him. They were yoo-hooing and waving up the respectable Sunday-quiet road.

Emma ran to him, her face tilted, and he caught her and swung her around, the bucket and spade threatening to batter him.

'I went in swimming and we saw a starfish. There was a women playing the organ and we sang Tell me the old old story – '

'The water must have been cold!' he cried, but she

179

shook her head and he loved her. He laughed at her, then settled her to her feet, and he held her hand until Kit came to him.

'Hello darling,' she said, without enthusiasm. 'Why didn't you telephone the time of your train?'

He stared into her face and saw that she had been happy without him.

'I wasn't sure which I would catch,' he said, and he ignored Linda and the soldier. He walked back to the house fast, Emma still gripping his hand, doing big strides with grunts of effort.

Then he steered Kit alone into the office. 'Get rid of him!'

'Who?' Her laughter, her air of happiness fled.

'You know damn well who.'

'If you mean Tommy, he is staying. He has nowhere decent to go.'

'I said get rid of him.' His voice rose as Kit raised her chin, the familiar red sparks of defiance flashing from her wide amber eyes.

'And I said he's staying.'

'Kit!' His voice lowered again, his teeth almost jammed. 'I am not fooling about. Get rid of him!' and Linda was in the doorway. Linda, stiff, her face poked forward and her hands clenched at her sides.

She ground out, 'If Tommy goes, I go too.' She came further into the room, her demeanour one of subdued threat. 'I'll go, Daddy. I'll go. He's my best friend. My very best friend.'

'Linda,' Bertie said quietly, his face as white as hers. 'You will do as you are told. You are still a child. In my care. Do you understand that?'

'I won't!' she said, then suddenly screamed so that Kit jumped with the shock of it. 'He's my lover. I love him to death!'

'Quiet!' Kit hissed. 'For heaven's sake be quiet. You'll have the neighbours hearing.' She rushed to close the door, then she turned to her husband and daughter.

'Don't listen to her,' she entreated Bertie as he sank to his seat at the desk. 'She doesn't know what a lover is. Not as grown-ups do!'

'I do,' Linda gasped urgently, frightened at the dead gleam in her father's eyes. 'I do. Tommy's kissed me. Hundreds of times. And I've kissed him too.'

'I know, dear.' Kit pushed her towards the door. 'You go out to him. Don't let him see you're upset. Go on. Make some tea. Your father has had a long weekend. He must be tired.'

Linda gulped and glanced at Bertie. He moved his head in a silent gesture for her to get out, but the awful headache had developed and the lights were flashing so badly he could barely see.

'Kit.' It was a heavy sigh. 'This is my house, my office. I am master here, and I do not thank you for encouraging the children to defy me.'

'Yes, dear.'

He knew she was humouring him and he wanted to stop it, prove he was still worthy of something better. He stood up, but the room began to sway.

Kit said from far away, 'You've been overdoing it.' When he didn't reply, she went on, 'I know how you feel about everything. I often feel the same.'

'It would have helped if you had come to Windsor. Backed me a little.'

And Kit told the truth. She said flatly, 'I could not have hidden the way I feel about Henderson-Hobbs. Everyone would have seen it. You would have been mortified.'

Bertie misunderstood and rubbed his forehead, trying to massage the pains away. 'Everyone fawned over him. Even me,' and Kit smiled widely.

'I'm glad you did. Flattery will get you everywhere. What did he have to say?'

'When he and I were alone? That there should have been no need to send Carruthers down for John. An efficient manager would have smelled a rat immediately and dealt with the matter.'

181

'Did he make any actual comment about John?'

'Oh yes. He said he was an up and coming young man with a fine future.'

Kit placed a hip on the corner of Bertie's desk and he came to her and kissed her on the nose. He said, 'I would like to get blotto.'

'We can't afford it.'

'Tom Buckley was on the train. He was drunk. For a few moments I almost envied him his lack of responsibility,' and as Kit's eyes widened with concern, he said softly, 'will you send the young man packing now?'

Kit shook her head. 'I discovered Linda has been reading a book. Heavy romance, I think. The sort you don't tell your parents about. Heaven knows what's in it, but it might have given her ideas. If Tommy goes she really might go too. I don't think she's in love with him. It's something of a schoolgirl crush mixed with pity because of his impoverished background. And, I suspect, she misses Elsie badly. They were good friends.'

Bertie went to the window, staring out at the patch of sky over the roofs going dark purple, and Kit said, 'You have a fine daughter, Mr Hemsworthy. She will be loyal to Tommy as long as she thinks he needs her. Be proud of her.'

'And if she lands in the family way – ?'

'You can blame me,' Kit said heavily. 'It will mean I haven't brought her up properly.'

Bertie watched a tram go past, looking slightly unreal, then he came back to Kit and patted her arm. 'At this moment,' he smiled whimsically, 'I'm glad you're frigid. Maybe I can convince myself your daughter is the same.' He walked to the door, unaware his words had stung. She snapped, 'You have a mind like a cesspit!' and he turned, startled, his brows up so his forehead became a mass of creases. 'Kit?'

'You have!' she stormed. 'Linda has just had her fifteenth birthday. FIFTEENTH! Her mind is full of rosy dreams of love. Pure love. Not desire. Not – ' She choked on the word, but got it out, 'blasted shagging!'

'Kit!' Horror hit him like a massive wave. 'Since when have you been conversant with barrack-room language? And in my office!' Disdain curled his lips and, unwittingly, he eyed her up and down as one eyes a mound of manure splashed against a wall. 'I am aware of what my child feels,' he went on tersely. 'You forget, I have been deeply in love myself – '

Kit's hand found the golden Rolls-Royce, with its golden pen, and it flew through the air towards him. He ducked fast but his cheek was grazed.

'You sod!' he gritted, his face blank with disbelief.

'Not me.' Kit was shaking, frightened of her own emotions. 'You! All these years you've thought I have no feelings, no senses.' She sat in his chair and put her elbows on his blotter, in an effort to hold herself still. 'Now you know differently. You're pushing me too far, Bertie. I, too, have had enough.'

In the kitchen Emma hunched her shoulders and tried not to cry. 'They're having a row,' she whispered, and Linda gripped Tommy's hand as he drew Emma to him before the fireplace.

'They'll stop,' Linda said anxiously. 'They're bound to.'

Tommy patted Emma gently, smiling. 'My ma and pa had rows all the time. Sometimes the winders got smashed. Elsie and me hid under the bed one time, outer the way. Everybody got barneys.'

'Not in our house.' Linda tried to sound sure of herself. 'Parents rowing are vulgar.'

Emma stared up at them both, her blue eyes and pink mouth in great unhappy circles of waiting for the next scene. 'I wish I had a puppy,' she sniffed, and stifled a sob. 'I could cuddle it then.' Both Linda and Tommy crouched to soothe her.

'Don't be frightened, Emma,' Linda whispered. 'A good row clears the air. Bunty says her mother always throws things at her father,' and none of them moved, until they heard Bertie go upstairs to the bathroom.

Silence reigned for more minutes, then Kit came along the passage, through the kitchen and to the garden. There she breathed deeply, taking in the darkening blue haze of twilight, and musing on how fast the year was speeding by. She bent, rubbing the shining silver and gold grains of sand from her legs. 'Linda?'

'Yes Mummy?' Quickly, anxiously.

'Did you make a pot of tea?'

Linda stood in the scullery doorway looking out. 'Yes, Mummy.'

'It's probably cold by now. Make another.'

Kit stayed out there, smelling the dampness already settling in the air, saying goodbye to what had been a free and easy day with the children, then she came into the house. 'Tommy?'

'Yes, Mrs Hemsworthy?'

'Your father was on the same train as my husband today. Apparently your father was drunk, and rather rude.'

She felt the tension jump between Linda and Tommy, and it crossed her mind that somewhere in Linda there had to be a seed of snobbishness that could be played upon. She said, 'Apparently, he – er – spat on the floor of the carriage my husband and his colleagues were in.'

Kit felt Emma come to her and clutch her skirt. She saw Tommy's face set as he made a decision.

'I'd best get back over St Thomas then, Mrs Hemsworthy. He might have gone to Ma Jeffries. She got her eye on my pa.'

Linda cried, 'No, Tommy! Don't go. Be with us.'

'I'll be back,' he promised, but Kit thought she heard no conviction.

He put on his khaki jacket quickly, combed his hair and pulled on his cap, looking in the mirror behind Kit's chair to check the angle of the peak, then he was marching away.

Linda's shoulders bowed and she went to the scullery, where the kettle was singing on the stove.

184

'It's been all spoiled,' she cried. 'Our lovely day spoiled. Just because Daddy came home. Oh I do hate him.' Then a thought occurred to her. 'Mummy!' she called, and turned the jet down under the kettle. 'I'm going with Tommy.'

As if those four words added impetus to the resolve, she dived to the living-room and through it. She was heading up the passage before Bertie, coming down the stairs, barked, 'Linda! Where are you off to?'

'With Tommy.' She didn't look back nor grab her blazer from the hallstand. The glass porch door slammed after her and Bertie's face was purple.

'Kit! What the hell have you said to her?'

Kit went to the scullery and turned the gas jet up. Then she turned it out. 'Emma!' she said. 'In the sideboard cupboard in the middle room is a bottle of port. Go and bring it, darling. I think I'll get rotten drunk.'

Emma grinned, the fear and tension gone. 'And me!' she urged. 'I'll be sloshed too.'

Kit watched her go, knowing no one was going to get sloshed, but a drink did seem a good idea, and Linda was running down the road, the thudding of her brown sandal-shod feet echoing in the hollow sound of Sunday evening, the street lights just pale orange shapes in the dusk.

Tommy didn't look around, but he felt devastated, and tried telling himself there were plenty of other girls. The trouble was that none of them were remotely like Linda. They didn't have that adoration in their eyes. And they knew so much there was nothing left for him to teach.

He heard Linda coming and slowed his quick march to a walk, then caught sight of a display of shirts spotlit in a shop window. It was a reason for stopping, pretending he was deaf to Linda's approach.

Her tearful panting voice said, 'Tommy. Don't go.'

He deigned to turn his head towards her, his bearing stiffly masculine. 'Don't know what yer panicking about. I'm only going ter see my pa.'

185

Linda looked from him into the window, shy of him. 'Do you like anything in there?'

'Not particularly.'

'I'll walk along with you.'

'You'll cop it off yer father.'

'I don't care. He's horrible.'

Tommy said nonchalantly, 'I'll have a set of civvies one day. A suit like that,' and he pressed his finger against the glass to point out a suit with yoked jacket and flapped pockets, while Linda cuddled against him, needing the warmth and strength that emanated from him, loving the rough feel and smell of the heavy khaki cloth.

They strolled together, looking in windows, choosing things for each other. Tommy held her hand, and said casually, 'I could never be an officer. Not unless there was a war. You get promotion quicker then.'

They took an hour to reach the swing bridge, then they stood on the quayside while the wind rustled in from the channel, spreading the smells it had collected on the way, rotting seaweed, dead fish, trawlers, the world on a green ocean, and Linda sighed before a background of black warehouses and cranes. 'Isn't it lovely?'

'Glorious,' said Tommy, and wondered if using such words would help him become an officer.

'Let's go down the sands!' Linda suddenly jumped and laughed, her face alive with anticipation. 'We can paddle.'

'It'll be pitch dark!'

'Oh come on!'

'The tide'll be out. It'll be all clay.' He looked down at her, at the open trust in her face, and knew that he loved her.

He looked from her quickly and extricated his fingers from hers. 'No,' he said slowly. 'You better go back home. It isn't safe down here,' then he laughed because her expression drooped. 'Or your Dad'll kick yer arse out.'

'Tommy. I could come to Aldershot. I don't go to school now. I could get a job.'

'Cor!' he jeered, moving from her. 'Who'd want you

hanging around waiting fer them ter come home at night? And what d'yer do when I'm out with other tarts?'

'You don't go out with – ' she gulped. 'Tarts.'

'How d'yer know what I do? I might be on the tiles every night fer all you know.'

'Take me for a paddle first, then I'll go home. Honest.'

He wanted to love her, right then, marry her, work for her, anything for her, but her pa was an officer. He said, 'All right, but no more mucking about. Then you stay home. All the time. I don't want yer hanging around my neck.'

'No, Tommy.'

They walked slowly, not speaking for a while, picking their way over hawsers and ropes. Somewhere an engine phut-phutted, and a very big, very black negro loomed up out of the night. 'Hi, man!' he welcomed. 'You two lookin' for a cosy corner where nobody see?' He chuckled naughtily.

'Hi Ebony,' Tommy greeted him. 'We're just walking.'

Ebony grinned. All white teeth and whites of eyes. 'Your pa come home all right. Maud said him and you can share that room with Ali and me.'

'OK.' said Tommy, without enthusiasm.

'So I'll tell her you're coming.' Ebony kept chuckling, and Linda drew from Tommy.

The black man loped away and she said uncomfortably, 'Will you sleep in the same room as those coloured men all the time now?'

'Seems like it.'

'It isn't nice. A white man in a house with coloured men.'

'Ma Jeffries got a big heart,' Tommy said. 'She don't mind what colour you are, nor if you get drunk every night. As long as yer pays yer rent.'

Linda wriggled her shoulders, not liking the change in Tommy's voice; as if meeting the negro had made him more common.

She said awkwardly, 'It is dark. I think I'd better

go home,' and they both turned back.

A ship hooted deeply and Tommy said roughly, 'After tonight, I'm not going ter see you any more.'

'Why? Because of my father?'

'Fooff! Him?'

'Then why?'

'Because, as I've said before, I'm a man and you're a kid. Look at you. Scared of black men.'

'I'm not!'

'You are. It was on your face and you were shivering.'

'I didn't bring my coat.'

They stood near the museum steps, the streets silent. She said, 'Did you know your pa was coming today?'

'I guessed it wouldn't be long. Ma Jeffries'll get him in the end. You watch.'

Linda walked from him. 'I'd better go. It is late.'

He wanted to go with her, but he turned away, not happy about the easy way she had taken his final farewell.

It was very dark when she got home and Bertie was at the gate, waiting, worrying. A cigarette glowed between his fingers and smoke billowed from his nose. He kept jerking his neck in little stretching motions, as if to ease the tension of wondering what had happened to her. She paused a few yards from him, then ran, scudding past him into the brilliant light of the passage.

'Lindah!'

She ignored him, her head up, defiant and angry.

'Lindah!'

Near the office door he hit her. A clip across the ear. She stumbled, fell into the hallstand, caught her foot in the slip mat and went down.

He heard Kit coming from the kitchen, and that other man was in his place, not throwing a coffee cup now, but standing to attention, wondering why the girl was sleeping at the foot of the stairs. She was in the way.

'Bertie! In God's name! What have you done?'

Kit crouched and cradled Linda's head, while Bertie loomed large, wide-shouldered and straight-backed,

188

beside the hallstand with its tumble of hats, coats and umbrellas.

She smoothed Linda's hair and whispered urgently, 'Darling. Come on. It's Mummy.' She tried to lift the fifteen-year-old but failed, and Emma was there now, watching, blinking with fright.

'Bertie!' Kit demanded. 'Help me carry her. You hit her down. You damn well lift her up.'

He came silently, like a sleepwalker. He stared down at Linda then raised her a little higher and kissed her cheek. The other man went away and Bertie groaned. 'Kit. Oh Kit!'

He carried Linda to the middle room where the big blue soft settee waited. He laid her there then knelt beside her, holding her hand and patting it. 'Light the fire, Kit. Call the doctor. Emma! Get a glass of water. Bring paper and firewood, please. Linda has fainted. We must get the room warm. We'll want a blanket too. Or a quilt.'

Emma ran and panted and brought a jug of water and an empty glass. 'I didn't know how much. Is Linda going to die? Will there be a funeral?' She ran away again and came back with paper and firewood, while Bertie's shaking hands caused the glass to play erratic notes as he held it to the water jug and poured.

Kit brought coal, matches, and soon flames licked and wood crackled. 'The doctor will come as soon as he can.'

Linda opened her eyes and Bertie murmured. 'You mustn't go over St Thomas. You mustn't keep going to the docks. It isn't safe for an old woman, never mind a young one. Why d'you think the police go down there in pairs?'

She sipped the water but refused to look at him. She said sulkily. 'Young girls live over there.'

'Not young girls like you. They know what to expect.'

'Elsie lived over there.' The barb was deliberate, but spoken softly. The corner of Bertie's mouth twitched, but he made no retort.

189

Kit hovered, watching for the rise of a bruise on Linda, the mark of a blow, but none appeared, and, stiffly, Bertie got to his feet. 'When Dr Sullivan comes,' he said, 'tell him I caught her on the ear.'

Kit was shivering, frightened. She had seen men walking the streets looking as Bertie had looked; stiff-legged, as if their torsos were in steel jackets, their eyes pale, red-rimmed, and their hair snow white.

They called it shell shock.

Was Bertie shell-shocked? Had he ever been shell-shocked? Fear made her cruel. 'You couldn't sink any lower if you tried,' but he didn't reply. He kept on climbing the stairs, and he went into the back bedroom. Elsie's room, Carruthers' room, Linda's room. Anybody's room. But mostly Elsie's.

He stopped inside the bedroom door with a sense of shock; he had half expected it to be the same, a double bed with Elsie in it, getting smaller and smaller as she dwindled into death, and he suddenly felt cheated.

He shook himself, cross with his weakness, and went to the window, his mind still confused. He had lost his temper, and coming here had been a mistake. Not a palliative.

Kit was right, he could sink no further. Yet who was she to pontificate? She had killed Elsie. Murdered her. Jealous, frozen bitch.

A light went on in a bedroom opposite and a woman drew the curtains. Bertie looked down, at all the back doors lining the narrow lane. His head ached, his heart ached. His very soul ached. He backed until his thighs hit the bed, then sagged onto it. He should have died with Elsie. Gone with her to that cloud she promised to be sitting on.

He thought of Linda, the foolishness of her, of not being able to explain to her what dangers were over there, the sort of men who sailed into the docks then wandered those streets seeking young girls. Who knew how many virgins woke up in the hold of a ship bound for the Middle East?

He thudded the palm of his hands against his temples, anything to hit away the thoughts, the muddle, then he stretched and breathed deeply. That was better. Get in charge of yourself, man.

'Bertie?'

He heard Kit calling, but he didn't answer until she tapped the bedroom door. 'The doctor has just stopped outside. Will you see to him, please? I'm getting supper.'

He went past her, then hurried down the stairs, light-footed, like a dancer, and the doctor had let himself in, stood under the passage light wearing his green pork pie hat and reddish plus four suit, the Gladstone bag in his right hand.

'Hello, doctor. Kind of you to come like this.'

The thick gingery brows came down like a shelf above the white-lashed eyes. 'And where am I likely to find the child?' Dr Sullivan looked up the stairs, hoping he didn't have to climb them.

'Not up there,' Bertie said seriously. 'Here. In the sitting-room.' Linda was in the deep armchair drawn towards the fire, her face pale as she watched the doctor's approach.

'Ah now, Linda girl. Where's the hurt, heh?'

'I don't hurt. Only inside.'

'Inside? You think you cracked a rib?'

'No. Nothing like that. Just sad. I hurt like I'm sad.' She sat, obediently still, and the gnarled but sensitive fingers pressed and prodded her scalp, but all the time her lower lip jutted slightly, and Bertie saw it. He waited for the examination to end, then he leaned forward. He said easily, 'I think she ought to go to hospital, doctor. She was unconscious for a while,' and Linda's bottom lip stopped jutting and began to quiver.

'Is that so?' The doctor looked at her with deeper interest.

'No,' Linda whispered, and shook her head. 'I wasn't unconscious.'

'Of course you were,' Bertie smiled. 'Your eyes were closed.'

'No.' She shook her head again. 'I didn't want to open them. That was all.'

Bertie moved to her, and laid a hand gently on her head, but she jerked from him, then her glance shot up and condemnation was there again. His hand stayed, wanting to grab her hair, force her to understand, but Dr Sullivan was saying, 'Well now, lassie, you go on in to your poor distraught mother. Tell her this old man of medicine is in sore need of restitution. A cup of good strong tea would be welcome.'

Linda half smiled, then drew herself off the chair and to the kitchen.

Bertie watched, wretched, wishing he could explain so many things.

'Now, Albert.' The wise old eyes glowered beneath the gingery bushy brows. 'I am of the opinion confession is good for the soul.'

'Kit probably told you.'

'Now what would there be for Kitty to tell?' The doctor sat in the blue chair with its velvet cushion, crossed his plus-foured legs so his green and yellow plaid socks became more apparent, and gazed up at Bertie.

'I chastised her,' Bertie said. 'Too forcibly.'

There was a pause and a small squall of wind made the French doors rattle, causing both men to look at them, startled, then at each other in silent agreement on the coming of winter.

'Have you told Kitty about the Somme?'

'She knows there was something.'

'You are not normally an aggressive man, Albert. It could be of value to talk about it, y'know.'

'It's all gone. Finished.'

'You're still a fine-looking man. I have no doubt that

192

if Miss Buckley returned from the dead she would find no change in you at all.'

Bertie stared into the doctor's face and wondered if the man was being deliberately insensitive. He didn't want Elsie back from the dead. He said, 'If she hadn't met me she might be alive today.'

'Nonsense, lad. The consumption was there already. Must have been.' The rugged Scots face was serious. 'On the Somme you blamed yourself for thousands of men walking to meet their maker, Albert – ' and Bertie wilted, his face collapsing like a small child's near to tears. 'I should have known,' he said softly. 'Seen. Learned.'

'If the men at the top didn't worry about it, there is no reason why you should go off your head – '

Bertie backed to the blue settee and sat quickly. There it was again, young men walking confidently in rows upon rows, having been told the enemy were annihilated, then the sudden shock of firing, slaughtering. Boys like Tommy Buckley. Mowed down. Screaming. Crying for their mothers. Their guts spilling out. Blood spurting.

Bertie said, as if he were alone, 'Carnage.'

The doctor's fingers tapped the arm of his chair. 'I would say you are in need of a good holiday, Albert. Thousands of men came home, and we all have to die sometime.'

Bertie didn't look at him; he was in two worlds, the trenches and the sitting-room, the noise of battle and the peace of home.

'Let me listen to your chest, Albert. Open up your shirt.' The doctor left his chair and uncurled his stethoscope from the bagginess of his jacket pocket. 'I'll give you a tonic, man. Take it regularly, and there'll be less fretting over other people and things you can't alter.'

'I don't fret.'

'You do, man, it's written all over you as plain as day.'

Bertie didn't reply. The stethoscope was cold but reassuring; it meant somebody cared, someone was trying to help. He said quietly, 'I think I'm going around the bend.'

'Heh?' said the doctor, as he removed the plugs from his ears and coiled the stethoscope back into his pocket, but Bertie didn't repeat his fear.

Kit came, bringing whisky and cigars. She had changed into a bright yellow dress of fine wool, and her glossy black hair was freshly arranged in a plait about her head.

'There, doctor, I've sent Linda to lie down. It's so good of you to come out at night like this.'

'Aye,' said the doctor dourly. 'I've just been prescribing a holiday for Albert. A second honeymoon, y'know?' and he saw Kit's face tighten and her amber eyes become veiled. He sighed and accepted the drink. He told himself there were some patients no mortal could help; they each created their own hell.

*   *   *

Big Tom Buckley had come up the platform of High Street station grinning to himself. He could see Bertie Hemsworthy striding out before him, scared. Tom wanted to laugh aloud. All fur coat and no knickers, them at the other end of town. He saw Bertie surrender his ticket and hurry to the street, and Tom felt free to enjoy a private conversation. 'You told 'im, boyo, you frightened the innards out of 'im, heh heh heh!'

The ticket collector leaned back a little as Tom gave up his ticket. 'Phew,' he said to the next stranger. 'Can smell it a mile away. Stale stuff too.'

Tom turned, hearing, leering, wondering whether to go back and knock the bloke's block off, but there was a copper, young feller, all sprung up ready to care fer himself. Watching.

Tom lifted his only hand in a derisory acknowledgement, and made an effort to walk like a teetotaller. He came to the courtyard and, ooooh gawd, the sun hurt his eyes. He squinted and the fresh air knocked his brain. He stood for a moment, pausing until he was more accustomed to it, and there was Maud Jeffries, waiting for him. He drew his stump across his mouth and grinned; a copper behind and Maud in front. Trapped, boyo. Good and proper.

Maud came, like a scraggy hen, to greet him, Ebony on one side of her, black as the hobs of hell; Ali grinning, showing off those coupla gold teeth like he was a millionaire slumming, and there was Stella. There was a piece of goods, Stella. Showed the old crone up.

'So you come then!' Maud was pleased. She had even powdered her nose.

'Aye,' Big Tom said, and as she put an arm about him and reached up for a kiss with naughty stars in her eyes, he thought she was better than nothing and they all looked the same in the dark anyway.

He said, 'You got a bed in your place fer a handsome chap like me?'

'Yer bloody drunk, Tom Buckley, and me got all poshed up for you an' all.'

Tom laughed, rocking his body back as little as was safe, and she scowled. 'An' I bin standing by 'ere waiting fer a real man to come out so he can protect me from the likes of 'im.' She jerked her head at the massive negro, who grinned widely and stuck his hands into the pockets of his loose grey flannels.

They all wandered down High Street, and Tom told his companions about Bertie Hemsworthy. Everybody laughed and lurched over the pavement with glee. 'Did yer tell 'im yer'll have his daughter? Did yer?' Maud was all wrinkled face and happiness. 'You old fool,' she cackled, and Tom hugged her with his left arm so her skinny feet left the ground, while Ebony had to walk in the gutter to make room for the merriment.

On the bridge Tom stopped, serious. 'This,' he announced, while Maud gazed up at him, 'is the loveliest place in the world.'

'Ooo gawd,' said Maud. 'You need another drink boy, come 'ome.'

By the time they got to Salubrious Terrace all Tom wanted to do was sleep, and he followed Maud's instructions up to the back bedroom; the room that used to be shared by Tommy and Elsie, when Gwen was alive and he was head of a family. In this house.

He groaned as he slipped his braces off his shoulders then sank to the mattress on the floor; four mattresses, and he wondered how many people used them and paid Maud rent for the privilege.

He remembered kneeling before the crucifix that used to hang on that wall over the fireplace, before Hemsworthy took advantage of Elsie, before they all took Gwen to bloody Malvern and let her die there, without him, before they put Tommy in the army . . .

He shouldn't have come back. He had no job in Dagenham, but he had no job here either, so where was the difference?

He rolled onto his side, the horsehair mattress hard and worn, he pulled the almost threadbare blanket up over him, felt the draught coming between chimney and bottom of the door, and began to fall asleep. Maud awakened him before he lost consciousness completely. 'Tom.' It was an endearment.

'Huh?' He didn't open his eyes. He wanted to be left alone.

'I got plans. If yer marry me we'll share 'em together.'

'Huh?' His mind said, go away woman, go away.

Her voice came again, 'So will yer, Tom? I'll look after yer proper. Will yer marry me?'

He sighed deeply. He knew there would be no sleep until he agreed, so he groaned again. 'Aye,' he breathed, 'anything you say,' and, with relief, heard her tiptoeing from the room and quietly closing the door.

When he awakened it was night, the candle flickered on the mantelpiece, and Tommy sat on the three-legged stool between the mattresses on the other side of the small room. Tommy leaned forward, in rough khaki shirt and trousers, his big toe sticking out of a hole in his thick woollen khaki sock. He said, 'Evening Pa. You got home then.'

Big Tom squinted, groaned and yawned. 'Gone all peace an' quiet.'

'Thought you'd be glad ter see me.'

'I gotta bucket fer a head.'

'Oughter keep off the booze.'

'And you oughter mind yer own bloody business.'

Tommy laughed. 'You don't have ter worry about me. I'll be back ter barracks soon.'

Big Tom sat up, stiff and ill-tempered, 'You still see that girl from the insurance?'

'Sometimes. Why?' Tommy watched his father carefully, suspicious.

'Nice girl. You oughter bring her over some time.'

'What for?'

'Me an' Maud getting spliced.'

Tommy got up from the stool and placed it back into the corner. 'I know what you did to her father on the train. She isn't coming over here again, ever.'

'You're on to a good thing there, son.' Big Tom rubbed the stump of his wrist across his furnace-swollen nose. 'She can come to the wedding, all posh like. We'll get a barrel in. Maud'll pay fer it. Give a nosh-up.'

'Her father wouldn't let her come. Not now. After what you done.'

'After what I done!' Big Tom was astounded. 'It's nothing ter what I will do, son. I'll get my revenge on that lot. Crippled my family life, they did. Killed it off.'

Tommy made for the door, his shadow dancing on the wall as the draught increased and fluttered the candle flame. 'Maud said to wake you. She got chips. In the oven. You better come and get 'em.'

Tommy's socked feet padded him down the stairs and to the kitchen where ten people sat or stood, the women and children looking starved, big-eyed and pot-bellied.

197

'Is he coming?' Maud stood before the grate, her hands on her hips, her head thrust forward.

'Yep. He's got big ideas though, hasn't he? Talking about having revenge on the Hemsworthys.'

'Take no notice.' Maud hit the air with a hand. 'He's not right in the head.'

'You going to marry him?'

Maud nodded as the gasp came from all lips. 'Need a man to help me in my business capacity, I do. The types I get in 'ere. a big man like yer father'll be worth his weight in gold.'

Ali sat on the arm of a wooden chair occupied by Stella. 'What he say, Tommy, about your girl, heh?'

'Wants her to come to the wedding.'

Everyone laughed, their eyes glittering in the gaslight as they watched Tommy standing in the doorway. 'That will be a great revenge on the Hemsworthys,' Ali cried.

'No!' Tommy stopped their laughter. 'It isn't just that. I think – ' he swallowed. 'I think he expects me ter – ' He went red, his short back and sides sticking up at the crown. 'I only just realised properly. He thinks her and me – Jesus Christ! I wouldn't. Not with her. She's a kid!'

Ali leaned forward, pinching one of the chips from the newspaper held in Stella's red-nailed hand. 'I know girls of twelve do it,' and everyone nodded agreement.

They heard Big Tom leaving the mattress, and Maud Jeffries said quickly, 'Listen 'ere, son, that Bertie Hemsworthy got money and position and power. Don't you dare ever lay a finger on 'is daughter. If you ever did we'd all be fer the high jump. All of us, fer encouraging her over 'ere.' She was wide-eyed, listening as the clump clump came down the stairs. 'Ebony!' she ordered. 'Get those chips outer the oven. Tommy, you find the vinegar bottle. Everybody be normal now. Eat yer supper.'

CHAPTER EIGHT

One Tuesday at the beginning of October John Davies sat on top of a sand dune and watched the Bristol Channel swerve and creep about the shores of Port Talbot. There were no waves in the humidity, only ripples that curled almost silently over each other. He linked his ham-like hands about his updrawn knees and felt fed up. In a rut. Frustrated.

He saw the snout of a fish break water, causing a circle of ripples, and he grinned; flies. Flies which caused fish to pop up. Flies which forecast rain. It would belt down.

He heaved his shoulders. Rain couldn't make his collections any worse, and there had been no new business for a fortnight. The black-covered book of rounds in his jacket pocket contained the names of every policy-holder and every cent they had paid over the last weeks. There were too many dashes in the columns where figures should be.

He felt energetic, like a tightly coiled spring, yet he had nowhere to go. He had canvassed his streets methodically, had done all that could be done, and now he needed fresh challenges. Promotion.

He lifted a pebble from the soft golden grains about him and threw it towards the sea, then he linked his fingers and cracked them noisily, watching for another fish, the sudden sparkle of a long silver-scaled body.

Nothing happened.

He might as well go home. Forget today. Hope tomorrow would be better. He stood, his turnups filled with sand, and plodded back to the road, his shoes squeaking with every step.

The air was salty, still, the tide sighing on the turn.

His bike was where he had left it, against the side of a garden wall, his macintosh rolled up and strapped to the grid at the back. Maybe there would be a storm; clear the air. Make everybody feel better.

He cycled languidly, long strong legs moving effortlessly and, at the base of the mountain, he dismounted and pushed the bike up the track.

With the sky coming nearer and greyer, the sweat rose on John's forehead and scalp, while a sheep called deeply, worriedly. Maybe, John thought whimsically, that call went on and on, from mountain to mountain, until it met the Brecon Beacons, and lost itself in the emptiness of the wilderness.

He came around the last high bush before home and the blackberries were there, ignored, shrivelling now, warning of winter and dark cold nights, of snow and the need for more peat and logs for the fire; the usual worry of how to get coal up to warm the kitchen; to warm young Buck who was sitting up these days and taking notice.

There was no smoke wisping from the old oblong stone chimney, no napkins on the line. He rested the bicycle down by the gate and looked more closely at the house. It stood out, starkly poised between the edge of the mountainside and nothing. The door was closed.

Today, with the humidity of lowering clouds, the sea as pewter-coloured as the sky, the farmhouse door was closed.

John moved fast, striding up the cinder path, then turning the great black wooden knob and going into the large kitchen. 'Maggie?'

She was sitting on the sofa, the baby a wrapped bundle in her arms, her face seeming to be squashed into narrow drooping folds.

Even as John asked, 'Is he asleep?' he knew it was more than that, worse than that. 'Mag! What is it?'

Her eyes peered at him from sockets that seemed

dragged down, like a bloodhound's. 'There's late you are,' she said tonelessly, and swayed the baby back and forth. 'I been waiting a long time.'

'I sat on the beach.' He flushed guiltily, going to her. 'It's been a murderous week . . .' His long awkward fingers became inordinately gentle as he carefully drew the edge of the white crochet shawl from the baby's face. 'What is it, Mag?' then shock caught his heart and panic made his eardrums roar.

'Oh Iesu mawr!' Great Jesus!

'I've sat here, John, for hours. Waiting. Nursing him. I couldn't leave him. Couldn't take him out. And no one came.'

John's anguished face stared from the baby to her. He whispered huskily, 'I'll get back down to Sion's, use their phone. Get a doctor!'

'An ambulance, bach. An ambulance. The fever ambulance.'

In the folds of white young Buck lay with eyes closed, his skin a mass of scarlet rash, his chin almost lost in the swelling of his throat.

'He only had a cold.' 'Maggie's voice cracked. 'I thought he only had a cold,' and John shushed her quickly, then he was running faster than he had ever run before, onto his bike, his bottom in the air, avoiding the saddle as his hands controlled the wheels hitting stones and ruts.

Fever! His son had fever!

His brain fired on: rich people had telephones in the house; could call a doctor straight away. People like insurance managers. Oh *duw Annwyl!* dear God! If only he was a manager. Didn't live where there was no road.

He rushed into the shop and used their phone. His voice was hurried but calm while his mind went on: that lavatory. That filthy bloody lavatory. The bluebottles when he forgot to buy lime. Maggie in there scrubbing the seat, breathing it all in, then nursing the baby.

He went back to the foot of the mountain and waited,

and when the doctor came the ambulance came too. Then the ambulance stayed where the streets began, and women put cloths across their mouths and locked their doors and windows.

John, the doctor, the nurse, the ambulance man with a great thick red blanket over his arm, climbed the mountain. They could hear each other breathing, struggling to climb faster, to make the bellows of their lungs and the pump of their hearts work harder. In the farmhouse, Maggie sat, crooning now at the scarlet unconscious baby.

The doctor knelt beside her, his Burberry swinging open, his bag also open, on the floor, beside his knees. He tried to look as if this wasn't serious, then took his hypodermic and gently rolled the baby towards Maggie. He uncovered the angry scarlet bottom, and Maggie began to cry as the needle went in.

Young Buck made a tiny sound, not a moan, not a sigh, and his eyelids with their thick brown curling lashes flickered slightly.

'There,' the doctor breathed, and nodded to the ambulance man. 'You can take him now.'

'No,' Maggie said, and although her voice was quiet, it was bordering on the ferocious. 'I'll carry him.'

'No,' John said firmly. 'Not you, cariad.'

But Maggie stood, her sagging face the texture of old flour. 'Put the blanket around me.'

And they did. Over the right shoulder and under the left, the baby folded into it on her right arm, then covered with it coming from the left. Welsh fashion.

Maggie went to the door surrounded by the doctor, the nurse and the ambulance man, while John delayed by the kitchen table to say a prayer of request.

Then he stared at the open doorway, and realised Maggie had not called him to follow her. In her stress she had not even remembered him.

He ran, ignored his bike and kept running, seemingly disjointed in his alarm and concern, springing over stunted gorse bushes to save the time going around them, and his sparse hair stood up on end while a streak of lightning sparked across the gently rolling summit of the mountain. He saw Maggie wrapped in the red blanket, the blue and white nurse behind her, the ambulance man and the doctor before her, each holding out a hand, palm up, as if to guide and save her. The thunder came in a faraway but threatening rumble.

'Maggie!' John screamed. 'Don't let the baby get wet! Keep him dry!' His arms flung out, he almost sprawled as he misjudged a jump.

The doctor drew aside from the others and waited, while the rain began, slowly pitting and patting the earth with big warning spots.

The nurse smiled soothingly and let John pass her so his arm could go about Maggie's back, as if he was trying to help her carry her load.

Around the ambulance the little side street was empty, grey, the windows showing only straight lace curtains and aspidistras in brass or china pots.

The ambulance man moved nearer Maggie. 'You better go back now, love. Come visiting later.' His arms reached out to take the baby.

'No!' Maggie snapped, and jerked to one side, her fingers spread to clutch Buck more tightly.

'You can't come,' the man said. 'It's the fever. The fever, love,' and, although his eyes were sad with sympathy, they were also hard with experience. 'You phone the hospital later on, then come and see him.'

Maggie lifted her head in fright and defiance and the rain splashed on her cheeks. 'No, No.'

The doctor nudged John, his gaze instructing, 'Separate them.'

John took Maggie's wrists and forced them from under the baby, the nurse moved in, and John knew he would never cleanse his soul of the look in Maggie's sunken, desperate eyes.

'No John,' she was pleading now. 'Be on my side, cariad. He's our son,' but the unconscious baby went, soundlessly, and John kept both arms about Maggie as the ambulance doors closed. 'I'll be there soon, my baby!' Maggie screamed in Welsh. 'Mamgi will stay with you!'

The doctor coughed discreetly. 'When you come visiting, Mr Davies, not up at Ynys, I'm afraid. There's no room there. In Swansea he'll have to go. You understand?'

Maggie and John stared at the man as he lifted his coat collar against the downpour. 'Ynys is only a small place in the crack of the mountains,' he went on. 'In Swansea it's a new hospital. Modern. Be better for him.'

Maggie stood in the middle of the empty side road, the rain falling more heavily, flattening her dyed black hair against her broad forehead. 'He won't come back,' she said quietly. 'I can feel it in my bones. He'll die away. Without me.'

The doctor hunched his shoulders. 'They'll be up to fumigate the place, Mr Davies. But you should burn what you can. The baby's clothes, everything,' and he was sidling towards his car.

John held the shivering Maggie and turned her towards the track, wishing she still had the red blanket, because rain was coming thick and hard now, great grey curtains sweeping at them, while the thunder was much nearer.

'He got wet,' Maggie said soullessly. 'When they took him from me. Out of the warmth of me and the blanket. Into the cold.'

'Mag,' he said hoarsely. 'We're getting away from here. I'm going to be a manager. I'll go to London and tell Henderson-Hobbs. Sit on his doorstep, I will, if necessary. I'll tell him, I've got to be a manager.'

Maggie sobbed and laughed a little at the same time. 'Being a manager won't stop my baby dying.'

'A better chance he'll have, when he comes home. Look now, Maggie. Two lavatories we'll have. One upstairs and one out the back. We'll have hot water in the taps and Buck'll go to college.'

Maggie stopped crying, the very ugliness of her face

a beauty in itself. 'Oh go on, John, I'm not as green as I look, mind.'

'Why not?' He had her attention, had stopped her crying. 'Bright as a button, he is. Can be anything in the world he wants to be.'

Maggie shook her head wonderingly and blinked the rain off her lashes. 'There's lovely that would be. If you could do it.'

His strong arm persuaded her up the track, her long full black skirt catching on straying brambles and ripping unheeded. 'He could be a doctor,' John said, 'or a solicitor. Imagine it, now, our boy a solicitor.'

Maggie held her face up to the rain and gazed at the clouds that hid God, and she knew that Buck would never become anything unless John became a manager.

They went into the farmhouse together, saturated, infinitely weary and frighened, and John realised all his proposal forms, books, and collections were still stuffed in his pockets. He unloaded them gingerly, and the marks of puce pencil had run in the wet, smearing purple streaks where pristine neatness was expected.

It was Tuesday. He had an account to do ready for tomorrow morning, and while his body ached and he wanted to nurse Maggie, he also needed promotion.

She knew his thoughts, could see them on his long irregular face, and she said, as she took warm dry towels off the brass rail before the mantelpiece, 'Get yourself dry, cariad. Put your pyjamas on, and don't you go to the office tomorrow. Let them lump it for once.' John took off his jacket and put it over the back of the old wooden chair in the lean-to, while the rain battered the corrugated tin roof and the wind began to howl.

He laid his soaking trousers and vest on top of the copper in the corner, while Maggie stood beside him in her enormous baggy bloomers and calico brassiere. A draught whistled under the doors and along the stone-flagged floor, and John, in knee-length flannel underpants, took her in his arms. He lulled her gently, swaying her as he swayed the baby on bad nights, then Maggie drew a deep breath and said huskily, 'Darro, there's cold it's getting,' but the rain had eased. She looked over John's shoulder, out of the little window with its wooden frame bent with age, and outside, miles away, across the distant Devon hills, a great rainbow arched, perfect in its shape and colours.

'Oooh look, John, there's beauty for you!'

'I bet it's a sign, Maggie. A sign everything will be all right. I'll poke the fire up and do some chips. Eggs, is it? Eggs and chips.'

She ran from him, eager to believe in signs and omens and, by the time they sat down to eat, the rain had stopped, the sky was clear, and the earth smelled rich and sweet.

Later, they dressed in their Sunday black and went sedately down the sheep track in the light of John's torch, their shoes sinking into patches where the ground had swallowed water instead of letting it cascade over, and they went to the side door of Sion's parents' shop.

'Is your mother in, Sion?'

Sion stared vaguely, lacking quickness of brain.

John said, 'Tell your mother Maggie and John would like to borrow the pony and trap.'

Sion nodded and retreated. He came back with his mother and father.

'What is it, John? Duw,' Mrs Roberts said, 'there's dressed up you are. Going somewhere posh then?'

'To the hospital. In Swansea. The new one. Young Buck got diphtheria.'

Mr Roberts moved back a step, and his wife put her hands to her face in horror. 'You can't mean it!' she gasped.

'We're sorry to trouble you,' John said in abject apology. 'But we don't know how long we'll be, so we can't take the train. Might not be one to bring us back, and a taxi won't know what time to get us either.'

Mrs Roberts gazed from between her hands. 'Oh, what

206

a terrible thing. The fever. Gone to Swansea too.'

Maggie made to move away. 'We didn't mean to contaminate you – '

'Oh duw duw,' Mrs Roberts seemed to awaken. 'If it's to come here, come it will. Through the shop, the way people cough and sneeze all over us there. Take the trap you, John. But cold it'll be. Sion! Come you, boy. Help Mr Davies now. Quick. And make sure the lamps are working properly, or lost Mr and Mrs Davies will be.'

She didn't invite Maggie and John in, and Sion didn't walk too close to them, but they were handed a big black umbrella, 'in case it buckets down again. You never know now.'

The mare knew her way to Swansea blindfold, and the streets smelled fresh. She lifted her hooves high in a trot, and Maggie and John bounced and rocketed the anxious miles with the roads still gleaming wet in the darkness.

They found the hospital easily enough and there were no high buildings here, only long low wards tucked into the narrow valley beside a wide road.

John tethered the pony to one of the young trees planted near the kerb, and set a stone behind the wheel of the trap, then he and Maggie went to the reception building and, from there, down to the ward door.

There a bright-faced nurse said, 'Oh no! I'm sorry. You can't come in. Not here!'

Maggie paused, one hand to her throat. 'I've got to!' she exclaimed. 'He's my only child. He needs loving!'

'Through the window,' the nurse smiled. 'All the visitors do that. They look through the window.'

Maggie's face lifted and her bottom lip jutted. She stepped forward, her buxom frame ready to move the nurse aside, but another couple came hurrying down the slope to the nurse, and they brought eggs and fruit and flowers.

Dismayed, Maggie realised she had brought only clean napkins and nightgowns. John handed the brown paper carrier with its contents to the nurse, and she pointed along the outside of the building. 'Just there,' she said quietly. 'The second window.'

She watched both couples go to their right places then she smiled and nodded and went in, shutting the door, closing away the well-lit glossy cream walls and the smell of fever and Dettol.

John's Adam's apple jerked up and down against the front of his collar as he whispered, 'Come on, Maggie. He might be watching for us.'

Maggie stared at the window, then in through it. It couldn't really be like this. Little children locked away. No loving. No kissing. No hugging.

The other woman was crying silently, leaning against the wall. She snuffled and smiled at John's bewildered stare. 'Dull, aren't I?'

'No,' John said, 'we feel the same way,' and looked through the window to a cot holding a small bundle, that could be anything.

Maggie and John watched as the nurse came into the room and moved the cot around, so they could see the face of the bundle.

It was Buck, and he wasn't watching for them. He lay on his side, eyes closed, swollen face hot and scarlet.

A great shudder ran through Maggie and her lips moved in silent repetitive prayer.

She and John stood there, watching the unconscious child until the other couple moved away and the four walked up the slope together.

At the gates the man touched his hat. 'Good night,' he said, but the woman hurried into the darkness, muffled in her misery.

John said steadily, 'Good job we've got the trap, Maggie love. We might never get a taxi here, and it's miles to the station.'

'Callous they are, John. Callous indeed.' A young woman came quickly along the pavement. She stopped. 'Hello Mrs Davies.' Her thin face was half covered with a scarf. 'What are you doing here?'

'My baby – ' Maggie said, not interested, then the girl lowered the scarf and smiled and Maggie said quietly, 'I know you . . .'

'We buy veg off you. Or rather my mother does. I live in Port Talbot, but I work here. I'm on nights. Just coming in now. Late too.'

'Oh,' said Maggie, as though she couldn't understand.

'My name is Jones,' said the girl. 'Freda Jones.'

'Oh?' said Maggie again, unable to respond, her brain numbed.

'Good night,' Freda smiled.

'They wouldn't let us in,' Maggie said. 'They took him and now they wouldn't let us in.'

'Oh no,' Freda bobbed her head. 'They couldn't do that.'

John took Maggie's hand and led her away.

The mare waited patiently, her broad head drooping, her hooves moving slightly as if to distribute her weight. John said 'Mag. D'you think we ought to go and tell Bertie? It is his son.'

'No,' Maggie said, 'Buck might be better tomorrow. We can tell him then. And it's late now, isn't it?'

John helped her aboard then checked the lamps before climbing up beside her. He took the reins and released the brake lever.

In the darkness, with no moon, and the streets gradually drying, the mare clip-clopped them the weary miles back to Port Talbot.

That night neither slept. They lay in the big flock bed holding hands, each pretending to be at peace.

Maggie heard the rain begin again, the wind start to whine in the chimney, and was ever more aware of the channel beyond the small township and sand dunes. She whispered to John, 'There's lucky we are, aren't we? At least our son is not on a ship,' and the wretchedness was like a live thing eating at her heart.

Her fears and imagination made her cold and she got up from bed and padded to the window. It was black out there, with street lights far below dimmed and distorted by the rain which hit the panes and ran to the sill.

'Maggie.' His voice came muffled from the bed.

'Yes love?'

'Let's go down and have a cup of tea.'

At twenty to five they heard the gate click. They shot startled glances at each other and ran for the door. Maggie was there first. 'Sion!' she exclaimed. 'God have mercy on you, boy, coming up in this weather. What is it? Tell me.' But she knew.

Sion stood in the tiny hallway, the rain running off his yellow sou'wester and yellow rubber cape. 'I won't come in,' he said, sniffing raindrops away. 'I wanter get back to bed, see.' His wellingtons gleamed with mud. 'It's the hospital,' he said. 'Phoned, they did, and Mam said we'd let you know – ' but his face went blank; he had forgotten what he had to let them know.

'Have some eggs, Sion,' Maggie urged. 'Free.'

Sion swallowed a breath. 'Mam says not to take anything.'

The grandfather clock swung its pendulum rhythmically, ponderously, and Maggie thought frantically. 'It's our lives it's ticking way. Ticking our lives away.' 'What did your mother say to tell us, Sion?'

Sion smiled with pleasure. He could not remember what the hospital said, but he could remember what his mother said. 'She says the pony's winded a bit but Dad will lend you the horse and cart, and don't forget to bring an umbrella.'

'Oh Iesu mawr!' Maggie breathed. 'He's not gone to his Maker then.' She turned to John where he stood in the kitchen doorway. 'If he was there'd be no sense in us going,' and her eyes were glassy with hope.

'We'll get a taxi,' John said quickly. 'Don't you worry now, Sion. Tell your mother not to worry at this time in the morning. We won't be long because they only let us look through the window.' The rain and wind came surging in as the door blew further open and banged against the wall.

'Where?' Maggie demanded, gripping her dressing-gown about her. 'Where will you get a taxi this time in the morning? You thank your dad, Sion. Tell him we'll be down now.'

'Have a swig of cider, Sion,' John invited. 'Keep the cold out,' but Sion was already backing away, waving his torchlight over the soggy ground as his wellingtons plodded back to the gate. 'I'm all right now,' he shouted against the wind. 'I'll tell Mam.'

Maggie closed the door, then ran back to the grate. 'I'll give him extra eggs for the same price when this is over. I will indeed.'

She and John left the lamp burning in the farmhouse window beside the Busy Lizzie; it made their leaving seem less terrible. They slithered and groped and clung to each other for support, while their eyes got used to the blackness and the wind, and their coats blew open and their legs got drenched.

When they reached the bottom of the mountain Maggie's lips were stiff with cold and wet, but managed to mutter, 'Darro, mun, my bloomers are soaking.'

'Ach i fi,' John said teasingly, while his mind kept worrying. 'You should never do it while walking like that,' and they both laughed, each trying to make the other feel better.

In the small yard behind the shop the stallion put his head down so his fringe fluttered against his blinkers; his hooves sent up silver splashes and, as Sion senior led the animal out to the street, the great iron-rimmed cartwheels rumbled. Maggie thought the wind might have moved Swansea much farther away; it was taking so long even to get started to go there.

'Oh dear,' she grumbled in Welsh as they finally left Port Talbot and bumped and swayed on the Swansea road. 'Fish! He must have carried tons of it in this cart, as well as onions. Stink, it does.'

John sat bent forward, the reins resting in one hand as he touched her with the other, giving an encouraging

211

but ever crooked grin. 'The rain'll wash it. Wash it all away,' and they both sat, waiting for whatever dreaded news lay ahead.

As they arrived at the hospital gates the sky was beginning to show a hint of dawn in the east, and the air had turned bitterly cold. The porter came out of his den and saluted them, but went back in fast, and still the rain lashed.

John jumped down to the road and led the stallion right to the ward with Maggie sitting in the cart, then he took the animal to a widely-eaved corner, hoping there would be a little shelter. He helped Maggie down, and they both bent their way to the ward door.

A young doctor met them, his face tired and unshaven. 'I thought it wiser,' he said gently, 'to let you know – ' The wind sprang at him, wet and furious, and he stepped back. 'You had better come inside,' he said tentatively, and Maggie hastened to obey.

She was a few steps nearer Buck.

The doctor noticed and gave an anxious frown, then went on, 'He has rallied again, but his temperature has been very high. We were – ' he shook his head a little, ' – very worried.'

'Is he alive?' Maggie stared at the face that seemed too young for such responsibility, then glanced around, startled that her voice had been so loud amid the bare walls, so piercing.

'You have a fighter there,' the young man smiled, as if, having let them in, he hadn't the heart to turn them out. 'You're soaked. How far have you come?'

'Port Talbot.'

The young man's face went blank, then, 'I thought I heard a horse – '

'Yes,' said Maggie and John together, trying to wipe their soaking hands and faces on handkerchiefs. 'A friend lent it to us. They're very good.'

The doctor frowned and blinked again, regretting allowing the attractive night sister to telephone these people, but then he sighed. 'Sister Jones will see to you,' and he gave Sister the nod to be especially kind, while he strode quickly and silently away, a slim form in a white coat.

'Is he going to die?' Maggie asked, and her voice was piercing again.

Sister Jones said, 'Sssh. The children are all sleeping. They do when it's almost time to wake them up. Come now to the kitchen. There's an electric fire. You can have a cup of tea before I take you to the room.'

Maggie looked at her glowingly, but didn't repeat the wonderful words 'take you to the room' in case Sister Jones realised what she had said and changed her mind.

John said, 'It's good of you.'

'Not at all.' Freda was polite. 'We aren't supposed to do as I did, but I had to let you know. It was up to you whether you came or not.'

'Oh, we'd come,' John breathed, and mentally promised her a great stock of vegetables.

Sister nodded, her hand already held out to guide Maggie away, and she took the umbrella that was sending rivulets over the tiles of the floor.

Ten minutes later Maggie and John stood in the little room surrounded by windows, and baby Buck was in Maggie's arms, her hands in rubber gloves, her body enshrouded in a white coat. 'Oh John,' she breathed, and glanced at the open door. 'He can't know it's me, not covered up like this. I'm doing no good at all.'

He nodded, silenced by the agony of the picture before him.

Maggie whispered. 'In your pocket. You've got chocolate drops. I'll try him with one.'

'Put him back,' he whispered in return. 'She said not to touch him. Getting her into trouble you are.'

'If he's going to die he'll have a chocolate drop. Quick now. Before she comes!'

The paper bag seemed to rattle like an oak tree crashing, and Maggie went on, 'If I hide behind the door she won't know,' and she scuttled into place.

She held the sliver of chocolate to the baby's lips and watched it melt against the heat of him. 'Lick!' she breathed. 'Oh annwyl,' my beloved, and the tip of the baby tongue appeared, the golden-brown eyelashes flickered, and Maggie's laugh was a suffocated sob. 'Good boy,' she breathed. 'Oh good boy for Mamgi.' She lifted him higher and dropped a kiss on his brow and, when she looked up, Sister Jones was in the room, eyes big with furious disapproval.

'Mrs Davies! You could be causing the deaths of other children. And you going round people's houses carrying the fever! Put him back at once!'

'I'll bath!' Maggie cried. 'As soon as I get home. John will fill the bath. We'll both bath. Boil the water in the copper. I've got carbolic soap. And Lysol.'

Sister Jones took the baby and put him in the cot, covering him, patting him, going to the trolley in the corner for a square of gauze and wiping the chocolate from his mouth. 'Now you had better go!' she said briskly, and Maggie left, chastened.

They hung up the white coats and left the rubber gloves on the shelf. They replaced their wet clothes and went out to the greyness of another Wednesday. The horse neighed, glad to get moving, the breath steaming from his nostrils.

*   *   *

On that same Wednesday morning the alarm went off in three hundred, Prince Edward Road at seven, and Bertie reached out a hand to stop it. He had slept well and felt more content because of it.

He turned his head and smiled at the dim outline that was Kit. She grunted and stretched. 'Did you hear the rain?'

'Rain?'

'The heavens opened. God help the poor devils out in it.'

'Yes,' Bertie said, and thought of the long sweep of beach, the high stone wall with the homeless lying before it.

'Policemen,' Kit yawned. 'Down the Strand. Pounding the beat.'

'Yep,' said Bertie, and wished she wasn't able to rile him like this so early in the morning.

During breakfast he shrugged his shoulders, then shuddered and shrugged again. Kit said, 'Someone walking over your grave?'

'Must be. I have an odd feeling. Waiting for something.'

'Like?'

'No idea.'

Linda lit the fires in the office and the middle room. 'Good girl,' Bertie said, and patted her shoulder. She was growing tall, too much like Kit, all legs and neck. 'Keep the damp out.'

She had used wet coal and it stank. Billows of smoke refused to go up the chimney, filling the house. Kit opened all the doors then flapped a towel around.

Bertie sat at his desk, hummed a few lines of 'Keep the Home Fires Burning', and promised himself he would remain calm. The night's sleep had proved his health was all right. A few more nights like that and his nerves would be back to normal.

He saw Linda looking like Cinderella, her schoolgirl hands thick with black sludge, her hair flopping over her face, her knees newly dirty from kneeling before the grates. He said, 'Linda, you would really like to go on with your friends, wouldn't you, to finishing school.'

'No.' She shook her head without looking up at him. 'I'm all right here.' She lifted the bucket of coal and the sticks she hadn't used and went from the room.

Bertie began to whistle tunelessly, telling himself something would turn up.

As the first agent came into the passage and hung his hat and trench coat on the hallstand, Linda was there, clean, smiling. 'Good morning.'

215

The agent grinned at her. She was becoming a corker.

By noon Bertie was rubbing his chin worriedly. 'Where the devil has John got to? You sure he hasn't telephoned or anything, Linda?'

She nodded, 'I'm sure,' but she was thinking of Tommy, wondering what time she could get out, get over to St Thomas.

Bertie left his desk and strode to the kitchen, the place feeling oddly empty now the men had gone, the air still holding the smell of cigarettes and wet clothes.

'Kit. There's still no sign of John.'

'He'll be in.' She slid a black iron pan of peeled potatoes along the hob, nearer the fire.

'He's never been late before.'

She wiped her hands on the white linen tea towel. 'Why not telephone the people in that shop? Maybe they know something.'

'Yes,' Bertie said politely, and returned to the office, but he didn't like the idea, nor the discomfort that was on him. He clapped his hands, trying to dismiss his worry. 'Linda! Why do I have you for a secretary? How about a cup of tea? Warm the inner man and all that,' and she laughed, glad of a reason to move about.

He watched her, wishing thoughts of John and Maggie didn't keep filling his mind. Thoughts of young Buck. His and Elsie's son.

By four o'clock he could stand it no longer. He shuffled the day's papers together and laid them ready for tomorrow. He gazed at the window then strode to the kitchen. 'Kit, I might as well get down the Sandfields. There's a death claim needs settling down there.'

'Will you be long?'

'Half an hour. No more.' He strode away again, whistling. He called from the front door, 'If John comes in, you'll attend to him. Won't you?'

'Of course,' Kit said, coming up the passage, and he went.

Linda came down the stairs. 'I'm going out too, Mummy.'

216

'So I see. Is Tommy home again?'

'I think so.' She was hedging.

'That lipstick really is too heavy for you, dear.'

'I like it,' Linda returned and a few minutes later she, too, left the house.

She walked sedately down the street, avoiding kids with their hoops and yodelling yells but, once around the corner, she snapped open the clasp of her handbag and took out the silvery snake bracelet. For a moment she moved it slowly, causing the red eyes to catch the light from the lowering white sky, then, smiling, she coiled it about her wrist and made for the tram stop.

She didn't hesitate at Maud Jeffries' open front door, and the smell of boiled cabbage, wet scrubbed wood, chimney smoke and too many people, no longer concerned her. She went on, up the bare stairs and tapped on the door of the gloomy back room.

'Come in,' growled big Tom Buckley, and Tommy stood there, trying to tidy his hair with spread fingers, as Linda hopped inside, then he glanced at his father, remembering this was what Pa encouraged, and he glowered at her. 'What're you pestering me for all the time?'

His father grinned, coming from the stool, big enough to block the light from the low window. 'Come on in, girl. Sorry there's no fire.'

Linda didn't glance about. She knew four men slept in there. She also knew it was the nearest thing to privacy that Tommy had. She said to Tommy, 'I was afraid I might have missed you.'

He scowled like his father. 'I told you not to be coming round here.'

His father drew up a spare orange box and motioned Linda to it. 'Hark at my boy,' he chivvied. 'Talking like he got a plum in his mouth.'

Linda ignored the proffered seat and smiled primly. 'He's trying to improve himself.'

'Improve 'imself!' Big Tom's voice boomed through the house. 'What'n hell for?'

'So he can be an officer.'

Big Tom looked at Tommy and guffawed.

'Him? An officer?' Big Tom's laughter was like great blocks thundering on her, and Linda said, 'Everybody has to improve themselves. Even my mum and dad.'

Big Tom stopped laughing, the back of his hand rubbing the base of his stubbly chin. 'I saw his sister improve 'ersel', and what good did that do, huh?' He gazed down at Linda and saw the courage there, and he grudgingly admired it. 'I'll tell yer this. If you wants him, you takes him as he is. Got it?'

Linda nodded quickly, eyes shining in the gloom, and Big Tom moved closer to her, liking her, resenting her.

'Light a candle, son,' he ordered expansively. 'Light two of 'em,' and he saw the bracelet gleaming on her wrist. 'Who give you that? Tommy?'

'No!' She drew her sleeve down to hide the snake, her inside anxious with diffidence of him. 'Ali did. And he bought one for Stella.'

'Ali did,' Big Tom echoed, and his face was drawn into a long O of thought. 'Hasn't yer pa warned you about taking presents off of black men?'

'He's not black!' she returned loyally. 'He's brown. And he's Tommy's friend.'

Big Tom looked at his son and his eyes asked, 'Why didn't you buy it for her?' then he was sitting on an orange box, and Linda accepted the other.

Tommy stared at his father, saw his father's contentment with the situation and struggled to stop it. 'Linda, I was just going for a walk. You coming?'

'Course she's not,' said his father. 'She'd like a cuppa tea.'

'No,' Linda said hurriedly, having tasted Salubrious tea, 'but I would like to sit for a minute. It's going awfully cold outside.'

'Well, now,' said Big Tom, making an effort to be a host. 'Is your pa all right?'

'Yes,' Tommy put in edgily, 'her pa is all right,' and received a warning scowl from his father.

'The insurance world is prospering?' Big Tom grinned, watching her closely. 'No worries there.'

'Oh yes there are!' Linda retorted. 'He's worried now. One of his agents hasn't paid in yet. It's paying in day, you see.'

Big Tom nodded as if he did see. 'Oh aye,' he said, then made a tremendous effort to cheer her. 'Maybe he'll pay in tomorrer.'

Linda nodded, then turned to Tommy, chattily. 'You know him. It's John Davies. The one who has Elsie's baby.'

The candle flickered and a door slammed downstairs, echoing hollowly in the barely furnished house, then Big Tom sat forward, the orange box beneath him creaking dangerously.

'What baby?'

Tommy said, 'You know what baby, Pa. You flung her out because she was expecting him!'

'Him?' Big Tom stared up at his son. 'You mean our Elsie had a boy?'

Tommy nodded, and Linda clutched her handbag to her, preparing to leave the situation she had created.

'Nobody told me she'd had a boy!' Big Tom stood up. 'Who got him? Huh?'

Linda said nervously, 'I thought you knew about the baby. I'm terribly sorry. I shouldn't have said – '

'Course you should,' Tom bellowed. 'It's the bastards in this house let me down. Nobody told me. Nobody told me I gotta grandson. Where's he at, huh? I want 'im 'ere!'

'You can't!' Linda got to her feet. 'He's John and Maggie's now. They bought him!'

'Bought him!' The big ex-steelman seemed to get bigger. 'Who'n hell had the bloody cheek ter sell my grandson? Don't I count? Don't no one never tell me nothing?'

Tommy stepped over a mattress to get to Linda, his head jerking as if mentally throwing his father to one side. 'You ask Maud, Pa. She knows about it. Everybody

219

knows about it. And if you'd stayed here, doing right, none of this would have happened.'

'Tommy!' Linda cried, as the candlelight made Big Tom's face grotesque in his fury. 'Don't say anything. Please. I want to go. I shouldn't be here. My father will be awfully cross,' and she ran towards the door.

'Your father!' Big Tom jeered and thrust out a clawing hand to stop her. He caught her hair and the nape of her neck. His fingers were hard, digging. 'Half a mo' love!' he roared. 'You're not going anywhere till yer tells me,' and he dragged her back to his great chest. 'That pansy bloody feller yer calls Dad. It was him sold my grandson?' He was quivering.

Tommy yelled, 'Keep yer maulers off her, Pa!'

'Shut yer trap!' came the reply. 'He sold him? He got money. How much, huh? How much did he make on my grandson? He going around now siring boys for sale, huh?'

Linda wriggled to be free of him, and when he let her go she stumbled forward, terrified and white-faced. She turned on the big man, her amber eyes sparking. 'My father is not a pansy – '

'He's a bloody lily-livered snob!' Big Tom roared.

'He's a gentleman!' she shouted, and heard Tommy laugh. It infuriated her still more and she swung her handbag in the air and backed to the door. 'I don't like either of you. You're both coarse and common.'

Tommy stepped after her but she hunched her shoulders. 'Don't come near me,' she cried, and Ali was outside the house, sitting on the windowsill, his brown face almost invisible in the semi-darkness. 'Hello sweetheart.' His voice was velvet, coaxing, as if he had heard every word upstairs. 'I'm on my way into town. Can I give you a lift?'

'You have a car?' She paused, surprised. She didn't look back at Tommy as he stood behind her, panting. She ran down the steps to the pavement with no clear thoughts, and Ali's hand was on her elbow, taking her across the road, avoiding the spread horse manure.

Everywhere looked alien, with dust like sand on the pavements, and empty cigarette packets and dirty newspaper in the gutters.

'Everywhere is so horrid,' she said, as if it suddenly mattered, and Ali helped her into the front of a little Austin seven, then he got in beside her, all Roman nose and hollow cheeks.

Tommy was at the car window. 'Linda! I'll see you tomorrow!'

She didn't answer. She wanted to cry.

'Linda!' He rapped the glass furiously. 'The middle market gate at half-past four!'

Ali drove away. 'Bye bye Tommy friend,' he called. 'Your papa looks for you. And boy, is that papa cross!'

Linda glanced at him and his laughter brought a wry smile from her. 'Are all men bad-tempered, Ali?'

'These days, yes,' he said. While his coffee-coloured hands steered the car through the narrowness between a lumbering tram and the kerb, he went on, 'Everyone has forgotten how to laugh, sweetheart. They still think of war and killing and starving and things like that.'

'Do you still think of things like that?' She sat, numb now, wishing she had been kinder to Tommy, wishing she hadn't mentioned the baby.

'Yes, oh yes, but I think of many other things. Nice things. Beautiful things. Like young women with eyes like flickering fires, lips that magnetise a man, and a heart that does not yet know where it may belong.'

Linda made a derisory sound. 'In your country the girls must look funny, if their eyes are like flickering fires.'

Ali swung the car past a milk float and its haggard grey mare. He said, 'I was talking about you, sweetheart. It is your eyes that – '

'Where are you going, Ali?'

'In through here.'

'But it's the private part of the docks!'

'Not private, sweetheart. Where the big ones come in.

221

The banana boats. You and Tommeee go to the South dock. Ebony and me, we belong in the Prince of Wales dock. There is also a North dock and a Beaufort dock – ' The car stopped. Ali rolled his window down, and the docks policeman put his head towards them, staring at Linda. 'Evening,' he said.

'Evening,' Ali returned.

'You got a visitor there?'

'I have advised her not to get out of the car. I am helping her, taking her home, but I must visit the ship first.'

The policeman looked Linda over, imprinting a mental picture, then grunted and stepped back. 'All right, Ali. See you,' and the car bounced on, over hawsers and chains that seemed to be streaming everywhere.

Linda said, with a tinge of excitement and awe, 'Is this where they have terrible fights with the drunks?'

'The silly people? Yes. The beachcombers and the sailors.'

'Beachcombers?'

'The down and outs that sleep on the sands. Beggars. Liverpool stiffs.'

'Elsie slept on the beach. And Tommy.' Linda's voice faded away, and Ali realised he had said the wrong thing.

'Oh, there are fine fights.' He tried to draw her mind from Tommy and Elsie. 'All punching each other. The police blowing whistles and using truncheons. A lot of fun. Prostitutes joining in – '

He stopped. Linda was gazing at him, wide-eyed. 'What are prostitutes?'

Ali swerved the car slightly, then laughed. 'Girls,' he said. 'One of them is the policeman's friend.'

'Does the girl fight as well?'

'She goes for help.' Ali grinned, gold-toothed. 'She runs for the police-box. A lot of people do,' and he heaved a sigh of relief as he reached his destination.

The little car stopped beside the longest, rustiest, highest boat Linda had ever seen. She bent her head to see it better and, as Ali opened the door and leapt out, the scent of docks filled the car.

Linda watched him. He was like a monkey, thin and agile, going up a gangplank, disappearing. She heard the gentle throb of an engine, the pat-patting of the water against the quayside, and she wondered about fights and girls, and foreign countries, where men like Ali said nice things about your eyes and lips, called you sweetheart, and bought you a bracelet just because you liked it.

Then Ali was back, driving out of the dock gates. He drove over the New Cut bridge and up Wind Street. Linda said quickly, 'This will do nicely, thank you, Ali.' Her hand was on the door lever.

'Ali will take you most of the way, sweetheart.'

'No thank you.' Her voice rose. Here was the border between town centre and the east end. She must not be seen with a coloured man. 'Ali. Please. I can walk from here.'

'Walk?' he laughed, his gold teeth catching the golden light from a passing street lamp. 'Are you ashamed of being with me?'

'Oh no!'

But she was, and her fingers remained gripped on the door lever. The car sped up Castle Street, High Street. 'I really would like to get out now.'

He swung left, past the public urinals in the middle of the road, and the western sky was a brilliant ochre where the sun had disappeared. There was a morass of traffic, crowds cramming the pavement and road, in the hard yellow light.

Ali said, 'An accident, I think.'

'Police too.' Linda could hardly speak. Reaction set in from the scene in the bedroom; the lingering hurt of Big Tom's fingers either side of her neck mingled with a longing for Tommy and a dread of Bertie.

'I'll get out here!' but the car kept moving and people could see her. She wanted to slide down, hide, but didn't

223

dare offend her driver. 'If you stop here!' Her voice was frantic, and he stopped beside the Albert Hall cinema, the queue stretching around the corner.

She sprang from the car, gasping, 'Thank you, Ali. So kind of you.'

He watched her, smiling, one brown hand resting on the gear stick. 'Bye bye sweetheart.'

The eyes of the queue were on her, impersonally curious, and Linda glanced at them, wishing Ali would drive away quickly. The commissionaire was calling, 'Two at sixpence!' and she was running down Cradock Street.

She ran into the emptiness of Northampton Lane, then stopped, panting. She felt awful. Cold. She took the snake bracelet off and put it in her handbag. She leaned against the stone wall until the banging of her heart eased, then she strolled on again, to the tree-lined pavement of Christina Street. There she emerged with her fears vanquished. She lowered her head as a secret laugh escaped her; she was really terribly silly. Fancy being frightened like that – of nothing.

Then she was striding her way home, to the western end of town, jauntily confident again, her handbag swinging at her side.

*   *   *

Back in St Thomas, high on the wall, Big Tom Buckley had stood watching Tommy rap on the car window. He saw the glint of Ali's teeth and eyes as the Arab bent to laugh goodbye, and Big Tom knew a fear he had not experienced since Elsie was a nipper. Ali was up to something. The bloody wog was after that girl, and that, to Big Tom Buckley, was more alarming than any threats he, himself, might make.

He saw the car nose away and he saw his soldier son turn and look up, as if undecided what to do next.

Tommy's fists were already clenched. He wanted to kick something. Kick someone. He marched across the road, daring the traffic to hit him. 'Pa!' He stood on the pavement and yelled up, 'You're a stinking rotten bloody tyke,' and people stopped to look and listen, then hurried on, knowing how fights could be.

Big Tom felt his face redden, felt his almost bald scalp prickle with anger. With one hand and one stump he could kill his own upstart, but the thought of Linda, the posh kid, getting into Ali's car, stilled him.

Tommy came to him, his confusion over Linda's departure mixed with fury over his father.

At the top of the steps Tommy paused long enough to take off his jacket, to roll up the sleeves of his rough khaki shirt.

'Pa!' It was a whisper that floated along the front doors and cracked walls, a whisper that said this fight was not to be a Saturday night brawl, not a kneeing of balls and gouging of eyes outside pub doors. This was a son wanting to cripple his father for the sins against his mother, and his sister, and his girl.

'Pa!' He walked slowly, his eighteen-year-old chin jutting, his eyes narrowed as he calculated the vulnerable points on his father.

'You remember, sonny,' Big Tom said scathingly, 'I've scrapped some since I could sit up, an' I've crippled some fer life. I wouldn't touch me if I was you.'

'You fight your way, Pa. And I'll fight mine. She was in the house ter see me. Not you. And you stuck yer nose in.'

'I didn't hurt her.'

Tommy squared up to him, and kids circled the two. A voice called, 'A fight! Come and see!' and Tommy lunged in at a tilt.

His fist whammed past his father's ear, then his father's only hand shot out and grabbed Tommy by the throat. The long fingers of the former steel-furnace man held the youth as a child might hold a teddy bear before screwing its head off, but still Big Tom's feet didn't move. A rare smile, a wicked smile, crawled across his big pored face, and he said, 'You got guts.

I'll say that for m'self. I gotta son with guts.

Tommy waited for the thrashing to come. He knew from experience that glossy-skinned pink stump could be more effective than a hand. It could punch, send sudden darkness into the brain, or send a pain that was seared with stars darting in an indescribable way. His ears began to buzz as the oxygen oozed from his head, and he felt his face begin to swell.

He kicked and missed, and all the time his father's strong ugly face grinned with pride. 'The army's making a man out o' you, boyo. The one good thing Albert Hemsworthy done fer this family was stick you in the army.'

Tommy felt his tongue curling, his father's head seemed to start floating from him, then he heard Maud Jeffries shrieking, saw the flagon raised, then slam down on Big Tom's head.

The fingers drew away from under his ears, his knees began to quiver, and he knew he ought to bash his father now, but he also knew he hadn't a chance in hell.

'There!' crowed Maud, watching the swaying, bewildered Big Tom. 'I don't like my man 'aving a fight on his own. I likes ter be in on it.'

'You skinny cow!' Big Tom snarled at her, and Maud lifted what was left of the base of the flagon.

'You want more?' she demanded, staring up into his grimacing face, and someone in the audience tittered.

Ebony loomed, white melon grin in the long shadow of the houses, and Maud said to him, 'I don't need yer help, black man, You go on in. We're going up the pub now. My fiancy needs a drink.'

Tommy watched painfully as he reeled against the house, his gullet trying to work, to swallow, his lungs trying to find rhythm again.

Big Tom stopped swaying and touched the top of his head gingerly, felt the stickiness of blood. 'You're a fine blasted old mare!' he bawled admiringly, and Maud preened, stretching to her full five foot two in height, then she turned and glared at Tommy. 'You been touching that girl at all?'

'No.'

'Not at all?' Big Tom added strength to Maud's demand.

'Not at all.' Tommy flung back the words.

'Tell yer what then.' Big Tom straightened his shoulders, magnanimous, ready to make amends. 'You tell 'er I apologise and get 'er to the wedding. We'll teach 'er a thing or two, won't we Maud?'

'Does she drink?' Maud wanted to know.

'Dunno,' Tommy said, not truly aware of the way the tide was flowing.

'Gawd,' said Maud. 'There's a man yer got fer a father.' Then, to the man himself, 'You better get that licence then, hadn't yer? I'll get the booze in. And the cake.'

Tommy began to straighten up, to walk away, and Maud shook the remains of the flagon at him. 'If you got any sense, boyo, you'll find another girl. One as understands us. Bring 'er to the wedding, 'ere in our 'ome.'

She turned and walked, shrivelled and overalled, into the house. She bustled into the kitchen and the cat was on the table again, licking itself. She swiped it mightily and it dropped to the stone floor then stalked away.

'That's better,' said Maud, and laid the remains of the flagon where the cat had been. 'Now I feels fine,' and she grinned at Big Tom as he came behind her, put his arms around her and gave a hefty squeeze.

CHAPTER NINE

On that same Wednesday, after Bertie and Linda had left, Kit jumped with shock as the telephone rang. She answered quickly, 'Hello! Unicorn.'

'Kit!' He was panting. 'We fell asleep. Maggie and me. I tried to phone you from the shop but they said it's out of order. Don't want me breathing over it – '

'John?' She was startled by his rush of words.

'I couldn't come in. I haven't done the account. The baby got diphtheria.'

'The baby?' She stared blankly at the phone, and his rush of words continued.

'They took him in yesterday. Sent for us. In the night – '

'In all that rain?'

'The doctor said he's a fighter.'

'I'm sure he is. Last night must have been the crisis. He'll be all right now.'

She paused and it was as if John had nothing else to say. She called gently, 'John?'

'What about the account?'

'Leave it for this week. Do a double next week. Like you always do at Christmas.'

'Six weeks they keep them in. The minimum. So many die – '

'He is in the best place – '

When John had concluded his call she sat, bewildered, glad the child was over the worst, but the shock of his illness renewed the memory of his birth, her ache of jealousy and unhappiness.

She mentally shook herself and finished off the filing

228

she had been doing. Part of her wanted to rush to the hospital, offer help, but a stronger instinct warned that Buck was nothing to do with her any more. He was no longer any of her business. No one ever referred to her about him, and she had long since stopped asking.

She leaned against the corner of the desk and felt isolated, not in on anything. Linda was exploring a world of romance, Bertie was wrapped up in romantic grief, and Maggie and John were strongly united in their mountain universe. Kit needed to talk, to hear a voice that was not laden with trouble.

She telephoned the operator, then sat, waiting, with the mouthpiece before her face. A little wave of relief clashed with a wave of disappointment; Head Office was empty. No one was replying. Everyone had gone home.

There was an uncontrollable wobbling all through her as she realised what she was doing. She had never telephoned him before, never contacted him nor given any sign she waited each Monday morning for the magical moment of eleven o'clock, yet now, for no feasible reason, she was calling him. In his office. He might not like it. He might even be rude.

Naively pleased she could have his number called without actually speaking to him, she continued to hold the black candle-like set, and to smile at it. Then, to her shock, the operator sang, 'You're through now, caller,' and his voice said brusquely, 'Yes? Who is it?'

Kit paused, suddenly unprepared.

'Yes?' he demanded again. 'Who is it?' and Kit placed the telephone back on the desk, the earpiece raised, ready to fit into the side grip. 'Well?' his voice scorned. 'You've dragged me from the end of the passage. Is it too much trouble to damn well speak?'

'No,' Kit said feebly, and picked the set up again. 'Robert. I'm sorry. It's me – ' She was truly trembling, delighted but nervous. Would this be the end of the Monday morning calls, the fantasies that took her through each week?

He didn't speak for a moment, as if he was frowning, peering at his receiver, wondering if he had heard aright. Then, 'Kitten? That you?' and his hesitancy, the slight unevenness in his voice calmed her.

'I'm sorry, Robert,' she apologised again. 'I expected Miss Gibbs to reply.'

He had recovered too. 'What does Miss Gibbs have that I don't?'

'Time,' Kit smiled, and pressed her mouth nearer the phone. 'I don't want to waste yours.'

'I have time,' he said, and she knew, by the way his breathing changed, that he had sat, probably at his desk. 'Everyone packs up here about four o'clock.'

'But not you.' Already there was gentle flirtation in her voice, the way it dropped a note, huskier, more intimate.

'No, not me.' He laughed quietly. 'I hang around hoping a certain Welsh lady picks up my telepathic messages and replies to them.'

'You mean you WANTED me to phone you?'

'I can't telephone you. How else can I hear your voice when I need it most?'

Kit chuckled derisively, warning herself he was spinning a line.

'I'm serious,' he said.

'Because I'm so far away,' she said unthinkingly.

'Meaning?'

'Oh nothing.' Alone in the office, Kit blushed with embarrassment.

'You must have meant something.'

'No, I didn't. Really.' She covered her words with laughter, and there was a small silence before he said deliberately, 'Kitten. You accuse me of being facetious.'

'Never!' She kept laughing, though she felt she was sinking into a trap she had made herself.

'You were saying I enjoy being two hundred miles away. That, as long as you are not here, in London, I can be serious.'

'No. I didn't mean anything of the kind. It was a

silly remark for me to make. I wasn't thinking.'

'If you were here now, beside me, I would be serious. I need you to talk to. I need you to look at. Kitten, I need you.'

Kit's fingers tightened about the stem of the phone, her brain slowing as if drugged by the unexpected outcome of simply calling his number, and she couldn't speak, couldn't reply. He went on more slowly, 'On this occasion you called me. Does that mean there are times when you need me?'

'I did just now.'

'Splendid.'

Her fingers moved on the set and she hunched her shoulders, hugging forward, wishing she could tell him so much, but sure she could never tell him anything.

He said coaxingly, 'And what was it you intended saying?'

The moment called for amour, for gentle words with tender meaning, but he had asked a question and Kit answered honestly.

'John Davies hasn't paid in yet, so our account will be late.'

She heard him exude breath, heard his exasperation, and the dread of upsetting him banished Maggie and John from her mind. She went on lamely, 'I'm sorry. I wanted you to know. I was going to tell Miss Gibbs, but she didn't answer. You did.'

Lies. Lies. She knew it and hated it. She had trumped up a problem as an excuse to speak to him, would have asked Miss Gibbs to put her through to him. Did Miss Gibbs know he telephoned her each Monday morning? Would her call have been food for gossip?

'Quite so,' he said calmly. 'But we still need your account first thing Monday morning. I suggest you wait until the last moment before doing it. Give the Davies man a chance to pay in, then bring the account to the office yourself.'

Kit glanced at the receiver as if she would see him

231

there, a man changed from friend to employer – or schemer.

'Me?'

'You, Mrs Hemsworthy.'

She could hear him breathing, waiting. Eventually she said warily, 'There are times when I don't particularly like you, Mr Henderson-Hobbs.'

He laughed indulgently. 'That means you invariably do like me, very much. So – ' and he moved as if he was lifting his feet off the desk and sitting forward. 'I will expect you here Monday. In time for lunch.'

'I can't – '

'Of course you can. You merely go the station, get on a train and leave it when it reaches London.'

'Bertie will wonder – '

'Did you ever wonder – ' He hesitated, then, ' – why Bertie found Miss Buckley attractive? Isn't it time you showed him that you are a woman all through?'

She sat with her lips apart, the tiny red flecks of excitement darting in the deep amber of her eyes.

'Mrs Hemsworthy?'

She ought to say no. Definitely no.

'Mrs Hemsworthy.' His voice was that of authority.

'Yes, Mr Henderson-Hobbs?'

'When you come up bring that white gown with you. I'll get tickets for the theatre Monday night.'

Night? She hadn't thought of night.

'I'll book you in somewhere.' He was planning, calculating.

'Mr Henderson-Hobbs! Robert! I can't possibly – '

'I'll tell Miss Gibbs to expect you. Goodbye Mrs Hemsworthy.'

'Mr Henderson-Hobbs I – '

The line was purring again, but differently, softly, as if all that could be done had been done, and Kit wondered whom she would eventually upset: Robert, by not going? Or Bertie, by not staying?

Bertie came home, swinging his arms, his homburg

at an angle on his head. Another Wednesday survived, but where in hell was John this morning? 'Only me!' he called, and Kit felt her spirits lightening; he was in a good mood.

'Tea?' she replied. 'Or coffee?'

'Tea.' He hung up his overcoat, watching his reflection in the hallstand mirror, straightening the knot in his white-spotted navy tie. He strode to the kitchen. 'What excuse did John give?'

'He hasn't been in,' Kit said, and was glad her back was to him, her hands busy with the kettle on the hob.

'Funny.' He scratched his head thoughtfully, then collapsed into his chair, his face grimacing at the depth he fell. 'I'll do something about this damn thing one day.' He slapped the worn rexine arms, and Kit knew she was not going to tell him about John's telephone call. Not just now. He was looking so much more like himself; she didn't want to see his face lose colour, his sudden concern for Elsie Buckley's baby.

She closed her eyes tightly as if the heat of the fire burned them, but it was the thought of Elsie and Bertie copulating that burned, deep inside her, to a tormented hatred, with a hatred of that hatred.

She turned blindly and poured his tea, passing it to him, and he stared up at her. 'Something wrong?'

'No. Why should there be?' and he nodded but, about half-past five, he sat at his desk, hearing the comparative silence of the street, and he worried about John, Maggie and his son.

'Kit!' he called as she came up the passage and stuck her head around the door. 'I'd better go over.'

'To John, you mean?'

'None of the men get up to this sort of antic unless something is radically wrong.'

She came into the room, wishing her tongue would tell him, but dreading him ever knowing. Bertie watched her without seeing her. 'I don't usually wet-nurse any of them.'

233

'Well don't start now. They may have been called away. It could be a waste of time going up that mountain. After all that rain.'

He looked sharply at the window. 'Quite dry now, and it won't get dark for a while.'

'You don't know if there's a train,' but he wasn't listening. His decision was made.

'Ring the station, Kit. I'll have a swill,' and his long legs were taking him up the stairs to the bathroom. He felt a mixture of things; pleasure because he was doing something he considered right, vexed because he was bothering over a man who never bothered about him, and nervous of his own re-action at seeing young Buck again, watching the Elsie eyes recognise and laugh at him.

The taxi arrived in minutes and Bertie plonked his hat on his head, checked he had his wallet, picked up his coat and strode out.

In Alexander Road the taxi met a morass of people, slowed, then stopped. Bertie craned to see why. A mare, her haunches jutting and eyes expanded with terror, lay on the road, rotted fruit squashed and trampled about her, the harness heavy, the shafts killing her frantic struggles. Men worked to free her and a tramcar behind the taxi kept clanging its bell.

Bertie swore under his breath. He could see the front of the station beside the driver's head. He tapped the glass, then paid the man off and stepped out to the road. Everyone was calling 'Whoa, there, girl. Whoa there!' and the terrified struggles of the mare's hooves clattered on the tramlines.

Bertie paused to survey the scene then lifted his head impatiently; this would not get him on that train to Port Talbot. He watched the crush of humanity and traffic in his endeavour to get across the road, and glimpsed a little car. In it was a small pale face with a fringe and young wide anxious eyes.

Linda?

Good God no!

Good God, yes!

The tram crawled forward, a policeman called, and Bertie saw Ali, a hawk-shaped nose in profile, the short but jutting chin.

Bertie waved a fist at the tram driver who dared bring his tram between him and the Austin seven. The car with Linda in it was gliding away, picking up speed. He yelled, 'Lindah!' and the policeman was beside him.

'Something wrong, sir?'

'Yes. My daughter – ' Bertie stopped, the car lost in traffic now, the fallen horse squealing loudly, the place milling with traffic and people and noise.

'Can I help, sir?'

Bertie stood between the tramlines, unable to run after the car, unable to tell anyone, certainly not a police officer, that his daughter, an ex-pupil of St Hilda's School for Young Ladies, was in a car with a coloured man.

A seaman! Bound to be. The only types found in Swansea. He belonged the other side of the New Cut bridge.

Bertie went on to the station, and at the back of his mind was a new worry; that coloured man had looked vaguely familiar.

He went quickly to the telephone kiosk. 'Kit? Linda just passed me. No, she didn't see me. Tell her I shall want to see her when I get in.' He left the kiosk and ran for the train.

Kit went back to the kitchen and, while she busied herself, reverted to daydreams, determined not to wonder why Bertie was quarrelling with Linda again. Nor what sort of upset there would be when the two got together. She mused on how you tell your husband his boss commanded you to London, but the question did nothing to stop the quivers of excitement rushing through her.

She made herself coffee, sat and cocked her feet on a dining chair. The luxury of it. The silence of the house. The self-indulgence of these moments.

She was a fool, she warned herself, to get all hot and bothered about a voice on the phone but, she argued, what harm was she doing? Twenty-four hours in London? Was it such a sin when it promised such pleasure?

The porch door slammed and Kit's feet shot to the ground. 'Emma? One day you'll smash the glass in that door!' but Emma was charging up the stairs.

Kit paused, wondering why Emma hadn't replied. The child was up to something she wasn't supposed to do.

Kit followed, not deliberately stealthy but quiet, and she peeped into Emma's room.

Emma was sprawled on the bed pulling strings of bubble gum from her mouth, concentrating, chewing then pulling again.

For a few moments Kit watched with a mixture of horror and fascination. The gum was rapidly re-chewed then spread across the front of the tongue and blown; a bubble formed and Emma blew harder.

Kit backed silently away. Gum was dirty, but obviously gave such pleasure.

Like love-making.

She went to the bay window in the front double room and stood watching the ochre sky turn the streets a hard yellow. Love-making. She had never seriously considered the term before. Making love. Was it possible to 'make' love? Weren't the words as meaningless as saying one could eat a horse?

Could Robert make love?

Would Robert make love?

She heard Emma go to the bathroom, the tank flushing, the taps running, and knew there would be grubby finger streaks on the white bath towel, then Emma was hopping down the stairs, thud thud, all secrecy over. 'Mummy?'

'Yes darling?' Kit stood at the top of the stairs.

Emma gazed up at her. 'I'm starving.'

Kit came down, feeling glad she was slim and beginning to realise she was a whole person in herself, not

236

just her husband's chattel. 'I suppose you could eat a horse?'

'Two,' Emma grinned, her second teeth firm and even. 'Can I get a slice of cake?'

'Yes,' Kit said, but her mind was working in unusual ways. Other couples wouldn't – couldn't – not a whole world being filthy. She wanted to laugh then, her imagination running riot. Yet, where did babies come from?

She was disgusted with herself, nauseated that her mind could give so much time to the degradation of women, yet there was also an awareness, as if she was on the verge of solving a scientific problem.

'And you?' Emma asked, all bright blue eyes, and a knife hovering over a slice of madeira.

'Me?' Kit exclaimed. 'Oh no. Not me!' then realised the question had nothing to do with her thoughts, and she laughed, while the excitement for Monday was still there.

When the fire was banked up and the wireless filtered light-hearted songs through the house, Linda came in, strolling down the passage like a tragic heroine.

'Did you see Tommy?' Kit drew Bertie's grey sock onto a wooden mushroom and prepared to darn the hole that presented itself.

'Yes.' Linda flopped onto the hard chair against the table, ignoring Emma crouched in the sag of her father's.

'Everything all right?' Kit glanced at Linda's pathetic expression.

'Yes, thank you. I suppose so.'

'Did you see your father?'

The pathetic expression fled, and the head that could droop in misery or toss in rebellion now jerked, startled. 'Why? Did he come looking for me?'

'No. John Davies still hasn't paid in, so Dad has gone to the farmhouse. He telephoned from the station saying he wanted to see you when he came in.'

'He always wants to see me. I never do anything right. I wish I could go away. Leave here for ever.'

237

Kit longed to cheer her, promise wonderful things – yet what could she promise? A land of unemployment, where the wounds of war were still fresh and some said there would soon be another?

'Blast!' she said, as the point of the needle punctured her knuckle. 'I'm fed up too, Linda. We all get fed up at times.'

'Why should you be fed up?' The challenge was there, the need to quarrel with someone and find an excuse to weep. 'You've got Daddy and the house and everything.'

Kit licked the spot of blood from her hand. 'I don't suppose Daddy will be long. John and Maggie are probably at the hospital.' She felt the interest of the girls quicken and she glanced at Emma. The child was bent forward, her chest almost on her knees. Both girls knew the next line was theirs.

'Why?'

'Because Baby Buck is poorly. Very poorly.'

The drama, the pathos left Linda, and Emma whispered, 'Has he got fits?'

'No.' The longing to nurse both daughters became stronger. 'He has diphtheria.'

Linda went to Emma and both girls squashed into Bertie's chair, their usually oval faces long with gloom. 'Will he die?' It was Linda.

'No,' said Emma stoutly.

'He might have to,' Linda argued. 'If there's room for ten in heaven, God will send the angel of death to get ten.'

'No,' Emma scowled.

Linda said impatiently, 'It's got to be somebody we love. Somebody precious, because it's our turn.'

There was a perplexed, sullen silence, then Linda whispered petulantly, 'I wouldn't mind if the angel took Daddy. Give us some peace.'

There was a long gasp from Emma, and Kit snapped, 'Linda! Don't be so nasty!'

'I'm not nasty,' she retaliated. 'He wants Elsie. Let him go to her then.'

'Come up to the table,' Kit ordered sharply. 'You can have supper and get to bed.'

The two girls hesitated, Emma with her fingers entwined before her, Linda ashamed of what she had said, but not prepared to retract, All three were startled as the front door bell jangled.

'Oh heavens!' Kit grumbled, harassed. 'Who can be calling at this time of day?'

Emma whispered, 'Maybe it's the angel of death.'

'Don't be silly!' Kit reprimanded, and quickly squashed her darning into her sewing basket.

Emma stood up, chin raised. 'I'll go and tell him to go away.'

Kit smiled as her younger daughter marched from the room, arms stiff at her sides, fear revolving all through her. Halfway up the passage Emma felt the wall, then stood on her toes to switch on as many lights as she could reach. She watched the glass on the porch door. And there was the outline of a man. A man not moving. Waiting.

Emma's eyes were popping with fright, yet she drew a quick breath, then opened the door so fast it caught against her feet and rattled, almost toppling her over. She gazed worriedly around its edge. 'Yes?' Her voice was piping.

'Hello Emma,' said Tommy. 'Linda home?'

Emma nodded, too overcome with relief to speak, and Tommy came in, taking his cap off and putting it under his arm. Emma let him pass her then she closed the door slowly, her eyes still watching for the angel of death, but Tommy went on, to the kitchen. 'Mrs Hemsworthy,' he said importantly, 'I'm sorry I've come so late, but I want to talk to Linda. Alone.'

'By all means,' Kit said, wondering why the histrionics and preparing to go to the scullery.

'No!' Linda called dramatically. 'I have no desire to speak to him,' and she was on centre stage again.

'Mrs Hemsworthy, as you know, my pa is home. He

239

and Maud Jeffries, my landlady – my pa says they're going ter get married.'

'Oh yes.'

'And pa says you can all come. Emma and all if yer like. He don't mind.'

'Oh?' Kit said; 'How very kind of him,' and put her hand to her mouth. 'We'll have to – er – think about it, won't we?'

She knew there was no thinking about it. The answer was no, definitely no.

Tommy hesitated, his practised entrance speech over, then, 'So if I can go to your middle room. With Linda.'

'No,' said Linda airily. 'I have finished with you.'

'You bin talking to Ali!' Tommy burst out, and Kit wondered if the ceiling was caving in. 'Ali?' she said. 'Who is Ali?' and all attention was on Linda. Emma sidled in and stood beside Tommy, her hands behind her back, her feet apart.

Linda gulped, made an odd gurgling sound, then lifted her head and said ringingly, 'Ali is my best friend. He works on the banana boats.'

'Ali?' Kit said cautiously. 'A foreigner?' and Linda nodded.

Kit sat. This was worse than the ceiling caving in. The spirit of coloured men had entered her home, her kitchen. 'Linda.' It was a breath rather than a name. 'Is this why your father wants to see you? You have been with this Ali? Today?'

The silence gave her answer.

'My God,' Kit breathed. 'Oh my God. You wicked girl. You naughty, wicked, silly girl.' Her gaze shot to Tommy. 'You knew about this? Who is he, this man?' Her face was ashen, her lips faintly purple. She turned to Linda. 'Don't you realise the danger you were in? What strange men do to young white girls?'

'He's not strange.'

'Don't be insolent, Linda. You're fifteen – ' and Kit

240

realised that, at fifteen, a girl might think she knew everything.

Tommy said urgently, 'She wasn't with him all the time, Mrs Hemsworthy. She and me quarrelled and she went off with Ali. He's Egyptian really, Mrs Hemsworthy – ' then inspiration hit Tommy. He added, 'Like Jesus Christ was.'

'Jesus Christ!' exclaimed Kit, bewildered and upset. 'What has He got to do with this?'

'He gave me a lift,' Linda said. 'That's all.'

Kit almost cried, 'Jesus Christ did?' but put both hands to her lips instead, stopping the blasphemy. 'Ali,' she said more quietly, 'gave you a lift.'

She longed for Bertie, for a voice, a personality stronger than her own. 'This – this Ali – he has a car?' She wanted to scream it. 'This – this – black man – ' Her fury broke out. 'Linda! Answer me. This black man. Does he have a car and did you get into it?'

Linda stared in horror. Her mother in a fury was a rare and awesome sight. Kit was slowly getting to her feet, amber eyes dark with threat, the long slim neck stretched with sinews reddening. 'Did you, Linda?'

Linda tried to speak and failed. Her father in a temper, striking her, her father demanding certain standards of behaviour, was expected, understood. This apparition before her was not expected, nor understood.

'Mummy!' and into the kaleidoscope of her mind came the memory of Kit in her nightie; Kit with a fat striped spider between her finger and thumb. Kit squashing. Slowly killing. 'Mummy. I didn't mean anything.' It was a whimper.

'Get to bed,' Kit hissed. 'Before I beat you.'

Linda ran, pushing Tommy to one side, and he went after her.

Emma would have gone too, scuttling like a scared mouse, but her mother said quietly, 'Emma. Get up to the table. It's time for supper.'

She went to the passage door and listened. Linda was

in her bedroom and Tommy was after her. Kit cried, 'Tommy!'

There was immediate silence, then hurried whispers floating along the landing.

Kit called again, less loudly. 'Tommy! You do not go into a young lady's bedroom! Kindly come out of there.' She went halfway up the stairs, looking through the bannisters until he appeared, then she nodded. 'Now I suggest you go home.'

'Yes,, Mrs Hemsworthy.'

Kit went back to the kitchen, she and Emma ignoring the sound of Tommy going, the porch door being closed gently, as if not to upset her still further.

By the time Bertie came home Linda had locked herself in her bedroom. Emma sat on the stool before the fire in her nightgown, a new awe of her mother keeping her wary. She heard her father come in and failed to stifle a little sigh of relief.

He paused at the hallstand, tired, his trouser legs wet from the searching tangling threads of bracken and bramble as he toiled up and panted down the mountainside. He hung up his hat, then stood watching it swaying slightly on the hook. Beneath the chandeliered light his reflection came from the mirror; he looked like Dracula, colourless, with sunken dark eyes and hair flattened by hours under the hat.

He grinned at himself, murmuring, 'Sure to get worse before it gets better, old chap,' and his reflection nodded, agreeing.

He went to the kitchen and was struck by the calmness of his homecoming, his wife and younger daughter just waiting, not talking.

His slippers were on the fender, the fire glowing; signs of winter.

He listened for Linda. Best to get it over. Do it now. 'Linda in?'

'Yes. You ought to change your trousers before you get a chill.'

242

'Where is she?'

'Upstairs. In her room.'

Bertie knew a sense of relief. 'You've dealt with her. You know where she was today.'

'She was with Tommy most of the time. He called here this evening. The other man is quite respectable.' She marvelled at her capacity for lying.

'He's a wog!' Bertie snapped.

'He's an Egyptian,' Kit retorted.

'You mean you knew about him all along? You connived with her!'

'Sit down. I'll make a cup of tea,' Kit said calmly, determined not to side with Bertie against Linda. 'Emma. Go up to the bathroom, please. I've left a pair of Daddy's trousers over the airing cupboard door. Will you bring them?'

Emma ran. She had to get back fast, hear it all, but there was nothing left to hear and, disappointedly, she handed the trousers over.

'The blasted house was empty,' Bertie called from the scullery as he changed, then returned to the kitchen. 'What a place in winter. The sky is almost touching the chimney, and when it grew dark it was impossible. Jet. You couldn't see your hand in front of your face.'

He sat wearily and Emma looked at her mother, waiting to hear the awful news again, Baby Buck was terribly ill with diphtheria. Emma's pink lips began to frame the message, her feet began to dance in her eagerness to tell, but her mother frowned at her, and Emma understood.

If the angel of death was coming for Daddy, it was better he didn't know about it. She scratched her ear and wriggled her shoulders as if her back itched. She said softly, worriedly, 'I think I'll go to bed.'

Bertie smiled, affection on his face, and he held out a hand to her. 'Good girl.' He presented his cheek and she kissed it, then she put her arm around his neck, hugging so his brows shot up with surprise.

'Good night, Daddy,' she murmured, then wriggled again. She looked at her mother then ran to her, craning to whisper.

Kit bent and the little voice hissed breathlessly, 'I don't want Daddy to die.'

Kit hugged her, whispering back, 'God knows that. He'll understand,' and Emma ran, embarrassed, not looking at her father, avoiding him, going up the stairs awkwardly, clutching the bannister rail.

Bertie said, 'What was that all about?'

'Secrets,' Kit smiled, and didn't tell him about John's phone call. She told herself he was weary enough; he could learn about the baby tomorrow, after a good night's sleep, but her conscience knew she might not tell him then, because it would mean he would get on with the account, realising John would not be paying in. The account would be posted as usual, not late, and she would have no excuse for taking it to London on Monday.

That night Bertie tried to throttle Kit.

He lay beside her on his back, trying not to think, not to worry. He said quietly, 'It's not like John, you know. He and Maggie seem to have disappeared off the face of the earth.'

'Did you go to the shop and ask?'

'Yes. No answer there either. Everywhere seemed dead, bleak. Gave me the shudders. I went to the farm-house twice, in case they hadn't heard me the first time. The front door's not locked. I tried it. I let the cat out actually . . .' His words tailed away and Kit lay in the darkness, staring at the ceiling, thinking Baby Buck was over the worst. Later on Bertie could go to the hospital, take toys and his paternal love.

'Try and sleep,' she said. 'You must be tired.'

'Did you warn Linda properly about strange men?'

'She knows she has to avoid them.'

'Are you sure he's respectable? He looked like a seaman to me. Here today and gone tomorrow.'

'Stop worrying.'

'We read such things in the newspapers, hear such stories. She's still a child, needs discipline.'

'Go to sleep, Bertie. I'm tired.' She closed her eyes and turned to her side, away from him, and Bertie had the ever familiar sensation of being rejected. He put his hand towards her and touched the base of her spine.

'Bertie! Stop it! I've told you. I'm tired.'

'My hand slipped.'

'It has slipped before,' and she curled away, her knees jutting from the bedclothes.

She screwed up her eyes, ashamed of her own lack of warm response, to want yet dread, to need yet spurn. She said softly, 'Good night.'

'Good night,' he retorted, but his thoughts were alive. How could a woman live as she did? Was he so repulsive she couldn't stop rejecting him?

His hands, drawn safely to his stomach now, clenched. What the hell was going on?; Emma whispering secrets and scuttling to bed, Tommy Buckley here again in defiance of his orders, Linda in a car with a flaming wog, John not paying in or notifying him of why. He groaned deeply as his thoughts clashed and fought each other, as the exhaustion of his nerves demanded rest.

He fell into a disturbed and lonely sleep, and his brain became confused with people; people in uniform, in mud, with fears, crying, screaming, bits of bodies being flung about, such helplessness, frustration, futility of life. There was a Hun piddling in the trench. Filthy swine.

Bertie crept up behind him, then sprang, his hands about the man's throat, a fierce fermenting desire in him to kill. Kill! His fingers sought the jugular and pressed and squeezed, and he was grinning, enjoying the thunder of shells, the flying of shrapnel, shrieks, the ghouls about him.

The flat of Kit's foot came back and up. He grunted and his hands flew from her throat. The bedclothes became a sea of upheaval and she escaped, still doped

245

with sleep. He bent, clutching himself, awakened wondering where he was.

Kit ran to the door and switched on the light, then ran back to him, her heart thudding with disbelief. 'Bertie! You were strangling me!'

His eyes were glassy, struggling against the light. 'Oh God no . . .'

They went downstairs and the fire was out. The house was cold. Bertie sank amid the cushions of his battered chair.

Kit made tea and gave him a cup. He sipped and told himself he would see the doctor. Pull himself together. He had stopped being a man, had let Elsie's death make him spineless. He went to the middle room then returned with the bottle of brandy. He tipped some into his tea, silently commanding his will to overcome his weakness. He lit a cigarette and felt the smoke scald his lungs, felt his tension ease. He said, 'I'm sorry, Kit.'

She said casually, 'I'm going to London on Monday. I can take the account with me, so there's no need to worry over it.'

His face went blank. 'You've already made plans?'

'Yes. Today.' At this moment she didn't care about him; he would have strangled her. She was no longer concerned about him.

He drew on the cigarette and sat back, his face curiously aware. He knew she would tell him as much as she wished him to know. No more.

She said, as she held her cup to her mouth, 'I telephoned Head Office late this afternoon. Henderson-Hobbs was there. I told him about John. He said the account still had to be in by Monday morning. I said I would take it up.'

Bertie gazed at her, knowing her, and feeling he could regain his command of her again. She had made plans, but if he denounced them, right now, she would obey.

She was his wife, his responsibility, his to have and to hold, and this was a moment of decision. He had just tried to strangle her, and she had not reviled him. She had kicked and damned near crippled him, but in self-defence. She had said nothing vindictive. He began to smile, to feel better.

'All right,' he said, and she was startled, looking from her cup to his face. She relaxed and began to laugh.

'You are feeling better,' she accused.

He considered while the draught came under the back door, over the floor of the kitchen and met the draught from the front door about his slippered feet. 'I've still got this odd feeling,' he said. 'I thought it was over Linda, but it isn't. I had it before I saw her with that man – a horse fell in Alexander Road.'

'Poor creature.'

'The feeling was strong on the mountainside. A sort of premonition. It's probably why I was trying to do you in. I was dreaming of war again. As if someone is dying.'

Kit shuddered, her thoughts fleeing to the hospital, the night stillness of wards, the laboured breathing of sick children. She ought to tell Bertie, but not now. Let him get some rest.

She went to him and kissed the top of his head. She put his cup and saucer on the table beside hers and then beckoned him. 'Come on. And this time, don't take your spite out on me.'

He was glad of her, proud of her. They held hands as they went up the stairs in the dark, creeping, trying not to breathe too loudly in case they disturbed the girls. They got into bed sighing and cuddled together, their cold feet and legs interlinked. He pecked a kiss on her ear and she giggled softly, knowing she was safe; he wouldn't touch her sensually now, he was too anxious to make amends for his dreams.

'Night dear,' she whispered.

'Night Kit.'

At seven o'clock the raucous ringing of the alarm found them still entwined in each other's embrace.

Linda heard them pass her room on their way down to

start another day; they were moving softly, but the stairs creaked after a night of stillness. She heard Emma too, Emma pattering to the bathroom, Emma running the taps, Emma delving in the airing cupboard for clean knickers and handkerchief.

Linda could stand it no longer. Jealousy surged, and she suddenly stormed out of bed. Emma was lucky. Emma was going to school, with the other girls, to play hockey, do gym. Greek dancing. She, Linda, had to be stuck at home, in the office. Her bare feet seemed to cling to the lino as she ran, the frilled edge of her nightie flicking about her ankles. She opened the bathroom door – it had no key – and Emma turned from the basin, a toothbrush held under the tap, her mouth full of toothpaste.

Linda pulled a face. With both hands she caught her lips and stretched them into a leer.

Emma spat. A great mouthful of thick white froth shot across the bathroom. She stood blandly, awaiting the reaction. It came dramatically. Linda shrieked and tore back to her room, the walls rent with her cries.

Bertie came charging up the stairs, his hair almost on end. 'Linda? For God's sake!'

She ran to him, her arms about his waist, her head on his chest as she sobbed, 'Daddy, oh Daddy. Emma spat at me. Just like Tommy's father spat at you.'

Emma stood on the landing in her knickers and vest, the toothbrush in her hand, and watched, the remains of toothpaste about her mouth, her eyes unconcerned.

'Daddy. It was horrible. All down my nightie! My lovely nightie!'

'Shush shush.' He held her gently, patting her head, but he was impatient, not understanding. 'Why d'you have to scream like that?'

'She spat at me!'

'If that's the worst that ever happens to you, you'll be damned lucky.' He pushed her from him. 'Now get dressed and stop making scenes and complaining.'

'I'm not complaining.'

248

'You are, Linda.'

Emma hurried silently back to the bathroom and turned on the tap.

Her father barely glanced her way as he went back down the stairs, and both girls heard Kit call to him, 'I can't think what's got into her. She used to be such a happy child.'

'It's that blasted Buckley family – !' then he stopped, as if he was saying things that shocked him.

Emma went down, washed and dressed, shining clean, her white-to-the-knee socks carefully turned over white elastic garters.

Linda slouched in, friends to no one.

Kit said, 'I need to nip to the shops this morning. Can you manage, Bertie?'

'Linda will manage,' he said easily. 'I think I had better visit the doctor.'

Linda smiled insinuatingly at Emma. 'I'll be fine,' she said. 'I'll be in charge of the whole place, won't I?'

'Yes,' said Kit, placatingly. 'The office as well.'

By half-past nine Bertie was sitting in the doctor's surgery, feeling foolish as he talked.

'You still need a holiday, Albert. Get one. Go to Scotland. Get the bracing air into your lungs.' The doctor leaned forward and tapped Bertie's knee, then he said quietly, conspiratorially, 'Stop being afraid it's the Somme all over again.' He studied Albert's face, knowing almost all and remembering. 'I'll fix you a bottle of something. Help you along.' He patted Bertie's knee with more vigour. 'We can't have you cracking up again. Get that holiday, lad. Get that holiday.'

Bertie smiled, and waited for the bottle to be prepared from the myriad coloured fluids in minaret-shaped glass containers on the many shelves. When he left, someone else's name had already been called.

He went to the street where even the dust and dung and petrol fumes smelled clearer than the waiting-room, and he whistled quietly as he walked.

A holiday. It would be good to have a holiday, if he could raise the cash. He paused in his stride, speculating, and a tall gangling man passed him, reminding him of John and setting up the worry again. It wasn't far to the station. Bertie looked at his watch. He could catch the next train.

He turned and began to run, ignoring the thoughts that called him a fool, the thoughts that said it was John's place to contact him.

He panted into the station and collapsed onto the corner seat as the train wheels slowly turned. He had to be in Llanelly, thirteen miles the other way, by two o'clock, and Kit expected him home to lunch first.

Blast John. Blast the way he seemed to take advantage of the friendship that had sprung up between them.

He reached the hollow emptiness of Port Talbot station and hurried through the streets, the mountain looming in dark shadow as a cloud protected this side of the sun, the houses about him tainted a garish yellow as the sunlight held the threat of more rain.

Then he began to climb, thinking of Maggie tugging the big black pram up here and John pushing his bike. Poor bastards. They deserved better.

He stopped for a moment, panting, unaware of how fast he had been climbing, and already he could see over the rooftops, see Mr Capriolli optimistically pedalling his STOP ME AND BUY ONE ice-cream cart, see women with babies in shawls wrapped to them Welsh fashion, one hand left free to carry baskets or control toddlers.

Bertie felt sad for them all and didn't know why.

The cloud moved across the sun, and the farmhouse was still empty. Bertie opened the front door and called, 'Hellohoh!' but got no reply.

The baby's pram was still in the corner, completely empty. The cauldron of cawl hanging from the hook in the chimney carried a slight film of soot, and there was an odd smell, as if Maggie had taken to over-using strong disinfectants.

Bertie felty angry. He stood at the window and watched through the little lace curtain as the cat pawed a hole in the front garden. The place felt cold, almost unused. He left in discontent, slamming the door hard behind him. The michaelmas daisies stood in peastick-supported clumps, their mauve flowers unmoving, and the headache came on, making him blink and walk faster. A cup of tea. He needed a cup of tea. Better still, a drink. A stiff whisky.

He hurried back down the track, and turned towards the shop, but it was packed with chattering, waiting women, and Bertie gave up. He made for home.

By the time he got there it was later than he thought and Kit wriggled her nose. 'You've been drinking.'

'Just one,' he said. 'That's all.'

'What did the doctor say?'

'Usual thing.' He glanced at Linda where she sat at the lunch table, and reflected the kid looked washed out.

'Which of the usual things?' Kit asked.

He turned towards her and smiled, not wanting her to know how blinding the jabbing headache still was, so he stretched and said, 'Fee fi fo fum, I smell grub cooked by Mum,' and everyone laughed. Kit came to him, half trying to ease her guilt about Monday, and he put his arm about her and looked into her face, then wondered; there was something in Kit's gaze he hadn't seen before. He tried to work out what it was: loneliness? Pity? Regret?

He kissed her without pressure and realised she was giving, not passionately, not invitingly, but giving.

He took time to look more intently into her eyes, shadowed as they were by the window behind her and, for the first time in months, something stirred deep within him, something young and comforting and welcome.

His lips quivered, wanting to speak, but there were

251

no words to explain, and Kit moved from him. He flopped into his chair and said, 'Any news of John?'

Kit paused in the doorway to the scullery and looked back. How could she tell him now that John had telephoned yesterday? Why let Elsie Buckley's baby intrude at this moment? 'I've been to town.' She avoided the question. 'But Linda has a list of all who called this morning.'

Within half an hour Bertie had left home again, and was on his way to investigate a fire in Llanelly.

CHAPTER TEN

Big Tom Buckley pulled on his boots then stood to stamp his feet more comfortably into them.

Ali lay on the mattress near the window. 'Are you going out, Tom?' he queried lazily.

'What does it look like I'm doing?'

Ali didn't answer and Tom said belligerently, 'No sign of a ship yet?'

'Not one going where I would like very much to go.'

'Where d'you want to go then?'

'Home. The winter here is too cold. I don't like it.'

'I don't like it either,' came the retort, 'but I gotta stick it,' and he clumped out and down the stairs.

Maud called from the kitchen, 'Going out, Tom?'

He went to her and the other women and children about her. 'I'm obeying instructions, woman. Getting a licence to stick my head in the bloody noose.'

She sparkled at him, her face loking younger, even though laughter wrinkled her more. 'Go on then, you. We'll have a night out ternight.'

'Got any money?'

'You got none?' She shammed shock.

'Stony.' He plucked his trouser pockets inside out so they hung beside his hips.

Maud went thoughtful and drew her thumbnail across her upper lip. 'I'll get another 'ouse, that's what I'll do. You c'n look after it fer me.'

He considered for a moment, then laughed a little and shook his head. 'All there, aren't yer?'

'All there,' she wriggled her hips and chuckled. 'You

253

do your bit, Tom Buckley, and I'll do mine. Is it?'

He went out and down the steps, buttoning his jacket with satisfaction; he had dropped in lucky there.

The bridge was up so he stood watching a ship passing through, on its way to the sea, the tang of salt strong on the air, and he surmised the tide was in. He considered the luck of Ali, able to choose a ship and its destination, then he was walking fast. He had a long way to go.

He reached the hospital gates and stopped at the lodge. 'My grandson's 'ere, mister. I came ter see him.' His attitude was pugnacious and the porter grinned. 'Oh aye. What ward's he in?'

'I expected you ter tell me. If you don't know what ward the nippers're in – '

'What's his name then? You just stay there half a mo'.'

Two minutes later Big Tom thudded down the hollow to the ward and peered through windows. Children gazed back and waved and giggled.

He waved back, scowling, telling himself he was losing his marbles; what did he want with Bertie Hemsworthy's bastard? Yet he went on searching, and didn't know he had come to say goodbye to the past, to acknowledge he would take another woman to him soon, and Gwen would never be mentioned again. Curiosity, he told himself, that was what brought him here, to see what sort of spawn his daughter had brought into the world.

When he found the right window his great scorched face fell in dismay. He hadn't expected this. Tommy had only said the kid was ill, he hadn't said the kid was struggling to survive.

For minutes Big Tom stood watching the cot, then he crossed himself: in the name of the Father, the Son and the Holy Ghost.

He turned to go back up the slope and Maggie was coming down, a basket over her arm, her body bedecked in the shot silk brown costume, her head balancing a large-brimmed brown hat.

For a few moments she stared at him, trying to remember, then she smiled. 'Elsie Buckley's old man!'

He nodded. 'I remember you,' he said. 'You were at the party. All in red. In the Hemsworthy house,' and Maggie's smile waned a little, also remembering.

He said, aware of her disapproval, 'I come ter see the nipper.'

'And did you?'

'Aye. Through the winder.'

She nodded, finding nothing immediate to say, then, 'Who told you about Buck?'

Big Tom hunched his jacket further onto his big shoulders and almost blushed. 'I thank you fer calling him Buck.'

'After your Elsie, poor soul. Though none of you cared about her nor care about him.'

'Now you hold on.' His belligerence swept back. 'I'm here, aren't I. Young Tommy told me and so I come.'

'And who told young Tommy?' Her gaze was as belligerent as his now.

'Linda, I suppose. The Hemsworthy kid.'

Maggie nodded and marched past him, the basket, with its kitchen towel cover, on her hip. 'So they know then.'

'They must do.' He turned slowly, puzzled, watching her go to the ward.

'You wouldn't think so,' she called, looking back.

'Yer mean they haven't been ter see him?'

'That's what I mean.'

Big Tom scratched his almost bald scalp and ruminated, as he clomped up to the gates, that Elsie had found herself a real bounder. Maybe he ought to find out where she was buried and stick some flowers on the earth above her, let her know bygones are bygones and he was taking another wife.

Then he went for the marriage licence while Maggie tapped the ward's office window, and a nurse came to a side door and took the contents of the basket.

Maggie said with a false note in her voice, 'He'll enjoy

the chocolate drops,' and the nurse in her blue dress and white starched apron smiled and nodded, and knew other children would enjoy the chocolate drops.

Maggie whispered anxiously, 'Can I come in? Just for a moment. I promise not to touch him – ' but the nurse silently shook her head, and Maggie moved away, the lost, bewildered expression on her face again.

She put the empty basket on her head, forgetting she was in Swansea where she didn't do such things, and she went to the window, staring in at the precious unmoving baby bundle, while tears ran down her cheeks and, deep inside her, were silent sobs.

She went back to the gates and the taxi she had bidden wait for her. As she climbed in, ready to return to the station, she forced her thoughts away from young Buck. She ought to get John's best shirt out and rewash it. There wasn't all that much time if he was going to London on Monday. He would see Henderson-Hobbs. Tell the man he needed that promotion. Tell the man he would work for nothing at first; he and Maggie would build up a district.

*　　*　　*

Early on Monday morning Kit wrapped the white jersey gown in black tissue paper and folded it into the bottom of her suitcase. She told herself not to go to London, she was being foolish and disloyal. But, when she looked around the room, at the bed, at herself in the dressing-table mirror, she knew she had to go. Or leave Bertie altogether.

It was a shock to realise she might be capable of leaving him, of leaving all the things she had accused him of spoiling. Instead of the interesting pallor some people associated with beauty, she now saw only a mottled lack of colour when she looked at her reflection. She was horrified at the self-dislike rising in her throat, a sort of nausea, but worse, because it was her disliking herself more than she had ever disliked anyone.

She put her clean nightie over the black tissue and the black Spanish-heeled sandals, then pretended they had been packed by accident, so not noticed.

Later she took the bulky package holding the week's accounts and all the week's collections off Bertie's desk, and she held her face up for Bertie's kiss. He hesitated, touched her elbows with both hands and kissed her between the brows.

It was as if each silently believed that this was an irrevocable parting, and neither had the temerity to do anything about it.

Kit glanced at the black candle-like telephone and hoped Henderson-Hobbs would remember she would be on the train to Paddington, not here waiting for his usual eleven o'clock call.

She wished she wasn't going, yet knew the wishing wouldn't stop her. A change of mind needed so much more. It needed a blotting-out of the last two years. Maybe it needed a blotting-out of the last sixteen.

Bertie handed her into the taxi and drew his wallet from his back trouser pocket. Self-consciously he held out two pound notes to her. Kit stared at them, startled; he was not only letting her go, he was giving her money to go with. For a few seconds she thought she loved him, maybe as one might love a poodle, then she took the money and the taxi drove her away.

She didn't look back. She didn't know if he remained standing at the gate, and she felt an ache like grief, wishing she and he could talk about secret things, explain and learn. And she did so wish she had told him about John and the baby.

Between Swindon and Reading she smiled at the other passengers in the carriage, then went down the corridor to the restaurant car. She sat and sipped coffee, the train swaying strongly, the pistons pounding and the whistle warning frequently. She worried about spilling the coffee on the starched white cloth and wished she smoked.

Bertie dimmed from her mind as Swansea sped more miles away, and the ever-growing nearness of London brought thoughts of Robert into focus. Her heart began to drum and nervous anticipation made the pit of her belly swirl.

Did he expect her to sleep with him? Tonight?

Would it be the end of the friendship if she refused? Would it be the end of Bertie's job?

In London she didn't attempt the underground or bus service, but took a taxi, and arrived outside the Unicorn Insurance building just before lunchtime. Here, in this street, was all the turbulence of the great city, the ambitious thrusting pressures, and Kit breathed it all in. She rested her suitcase on the kerb and took her vanity mirror from her purse. She dabbed her nose with her powder puff, removing two specks of black engine soot, straightened her white helmet of a hat and smoothed its bold white feather into neatness.

Her toilette over, her handbag under her arm, she lifted her suitcase and entered the Unicorn building.

The door porter watched her through the walls of his glass sanctuary, raised a hatch and called, 'Hoi, miss!'

Kit turned and flushed, his lack of finesse forcing her guilt to surface. 'You called me?' Her fear of losing control, of showing her lack of confidence, made her haughty. She didn't move, considering him, her carefully shaped and combed brows raised in a question that looked like disdain.

'You can leave that bag of yours 'ere. No sense in carting it upstairs.' He grinned, grey-uniformed and aware of his own importance; Guardian of the Gate.

Kit smiled, appreciating his thoughtfulness, and he hurried out of his sanctum. 'Which office d'yer want, heh?'

'Mr Henderson-Hobbs.'

He tweaked his nose in secret glee. Something going on here, all la-di-dah. 'Up in the lift. Top floor. I'll show you.'

With boots pointed at ten to three he pompously led her along the corridor. He saw her into the lift and showed her which button to press, then he watched the doors close on her and she glided heavenwards.

Miss Lilian Gibbs met her, but only because Miss Gibbs had been to the Ladies Room and hoped to get back to her desk before her absence was noted.

'Yes?' she queried as Kit approached.

'Mr Henderson-Hobbs' office, please?'

Lilian Gibbs opened the door of her own office and went in, then she remembered. She turned to Kit. 'Are you – ? Yes, of course, I saw you at the banquet. You are the manager's wife from Wales.'

Kit didn't like the way it was said, as if London was condescending to recognise Wales. 'Mrs Hemsworthy,' she said. 'I have reason to deliver last week's account.'

'That's right,' Lilian smiled. 'I was instructed to thank you very much for your trouble.'

Kit's jaw dropped slightly, but then she smiled and the disappointment failed to reach her eyes.

'There's a note here for you.' Miss Gibbs took it from the top drawer of her desk. 'Mr Henderson-Hobbs had to go out.'

Kit took the envelope, humiliated, thinking of the white gown in its black tissue wrapping.

'Thank you,' she said charmingly, and noticed the diamonds of her engagement ring sparkling, as if to remind her she belonged to Bertie.

She walked away quickly, straight-limbed and arrogant in her tailored navy serge costume. Blast the man! He had made a fool of her in the same way that he continued to make a fool of Bertie. You will get the sack. You won't get the sack. You will go to the theatre. You won't go to the theatre.

She felt small and demoralised.

The porter grinned as she reclaimed her overnight case. 'Good day, miss.'

'Good day, and thank you.' She went out to the street.

No idea of where to go or how to get there. Thoughts of home beckoned but, to come all this way and see nothing, not even the wond'rous lights of Piccadilly?

At the corner she stopped, lost, not knowing which way to turn nor what to do, the manila envelope still in her pocket. Impatiently she drew it out and considered flinging it away. It would be an apology, of course. Words that meant nothing to the sort of idiot men picked up for fun; Bertie with Elsie Buckley, her father with Chinese girls, Henderson-Hobbs with whom? Half London? He was attractive enough. In an ugly sort of way.

An open-topped three-wheeler Family Morgan stopped beside her, and Henderson-Hobbs called from behind the steering wheel. 'Like a lift, Kitten?'

She laughed. She wanted to swoop onto him, cry out rude things like, 'You silly ass,' but said nothing, only laughed, her eyes shining with happiness. He joined her at the kerb, flung her case to the back seat, then helped her into the front. Traffic manoeuvred around them but she felt miraculously alone with him.

'Robert! You idiot!'

It was as if they had always been together. As if they belonged together. Two people who understood and accepted each other, but had not yet made love. For a second he stood looking down at her, a little smile flickering about his mouth, then he hurried around the car and cocked his leg over the driver's door. He glanced up and down the road, prepared to slip into his seat, and there was a chap going up the Unicorn steps.

The fellow saw him and backtracked to the pavement. He raised a hand in greeting, and Robert wondered where he had seen that long crooked face before. He acknowledged the greeting then turned from it. Kit glanced back but saw no one. She laughed up at Robert and his attention flew to her.

He drove on and Kit opened the letter and read it. All it said was, 'I shall pick you up. Forget insurance. Forget respectability. Anticipating and happy. H.H.' She leaned towards him, confident nothing private could happen in an open-topped car, in a London street at lunchtime.

'Mrs Hemsworthy?' he said, without looking at her.

'Mr Henderson-Hobbs?'

'Are you going to sleep with me?'

She drew back, shaken, but he was laughing; it was fun, all fun. 'Oh no, sir,' and she was glad she had not unpacked the white jersey gown, and stayed home.

She didn't ask are you going to sack or transfer my husband? That would be insurance, and he had ordained that insurance be forgotten.

They lunched at the Savoy, and Kit felt she had been bred to it. Her eyes laughed into Robert's and she thought how young he looked, how fresh-faced; how being born into the security of money gave people that certain air the poor or struggling could never achieve.

Then she sat in the car again, expectant, her nose a little shiny, her lipstick not repaired. 'Where to now?'

He drove quickly, the picture of that man's crooked face in his mind. He said, 'The afternoon is yours. I'll pick you up about seven.'

'Where are we going then?'

'I thought you might enjoy a play at St James'. Gertrude Lawrence and Gerald du Maurier are in it.'

'What's it called?' She wanted to hug herself with pleasure. A London theatre? All dressed up? With Robert?

'*Behold We Live.*' He glanced at her, half smiling, and she wondered if he was sending her a message, and she was content to agree.

He dropped her at her hotel awning and returned to the office.

At three o'clock Miss Gibbs announced, 'A Mr John Davies to see you, Mr Henderson-Hobbs,' and Robert remembered the man on the steps. He slapped his brow. Of all the thousands of people rushing around, it had to be John Davies arriving as he met Kitten.

He blew out his lips in self-exasperation; 'Well,' he said

to Miss Gibbs, 'show the fellow in. Let's find out what he wants.'

John trod the Unicorn's grey carpet with renewed confidence. It wasn't blackmail. It wasn't anything, but he knew, and thought Robert must know, that a promise of promotion meant Bertie would not be told who Kit had looked so happy to be with.

John sat opposite Robert's desk as if he had designs on changing places.

Robert offered him a cigar and John refused. 'Rarely touch them.' It sounded like a judgement from Jehovah.

'So . . .' Robert said, refraining from smoking himself, shutting the cigar box slowly and quietly, 'why do you want a chat with me?'

John leaned forward, bony knees in best black, his big knuckly hands dangling between them, his fingers firm on the rim of his black felt hat. 'I came around earlier on. Just to see where the place was – '

'I recognised you,' Henderson-Hobbs smiled. 'I often take a decko first if I feel nervous.'

'I'm not nervous.'

'Good. I understand you are to submit a double account this week.'

'Yes.' John was taken aback. 'Mrs Hemsworthy said – '

'Naturally. You will see Mr Hemsworthy as usual on Wednesday, paying in then, so what is it you wish to chat to me about?'

John hesitated. The boss's attitude could be a bit inhibiting, in spite of the smile.

'I'm not getting on fast enough,' he said pointedly. 'I want my own district.'

Robert's eyes became slightly hooded but interested. He sat back, his head in an I'm listening gesture.

John lunged into his story: Welsh, ambitious, desperate, while, not far away, in a discreet hotel, Kit threw out her arms and twirled in the pleasure of being away from it all.

That evening, when Robert came again to the hotel,

she was soignée and waiting, her body swathed in the white jersey gown, the pointed toes of her sandals peeping from beneath the fishtail hem, her hair plaited and coiled about her head.

He stood for a moment, admiring, his top hat held by the brim at his side, his theatre cloak lined with scarlet.

The snobbery in Kit was more than satisfied, and she stood aside to allow him into her room, allow him to place the stole she had bought that afternoon about her shoulders, then she drew it to her, seeing him in the mirror, eyeing the gown, the way it covered so much, yet showed almost everything.

She reflected that, if ever she undressed for him, he would receive no shocks.

When she turned she did so deliberately, knowing she was being provocative, unexpectedly aware she had some kind of sensual power over this man. It was all so unlike being with Bertie.

Robert stayed close to her, recognising and amused by her behaviour. He handed her her black evening purse from the bed and, as they left the room, he put out the light and made sure the door was properly locked.

He didn't touch her, not even a fingertip against her arm as they entered the lift, and Kit felt a strange tightening in her, as of anticipation, suppressed excitement.

She felt sure that, for all this man's influence in the world of insurance, she was his ruler now. He would do nothing to offend her. Not tonight.

By the time they took their seats in the stalls Kit had completely forgotten Swansea and everyone in it. Here was the dream of escape come true, and it didn't occur to her that Elsie Buckley had experienced much the same each time she entered three hundred, Prince Edward Road. For Kit, here was succour, the glitter of evening dress all about her, the perfumes of women, the cigars of men, the artificial world of the stage and the crescendo of applause. If the King and Queen had been

263

in the ornate box above her she could not have felt more spiritually elevated. It was what Lorraine had brought her up to expect, and what Bertie had failed to give her.

Then she and Robert were just two in a throbbing mass surging from the theatre, having to readjust from the brightly-lit world of make-believe to the chill darkness of lamplit streets.

They walked quickly to the car, got in, slammed the doors on themselves, and Robert said, 'I have never married, you know,' and Kit didn't answer.

He glanced at her in the darkness, his right hand pale on the steering wheel where the glow of street lamps caught it, and Kit was terribly aware of him, an indefinable something that was warm and necessary to her.

Robert suddenly jerked his arms and shoulders and gave an exaggerated sigh. 'Supper!' he exclaimed. 'I think that is next on the agenda.'

And in this restaurant was a table in a secluded corner, with candlelight, and a pink rose in a crystal vase. There was a small orchestra, a space where couples held each other and waltzed, and tried not to think of tomorrow.

Robert ordered the meal, watched her sip her Martini, then suggested they dance.

For the first time ever Kit went into Henderson-Hobbs' arms and thought her breathing would stop. She regretted marrying Bertie, regretted living in South Wales, and she wished her heart didn't throb so, yet the sensation was divine.

Robert's cheek was against her ear. She and he could dance close together, not step on each other's toes, and she wanted to stay against his warmth, sensing the vibrations of him as their bodies moved.

Neither spoke. There seemed nothing to talk about, and neither looked at the other as they returned to their table. Robert acknowledged no one, and Kit wondered if this was because he had brought her where he was unknown. Hidden her away.

When he took her back to the hotel he travelled up in the lift with her, and the thoughts drummed into her brain; would he? Wouldn't he? There was also the fear that she would let him, and the fear that she would fail.

But he left her at the door, his eyes sober. He kissed the palm of her hand, then strode away. He paused only halfway along the corridor, turned and gave a half salute, then he was in the lift, going down, and she still hadn't asked about Bertie.

She wrapped the white gown away with the sandals and purse and, when she finally put out the light and settled to sleep, said a little prayer, 'Thank you God for today, and forgive all my yesterdays.'

There was no adding 'and all my tomorrows' because there would be nothing to forgive. There would never be another trip to London without Bertie. In retrospect, the dancing scared her. There had been no way of knowing her body could react like that to any man. And she vowed never again would there be any dancing with Henderson-Hobbs.

He telephoned her next morning, laughing, as if his few hours in bed had renewed and refreshed him.

'Good morning, Mrs Hemsworthy,' and Kit laughed back, her eyes still asleep, the bed warm about her.

'Good morning, Mr Henderson-Hobbs. How are you?'

'Splendid. Infinitely splendid. And you?'

'I don't know. I haven't awakened enough to find out.'

'Ah.' His voice lowered a note. 'And what was it you dreamed of?'

Here was her chance. In bed, the environment she only ever shared with Bertie, and Bertie's presence came to the fore.

'My husband.'

He laughed deep in his throat. 'So you were lonely in bed.'

'No,' and her voice held no intimacy, no familiarity. 'I dreamed that I had a wonderful night out with a wonderful man, then I felt I had been on holiday while

265

my husband slogged for an insurance firm. He needs a holiday too.' She didn't mention the dark blue rings around Bertie's eyes, nor the risk of a nervous breakdown, because employers don't want employees who can't stand the pace.

'Has he had a holiday this year?'

'No. Our last holiday was in a tent. It rained and thundered and the stream overflowed and washed us out.'

He laughed, but it was a different sort of laugh, a laugh that meant a creased forehead and hard thought.

She waited, her eyes open now, looking at the smooth white ceiling, and he said cautiously, 'I'm sending some of my top men to Bournemouth at the end of this month, for five days. It's a conference. We're considering reorganising the firm. Shifting people about.'

Now Kit was wide awake, her brain clicking fast. His top men? Bertie would love it. Boost his morale. Shifting people about? To Merseyside? No hint of the sack?

She thrust her fingers through her mass of loose black hair and sat up.

Robert said, 'Do you think he would appreciate the idea?'

'I shall ask him. Shall I?'

'No.' It was the businessman instructing. 'He'll receive the usual official notification.'

'You mean he'll have no choice?'

'His choice is in your hands right now. Is it Bournemouth or not?'

'Oh, it's Bournemouth,' she returned, a little awed at his decision-making, at his expecting her to think as fast as he.

'Right,' he retorted. 'I'll attend to it personally. Are you lunching with me today?'

She felt her body wriggle, as if trying to cuddle itself, and her hand was warm as it caressed her naked shoulder. 'No,' she said quietly. 'I have promised to be home by one.' She hadn't, but felt it wiser to end her visit to him now, while it was still sweet, and besides, she had to shop for take-home gifts.

There was a slight pause, but he made no attempt to dissuade her. 'As you wish,' he said, and she regretted refusing him, wanting to lunch with him, to see him and enjoy him. 'Thank you Robert. For everything.'

'You are charming, Kitten.'

'You are – ' He waited, but she didn't say fascinating, she said 'very kind', and a moment later he was saying, 'Thank you, Mrs Hemsworthy. Goodbye.'

'Goodbye, Mr Henderson-Hobbs,' and she lay quietly, not even replacing the telephone on the bedside table. Her thoughts were now steadfastly on Bertie.

She had to find some way of telling him John had telephoned, that the baby was ill. In hospital. She planned to take the rest of the day to work it out.

* * *

John had got home from London the previous day, as Maggie was returning from evening visiting at the hospital, and neither had good news for the other.

They went to bed talking little, and cuddled together wondering what the future held.

Then came the expected and dreaded knocking on the front door, and John went down to answer it with the lamp held above his head.

'Sion?' He peered at the white face amid the blackness of night.

'Yes, Mr Davies. It's me. The hospital – '

'Thank you, Sion. Go on home to bed, you. Good boy. We expected it.'

He closed the door and Maggie was behind him, not speaking, huddled in her dressing-gown.

Their clothes were ready before the banked-up fire, their eyes wide with the tension of the past hours.

'Good job that doctor warned me,' Maggie said tremulously. 'When he come out of the ward to tell me I thought I would die too. Good he is though. I told him you were away, in London – '

267

'I came home as soon as I could, cariad. I'd have come to the hospital after you if I had known.'

Her voice was erratic. 'After travelling all that way? Oooh, duw duw. To London and back in a day, then go all the way to Swansea? And no good could you do there. Me neither. I could only come home – '

Her plump hands fumbling with her clothes, the big kitchen cold, the clock ticking laboriously towards half-past one.

John asked, 'Shall we take the chocolate drops?' as if to make her believe there was yet hope.

Maggie gave a little nod, but her head was down as she climbed into the big black skirt, tears dripping to her bodice. 'Maybe he'll like one,' she snuffled.

'Do him good,' said John, without heart. 'Like cocoa.'

The horse and cart were waiting in the lane beside the shop, the side lights burning, but there was no sign of the Roberts family.

Bleakly Maggie boarded and unfolded the grey blanket John handed up to her. She opened it and, when John climbed up beside her, she tucked it around them both.

John flicked the reins and the cart rumbled to the main road. Everywhere was still and silent but for the sound of themselves.

At the hospital Sister Freda Jones waited and, in the strained silence, Maggie and John put on the white coats and rubber gloves.

In the small room Maggie stood beside the cot and murmured, 'I think I need a chair, cariad,' and Sister hurried away.

When she and the nurse returned, with the high-backed armless chair, Maggie had Buck in her arms, and John stood, legs spread, as if ready to defend her.

Sister Jones rebuked quickly, 'Mrs Davies!' and, with the chair placed in the corner, she advanced on Maggie. 'He has to go back in the cot. Keep warm.'

'Don't come near, cariad!' Maggie said softly in Welsh. 'Almost a week you've had him, and done no good. Now it's my turn. My love will cure him, Freda Jones.'

'Mrs Davies! Please! You're getting me into trouble!'

'Scream you,' Maggie taunted. 'Call the doctor. The fire brigade if you like. Get the matron out of bed. But in my arms he is now, and there he's staying.'

Sister hesitated, hearing the crack in Maggie's voice. 'Oh come now, Mrs Davies.' She tried to soothe.

'I gave him up once – ' Maggie swayed Baby Buck gently to and fro, her right hand pat-patting the small of his back, the heat of him burning through the clothes about him, ' – for the ambulance. And he got pneumonia. Neglect!' Maggie drove the accusation around the room.

'Maggie,' John entreated softly. 'Don't go getting all worked up. You'll upset the baby.'

She blinked fast, her face thinner than a week ago, and she nodded at him, gulping back more words of accusation.

'Sit down now,' John persuaded her, and it was as if the nurse and sister were no longer there, because neither said a word.

Maggie sat and the baby face moved slightly. Maggie saw it and gasped. 'Oh John! How right you were,' and she didn't notice the nurse and sister glide from the room. She said, 'Help me, love. Open this silly white coat. Get these gloves off. Smell they do.'

She murmured to the baby, promising never to leave him again, and she opened her coat and her blouse and brought her breast up from inside the big brassiere. 'There, my child. Feel Mamgi warm and soft against your cheek.' She swayed back and forth, humming a little tune.

John stayed until about five o'clock. By then Maggie was sitting back in the chair, her brassiere wide open, the baby face squashed against her. John kissed her and promised to return after he had given the horse and cart back to Sion senior.

Maggie nodded, but he knew she was too preoccupied

with the baby to notice him, and he had a special task to do.

The lavatory.

As dawn came coldly over the mountain tops, he stood in the garden and wondered where God was when such help and understanding were needed here.

He dug as if crazed, his arms and shoulders strong with frustration and despair. He sweated in the chill of day and he trundled the wooden hut from the old hole to the new. He checked the latch and promised himself that fever would never have the chance to get at his family again. He would be a manager. Buck would come home to a finer future.

He put the spade away and washed his hands in the cold water gushing from the outside tap, wiping them on a strip of sacking. He went into the lean-to, and came out again carrying an enamel bowl piled high with wrung-out washing, a bag filled with dolly-pegs over his wrist.

He worked quickly, worrying. A week ago tonight Buck had been taken into the ambulance and, for that week, his job had suffered. Yesterday no collecting at all had been done. He had been in London. Today he should do a double account.

His awkward fingers tried to rush, dropped a shirt onto the earth and snapped a peg in half, but a breeze was rising. The clothes began to billow.

Then he heard Maggie sob.

He turned, startled, thinking she was behind him. He felt as if his soul had succumbed to mourning, and he left the still half-filled bowl and the bag of pegs on the path.

He needed to get to Maggie.

Far away she was still sitting in the soft leather chair beside the cot, cuddling the baby to her, staring at the little scarlet face, not believing the dreaded had happened so easily.

The baby lips were still pink, the baby fist still curled

270

against his chin, but there had been that long deep sigh, that odd rumbling, groaning sound as his lungs emptied.

'Oh Iesu Mawr!' Maggie moaned. 'Great Jesus, don't do this to me,' and terror curdled in her soul.

She lifted Buck upright before her, and shook him. She breathed his name, her own heart struggling to beat against the shock and disbelief. Then she screamed, 'Sister! Sister!' and sat with Buck hugged tightly against her, her fingers clawed into the white blanket.

Feet ran, padding down the corridor, and Sister's face was agape with realisation, her arms and hands outstretched. 'In the cot, Mrs Davies! Put him in the cot! Do yourself up!'

'No!' Maggie wailed, and her face was a grimace of wide wet mouth and bulging tortured eyes. 'He's mine. He's mine.' Her voice broke, ready to shriek, and Sister slapped her face lightly, her fingers sinking momentarily into the soft loose folds of Maggie's cheek. 'Nurse!' she ordered. 'Call Doctor, then make Mrs Davies a cup of tea. Quickly!'

The dead baby was put in the cot and covered as if alive, and Maggie's blouse was pulled closed, her white coat buttoned and the rubber gloves dragged back on as she still sat. Sister crouched by her, glaring into her face. 'The sack! D'you want me to get the sack? And what good would that do? Who'd care for the other mites? Go and see them in that ward.'

Maggie moaned, and Sister caught her under one arm and heaved. 'Come on. Into the kitchen. You ought to have a bath and all. Be scrubbed.'

Maggie got to her feet but swerved to the cot, 'Oh annwyl . . .' my beloved, she moaned, and sank slowly to her knees. 'I told them,' she sobbed. 'I told them I wanted to go in the ambulance with him. Caught cold then, he did. Taking him from the warmth of me, out into all that rain.'

'Mrs Davies.' The nurse was back, white-faced. 'Mrs Davies. Come and have a cup of tea?'

Then the doctor was there, serious, covering Buck's head with the sheet, and Maggie clung to the cot rails, suddenly very old.

'Oh annwyl,' she moaned, and pleaded with God to return breath to her baby's body.

The nurse, the sister, and the doctor got her from the room. She was sagging, as if boneless. They put her into an armchair in the staff-room and were still watching her when John rushed in, hot-faced, the cost of a taxi gone from his pocket.

Maggie held out her arms to him. 'Why us?' she cried. 'Great Jesus. Why us?'

CHAPTER ELEVEN

Big Tom Buckley sat on the doorstep of Maud Jeffries' house and scowled, the stump of his right wrist resting in his left hand. He saw the sole of his right boot was flapping off again. He had nailed it on twice. One nail had come through and torn his big toe. He had stuck a layer of cardboard in as protection. Now this.

He examined the boot, cursing softly, then scratched the tip of his ugly red and purple nose. He scowled at the kids playing football on the hardened patch of ground between him and the top of the wall; they were bare-footed, almost bare-arsed, snotty-nosed, and winter hadn't set in properly yet.

The football was a battered leather cover stuffed with newspaper, but it tolerated the kicking. It came whizzing at Big Tom's head and he dodged, then he moved from the house, stiff, surly. That used to be his house. His and Gwen's, with young Tommy and Elsie.

He spat fruitily.

He missed Gwen. She shouldn't have gone to Malvern like that. And died. That was flaming Hemsworthy for you. Sticking his stuck-up nose in.

He missed Elsie. And he had never really seen the baby. He wished now he had seen the baby. When it wasn't ill. Must have been a fine little nipper.

The hurdy-gurdy man stopped on the other side of the road. From his stance above the stone supporting wall Tom could see the man in rags. Army greatcoat, and boots that were too big for him. Any fool could see they were too big. They were turning up at the toes.

Tom grinned. Army boots with bloody great studs in 'em, turning up at the toes. Must be crippling him.

The organ-grinder turned the handle of the organ and the notes tinkled out, drowned now and then by the heaviness of traffic, but Tom knew the tune: 'By the side of the Zuider Zee, Zuider Zee . . .'

'Hoi!' he bawled playfully. 'Ain't you got nothing better?'

The organ-grinder grinned and nodded, knowing the yell was for him, but not hearing the words. He put his old grey cap upside down on the top of the organ and took his red-trousered monkey on his shoulder, its brown inquisitive eyes watching the children and mongrels gather.

Elsie used to listen for the organ-grinder. Danced sometimes for him, laughing and singing the Zuider Zee. Tom put his hand in his trouser pocket and felt for money. He found four big pennies. One looked brand new, gleaming copper with the date, 1933, stamped beneath Britannia and her shield ruling the waves. He flung it into the air and heard it tinkle as the traffic was momentarily silent, and with the silence came Maud Jeffries, up the steps.

'Throwing yer money way again, Tom Buckley. No wonder yer never pays me no rent.'

'He needs it more than you do.'

'Don't you believe it. There's money in begging these days. Everybody's doing it.' She stood grinning at him, her grey bun screwed tightly on top of her head, her black shawl caught with a big safety-pin on her chest, one arm about a large white loaf of bread. 'I been making arrangements fer the wedding,' she said. 'The cars'll cost two pounds ten and a cake'll be ten bob.'

'A cake? Cars? You don't need all that!' He was aghast.

'An' I got another 'ouse,' she went on, as if she hadn't heard him. 'So you c'n get over there'n clean it up. Make sure there're no bugs nor rats. You c'n have the front bedroom there, just fer you'n Tommy till we're hitched, then I'll join yer.'

274

'To live?'

'Not ter die, I'll tell yer that much. You'll be my old man then, won't yer? You'll do the work then, boyo. I'll help, don't you worry, until yer learn the ropes. And later we'll buy a big house and turn it into a hotel.'

She gazed up at him, pleased with herself, and Tom gazed back, his brain slower than hers.

'All right?' she demanded.

'Yeah,' he agreed. 'As you say, but I gotta go now. Got my own business to attend to.'

'Like what?'

'Like seeing a man about a dog,' then he grinned at her, his method of charming. 'You going ter wear white then? And a veil with orange blossom and that?'

She laughed, her eyes twinkling at him, and he strode past her, then down the steps. He needed time to get adjusted. A hotel? Godamighty! Are all women like that? Grabbing? Wanting more?

Elsie had wanted more. Deserved more. She hadn't deserved to be used by sodding Albert Hemsworthy.

His fingers found the remaining three coppers still in his trouser pocket. He could have a mug of strong ale . . . or he could get two eggs for the baby.

TWO eggs! There'd be nutrition for him.

He strolled casually now he knew where he was going, his flannel shirt still open to the waist, his loose sole click-clicking against the pavement. He kept his shirt sleeves rolled up and stopped to look in shop windows. He didn't want anyone knowing he was going to spend his last stever on two eggs, then take them to the hospital over two miles away.

Once across the New Cut bridge and out of the salty slimy tang of dockland, he walked faster, but still slouched, naturally disgruntled. He saw a sign fixed to a lamp post warning a two pounds fine for spitting in the street. So Big Tom spat, and murmured, 'That to them,' then went on.

He limped through the gateway of the hospital as his

big toe became more troublesome and he went down the slope to the wards. He enquired. He listened and, at first, shock stopped him hearing. 'What d'yer say? Gorn? He was my grandson!' He glared, and the nurse smiled kindly and touched his arm as if to send him away. 'His mother and father will attend to him,' she said softly.

'Where is he now, huh?'

'In the mortuary.'

He turned from her, hurt and bewildered, and stamped with his flapping sole back up the slope.

On the street there were trees. Posh. Trees planted in the pavement. And a grass verge. Over rooftops he could see the channel. Not the docks part with cranes and galleys and funnels, but the lovely part, the Mumbles, where there were oyster beds and folk with so many jobs they could choose.

He looked at the brown paper bag in his hand; the two eggs, pale with pointed ends, as if the chicken had struggled, constipated.

He held the bag out, in the centre of the pristine pavement, then he dropped it. He heard the eggs crack, but nothing appeared, no yellow goo, no sticky colourless white, so he rammed the heel of his better boot onto it, and he kept ramming, as if he was ramming all his loneliness, all his lack of understanding, into the faces of those who knew nothing about it and didn't care anyway.

He wandered on, down to Sketty, a land new to him, and there were the pubs, two of them, facing each other. But he had no money. He stood in the porch of one and sniffed, taking in the smell of booze, filling himself with it, then he strolled out, defiant. In a month he would be his own boss; a married man, in charge of two dosshouses. A man of commerce.

He'd show 'em. In fact he'd start now. He'd go home thataway. Down there. Past the posh park, and he would go along Prince Edward Road . . .

He walked, chuckling. He would get to number 300 and he would gob extra juicily, right in the middle of those fancy red tiles between Bertie Hemsworthy's gate and front door. He would settle the swine who'd put our Elsie in the pudding club, then banished her from his house when her belly was growing.

As he strolled he tried not to hear the flopping of the loose sole. He wished more than ever before that he had a right hand. A left hand to hold the swine. A right hand to smash him.

Pulverise him. Fragment him.

Forgotten was his own evil-tempered disapproval of Elsie. Now she was his dear girl, the kid who had been led astray, led to her death by a man who had money, position, power. A capitalist. Hang the bugger!

Prince Edward Road wasn't as near as he had imagined, and when he did reach it he found it was long; house after house, all with imposing front doors above a marble-topped step.

He knew three hundred. Had been there before. He stood before it, tired, jobless now for three years. Hadn't he walked with the crowd of other unemployed men to Dagenham, seeking work in the new car factory there? Hadn't he got shot at by a Dagenham fool who wanted to keep him out? Hadn't he come home to nothing, while this swine lived in luxury, preying on young girls?

He spat. In the gutter. Somehow it wouldn't look right on those red tiles. Sort of blasphemous to Elsie and her bastard son.

He needed a drink. A pub. The fellowship of loud male voices, the smell of beer slopping on tables, a sawdust-covered floor, the acrid inhaling of cheap tobacco smoke.

Gawd! He needed a drink.

Linda saw him. Linda, that early Tuesday afternoon, while her mother was still in London. Linda, weary of typing letters with two fingers, of rubbing out until bits of eraser littered the inside of the black-keyed machine. She wandered to the window, fenced in by a job she needed but didn't like, and there was Tommy's father.

277

Joy overwhelmed her. Tommy had sent a message! Then another thought filled her mind: Tommy was in trouble. Tommy was going to China? Or India? Or somewhere awful.

She forgot her fear of the ex-furnaceman. She ran to the porch door and opened it, then stepped out, onto that black and white marble step and waited, her lips apart, allowing a glimpse of her young shining perfect teeth.

'Mr Buckley!' She was panting, her hands clasped in anticipation.

He hadn't expected her. Hadn't thought of her. He removed his cap and rolled it up, holding it before his chest. She was a lady. He had seen it before, but not like this. A real lady. She had class coming out of her earholes.

'I bin to the hospital,' he said, awed by this new dimension of her, 'and I come ter say sorry.' He hadn't, but now it seemed opportune and right to do so. Gentlemanly.

'Say sorry?' For a moment she was unaware of his meaning, then she remembered the scene in the back bedroom of Salubrious Terrace and went scarlet, her shoulders liting as if to protect her head from his hard clutching hand. 'Oh – ' She thought quickly, of the terrible way he lived, of the gloom about him, and said, 'We all get our off days.'

She wondered whether to invite him in. It was rude to leave him outside, yet she didn't think it wise to do anything else.

She had an idea. 'If you wait a moment, I'll tell Daddy you're here.'

Daddy! Suddenly Big Tom didn't want to meet Daddy. Not now. Not until he'd had a drink. You couldn't slosh a man just like that. Not when you needed a drink.

Daddy came striding, an impatient frown on his face. 'Mr Buckley!' He flung out an arm, gesturing Tom from the gate. 'Look for your son elsewhere. He is no more welcome here than you are.' Bertie drew Linda in, and prepared to close the door.

278

'My son!' Tom jeered, and wished he had spat on those tiles. 'Not my son now, Mr Soddin' Hemsworthy, sir. It's yours. And he's dead. Get it? Dead.' Tom felt a delight at seeing the insurance manager's face change to an expression of high dudgeon: the bloody idiot didn't believe him; think he'd come round here ter tell some damn fool story like that? So he repeated it. 'A gonner! Your son is done for. Corpsed!' Tom poked his forefinger towards Bertie. 'And he was my grandson, and you didn't 'ave the backbone ter come and tell me. To tell me my girl's kid was at death's door!'

Bertie's mouth was open, his gaze darting from the pointing finger to the wrathful face, then he laughed deeply, derisively, his lips curling as he watched Big Tom but flicked a hand so Linda would know he spoke to her. 'Phone the police. Now. Fast. Get the Black Maria. I want this man arrested for intimidation, disturbing the peace!'

Linda's feet moved in dismay but she stayed beside him. 'Daddy – '

Tom Buckley opened the gate and came in, his great shoulders hunched. 'You're a sewer rat, Mr blasted big 'ead. Get the police. Fetch 'em. I'll wait. Get it in the papers. Let 'em all know you disown yer own son even when he's laid out. Ready fer his box.'

'Get out!' Bertie stormed, his face ashen, his fists tight to his sides. 'Or I'll fling you out myself!'

Linda caught the edge of her father's jacket. 'Daddy don't! Daddy!' then, 'Daddy. The phone is ringing!'

'Well answer the blasted thing, and you, Tom Buckley, shove off. Get your rotten trouble-making tongue away from my property!'

Tom lifted his stump of a wrist so it jutted from his sleeve, shining and pink and threatening. 'I've bin wanting ter give you a pug in the lug, mister, fer a long time – '

The telephone still jangled and Linda ran to answer it, panic-stricken. 'Hello?'

The sharp Welsh voice demanded, 'Kit Hemsworthy?'

'No. It's me. Linda.'

'Get your father to the phone, Linda. Tell him it's Maggie Davies.'

Linda turned and ran into a chair, gasped and saved herself but left the chair on its back.

The men were almost nose to nose, grimacing, each waiting for the other to make a false move.

'Daddy! It's Maggie on the phone! Maggie Davies!'

Big Tom became aware of her voice first. He looked quickly at her then back at Bertie, his chest heaving. 'There,' he leered. 'Get it from the horse's mouth,' and Bertie began to wonder.

'Don't you go,' he glared at Big Tom. 'You and I have business to clear up. You flung Elsie onto the streets. I took her in. Me and my wife.'

'The phone, Daddy!'

'Yah!' sneered Tom Buckley. 'Yer shitarse!'

Bertie flushed, the purple vein in his forehead swollen and throbbing.

He strode to the phone, kicking the toppled chair out of the way. 'Yes?' he barked into the receiver.

Maggie spoke slowly and deliberately, determined to wound. 'Your son, Mr Hemsworthy, is dead. Gone to his mother. God bless her. And I hope the news sees you in hell – '

'Maggie!' He felt ripped apart. 'What's going on? For God's sake!'

'You need God, Mr Hemsworthy. That you could say you wanted your son in one breath, then not go near him on his deathbed.'

'Maggie!' It was a scream, dreadful and agonising. 'I didn't even know he was ill. I still don't know.' He stopped, panting and distraught, then went on, less loudly, 'How can I know if you don't tell me?' The wires hummed and he cried, frightened, 'Maggie? Are you still there?'

'Yes,' she said quietly. 'I am still here, Mr Hemsworthy,' and they both went silent as if to draw breath.

Bertie said, 'God alive, Maggie, I honestly didn't know. This is terrible. A terrible shock. You've done what you wanted. You've put me in hell.'

Still Maggie remained silent.

He went on brokenly, 'Tom Buckley just called to tell me and I didn't believe him. I was going to call the police to have him arrested. I've been worried sick about John not paying in. I've been up to your place twice. I let the cat out – '

'Your wife knew.'

'Kit? She couldn't have. She would have told me. She loved Buck. Wanted us to keep him!'

'Your wife knew.'

'Dear God. I'm sorry. Oh dear God.' He lifted the toppled chair and sagged into it. 'Maggie – '

She didn't speak.

'Did he have an accident? Was he hurt? Did he cry?'

Bertie wanted to cry, still trying to believe this was a macabre joke. None of it made sense.

'No,' Maggie said quietly. 'He didn't cry. Not once. Not all the time. And he didn't have an accident. I wouldn't let him have an accident. Adored him too much I did, for that. I was nursing him when – when – ' She began to sob, and Bertie put out a hand as if to reach her, but there was only the cold hard wood of his desk.

'I'll come over, Maggie. I'll be with you as soon as a train can get me there.'

'Yes,' Maggie said, still unforgiving. 'It's the least you can do.'

'Is he home with you now?'

'No. He won't ever come home again. It was the fever.'

She replaced the receiver in the kiosk, and Bertie turned to see Big Tom standing in the office doorway with Linda peeping around him.

Bertie looked into Linda's eyes and saw the guilt. 'Linda! You knew he was ill!'

'Oh Daddy.'

Other footsteps came running into the house. Emma,

281

hot and red-faced from rushing. 'I've come to tell you I'll be late home tonight. Miss Griffiths says – '

'To hell with Miss Griffiths! Emma! You knew Baby Buck was ill?'

She nodded dumbly, alarmed.

'And now he's dead!'

Emma moved closer to Big Tom's side, seeking protection, her eyes suddenly enormous and very wet. 'He had to, Daddy. Or God would have – '

'My own daughters taught to be cheats and liars. To me. Their father!'

Red lights flashed in Bertie's head. He thumped the desk so the pens, the pencils and the papers jumped. 'And my wife. She knew. Your mother knew!'

It was a double whisper. 'Yes, Daddy.'

He tried blinking the stabbing headache away. 'You, Mr Buckley, can take your leave. There is no further link between yours and mine. Good day to you.'

Big Tom paused, the two girls tucked tightly against him in the passageway.

'Mr Buckley!' Bertie cried. 'Get out!'

For a few seconds longer Tom stood there, his face a mask of apprehension, amazed at what he was witnessing. Yet Hemsworthy wasn't bashing anybody, wasn't storming to get drunk. He said, as if ashamed of being an intruder, 'I'm sorry, guv'nor. I didn't know – '

Bertie nodded as if understanding, but his voice was curt. 'Get out!'

Linda pushed between Big Tom and the door frame. 'Daddy. You can't quarrel with Mr Buckley. I'm going to marry Tommy.'

'You, my girl, are going to have a tanned arse. Mr Buckley. I told you to go.'

'Daddy! I'll go too. I'll go to China with Tommy!' Her chest was tight with fear and rebellion. 'You quarrel with everybody. It makes us all unhappy.'

Emma squashed forward too, and Big Tom looked down at her and Linda, his own fury lost amid the conflict he saw here. 'Mr Hemsworthy – Captain sir – '

'Get out, Tom. It wasn't right that you should know before I did.' Bertie's voice mellowed with weariness, and slowly Tom backed. In the porch he drew his sleeve across his mouth and said softly, 'If you two kids need a friend, come on over to us,' then he went, the sole of his boot flipping, flapping, as if preparing to trip him.

Emma gazed despairingly after him, then gasped, 'I've got to go back to school. We're practising the Christmas concert,' and she ran, her dark hair bobbing about her ears.

Linda went into the office and stood silently watching her father.

'I'm going out,' he said. 'I need to see Maggie and John. Get the truth. Your mother will be back from London before I get home. Tell her from me she should have stayed there.'

Linda watched him go, then ran upstairs. She tipped her school satchel empty onto her bed, then refilled it with clean socks, knickers, cardigan, nightie and her post office savings book.

She hurried to the kitchen, and took the shilling piece that was kept on the mantelpiece for the electricity meter, then she went to the biscuit tin in the pantry and took the coal money, the milk and laundry money.

Quickly she scrawled a note and put it on the pink blotter on Bertie's desk.

The telephone rang beside her and she walked past it, her navy beret on the side of her head, her satchel over her shoulder, but the phone kept ringing and, at the porch door, she turned back, unclipping the receiver and speaking tonelessly. 'Unicorn Insurance Company.'

'Linda?' Lorraine's voice came clearly over the wires. 'That you, darling?'

The wonder of hearing her grandmother's voice at that emotional moment made Linda want to cry and she couldn't reply.

'Darling? Linda?' Lorraine's voice became anxious.

'Yes, Grandma.'

'Are you crying, child?'

'No, Grandma.'

'Well, what is it? You sound all sniffly.'

'It's a cold. A cold in my head,' Linda lied quickly as if Lorraine could know she was packed and leaving.

'Why are you in that office with a cold? You ought to be in bed. Where's your father?'

'Just gone out, Grandma.'

'Your mother then. For heaven's sake dear!'

'She's gone to London. John Davies didn't pay in last week,' sniff sniff, 'so the account was awfully late, and Mummy has taken it to London.'

'Oh dear,' breathed Lorraine. 'And no one told me a thing. I am so glad I phoned, darling. You've all been on my mind so much. When are you leaving school? Is it this term?'

'I left, Grandma. Last July.'

Lorraine went silent, then, cautiously, 'Are you staying home now? All day, I mean, even when you aren't poorly? I thought you were coming up here. To Malvern.'

'I can't go to finishing school now, Grandma. Daddy might be getting his notice. Dismissal. So Mummy doesn't have much money – '

'Piffle! Your father is punishing the lot of you for his foolhardiness. Your mother actually goes on her knees to scrub that kitchen floor! Now listen here, darling. You must finish your education. You can't be stuck in that great house like this . . .'

Linda hugged the phone and thought of escaping to finishing school; visions of dormitory frolics rose before her; hampers and midnight feasts. Friends. And Tommy being an officer, coming to visit her. All the girls swooning over him, green with envy.

'Darling?'

'Yes, Grandma?'

'Go to bed now. Have you any lemons in the house? Make a lemon drink, and the moment your father comes

284

in tell him to wrap some goosegrease on a flannel about your throat. I won't keep you now, dear. Tell Mummy I will phone again tomorrow to see how you are. All right?'

'Yes, Grandma.'

'Oh dear.' Lorraine was dithering. 'Better still, ask Mummy AND Daddy to ring me the moment they get in.'

'Yes, Grandma.'

Then Grandma had gone, and Linda didn't make a lemon drink.

She ran away from home.

Kit arrived at High Street station in the early evening and no one was there to meet her.

She stood for a while at the kerb with her suitcase on the ground beside her, then, as the yard cleared of travellers, she felt increasingly conspicuous. Bertie should not keep her waiting like this. She had promised she would arrive at this time, and he should be here to meet her.

She stalked to the telephone kiosk and rang the office. There was no reply.

She pondered. If Bertie had been held up and she took a taxi, he might get here, not find her and hang around for the next train.

Taxis were returning to the station, lining up, their drivers eyeing her curiously then surreptitiously. They knew how long she had been there.

She checked the contents of her purse. The hotel had not been cheap and she was loath to spend more, but as the first drops of rain fell and the cold began seeping into her, she beckoned a driver.

She arrived home to find the house empty. No kettle boiling. No fire. No welcome.

Pettishly she took off the white velour helmet and flung it to the table, the proud feather in it bending and folding.

This was a dreadful anti-climax. She had left London in a state of guilt, ready to confess her wickedness to Bertie, beg his forgiveness because she had spent last evening, socially, with another man.

She had expected recriminations. She might even have cried. She had not expected nothing.

The telephone in the office rang and she hurried to answer it. 'Hello. Unicorn Insurance Company.'

'At last!' came a furious male voice. 'Are you all on holiday there?'

'I'm sorry. Have you had trouble getting through?'

'I've been ringing all afternoon and got no reply.'

'I am sorry,' Kit repeated, and alarm bells were ringing. The place empty all afternoon? 'What can I do for you? This is Mrs Hemsworthy.'

'I keep telling your office about no one calling on me and now I've had a letter saying I'm lapsed.'

'Oh dear. Can you give me your name and address, please?'

'Madam. You should know it by heart now. My name is Browne. With an E. I work at the docks – '

'The docks? We don't have an agent calling at the docks – '

'Precisely. And I am not at home when your agent calls at my house. So now they've lapsed me, and I'll lose all I have paid in.'

Kit thought hard. 'I do remember,' she said slowly. 'You have written to us, haven't you? Isn't it possible someone tried to see you?'

'No one. And I will thank you kindly if you would give me some attention.'

'Yes, Mr Browne, of course. I shall most certainly attend to it at the soonest possible moment.'

'I shall write to your Head Office. They should be informed of the situation.'

'I assure you – '

'And I assure you, Mrs Hemsworthy, your service is not good enough.'

He rang off sharply. Kit hung her receiver up gently. The morning's mail was on Bertie's desk unopened, and there was the note in hurried schoolgirl handwriting. 'Dear Everybody. Do not look for me. I am

286

going to be with Tommy. For ever. Linda.'

Kit read it again, partly shocked, disbelieving, then realising she had been expecting it for some time.

She went to the kitchen and made herself a cup of tea, then she lit the fire. All the time she listened for the front door opening, for Linda to scowl in, to explain the note had been a mistake, for Bertie to fling his hat to the hallstand, for the chatter of voices. And where was Emma?

She went to the office and tried to work, but her family was missing and she couldn't concentrate. She put the stone hot-water bottles in the beds, and the girls' nighties over the oven door beside the fire to warm. She set the table for supper, four places, and she kept patting her hands together and telling herself not to panic.

At last the porch door flew open and Kit ran to call, greeting, switching on the passage light. 'Emma? Where have you been until this time of night?'

'I told Daddy. It was special. I'm in the Christmas concert and we had to stay to practise.'

'But it's gone seven o'clock!'

'We had tea in the hall, then we cleared it all away and planned the concert.'

Emma stood, not understanding her mother's lack of correct response. 'I told Daddy. I did.'

'All right. You told Daddy. But why isn't he here? And why should Linda run away today?'

Emma dropped her satchel at the bottom of the stairs and waved her arms helplessly, then thought up a solution. 'She felt like it today.'

Kit crouched to see into her daughter's face more clearly and Emma's cheeks were pink from rushing, her thick dark fringe pushed up in sweaty stiffness. 'Tell me about it,' Kit invited, and Emma put her arms about her mother's neck, her blue eyes big. 'Miss Griffiths told me to come home and tell you and Daddy I would be late because of the concert.'

'Yes?'

287

'And there was a terrible row. And Mr Buckley was here and Maggie Davies was horrid – '

'She was here too?' Apprehension filled Kit's face. So Bertie knew the baby was ill, that she had not told him. She sat on the lower stair, her legs feeble, and Emma struggled to retain her hold, frightened at the way the colour of her mother's face had changed. 'Yes, darling. I'm listening.'

It was Emma's turn to crouch now, staring into her mother's eyes with deep concern. 'And Mummy . . .' It was a pathetic unwilling whisper.

'Yes, my darling?'

'Baby Buck is dead.'

Kit's hands caught the featherweight little body and held it close, while the small voice went on huskily, 'God did send the angel of death, and Daddy was shouting, and Linda said she would go away.'

The lump in Kit's throat felt real, solid.

'Oh darling,' she choked. 'If only I had told him.' She released Emma and found her handkerchief, using it to rub the tip of her nose hard as she tried to think clearly, not to rush into more problems. 'A cup of tea,' she said, and managed a smile at her younger daughter. 'Be together.' She stood up and took Emma's hand, coaxing her to the kitchen, murmuring, 'The baby dead . . . I wonder where Linda is . . .'

'In China,' Emma piped helpfully.

Kit gave a suffocated laugh. 'Why China?'

'To find Tommy.'

Kit lifted Emma into Bertie's chair, wanting to hug her, keep her close emotionally and physically. 'He's not in China. He's up near Aldershot somewhere.'

The clock ticked, the fire crackled, the telephone was silent, the porch door closed.

Linda had left home. Baby Buck was dead. Dead.

Memories swamped her: Baby Buck chuckling before he was given a name; dribbling, sleeping, screaming, sucking hard on his bottle, burping, content as she held his legs in the air and flicked powder on his pink bottom, his nappies in the bucket in the scullery; all before Maggie came and stole him away.

Kit wondered if her heart would ever heal. Her brain searched frantically for something to do, some way of helping someone, if only herself.

She made the pot of tea but didn't drink. She left Emma with a fresh currant cake and knife and went to the office. She had to get in touch with Aldershot. Find Linda. Her body trembled with a mixture of fears as she awaited the operator's pleasure then, although Aldershot wanted to be helpful, what was Private Buckley's number?

'I'll call you back,' she cried, and ran to Linda's room. She scrabbled in drawers, and eventually found Tommy's number in Linda's bible under her pillow, along with a silk text that entreated, Suffer Little Children To Come Unto Me. Kit murmured intolerantly that He didn't have to take them so young, and ran back to the telephone.

Aldershot could do nothing immediately, they said. They would make enquiries. Probably ring her back.

'Where is China, Mummy?'

'I don't exactly know, darling,' she lied rather than try to explain. 'We'll look at a map tomorrow.'

She put Emma to bed and stayed until the child was sound asleep, still pink-cheeked, then, leaving the bedroom door open and the landing light on, Kit crept downstairs to worry.

She sat in the office, so cold she put her coat on and huddled into it. She watched the telephone, urging it to ring with news that would bring relief.

It did.

'Mrs Hemsworthy?'

'Tommy!' She wanted to hug him, thank him over and over. 'Oh bless you for ringing. Is Linda with you?'

'No!' He was startled. 'I don't know nothing. Isn't she home with you?'

'Tommy. Listen. I've just got back after a business trip. There is no one here but Emma and me. There was a note from Linda on my husband's desk saying she has gone to you.'

'Mrs Hemsworthy.' His voice began to rise with anxiety. 'Shall I tell the police?'

'No!' She gulped with shame at the way she was putting respectability before the safety of her daughter. 'We'll give her time . . .'

'I'll watch out for her and if she comes – '

'When she comes, Tommy.'

'When she comes,' he stood corrected. 'I'll phone you again.'

She sighed, feeling she could do no more just yet.

The sound of the receiver going back into its rest seemed over-loud, and she sat another hour, waiting. At nine o'clock Tommy phoned again, his voice full of confidence and self-importance now. 'The sergeant just told me, Mrs Hemsworthy. They picked Linda up. She's on her way here.'

Kit went to the kitchen, her knees sagging, and drank a steaming hot cup of tea while she screwed up her eyes to keep tears of relief away.

Bertie arrived home after midnight.

Kit heard him creeping in, and she sat in her chair facing the kitchen door and waited. If there was to be a row, let it be now. Keep nothing back. Let him have the lot. The anger. The resentment. The jealousy.

The kitchen door opened and he came in. She stared coldly at him, her veneer of calm well in place. She said, 'You have been drinking.'

'I have been to the club.' He stood, brooding, his hat on the back of his head, his hands in his trouser pockets, his jacket open, his tie loosened.

'You look uncouth.'

'You look beautiful, but you're a viper. I dislike you intensely.'

One corner of Kit's mouth tilted. 'The truth at last.'

He swayed a little. 'I thought I married a woman. I married a gatepost.'

Kit watched him for a full minute. He wasn't just tipsy, he was strange. She reconsidered her ideas of battle and said quietly, 'Shall I make black coffee?'

'I'd prefer milky tea.'

'I shall make milky tea.' She got to her feet slowly, as if nervous of jolting him.

'You are a cheat by nature,' he goaded, 'and you are training our daughters to be the same.'

'We will discuss everything in the morning.'

'You will tell me now what you should have told me last Wednesday.'

She moved to the table and Bertie moved with her. His long slim hand shot out and grabbed her wrist; he squeezed and she squealed. 'Bertie! You're hurting me!'

'My son is dead.'

Kit felt a drumming in her ears, knowing the depth of his sorrow, sensing his anguish.

'I'm sorry,' she said quietly. 'I am. Terribly sorry.'

'Cow!'

Startled, she gaped into his face. 'Bertie! You've never used that word before!'

'I can think of others. You took your white gown to London.'

She tried to spin from him, but his grip was tight. 'How do you know?'

'I looked. In the box on top of your wardrobe.'

'You pried? Spied on me?'

'This is my house. I am master here. You are my wife.'

'You brought your tart home. Had your bastard son born here!'

'Shut up, wife.' His lips were drawn tightly. 'If I had every tart in town the blame would be yours. When did you ever want me? When did you ever say you loved me without your eyes wavering under the weight of your lies? There's a nasty smell about you, Kitty Nolan – '

She snatched up a fork and stabbed it into his hand.

She watched the four white punctures gradually turn pink, then red, and the blood began to ooze.

'Look!' she said disgustedly. 'Whisky. Pouring out of you.'

He didn't release his hold. He said, 'I feel like raping somebody,' and her fear became even more real. She tugged her arm, struggling to free herself, and he smiled, inclining his head. 'Darling, you have taken me without wanting me. Now it's my turn to take you. Without wanting you. Because there isn't a tart available at the moment.'

'I'll kill you!'

'Not till I say so, and then I won't mind. Buck will be buried with Elsie. I will go in the same plot.'

His very calmness, coldness, quelled her panic. This was a man who had killed Germans, face to face, had ordered others to do the same, had climbed over corpses to create more corpses. This was what loyalty to King and Country had made him.

The remembering inexplicably found her easing, speaking more quietly, staring down at the waiting cups, the plates arranged for supper, and he swung her to him, lifted her face and rammed his mouth on hers. Kit put up her free hand and removed his hat, throwing it wherever it might fall, and knew that Bertie needed her, all of her, physically, mentally – and maternally.

It was she who led him up the passage and to the bedroom. In the darkness she got into bed naked, and the water bottle thrust painfully against her hipbone. She winced, then lifted the now useless thing and leaned out to stand it on the floor. Her flesh erupted in goosepimples and she closed her eyes. Please God make me love him, please God make me responsive.

She kept her eyes closed and, to her, he became Robert Henderson-Hobbs. Robert in the blessed darkness. Robert possessing her, receiving her love. Making love.

A little later Bertie lay beside her with his hand on

her belly, and she felt tears running down her face. She couldn't understand why.

She sniffed and sat up. She found her handkerchief under the pillow, and her nightie on the chair beside the bed. She used one and put on the other, and Bertie's hand didn't leave her, slipping from her belly to her thigh and resting there.

When she lay down again she said softly, 'Carruthers was right when he said you are not likely to get the sack.'

'Oh yes.' His head was turned from her.

'Henderson-Hobbs implied as much.'

'Did you pay a ransom for the information?'

'No. He didn't ask for one.'

'Why the white gown?'

'He took me to the theatre.'

'Then?'

'He left me at the door of my room in the hotel.'

'Just like that.'

'Just like that.'

They lay silently, each feeling the heat of the other, until he said, 'I'll have to move. Go to the bathroom.'

'I'll go down. Make coffee.'

'I prefer tea.'

She shrugged and struggled from the blankets. 'I suppose there'll be no account from John again this week.'

'To hell with accounts. He was my son.'

'And what about your daughter? Linda. Where is she?'

'She's in Crookham,' he said unexpectedly. 'It's not far from Aldershot. I got through to them from the club. She'll be all right. They'll send her home.'

Kit bit her bottom lip; so he had thought of the girl, taken the trouble to seek her out.

She said with a deep sigh, 'I'll make the tea and cut a sandwich for you.'

He didn't argue and, when he sat in his chair, eating, he watched her closely. He had not enjoyed having her.

He had wanted to rape, to hurt, to wreak vengeance, but for the first time ever, she had responded.

Now he felt nauseated by the whole horrible business.

He remained naked, hoping Kit would be upset, remonstrate, accuse him of vulgarity, but she didn't. She made the tea and handed him a scalding hot cup. She said calmly, 'Don't spill it. You'll ruin yourself for life,' and he felt cheated again.

CHAPTER TWELVE

Linda stepped out of the Staff car that brought her from Aldershot to Crookham, and she thought it all lovely, like Queen Mary arriving to inspect the troops.

She thanked the WAC driver prettily, then walked towards the two uniformed men waiting at the camp gates.

She smiled at Tommy, but the sergeant was senior, so she stopped before him, and saluted. A fine salute. As taught by Captain Albert Hemsworthy.

The sergeant saluted back, taken unawares. 'Evening miss.'

'Good evening, Sergeant. Isn't it cold?'

'It is, miss. Very cold.' He wondered who the hell she was, how in hell Buckley had got involved with her, and what he ought to do now. He excused himself and went to the car, calling, 'At ease, Buckley. Dismiss,' and Tommy and Linda were away, turning down the badly lit road, amid the sighing blackness of trees.

'Linda! You bonkers or something? Comin' here? Yer father been on the phone, and yer mother. You gotta get home again before there's more trouble.'

'I can't ever go back there. We had an awful row with Daddy. He'll hit me if I go back, I know he will.'

'You can't stay 'ere for ever!'

'I'll sleep out. On the grass.' She snuggled up to him, her hand catching his.

'Cor! Yer freezing!'

'I was so afraid you'd gone to China.'

'I told you. I'll come home first.'

'When are you going?'

'How do I know? I'm only a private.'

He kissed her, because she was shivering with cold, and if his lips were on hers she would stop talking about China.

He said then, 'They arranged for you to stay in some woman's house. I'll take you there.'

'Not yet,' she argued. 'Not yet.'

'I gotta get back to camp.'

'I came all this way – '

'In the morning you go home.'

'No!' she snapped, and in the gloom of the trees he could see the white of her face, the angle of her head.

'You got to, Linda, You can't stay here!'

'I've nowhere else to go.'

They walked slowly, his arm about her as the satchel was moved out of the way, and toads hopped across their path.

'I love you, Tommy.'

'Yea, but yer a nuisance.'

'There are camp followers.'

'Not with this camp.'

There was silence except for their slow footsteps. An owl swooped overhead and Linda squealed, so Tommy kissed her again, long, sweet and caring.

Next morning she left Crookham by bus, the road stretching starkly empty behind her, the silver birch trees bereft of leaves.

She went to three hundred Prince Edward Road, and the front door was drawn to. She stood forlornly at the gate, hoping someone would see her and encourage her in, but no one did. She quickly opened the glass door and listened, then went in.

The house was empty, but full of familiar smells. Home. She crept to the kitchen and everywhere was so tidy. Even Daddy's cushions were all plumped up, and on the mantelpiece, propped against the clock, was a note: Linda darling, I have to nip to the shops. Won't be long. Mummy.

296

The telephone rang in the office and she instinctively ran to answer it. 'Hello?'

'Lindah!' It was Bertie. 'So you're back. I'll be home straight away – '

She replaced the receiver, cutting her father's voice off, her heart drumming, her delicate nostrils stretched with the shock of hearing him so unexpectedly, hearing the impatience in his voice that could only mean more rows, then she was out of the front door again, running down the street.

Tom Buckley saw her while he sat on Maud Jeffries' windowsill, and he stood to greet her.

'Hello,' she said to him, as they met at the bottom of the steps. 'I've been to see Tommy and I want to live here.'

Big Tom's brows rose and he buttoned up his shirt to be respectable.

'What's yer pa say?'

'I don't live there any more.' She stared up at him and he nodded, accepting if not completely understanding, then, as she went to move forward, he barred her way. 'Maud don't want you in her house.'

'You said if ever I need a friend – '

Big Tom rubbed his mouth, then the top of his head, then looked at a tram rattling past. 'They'll be stopping all them soon. We'll have buses.'

'Yes,' Linda said, and wondered if he was going to frighten her again. She said quickly, 'I'm going to see Mrs Jeffries,' and dived past him.

Maud sat at the kitchen table peeling onions, tears streaming down her narrow bony face, the cat preening beside the bowl.

'Oh it's you,' she said. 'Tommy's not 'ere, so what d'yer want?'

Big Tom came in and said, 'She's run away from home.'

'Godamighty.' Maud flattened a tear with the back of her hand. 'What she expect us ter do about it?'

'She wants a mattress.'

'Huh. Gotta hope,' said Maud. 'There's no room fer her sort in this house,' then she rested her hands with the knife and half-peeled onion on the table and looked into Linda's face. 'Where you bin all last night?'

'With Tommy.'

'Oh aye,' said Maud and shot a glance at Big Tom. 'We better ask Stella then. She got a nice room all to herself, around the corner. Yer better wait here till she pops in.'

Everybody popped in before Stella, and they all sat talking, scratching, sniffing and deciding it was a hard life, a rotten world and the sooner we're all dead the better.

When Stella came Maud made tea and let it stew on the hob so it would look stronger, then she ladled thick glutinous tinned milk into the cups because the sugar in it was good for you. The resultant drink smelled and tasted of onions.

Stella leaned towards Linda, her hair very golden today, with no dark roots, and said, 'I bet your dad flung you out,' while Linda stared back into the blue eyes and experienced the sympathy she so desperately needed. She nodded.

Everybody relaxed. Everybody sighed a long 'Oooo,' with a depth of understanding.

'Cos he don't want yer being friends with Tommy,' Maud said flatly, and the whole room knew she was right.

They had no money, no expectations, few belongings, but they knew about our Elsie and that man.

And this poor child with him for a father!

Ali said, 'You come and sit by me, sweetheart. We will care for you.'

'No,' said Stella quickly. 'It's best she comes with me.'

Maud cupped her narrow chin in her hands. 'He'll come after her, mind.'

Stella said quietly, 'Then nobody seen her, have they.'

There came a long ruminating silence, all considering the wisdom and dangers of such a scheme, but eventually it was arranged. That night, Linda unpacked her satchel in Stella's room two streets behind Salubrious Terrace, higher up the hill. She got into the winceyette nightie, then dived into the brass-knobbed bed with Stella.

Stella's hair was rolled in pipe cleaners. The blankets were thin and tickly; there were no sheets, and the pillow cases were old flour bags. The whole place smelled of mice, but Linda felt it was another adventure, and when she did think of Mummy and Daddy and Emma, she told herself she didn't mind never seeing them again. She would rather stay here and wait for Tommy.

Bertie came to Salubrious Terrace that night, but didn't get past the top step. Boys had given ample warning of his arrival, and Maud was there with her arms folded across her flat chest.

'And what d'you want?' she demanded perkily.

'My daughter.' Bertie was tight-mouthed in the gaslight coming from the passage.

'She ain't 'ere.'

Bertie watched her and decided she was not a liar. 'You sure?'

'Wouldn't 'ave her here. A young girl like that? And me with a house full of men?'

Bertie looked around helplessly. These people had big hearts when they thought they were right; he wouldn't get anywhere questioning the crone. He said, as if resigned, 'If she does turn up, you'll let me know, won't you?'

Maud rubbed the tops of her folded arms. 'I'll tell 'er ter phone you herself.'

Bertie hesitated, in case the old woman knew more than she appeared to, then he said, 'She went to Aldershot yesterday and saw Tommy, but they tell me she left there this morning.'

'Oh yes.'

'Yes.'

Maud said, 'I'd look among her friends if I was you. She wouldn't like ter be with me now, would she? She'd

299

like a feather bed, that one. She got any money with her?'

Bertie nodded.

'Then don't you worry. Right as rain she'll be.'

Big Tom came up, smelling of the pub. 'You worried about something, Mr Hemsworthy?'

'My daughter, Linda. Thought she might be here with you.'

'Aye,' said Big Tom meaningly. 'I know what it's like ter be worried about a daughter. Wondering if she's with some bloke an' how he's going ter treat her.'

Bertie went home to Prince Edward Road. 'No,' he said to Kit. 'Don't phone her friends. We don't want them knowing,' then he sat in his chair, and hoped Linda would have the sense to come back in time for Baby Buck's funeral on Friday.

*　　*　　*

On that day Maggie lifted the latch on the old door of the lean-to and opened it. The sun was shining. She would have liked it to be drizzling. She would have liked God to have cried for her and John and, she thought, for Bertie Hemsworthy, the man whose child had been sold, and died, without him knowing.

Draped in mourning she gazed at her husband where he stood at the bottom of the garden, his back to her, his suit new and black but not fitting very well. He was staring out over the small town below, towards the white mist that had covered the channel for two days. Sounds carried on the still air and, even up here, she could hear the moaning of foghorns.

Such plans they had had. Buck grown big and strong. Buck being a scholar.

Now it was all gone. All the hopes, the chuckles, the tantrums, the clutching wet fingers. All in the pine box at the hospital, while inside the house were flowers and wreaths from so many people.

Maggie wanted to call John, but she also wished he

would come to her, help her. She left the stillness of early winter and went back into the house, where drawn curtains caused near darkness and an emphasis of grief.

The first mourner came, then the second. Sion came with his mother and father, their shop closed for the day. Big Tom Buckley came, the sole fixed once more to his boot and the leather uppers brushed and rubbed.

By the time the minister came, the house, the back and front gardens could hold no more.

Bertie sat at the top of the stairs, not wanting anyone near him. Kit stood in the lean-to whispering to Maggie. 'I brought a cake and a ham. I thought – '

'Yes,' said Maggie. 'Thank you, but the food is all ready. Never short of food in this house. I only have to put it out after.'

'Are you going to the cemetery?'

'Yes. Of course.' Maggie was indignant at the question. 'See the lamb put to rest with his mother, poor girl.'

'It's a long way.'

'We'll all go. And others will meet us at Oystermouth.'

Kit nodded, aware her gifts of food were unwanted, and she put her basket on the lid of the copper, then she smiled at Emma and fretted about Linda.

Maybe the girl would come home today. Surely she would come home today, yet the front door was locked. She calmed herself with the knowledge that Linda knew where to find the key. It was lying along the row of nails under the office windowsill.

She glanced at her wristwatch. There was shuffling in the kitchen. John came for Maggie, ignoring Kit, and the dreadful silence fell a moment before the drone of the minister's voice began. It was the man who had christened Buck in the Church of England.

Emma snuggled closer to her mother's hip and resorted to sucking her thumb. Kit kept a hand on Emma's ear, pressing the child's head to her.

She wondered about Bertie, wondered if she dared break the custom of women being separate from men,

301

and go to him, but it was too late now. The crowds prevented it.

The place became airless and Kit thought of Elsie's funeral; the curtains drawn for ten days after, no laughter, no raised voices, no quick movements allowed. Had Elsie called her baby to her? Taken him?

Then, blessed be, the minister's sermon was over; there would be a service at the graveside, but now Kit was able to move forward, into the kitchen, Emma still clutching her.

Men filed to the parlour, on the other side of the foot of the stairs, then came out, each carrying some of the flowers or wreaths. Maggie seemed composed, unsmiling, while women nudged each other, eyeing her meaningly, but saying nothing.

Kit turned from her, a little disappointed in the apparent lack of feeling, and Bertie was coming from the parlour, his face sallow and thin with tension, a great bunch of yellow chrysanthemums held high in one hand, putting on his hat with the other.

Kit wondered how many here would guess he wasn't just John's employer paying his last respects, but the child's father, erstwhile lover of Elsie Buckley, the girl who had loved bright yellow flowers.

The minister waited on the path, his surplice very white, the crocheted hem stiff with starching. Everyone toiled down the mountainside behind him, some of the gorse and blackberry bushes now gone, where Sion and John had been busy with scythes.

Kit saw Maggie walking alone, with a big-brimmed hat on her head, the black veil obscuring her face, and went to her. They walked side by side, but neither spoke to the other and no one attempted to crowd them.

Emma stumbled and sneezed, walking between Maggie and Kit, a hand gripping each skirt, and somewhere at the back a woman began to sing 'Nearer my God to thee . . .' Other voices joined hers; it became a dirge that made Kit's inside tighten with the grief of struggling to exist.

At the foot of the mountain the empty glass-sided hearse waited with a procession of cars and horse-drawn vehicles. There were no people waiting here, not a dog nor a cat, only those coming from the mountain, and every house had its curtains drawn.

Bertie, John and Big Tom slid the flowers and wreaths onto the top of the hearse and, when that was laden, they placed them carefully around the edge of the inside, so obviously leaving space for the little coffin.

Big Tom crossed himself, and Kit ran to him. 'Mr Buckley! My Linda! Have you seen her, please? I'm not asking where she is, I'm asking have you seen her. Is she safe?'

He nodded briefly. 'She'll come ter no harm, Mrs Hemsworthy, but she's not in our house.'

'You do know where she is?'

He paused, seeing the stress, the pleading in her eyes. 'The girl's all right, but don't ever tell 'er as I said so,' and Kit had to move back as more flowers were brought and arranged. Then the men sorted themselves into cars, the women taking to the traps and carts, everything draped in black.

For a second Bertie turned, as if averse to undertaking the next part of the journey, his eyes very dark as he looked at Kit, and Kit stared back, into them.

She felt momentarily that he needed her and, thrusting Emma aside, she ran to him. 'Darling!'

'Sssh!' he said, and it was as if she had snapped him from whatever world he had been in.

'Bertie!' She had a conviction that this moment was important. This moment could save her marriage, but he threw it away. He said, 'Be quiet. I'm all right.' His voice was brisk, dismissive, and she guessed he had been thinking of Elsie, walking with Elsie, while she, his wife, had been an intruder.

She clutched at his jacket, a last-minute bid to hold him, and his pocket was heavy. She tugged, preventing him getting into the car with John and Big Tom. 'What's in your pocket?'

But she knew. She had felt the outline of it, though she didn't want to believe. 'Bertie! What's in your pocket?'

He drew out the big key of the front door at number 300 and held it in the open palm of his hand.

'Linda will be locked out,' Kit murmured, shocked.

'Teach her a lesson,' he returned, and she snatched the key while he climbed into the car, and he didn't look at her again.

The key was six inches long, iron, not made to be carried about, and Kit clutched it to her. She tried telling herself he hadn't brought it deliberately, he wouldn't be so unkind. He had merely forgotten to leave it under the windowsill, but the niggle remained. Bertie didn't give a damn for her or her daughters.

She looked into Maggie's face, the black veil unmoving in the stillness of the day, and Kit blurted, 'Maggie! You ought to be in the front car with the men!'

Maggie's eyes were dead, watching the hearse. 'You have two children, Kit,' she said tonelessly. 'I have none. Don't grieve your other losses.'

Kit looked around for room for her and Emma and was beckoned by a woman in a trap. 'Here, love!' she called. 'You can squash in here.'

Kit obeyed, but resentment was growing: she who had, not so long ago, had a car, to be travelling now like a peasant. She drew Emma onto her knee and stared into space.

Few spoke all the way to Swansea. As they travelled through Skewen the rain threatened, and a woman put up a big black umbrella, but the cloud passed, and still no one spoke.

At the hospital in Swansea the cortege stopped and everyone alighted following John, Bertie and Big Tom.

The shock for Kit was infinite. There, behind a glass partition, lay Baby Buck, his face waxen, his tiny hands on his chest, his body enshrouded in white satin padding, with arum lilies at his feet, the lid of the coffin standing beside him.

Kit saw the top-hatted undertakers go into the room, their hands in rubber gloves, their black suits hidden beneath the hospital white gowns, then she was moved away by pressing hands and gently coaxing voices.

Everyone went back to the pavement, and soon the coffin came and was thrust into the hearse amid the flowers.

Somewhere near the kerb Maggie shrieked and began to scream for her baby. John rushed to hold her, her sobs becoming embalmed in Kit's heart with a form of forgiveness for all the wrongs she thought Maggie had done her.

'Sssh . . .' everyone breathed, and some walked a few yards away to try and escape the atmosphere of sorrow.

Bertie came to Kit. He looked like death himself and she wanted to touch his face, say something that would ease the strain between them, but thought it too late.

He left her and got back into the car.

She knew she could go no further. She stepped back, into the hospital grounds, holding Emma's hand, and the funeral went on its way, to the hill plainly visible from outside the hospital, the hill where Elsie had lain for eight months.

Kit waited a little longer, stonily calm now, waiting for the claustrophobia of misery to ease, then she and Emma walked home, breathing the clear air, wondering if Linda would be waiting at the gate.

As they stood before the hallstand, removing their coats with the black ribbon bands on the arms, and their hats with the black ribbon bows, Kit said, 'Emma, will you look out for Linda, darling, please?'

'Yes, oh yes.' It was almost a sob forced between brand new front teeth, and the seven-year-old went charging up the stairs.

'Darling, Why not watch from the office?'

Emma was already rushing along the landing. 'I can see more up here. I'll see her and she won't know I'm spying.'

305

Kit thanked God there was one little problem solved then went back to the front door, opened it, placed the coconut mat before it and looked along the street again.

She glanced into the office; it needed dusting. Maybe tomorrow things would come back to normal. Linda might be home and Bertie – What was Bertie going to be like? Would he grieve over the baby as he had grieved over Elsie?

She watched the clock, timing the funeral. Five miles to Oystermouth, to the graveside. Ten minutes, maybe fifteen, for the service.

He should be home.

The hours passed.

She decided he had gone back to Port Talbot, gone for the meal that followed every burial.

The evening came and went.

He arrived at gone eleven.

He slammed the front door and bolted it so noisily Kit guessed he thought she was in bed, and he was all set to awaken her. He went on, up the stairs and into the bathroom. Water gushed and gurgled then he was marching along the landing.

Kit sat, deadening the nerves that had become strung with anxiety, then she wound the clock, locked the back door and took Bertie's slippers from the fender.

She marched purposefully up the stairs, paused to peep into Emma's room, then went to the main bedroom.

Bertie was in his pyjamas, sitting in the basket chair. He looked up from a book coldly and removed his spectacles. 'Why weren't you at the graveside?'

'Because I have been waiting for my daughter to get over her fear of you and come home.' Kit flung one slipper at him, then the other. The first he dodged, the second caught him on the neck.

There were a few seconds of silent shock, of Kit standing with her feet apart as if awaiting an attack.

She said, 'I'm finished with you. That any man could deliberately lock his daughter out! She had the right idea. She's gone, and if she has any sense she won't come back. I shall do the same.'

'You bloody won't!'

'I bloody will!' She opened the neck of her dress, then lifted it over her head. 'I shall sleep beside you tonight because it's my duty while in your house. But tomorrow, that is the end. I shall take Emma with me.'

He stood before the empty black grate and waved the slipper that had lodged on his shoulder. 'You will do nothing of the kind! I shall not allow it. You are my wife. You will stay where you belong.'

'You are supposed to be my husband. You walk around like a zombie, pretending to be in agony over the death of Elsie Buckley, yet you banish her brother – and so my daughter – from YOUR house. So, all right, Albert Hemsworthy. Keep your house. And your office. In fact –' Kit scorned, her nightdress coming down over her head, 'you can stuff the lot up your arse!'

She suddenly felt marvellous. Rarely before had she been so crude, common, vulgar. This was a new challenge. Freedom.

She brushed her hair vigorously, then jumped into bed. She wanted to laugh. It was heady. Reaction from the funeral; Baby Buck's face as waxen as a doll's.

Bertie was temporarily speechless, standing in his baggy striped pyjamas with a slipper in his hand.

He said, 'Somebody put you up to this.'

'Are you getting into bed or aren't you?'

'Henderson-Hobbs! Bloody Henderson-Hobbs! He wants to pinch my wife! John saw you with the man, acting all girlish!'

'How lovely. You have a wife capable of being girlish at forty-two. What a pity you can't keep her.'

His face began to go from astonished white to furious red, and Kit told him, 'I have had my say. Now you can put out the light.'

He stood disbelieving, so she got out of bed and scampered to the light switch herself, her pink voile nightie wafting. She returned to bed and lay panting.

Anything could happen.

For a while he didn't move and she was tempted to speak. As her gaze became accustomed to the darkness she saw him, his arms relaxed, his head drooping, and she thought of Carruthers' words; few can tell the difference between pure love and desire. Had Bertie experienced both? And right now, his love child was spending his first night buried in yellow-brown clay-like soil.

Kit felt an urge to put the light back on, revoke the terrible cruelty she had inflicted during the last ten minutes, but it was done. There was no going back.

He collected his clothes from the chair, and whispered as he padded around the foot of the bed, 'I'm not tired. Maybe I'll telephone Crookham again. Maybe Linda went back there.'

Kit didn't answer. It was chilling to find he was not coming to her, and she made no effort to say she had asked Tom Buckley today about Linda.

She heard the front door open and close stealthily, heard Bertie's footsteps going from the house, and she lay until she heard him come back, then she dozed.

It was a new day when she sat up, the place beside her still empty.

She got out of bed, slipped into her dressing-gown and went downstairs.

Bertie was sunk into his battered chair, his chin on his chest, faint snores coming from his slightly open mouth. Twenty-four hours' dark growth surrounded his jaws, and dark blue shadows circled his eyes.

Dead cinders were low in the grate, a used cup was on the table; cocoa and the last of a packet of digestive biscuits.

Bertie had eaten.

She went to the scullery and filled the kettle, knowing they all had to continue to exist and, when she returned to the kitchen, he was trying to awaken, raising his eyelids as if magnets secured them.

He said, 'Linda is over there somewhere. Tom didn't deny it, but he wouldn't admit it either.'

'You got him up? About two o'clock in the morning?'

'The whole street almost. He didn't mind. I agreed I'm a rotter. I apologised. I don't think he'll spit at me any more.'

'D'you want a cup of tea?'

'Please.' His bleary gaze watched the steaming brown liquid flood from the spout of the china pot and, as she handed him his cup, he said practically. 'Kit, If you walk out on me, I'm finished.'

'Rubbish!' but her heart lifted, and a little excitement swelled inside her. 'Since Elsie died you haven't been aware of me –' Now, she thought, ram it home. 'You loved her. You still love her.'

He sipped the tea, his manner languid. 'A different type of love. I carried a lot of guilt.'

'Because you were older than the boys who taught her all she knew?'

'Because we had so much more than she would ever have. And I threw her out when she was ill, expecting Buck.'

'Did you know she was ill?'

'No.'

'Did you know she was expecting Buck?'

'No.'

'Then stop feeling sorry for yourself.'

'I feel so bloody whacked these days.'

'Reaction. The war. The idea there's another on the way. It has all piled up.'

'It's not that simple.'

'Everybody feels guilty. I do.'

'You?'

Kit flushed with embarrassment and took the teapot to the scullery, emptying it in the sink, swilling it thoroughly under the tap.

Bertie creaked himself out of the chair, his cup of tea on the fender, and followed her, his shirt and trousers rumpled, collarless and tieless, his hair shapeless.

'Guilty about what? Leaving the funeral like that?'

'About not liking bed.'

'Bed?' It was evident that had been furthest from his mind. 'You mean in bed, when we – '

She was blushing hotly now, one hand clasping the handle of the teapot, the other clutching her dressing-gown about her as if he were a strange man intruding.

He rubbed his chin then went back to the kitchen. He stood with his back to the grate. 'I don't suppose you can help it. You're made that way,' he said, and Kit wanted to fling the teapot at him as she had flung the slippers. Why couldn't he see, she wasn't 'made that way'?

She said, 'I'll call Emma. She'll be early for school today without any trouble,' and she left him to finish his tea.

When all three sat down to breakfast she felt him looking at her, but she didn't look back.

When the mail shot through the letterbox Emma ran for it, leaving her chair at the table without permission, her face intent on only one thing.

She brought the bundle to the kitchen and handed it to her mother. She was pouting, glowering at her father. 'And what,' he asked, 'has got into you?'

'There's no letter from Linda. And she's in China.'

Bertie turned from her, his face expressionless, and Emma got back onto her chair. Bertie said quietly, 'Another Linda,' and Kit smiled at Emma and passed her the small glass dish that held the Silver Shred.

She recognised the long white envelope from London. Robert, of course. The conference. She passed it, unopened, to Bertie, and he slit the end with the bread knife.

Kit opened a small blue envelope that was covered in grubby fingermarks and smelled of fish. She read the letter inside, then said, 'That chap at the docks is still complaining. He deserves a big bonus on his endowment. No one has collected his premiums and he's been lapsed. He telephoned the other evening. A Mr Browne. With an E.'

Bertie looked up, his face questioning.

Kit said, 'You remember.'

'Write and tell him I'll call personally next week.'

Kit sighed; it was as if Bertie thought she hadn't the courage to leave him. Pity for him stirred in her again; that such a man, so superior to others in appearance, personality, and potential should have descended to the level of Elsie Buckley.

Ten minutes later he was in the office.

As Kit cleared the breakfast table she gathered up the mail, and the letter from Head Office was still out of its envelope. She read it; the conference was in Bournemouth from the evening of Friday 24th November to the morning of Wednesday, 29th November. Mr Hemsworthy was requested to present himself. The main topics for discussion were expansion plans within the company and an extension into other forms of insurance.

Bertie had read it but not mentioned it. Kit wondered if he would be contrary and not go. If that happened, how would Robert take it?

CHAPTER THIRTEEN

Maud wore pink and Big Tom was glassy-eyed before they set out for the registry office. Almost everybody came. It was like a procession or, as Tommy laughed, a Whitsun treat. He wore a grey suit and looked more spiffing than Linda had ever seen him.

The kids from the terrace all had trousers that had bottoms in, or knickers that had a crotch, and all pulled their socks down so the holes were hidden under, inside their daps.

Some of the women cried a little because it was all so beautiful, and one of the toddlers refused to give Maud the horseshoe made from silver paper.

The policeman outside the police station in Alexander Road saw them wandering along the pavement, the deed done, confetti splattering everywhere, so he held up the traffic while they crossed the top of Orchard Street, then they all crammed into the Adam and Eve. Big Tom made a trio with Ali and Ebony and sang Nelly Dean, their voices blending in harmony. 'You are my heart's desire . . .' As Maud said later, it tore at everyone's heartstrings.

Linda and the kids wandered around Woolworths' until the yells and laughter came down High Street, then the parade was all joined up again, with the kids stuffing the chocolate they had just nicked, and skipping about with cold noses and blue lips.

Back at Salubrious Terrace the cake waited beside the cat in the centre of the table. The bride entered, swiped the cat, and opened the first bottle of gin.

Everyone packed in and drank the couple's health, while Big Tom took up position as caretaker of the barrel fitted in the scullery. They all had corned-beef sandwiches and someone gave Maud a present on behalf of her lodgers.

There came a silence. Then there was a scurrying and other presents appeared, some wrapped so hastily Maud guessed the vase or jug had just come off someone's mantelpiece, but she loved it all; her cheeks glowed a different colour from her rouge, and her grey hair gradually straggled from the bun on top of her head.

Maud put on her pinny to save her new dress, and the barber came over from the shop, then the butcher, while Big Tom sat on the rickety scullery table and sang loudly, 'I like the girls who do. I like the girls who don't. I hate the ones who say they will, and then they say they won't.'

Maud and Tommy brought him into the crush of the kitchen and urged him to sing it again. There was general goodwill, tangy breath and hot bodies, babies sleeping at their mothers' breasts, and everyone sang in dreadful chorus, 'But of all the girls I like the best, I might be wrong or right, is the one who says she never will, but looks as though she might.'

Everyone burst into laughter and Linda sipped her second gin and lemonade. In the passage Tommy pushed her against the wall and kissed her greedily; she pushed him away and didn't like his smell. He whispered, 'This is my last leave, love. We're off ter China.'

So she clung to him, his neck soft against her face, and he kissed her again and again until she thought he would eat her.

People passed them, edging sideways not to interrupt any youthful longings, and Tommy pressed his thighs tightly against her and whispered, 'Linda – . Let me love you before I go . . .'

'You are loving me,' she whispered back, and snuffled against him, her lips uplifted. Ali came from the kitchen.

313

'Hi, you two lovebirds!' he called. 'What you at? It's Maud's wedding, don't you know.'

Linda laughed at him, shiny-eyed, 'Where're you going, Ali?' and he leaned towards her so Tommy had to move aside. 'To get more lolly, sweetheart. The party's going flat.'

Ebony was behind him, laughing, all coal-black face and white melon smile. 'We'll kidnap you, heh, little lady? Carry you away,' and she went with them, gaily, leaving the thwarted Tommy.

He returned to the kitchen, scowling, while she got into the Austin seven with Ali and Ebony. Ali honked the horn and yelled gleefully through the opened window, 'Make way! Make way!' while Linda leaned against Ebony in the back and wondered why he wore perfume, and why gin and lemonade made her feel sort of giddy and sick.

She said, 'Where do you keep your money, black man?'

'Me?' laughed Ebony. 'I have no money. I never have money.'

'Ali's money, then?'

Ali called while the car veered across the tramlines and back again, 'I got no money neither. It's all gone on the barrel.'

Linda sat up and asked. 'So where are we going?'

'To borrow some,' they said. 'Off the men on the ship. They can come to the party too,' and they laughed and sang all the way to the docks, teasing the policeman at the gates, telling him Linda was a white slave, and she nodded and watched him frown, and wished she had stayed with Tommy.

* * *

Bertie lit himself a cigarette and added to the smoke in the tram, then he alighted in the centre of town and stood on the pavement, too tired to continue working. He wished Kit would go back to being her old self, dependable, cool and calm.

He took out his book again and ticked off the addresses he had attended to, totalling the cost of a fire he had investigated, telling himself it had probably been arson, but the woman needed the cash . . . It was then he thought of Head Office and the conference at Bournemouth. Two weeks come Friday. He finished his cigarette and dropped the butt where it might keep clean and be found by a down and out. Bournemouth could be a bit of a break. Leave Kit to herself for a while. Give her a chance to calm down.

He walked quickly. A Mr, who was it? Browne, with an E. He smiled at the emphasis on the E. Better get down there. Sweeten the poor chap.

By the time he reached the docks entrance his hat was on the back of his head and he was whistling, striding as if he had never been tired or worried, and the docks police saluted him cordially. 'Nice day.'

'Gets dark early,' Bertie said, because it was cold and grey, and the dock water looked filthy and sluggish. 'I have a client down here. Wants to pay his insurance.'

'OK,' returned the officer, polite but not interested, and Bertie went on, over the cobbles and tramlines, the great rusting chains and hawsers. He didn't like the atmosphere, the way the smaller boats rose and fell. There were men heaving great loads, cranes swinging, coal trucks shunting, clanging and echoing up into the Tawe valley. And over all was that distinctive docks stench.

The little Austin seven with its dented door was at the quayside, and a coloured man was getting out; a small, lithe, ugly sort of man with a face like a preying hawk. Bertie knew him vaguely, had seen him before, but where? A massive negro slid from the car and stood helping a piece of goods out. Bertie sniffed disparagingly, then: Linda!

In an inexplicable flash Bertie remembered the group outside the station, waiting for Tom Buckley, the bracelet glinting on the blonde's wrist. The image became

315

tangled with the serpent bracelet with the red eyes claimed by Linda, and the jigsaw slammed into place.

That crone and those men. Linda receiving presents!

He screamed at her. 'Lindah!'

He would kill the sods. All of them. 'Lindah!' He charged, blind with fear and fury, arms raised, feet flying.

A ship's funnel boomed, deadening all other sounds. For an instant the seagulls squealed and wheeled in silence, the men etched in slow motion, then everything was normal again. A gull shrieked and swooped, yellow-billed and black-legged, on a bollard, wicked, threatening, white wings outstretched before folding like old screens. And that darkie had his arm about Linda.

They were taking her aboard!

'Lindah! Keep off! Lindah!'

He was frantic, the sound of his feet banging in his ears, and he seemed unable to cover any distance at all. 'Lindah!'

She was laughing, tossing her head. Another bloody wog was up on deck waving to her. 'Lindah!'

If Bertie saw the anchor rope it didn't register; wet and black it writhed along the quayside and he fell over it.

He saw a banana boat turn upside down, heard his arm snap and his head crack as the quay wall shot up and hit him, then the water was ice, stinking, foul-tasting. Bits of wood slapped his nose and brown froths of scum clawed his face. His eyes stared in shock and his lungs filled with the vileness of oil and salt. His good arm rose but he sank, and his mind went into oblivion.

Linda heard the last shriek, saw men in great wellington boots and roll-necked jerseys running, felt Ali's arm drop from her waist and heard the laughter go from Ebony. Voices shouted in Arabic, then she was hurrying after Ali as he sprinted up the quay.

She stood then, beside Ebony, watching the men bring someone from the dock, an elderly-looking, thin, white-faced, bedraggled, unconscious man whose right arm dangled as if only the skin held top and bottom together.

They dropped him onto his stomach on the cobbles between the railway lines, and one man knelt over him and began pounding his shoulder blades so horrible sicky water shot from his mouth.

Daddy!

Petrified and silent she watched. An ambulance came, all fuss and noise and busy men in uniform. They took Bertie on a stretcher and someone had all the papers out of his pockets, water dripping and running everywhere. 'The pencil's run, mun. You take 'em,' and when the ambulance had gone and the men moved away, muttering, praising each other, Ali said, 'Sweetheart. What is it with you?'

'It's my father!' She was stunned and shocked. She had done this. She had said God could take Daddy, but she hadn't said God could take Buck AND Daddy.

'I have to go home now,' she said. 'Mummy will be on her own. Please tell Tommy.'

Ali brought the car to her, wishing he had a shawl to wrap about her, glad he had somewhere to take her, away from his responsibility.

Ebony said, 'OK man. I'll tell Tommy,' and he loped away as if he was back in Africa, covering ground easily, to get to Salubrious Terrace.

Ali didn't get out of the car at Prince Edward Road, not even to open the door. He sat looking straight ahead, knowing he was in the wrong part of town for a coloured man. He waited until Linda was on the pavement, until she said, 'Thank you Ali,' then he drove away. Fast.

Kit saw the porch door open and ran to it. 'Linda! Darling. What a naughty girl you've been. When your father gets home – ' Then, quietly, 'What's the matter? What has happened?'

Kit telephoned Dr Sullivan. When he came, he attended to Linda first, soothing her, advising Kit, then he sat, all rust-coloured plus fours and jacket. 'And what was Albert doing on the docks, heh?'

Kit sat opposite him with Linda leaning against her.

She said, 'We've been worried about him for some time.'

'And rightly so,' ruminated the old man, licking his lips. 'He's been in a pretty muddle. He's like two men, you know, Kitty girl. One needing you, and the other thinking he's still twenty-one, wanting young Elsie Buckley. Not an enviable position to be in, I can tell you. Not when you're a respectable man like Albert.'

Kit moved her shoulders uncomfortably. 'I telephoned the hospital straight away. They said – well, he was crying. Not sobbing or anything. Just crying. He did that after Elsie died.'

'Do him a world of good. Wash the tension out of his system.'

The clock ticked, the telephone rang and stopped again.

The doctor said, 'And what is it you think I can do for Albert, Kitty, heh?'

She smiled wanly, wondering just what any man could do for Albert. She said, 'The hospital will care for him for a while, but what comes after? Is he heading for a nervous breakdown? He had one on the Somme. He hasn't told me much about it, but I put the pieces together.'

The heavy gingery head nodded slowly. 'Thousands of men had breakdowns. Some were shot in the back by their own officers as they ran away. It was war, Kitty. War.' The doctor heaved a sigh and straightened his shoulders. 'He'll be in need of convalescence, y'know. Can you afford that?'

She nodded quickly, but didn't dare ask how much she would have to afford.

That evening she bathed and dressed carefully. She told the girls to be good, she was going to visit their father, but she only got to the front door. There the cold night air hit her and she experienced the same sensation as at the funeral. She couldn't go. It wasn't just the distress of seeing Bertie crying, in pain, it was also entering hospital, with all its dreadful connotations.

Linda and Emma looked up silently as she came back into the room and slowly took off her coat. She said, with a forced smile, 'We'll leave him to rest for a few days, shall we?'

Emma bent her head to her homework on the card table behind the kitchen door, and Linda struggled with a ball of wool, her lips silently forming instructions to the needles. 'One purl. One plain.'

Kit stood for a moment, still undecided, duty calling one way, emotions calling the other. She was married to Bertie, had promised to honour and obey; in sickness and in health.

Emma sighed as if her problem was insurmountable. 'I can't do long division.' She looked up at Kit, and there was no more indecision.

Kit changed back into her woollen dress, helped Emma with her homework and Linda with her knitting. It seemed Tommy was to have a pair of special Linda socks.

Next morning, when the telephone rang, Linda was there to answer it. Kit said, 'It's probably that poor Mr Browne with an E. I don't suppose your father got to him.'

Linda laughed and ran. 'Hello?' She called down the passage, 'Mummy! It's Grandma.'

'Tell her I won't be a moment,' Kit said, and Linda ran back into the office to tell Grandma all about it.

Grandma was entranced and horrified. 'Linda. Darling. Please don't speak so quickly. I can't quite catch what you are saying. Your father really should arrange elocution lessons for you. Now, begin again.'

'Well, I am home at last.'

'Home?' Grandma was curious. 'Where have you been, dear?'

'To Crookham. I went to visit my boyfriend.'

'Oh darling girl! How wonderful. Do I know the family?'

Lorraine sat in her luxurious detached house in Worcestershire and waited delightedly. She said to her

319

husband in an aside, 'Linda seems to have a rather special boyfriend.'

'Bit young,' the colonel commented, and eyed the new maid speculatively, as she apologetically hurried into the room through one door and out of another.

'He's a soldier, Grandma.'

'A soldier?' Grandma developed reservations. Linda had not said, 'He is an officer cadet,' but 'he is a soldier.' Lorraine's perfectly shaped brows rose slightly. 'Soldiers can be the very devil, you know dear,' and her husband leaned forward, listening.

'What rank?' he whispered.

'What rank, darling? Grandpa is asking.'

'A private up to now, but he might be a general one day.'

Lorraine suffocated a gasp, then mouthed at Grandpa in horror. 'A private!' and Grandpa sat back, gradually turning a little puce. He said in an undertone, 'That damned fellow Kitty married is half-baked. No wonder he got no further than captain.'

'Sssh dear. I'll find out more.'

The colonel nodded and sat back, wondering whether to light his pipe.

'Darling? Is your daddy there?'

'No. He fell in the dock. He's in hospital now.'

Lorraine stared at the mouthpiece, then at her husband. 'I think we had better get down there,' she said, her refined voice quivering. 'Pack a bag, will you? I can't think what Albert is up to. The child not going to finishing school, fooling around with a private, and now Albert goes diving into the dock.'

'Heh what?' said the colonel. 'Some sort of competition, I suppose.'

'Get the car out.'

'Hi, I say, old girl. Ease up a bit, what.'

'Linda? Tell your mother I'm longing to speak to her. Tell her we are coming down.'

Linda ran to the door again and called, 'Mummy!'

320

and the tone of her voice brought Kit, a teacloth still in her hand.

'I told you to tell her – '

'She says they're coming down.'

'Oh no!' Kit strode to the phone. 'Mother?'

'Darling, you poor thing. You must be desperate for help. How on earth did Albert get into the dock? Was the man drunk or something?'

'Mother! Bertie does not get drunk – '

'Of course not, dear. It was a slip of the tongue, I am sorry. But Linda, how lovely.' Kit made a little moue at Linda, recognising the fake pleasure in her mother's voice.

Lorraine probed, 'She went to Crookham. Did you go with her?'

'No Mother, I didn't.'

'Well,' Lorraine tried to think diplomatically. 'Someone chaperoned her. Didn't they?'

'No Mother.' Kit's voice was brittle. 'She went alone.'

'Darling!' Lorraine thought of the smelling salts but settled for fanning herself with her manicured hand. 'Surely you didn't let her go to see some riffraff completely alone?'

'To what riffraff are you referring?'

'Oh come now, darling. I am your mother.'

'He happens to be a friend of the family.'

'Oh . . .' Lorraine went silent.

Kit sat with the teacloth in her lap and said quietly, 'He happens to be Elsie Buckley's brother.'

The silence from Lorraine became ominous.

Then the colonel's voice rumbled down the wires. 'Kitty. You are letting the family down, y'know old girl. If you choose to have gels you also choose the responsibility for them. Your mother is concerned, and so am I. We intended popping down to see you sometime anyway.'

'Father. This is ridiculous. The family name is not besmirched. I am no longer a Nolan. I am a Hemsworthy.'

'Lorraine still feels we ought to see you. Clear our own minds – '

Lorraine took the phone from him. 'Darling,' she cooed to Kit. 'It will be lovely to visit you. We can stop the night at Ross. There is a wonderful hotel with the gardens overlooking the Wye. Bye bye, dear.'

Kit put down the receiver and rubbed her forehead. She didn't think she could tolerate her parents' interference. Linda went to the window.

Instinctively Kit knew her daughter was watching for Tommy. She said, 'Are you expecting him this morning?'

'He didn't say, but this is his last leave before he goes abroad. I came straight home yesterday. I didn't say goodbye.'

Kit's shoulders sagged. Linda looked so pathetic, yet had caused so much worry and stress. 'If you want me,' she said, 'I'll be in your bedroom. Shifting everything into Emma's.'

But Tommy didn't visit until next morning.

He stood on the front door step with a thin bunch of forced daffodils. He looked a model of spit and polish. His cap was on straight, his heavy black boots so shiny they reflected light.

'In here,' Linda said quietly but urgently. 'Mummy's upstairs. Seeing to hot-water bottles. My grandparents are coming.'

'Everybody'll be coming,' Tommy said. 'When someone's ill everybody comes.'

They stood gazing at each other until Linda shyly moved closer to him, and he said softly, 'I'm sorry.'

'Oh he'll get better,' Linda retorted, and stuck her nose into the yellow of the flowers.

'Not your father, silly. Us.'

'Us?'

Linda watched him, trying to remember, and then it came, the cuddle in Maud Jeffries' passage, his urgent plea to love her. 'Oh well,' she blushed. 'We were a bit tipsy, weren't we?'

Tommy's forehead puckered. Was that all it meant to her? 'I wasn't,' he said curtly. 'I meant it.'

'Oh all right. I wasn't either, but I didn't want you – '

Kit came rushing down the stairs laden with used towels, a broom, and a bucket filled with odds and ends, wisps of black hair loose beside her ears. 'Linda!' then she saw Tommy. 'Oh hello.' She flung him a smile. 'The bride and groom gone on honeymoon?'

'Yes. They went to Mumbles yesterday on the train, and they've gone ter Singleton Park today.'

'How nice.' Kit tried not sound patronising, but her inside shuddered. Mumbles on a grey November day? The wind bitter, the sea like something out of a filmed storm. 'I hope they'll be very happy.'

She hurried to the kitchen and Linda and Tommy followed. He said easily, 'Maud is making plans. She says she wants a hotel. Somewhere posh, yer know. Like Penarth.'

'Oh yes.' Kit managed another smile, and wondered about the ambitions of this Maud Jeffries, and the expensive houses and rates in Penarth.

'And if they do, my pa will be manager.'

Kit paused in her rush to the dirty washing basket in the scullery. So even Big Tom Buckley wanted to be a manager. Supreme ambition for all: be a manager.

She hastily dumped the towels, then came back to the kitchen. She smiled at Tommy. 'That would be lovely, if your pa did become a manager,' and thought she saw him grow two inches. 'Linda, will you fold the dirty washing into the dirty pillow cases please? If I don't hide them your grandmother will wail about the inconvenience she's causing.'

Tommy grinned, the dimples in his cheeks again. 'Can I help, Mrs Hemsworthy? I can chop sticks. Get coal in.'

Kit straightened her body and laughed. Bertie was not going to walk in and disapprove; she was missis for a while. 'Go ahead,' she encouraged. 'You know where everything is. You've done it before.' Linda beamed, and went to the scullery as Tommy took off his jacket and rolled up his shirt sleeves. Linda said happily, 'The axe is beside the blocks. You'll see them,' and Tommy paused long enough to drop a kiss on her cheek.

Kit put her hand to her mouth, wondering if she was wrong in allowing them to believe she approved the friendship, but decided this was no time to worry. The colonel loved home-made cake. The whisky bottle needed replacing with a full one. She hurried to the larder, checking her food stocks.

By the time Lorraine and the colonel arrived the house looked faultless.

'Darling!' Lorraine carolled, as she swept in, all expensive perfume, marcel-waved silvery hair, and mink coat. 'Your father took such an age to get here.'

'We did get here,' he humphed, and stood a single suitcase at the foot of the stairs. 'The roads are not built for cars.'

'Why blame the roads, dear,' Lorraine chided. 'Though we did stop for lunch. Salmon, darling,' she cooed at Kit. 'Fresh from the Wye, and delicious.'

Then she concentrated on Linda, her arms held out, but Linda didn't go to her, and Lorraine's gaze shot to Tommy. 'And who is this young man?' she asked imperiously.

'My fiancé,' Linda said, knowing what Grandma was thinking, and stepped nearer Tommy. 'One day we're going to be married.'

'How nice,' said Lorraine, while the colonel thought the old girl could certainly carry it off.

He looked at Bertie's chair, decided it was past providing his type of comfort, then looked at Kit's. With both his wife and daughter in the room drawing invisible swords, it would be wiser not to sit in either, so he groaned patiently and sat on a hard chair at the table, then he took his pouch and pipe from his jacket pocket.

Neither Kit nor Lorraine could prevent their noses twitching with dislike as the colonel packed, prodded,

324

lit up, puff-puffed, and sent clouds of smoke ceiling-wards, but Tommy grinned. 'That's Bondman, sir.'

'It is indeed, young man, and what did you say your name was?'

'Buckley sir. Thomas Buckley.'

The colonel thought his wife would expire.

Kit was laughing, aware her father was willing to toler-ate the private. 'Come on, Linda,' she called. 'Make a pot of tea, and you, Tommy, be the colonel's batman and take his and Mrs Nolan's bag upstairs. The back bedroom.'

Tommy went, aware of the embarrassment his name engendered, but also a little surprised that a colonel could sit and puff such a dirty old pipe. In fact, the colonel seemed the sort of man who could well have a hole in his slippers. Tommy laughed to himself; he liked the old codger, in spite of him being a nob.

In the kitchen Lorraine was in Kit's chair, her brows up. She said to Linda, 'Darling, never mind the tea. Come and talk to grandma. You aren't serious about this young man, are you? What can he offer you?'

'Love,' Linda said candidly, standing before Lorraine. 'And he's big and strong and brave and true.'

The colonel eyed her through clouds of smoke, and stretched his neck a little as he thrust his head forward.

Linda turned back to the tea-making, and Lorraine signalled deep distress to her husband. 'And what of Albert?' she said, as a cup and saucer were handed to her. 'How is he?'

'I have no idea,' Kit said calmly. 'I haven't been to see him.'

Lorraine sat upright, the cup steaming before her. 'But darling – '

'Mother. When things have been awkward between you and Father I have not interfered. Now I ask you to afford me the same courtesy. Mind your own business.'

'Then you must allow your father and me to help in other ways.' Lorraine nodded to the colonel who nodded back. 'I shall take it upon myself,' said Lorraine majestically, 'to set Linda upon the right road. I shall visit the school in Malvern next week and, if I consider it worthwhile, I shall come for her, take her to see the place, to meet the staff and, if she likes them, she will go. For a year.' then, 'Unless she needs two.'

'Bertie will never allow it.'

'Piffle to Bertie. Once the matter is attended to he can do nothing. And I am certainly not prepared to stand any nonsense from you, Kitty. Linda is coming under my wing.'

'Grandma – ' Linda said.

'Quiet, child. I love you, and I will take care of you. Grandpa? Isn't that correct?'

'Correct,' echoed Grandpa, and wondered if his pipe was going out.

'Grandpa,' Linda tried. 'I don't want to go to finishing school. I want to be with Tommy.'

'Humph!' growled the colonel. 'If he's at Crookham he'll be going abroad soon – '

'He is, Grandpa. To China. This is his last leave.'

The colonel's pipe had gone out, so he took the *Daily Express* off the other chair beside him, put it on the table and began scraping the bowl of his pipe out on it.

Linda stood beside him, her arm across his back. 'He could be a general. I know he could.'

'Field marshal,' Lorraine said disparagingly, and her husband glanced across the room at her.

'Some young fellers have possibilities,' he said. 'Unfortunate that he was born in the wrong bed. Influence. Right background. Make a difference, y'know.'

Kit said quickly, 'He does have the right background.'

The colonel's head jerked and he dropped the pipe-scraper.

'You,' Kit smiled.

Lorraine called, 'Kitty, darling. How dare you!'

Kit sighed and sat at the table opposite her father. 'All right. Do nothing. Both of you preach about the help you can be. Write a couple of cheques and feel your promise has been kept.'

Lorraine leaned forward and placed her tea on the fender, shielding her face from the heat of the fire. 'Really Kitty. Even when you were younger you were impossible. Sometimes I wonder if there is anything of me in you at all.'

Tommy came back down, self-conscious, not seeking a chair but standing near the door, wondering whether he ought to be at attention until the next instruction. The colonel began puff-puffing again, the stem of the pipe between his teeth, his gaze on the bowl of tobacco. He then said, 'Think I'll smoke this outside. You ladies are a delicate species. Why not join me, young feller.'

The colonel left his chair, packed his baccy pouch away and ambled through the scullery to the small garden. Tommy paused, not believing what he had heard. Lorraine said, 'Oh for heaven's sake, young man, go. Pander to my husband. He does belong to the Corps of Colonels. One never knows what that crowd get up to.'

Tommy went, striding. He had never heard of the Corps of Colonels, but he was willing to learn.

Linda stared after him, then at her mother. Kit said, 'I think, when Tommy comes back in, you had better suggest he goes home.'

'Mummy,' Linda whispered. 'Can I go out with him tomorrow? It's his last day.'

Kit nodded, and Lorraine lifted her tea off the fender, her attitude one of pained resignation. 'My life,' she sighed delicately, 'seems to be made up of some sort of steeplechase. I really don't know how I cope.'

'You poor darling,' Kit smiled and, by supper time, Lorraine was triumphant. Kit was a little pleased, and Linda was aware her future was about to be settled. Mummy whispered it was up to Tommy if he wanted promotion during his six years of service.

The colonel succumbed to Bertie's chair, aware he would have difficulty lifting himself out of it, but Emma was curled on his lap, whispering that he smelled better than anyone else in the world.

Just after lunch on Friday the colonel tucked his wife into the front seat of the Bentley, kissed his daughter and granddaughters, then drove away, making for the Cotswolds.

Kit thought thank God that out of bad comes good. There would be little need for her to worry about Linda or Tommy now. With Linda in finishing school, and Tommy in China, the social strata of life would do the rest.

But in the meantime money was needed, money for Bertie's convalescence, and money to put in Linda's post-office book; the girl couldn't go away empty-handed, and the Unicorn Insurance Company seemed to have come to a standstill in Swansea.

Kit resolved to make a start.

On the Saturday a small advertisement appeared in the local evening newspaper: LADY CANVASSERS REQUIRED. COMMISSION ONLY. TRAINING GIVEN. HOURS TO SUIT. BOX 358.

Kit sent Linda to collect the replies the following Wednesday lunchtime and, on Thursday morning, she left Linda alone in the office while she went to call on each of the applicants.

On Friday morning the postman brought a picture postcard of the centre of Southampton town. It was addressed to Miss Linda Hemsworthy, and the message on the back was written in pencil. 'I will love you always.' There was no signature.

Linda went to her bedroom to cry.

Kit took the accounts to the kitchen and spread them on the table, her back to the fire. The clock ticked and the house seemed lonely and unusually silent. Bertie had gone. Tommy had gone. After Christmas Linda would also be gone. Kit bent to the figuring.

On Saturday the accounts were finished and posted. On Sunday Kit asked the Lord's forgiveness for working on His day, and had the six women in to learn something about insurance.

She didn't visit, nor contact Bertie.

Her canvassers began on Monday morning, together, so they could share their failures and successes, as well as eat faggots and peas in the tiny shop in High Street at Kit's expense.

Kit well remembered the trouble John had been in when he and Maggie had taken on a canvasser, but she was in a mood of rebellion and freedom.

At the end of the day she hurried home feeling wonderful, tired but content. She could do it. Today had proved she could expand this area. Build. Build.

She fed her two daughters, sent them to bed, then worked in the office until midnight.

She felt released. No one to please but herself. She stood in the centre of the office, laughed at the portrait of Claud Hobbs and stretched. She went to the middle room and plumped up the cushions. The place was dusty; her next ambition was to get a woman in as housekeeper.

She went back to the office and sat in Bertie's chair. She cocked her feet onto Bertie's desk, her heels on his beloved pink blotter. The note on the pad in Linda's handwriting said that, this morning, Mr Henderson-Hobbs had phoned. He was another who didn't seem to matter any more. Her fear of Head Office had gone. She could build this district. Double it. Treble it. She knew it. Women canvassers were being given business by other women who needed insurance. Bertie's job was safe. They would never shift him while the business kept pouring in. And women worked for next to nothing.

The following Friday while the great blue Head Office account sheet was spread over the kitchen table like a poor man's cloth, Kit counted rapidly on her fingers and the front bell jangled.

Today she felt rather tired. There had been moments when her thoughts turned to Bertie, and she was a little forlorn that he had not contacted her. No one had contacted her. Not even Maggie, while John had posted his accounts in.

The bell jangled again and she tidied her hair quickly,

whipped off her apron and flung it to a chair, and went to see who needed attention.

He smiled, confident he was welcome. 'Good afternoon, Mrs Hemsworthy.'

She hesitated, only a second. 'Good afternoon, Mr Henderson-Hobbs.'

For a moment she felt happiness, then a quiver of trepidation; had he heard of the canvassers and brought retribution?

'I assume your husband is in Bournemouth?'

'Bournemouth. Why should he – ?'

'The conference.' He leaned forward, towards her, his gaze wary. She wasn't reacting as he had expected.

'Oh?' Her eyes took on a sparkle, became a deeper amber, almost tan. 'The conference? Yes, of course.' Then, nervously, 'Would you care to come in?'

He carried no baggage, not even a briefcase. He apparently had no intention of staying.

She was very pleased to see him.

She took his hat and gloves, noticing the gleam of cleanliness and golden lights in his blond hair. She laughed into his eyes, and he laughed back, this man who looked like Bertie, yet had so much more in the way of style and breeding.

He and she stood in the narrow confines of the passage, and she was aware of the strong sense of intimacy, yet still he didn't touch her. He saw the office door was open and nodded to it. 'The inner sanctum?'

'Absolutely,' she laughed, and he went into it. She rushed past him and sat in Bertie's chair, at Bertie's desk, then smiled, embarrassed at her silly action. It was as if she had been protecting Bertie's empire.

Robert watched her whimsically, then gazed around. He grinned at his father's portrait and said, 'That flatters the old boy.'

She nodded, leaning forward onto the desk, as if to show she was the owner, and he said briskly. 'The accounts? They have been posted?'

'No. Not yet.'

'Who is responsible for doing them?'

'I am. We are.' She felt trapped, disillusioned. He had not come to see her while her husband was away; he was not seeking a clandestine affair. She said, 'I'm in the middle of doing them now. In the kitchen.'

He nodded again, as if humouring her eccentricity. 'Shall we see them?'

'Of course.' She felt nettled, and it sounded in her voice. So he was investigating the sudden flow of new business. 'Will you follow me?'

'Thank you.'

She hurried past the hallstand, asking herself if he had noticed Bertie's overcoat there. Would he wonder why Bertie was away without it?

She led him to where the fire glowed, the great black iron kettle sang, and her apron had slipped from the arm of the chair to the floor.

He ignored all that. He went straight to the table, to the account sheet, and bent over it. He didn't need his fingers to count. It was as if his brain held some sort of magic, and calculated easily. He glanced at the front of the sheet, flicked it over quickly and checked the centre and the back.

Kit stood aside and watched. Had she made a mistake? Was there anything that looked as if she was on the fiddle? What if he suspected dishonesty? Was he searching for a reason to sack Bertie? A sick sensation caught in the base of her chest, then she lifted her head indignantly. 'It is all correct. I am perfectly honest.'

He paused in his checking to look at her, then came the little nod again and a smile in his eyes. 'Of course, I had forgotten. Fraud is probably a touchy subject with you,' and he went back to checking.

She made tea, ham sandwiches, got fruit cake from the tin and put it on the one-legged glass stand. Emma came in, planning to spread her homework around and eat cake. She wriggled her nose and said, 'Hello.'

'Hello,' he returned. 'Am I in the way?'

'No.' She pushed her fringe back in dreadful exasperation. 'The accounts are always more important than we are.' She picked up her books again, tucking them in her satchel. 'I shall go upstairs. To my room. In the cold.'

'Put your coat back on,' Kit smiled. 'I'll call you when food is ready. You can have it upstairs.'

Linda came from her bedroom, peering over the banisters. 'Who is he?' she whispered, and Henderson-Hobbs rolled up the thick blue paper sheet and said, 'I shall retire to the office, Mrs Hemsworthy. I suspect I shall find it more compatible,' and Kit smiled at everyone as if she had no fears. Or dreams.

Kit gave him the keys to everything. Let him look. Let him pry.

When he had left, her children sat down to tea, their gaze now and again sliding to their mother. They had heard the whispered invitation, 'To the hotel, Kitten. I need to see you alone.'

Later that evening Linda and Emma were put in charge of the house, and Kit came down the stairs in a midnight blue velvet suit. The girls had seen it before, but they had never seen Mummy look like this.

She was glowing.

The jacket was tight-waisted, short, with a peplum. The skirt fitted to the thighs, then flared to the shins, swinging. A narrow coney fur covered her shoulders.

She checked her small black handbag and kissed her daughters. They made no sound, but their eyes were wide and curious.

'Be good, my darlings. I might be very late, so get yourselves off to bed,' and there was an air of fatalism everywhere.

She climbed into the back seat of the taxi, disappearing into the darkness, but still waving to her daughters as they watched from the lit office window, then she sat back, silently counting to ten, trying to breathe against the horrendous banging of her heart while the excited apprehension got worse.

The hotel frontage was brightly lit, the pavement looking unreal in the glare of electric lights. The commissionaire hurried to the taxi and opened the door for her, and she saw the sudden admiration and respect on his face. Her confidence soared.

She paid the driver with a hand that was steady, then the lights shimmered on the velvet, her narrow waist and swaying hips.

The driver and commissionaire exchanged glances, then parted, the taxi mingling with the greyness of High Street and the scent of pubs and clubs.

Kit was aware of it all as she went into the foyer, then stood, awaiting attention.

It came fast, the bellboy directing her to the lift, taking her up and silently sucking in the subtleness of her perfume.

She didn't need to seek Henderson-Hobbs' suite of rooms. The door was open and he stood there, waiting. Momentarily unnerved she paused in the corridor, while he appeared before her, his tuxedo immaculate, the pink satin jutting from his breast pocket; a man who knew how to dress and was worthy of fine tailoring.

He held out a hand and she went to him, then he guided her into the room. It wasn't much. Everything was somebody else's, had been used by many others, but there were roses on the round table with its beige lace cloth, and there were roses in a large vase on the floor beside the fireplace.

Kit gazed at Henderson-Hobbs and smiled. He, too, had made a special effort.

She allowed him to remove the coney fur, regretting its loss, yet her shoulders weren't naked. The blue velvet caressed her throat, held high with small gilt poppers.

'You look very beautiful,' he smiled, the fur over his arm. 'Even more than before.'

She had come to him, dressed to kill, and he was experienced enough to recognise the signals. The lady was willing.

The point of his tongue touched his bottom lip, and he put the fur in the bedroom then, leaving the door open so the bed was visible, he returned and suggested she sit on the deep settee.

Kit looked at the bed, at the roses, and at him, wondering what his approach would be; if she would resist. If, maybe, nothing at all would happen, Yet the hushed atmosphere of the room warned of intimacy.

'What would you like to drink?' His body was inclined slightly towards her, his face patient, the hunter afraid of pulling the trigger too soon.

She laughed. 'A cup of tea,' and he strolled to the bell pull.

'No!' she cried. 'No. I was joking,' but in that instant she learned a lot and her brain logged it away; a man will oblige all niceties before he takes a woman to bed.

She thought fleetingly of Bertie pleasing Elsie, of Elsie knowing more about men than she, Kit, a married woman, until now. 'It' was the power. Not good cooking, laundering, typing. Yet she had been taught to refuse 'it', not to co-operate.

'I'll have a whisky and lemonade,' she said, and undid the top poppers on her jacket.

Henderson-Hobbs gave a slow half smile, his green eyes warily speculative, and Kit began to feel supreme. Here was another challenge; he was in the palm of her hand. How long could she keep him there?

She went to the settee and sat comfortably. He brought her the drink. He sat opposite her and she crossed her knees, the sheer silk of her stockings glamorising the gentle curves of her legs. It had become a game, a game of catch me, and she was on the verge of enjoying it.

This man was not her husband, did not own or possess her; she had not religiously promised to love and obey him. The only hold was attraction. And she liked him. The ultimate aim was security. He could provide that.

She sipped, and became aware of the faint vibrations

surrounding them both. She said brightly, 'I haven't been in this hotel before.'

'Neither have I.' He smiled, then, 'You brought in a lot of new business this week.'

'Yes.'

'Did your husband canvass it alone? He doesn't appear to have any help.'

She uncrossed her knees and said simply, 'My husband hasn't gone to the conference. He is in hospital.' She watched him as he looked into his drink. She decided the evening was going to be a fiasco. She had been a fool to expect anything else. She said, 'He fell into the dock.'

Robert looked into her face and began to laugh. 'He did what?'

'Fell into the dock. Someone in your office sent a Mr Browne, with an E, a lapse notice, and my husband was on his way to rescind it.'

Robert sat back and crossed his ankles, still laughing. 'I take it he intended swimming to the policy-holder.'

'He fell in, and was dragged out, unconscious, with a broken arm and concussion.'

His laughter died away. 'Oh! I'm sorry!' Then he asked, 'How are you managing? I imagine he will be laid up for some time.'

'I took on six women canvassers last Monday. They're working for commission only. I got the idea from John Davies,' and when he made no comment she reminded him, 'He employed an Italian. Carruthers disallowed it.'

'And so Carruthers should. Davies has no authority to employ another in our name.'

'And I have?'

He paused, watching her, the smile hovering on his lips, then, 'Certainly you have.'

And Kit's business confidence grew. Casually she asked, 'Do you have plans for John Davies? I understand he came to see you.'

335

'He did, and no, no plans. Everything hinges on the outcome of the Bournemouth conference.'

'Shouldn't you be there?'

'I will be. This time tomorrow.'

Kit laid her head back. The tension had gone and some of the fear had gone with it.

He smiled. 'Will you dart away, Kitten, if I sit beside you? Shall I – ' he said softly, 'top up your glass?'

'With lemonade,' she agreed, and he obliged.

He sat beside her. 'I ordered supper for later on,' he said. 'I thought you might like it.'

She turned to him, appreciating him, and he put a hand to her face, his thumb caressing her lips. 'If I kiss you. Very gently. Will you scream?'

'How do I know?' she asked. 'Until you try.'

The small whimsical smile filled his eyes again and she leaned towards him.

'Mrs Hemsworthy,' he muttered. 'I think you are about to teach an old dog new tricks.'

'Mr Henderson-Hobbs,' she returned, 'this old cat has everything to learn, and no opportunity in which to learn it.'

He spent such a long time doing so little she thought she wasn't going to learn anything at all. She closed her eyes and his kisses remained light, only tasting, then she let him remove the blue velvet jacket, and his hands were warm, caressing her shoulders and neck above the lace straps of her petticoat.

'Mrs Hemsworthy – '

She opened her eyes quickly. 'Mr Henderson-Hobbs? Robert?'

'Are you so overwhelmed by my charm that you are too faint to move?'

She chuckled and closed her eyes again. She felt his mouth approach hers and she kissed him, her fingers against his throat, trailing and teasing. Mr Henderson-Hobbs wriggled closer, his thigh hot against hers.

His kisses became an embrace. He drew her to her

feet and she stepped out of the blue velvet skirt. Together they walked to the bedroom.

It was unlit, a gas fire flickering uselessly, and she gave the door a little push to close it, needing the darkness.

She lay on the bed as if preparing for a medical examination and heard him undress then, in the minute glow spread by the fire, he stared down at her.

'Kitten,' he breathed. 'I want to see you. All of you,' and her throat said a silent, 'No!'

He knelt beside the bed and his hands came to her thigh, unclipping the suspenders, slowly peeling the stocking down.

Kit lay watching him from lowered eyes, her heart tightening, 'Robert – '

'Ssh, my sweet.' He was smiling, removing the second stocking, looking at her bare legs. He kissed her insteps, then the gentle sweep of her shin, her knee, then her thigh.

She gasped and he paused, smiling up at her. He stood and leaned over her. 'Kitten.' His voice thickened, had an edge like sand. 'Don't be shy of me.' He bent and kissed her mouth while she lifted her face to him, her fingers moving to the soft strong warmth of his neck, rising, combing through the golden thickness of his hair.

She waited for her fantasies to come true, waited for the divine throbbing that would herald desire.

The tip of his tongue teased hers, then sped lightly in little kisses to her lace straps. 'I must see you. Love you.'

In the darkness she saw his eyes, the glint, and she heard his breathing change, became more aware of his eagerness to possess her.

'Robert – '

'Dearest . . . Dearest . . .' His right hand left her and reached for the bedside lamp. 'I must see you. Adore you.' He switched on the light and smiled into her eyes. His fingers touched her throat, caressing, preparing to undress her.

For moments Kit felt she couldn't breathe. There was

the dread of him seeing her ugliness, the sallowness of her flesh, then in dread, she swung from him. 'Robert! I'm sorry. I can't!'

There was a tortured lull, a shocked silence, then his hands clutched her, pulling her back onto the pillow. She stared up at him, wanting him, but dreading him suddenly despising her body, seeing its faults. Yet she hoped, fleetingly, that this could still be her dreams come true, this could still be making love, but she knew it wasn't. It was making lust.

She lay quite still, and he peeled her petticoat down. He saw the small breasts and she didn't move. She awaited the derision. He stared at the gentle swells and pink nipples before him and breathed, 'You are beautiful. Perfect.' And she didn't believe him.

He sensed the tautness of her and his gaze met hers as if he was trying to read into her soul. 'Kitten?'

'I'm sorry,' she whispered, and her eyes were damp with tears of mortification. She said the only thing that came to mind. 'I belong to Bertie.'

Robert waited, his lips apart, his naked chest heaving as he breathed, then he moved right away and sat on the edge of the bed.

Kit murmured, 'I am sorry. I suppose I am naturally frigid.' She didn't add, I am also sickeningly disappointed.

He stood up. 'Not naturally frigid, Kitten, just naturally scared.'

She looked away from him, her face hot, her body shivering, wishing he hadn't switched on the lamp. 'I'm sorry,' she repeated. 'So sorry.'

'I could end your husband's career,' he said quietly, and she moved away and sat on the other side of the bed, looking back at him. 'You do what you think is right. And I will do the same.'

She stood up, preparing to return to her skirt and jacket, and he gave a little laugh, almost a gurgle. 'Kitten, surely, inside that frightened woman there is a passion trying to get out.'

'I know,' Kit laughed sheepishly, and moved to the door. She noted that, naked, he looked even more like Bertie; two dangling arms ready to clutch, two legs with knobbly knees, a lot of flesh and a weapon that failed to fascinate her.

'Get dressed,' she smiled kindly. 'I like you better that way.'

He jerked his head ruefully. 'I said you would teach me new tricks. This, Kitten, is the newest trick of all.'

She left him to dress and she put on the velvet suit, then she sat on the settee with her shoulders bowed. Now her refusal was final she felt foolish and immature.

He came to her and kissed the back of her neck. 'My fault,' he said quietly. 'I rushed you. If I must lust after another man's wife, I must remember she isn't easy to catch.'

'Are all women like me?' She couldn't look at him.

'The nice ones are.'

He crossed to the bell pull and tugged three times. 'Supper,' he smiled. 'The signal to bring it.'

They ate in near silence and, when the cold chicken and salad was finished, he dabbed the serviette to his mouth and said, 'Kitten, Albert doesn't realise how fortunate he is.'

Kit moved a shoulder shyly.

He went on, 'Are you afraid I'll dismiss him?'

'Yes.'

'Yet you are so afraid of me that you would refuse again?'

'Probably.' She eyed him then, admiring the fact he had not lost his temper. She said, 'I take it you are a man of vast experience.'

'Not vast enough,' he replied and, half an hour later, she was home, drinking cocoa, wondering what would happen now.

She had to wait another week, then there came one of those long white envelopes with the Unicorn insignia on the back. She opened it feverishly.

It contained a statement, set out in the form of a circular.

It was bald.

'To all Managers:

The First conference of the Unicorn Insurance Company was held . . . It was agreed . . . Commission to managers to be raised by one percent . . . Commission to agents will remain unaltered . . . The basic salary of all managers will be dropped by five shillings.'

'Good God!' Kit exclaimed in the emptiness of the office. 'The rotters!'

'It is anticipated these measures will prove a greater incentive in the aim to increase all areas . . .'

Kit's gaze flew on, her lips moving as she silently read, her mind deriding, blah blah . . .

Then it came: – 'We are pleased to announce the promotion of the following men: – '

And there it was, among half a dozen others: 'Mr John Davies, of the Swansea District, will be opening up the Carmarthenshire area . . .'

Kit let her head sag into her hand. So John had got it. Maggie would be a manager's wife. But not in Swansea.

Thank God. Thank God. She ought to tell Bertie.

She was near to crying with relief; so many months of stress, of waiting, and here it was.

There was an end note from the chairman. He had visited all districts, and it was unlikely any further changes would be made in the foreseeable future . . .

The telephone rang. It was Maggie, panting. 'Kit! Oh cariad. My man got it. Would you believe? And he's out so I can't tell him till he comes in. My John! A manager . . .'

Maggie was crying and Kit wanted to cry with her, hug her and be friends into eternity. She said, 'Maggie. Let's have a party,' and while she said it she wondered if it was too soon, if the mourning of Maggie would prevent such frivolity.

'Oh Kit, lovely that would be. Oh duw duw . . .'

A pause, filled only with Maggie's panting, and Kit

reflected she must have run all down the mountainside to Sion the shop, to tell the Hemsworthys the news.

'I wish – I wish – ' Maggie was sobbing. 'I wish my baby – '

Kit didn't answer. She was grieved about the baby, grieved in so many ways, yet now his death seemed to have presaged the end of an era.

The end of Buckley intrusion.

She said tremulously, 'Right then, Maggie. We'll arrange a party. What about Christmas?' but her mind was shouting, 'I must see Bertie. Tell Bertie.'

Maggie went off the line, laughing yet still crying, and Kit called up the stairs, 'Linda? Darling? What are you doing?'

'Sorting my clothes.' Linda came to the top of the stairs, no longer sullen. 'Grandma said she wants a list of all I haven't got, then we'll go to London on a shopping spree.'

Kit leaned against the wall, wondering why she had allowed Bertie to lay down the law for so long, why she had let pride stand in the way of her daughter's future, preventing her from asking Lorraine for the help she so obviously loved giving.

She called up, 'I've had a rather important letter. I shall have to take it to the convalescent home – '

'Can I come?' Linda charged down the stairs.

'No darling, no. Daddy hasn't seen any of us since the day he fell in the – ' She began to giggle, a mixture of merriment, and a vision of the sometimes pompous Bertie falling in the dock, and horror that such rancour could have grown between them. 'You and Emma come with me this evening.'

The telephone jangled, demanding, and Kit almost flew to it, arm outstretched.

'Good morning, Mrs Hemsworthy,' he said, and she had to think. Was it Monday? Eleven o'clock? Heavens!

'Good morning, Mr Henderson-Hobbs. Isn't it a glorious morning?'

'Pouring with rain, actually.'

'Is it?' She glanced at the window and couldn't see the street for the wet cascading down the panes. 'So it is. I had forgotten. I've just read the letter from your office. The news, Maggie just telephoned. She's delighted. I'm so relieved.'

She stopped abruptly, confused; she had been out of control. 'I'm sorry,' she said. 'You must think me very silly.'

He waited for her words to die away completely before he said, 'Mrs Hemsworthy, you sound delightful. Warm and friendly.'

She laughed, her mouth wide. 'Mr Henderson-Hobbs, you are spiffing. Thank you for not sacking Bertie, for promoting John, for a lovely supper, for – for – '

'For?' he prompted.

'For being nice to me.'

There was a long silence before he said flatly, 'Goodbye, Mrs Hemsworthy. It has been an experience knowing you.'

'Thank you,' Kit said and, although the line went dead, she kept it against her ear, as if part of her longed for his voice to return. But, she told herself, it was as well, because she was Bertie's wife; she belonged to him, for ever and ever.

She telephoned for a taxi and powdered her nose. Speed seemed so important now. Maybe she was already too late.

She arrived at the gates of the convalescent home with spots of pink on either cheek, as if running a fever, and she walked hurriedly up the drive, a north wind cutting into her, whipping the rain into her face. Inside the building it was over-warm, cloistered, faint echoes sounding, and muted voices far away.

She had to ask which room her husband was in, and how to get there, but Bertie had seen her arrival. He stood at the end of the corridor, waiting, his striped pyjama legs beneath the dressing-gown as familiar as anything could ever be.

342

'Kit,' he called, to attract her attention, and the wind had buffeted her hat to one side while her face shone with rain and pleasure.

She waved the letter in greeting. 'Everything is all right. John has been promoted to Carmarthenshire. Lorraine is sending Linda to finishing school. Tommy's gone to China.'

She didn't get around to telling him about Big Tom Buckley and Maud Jeffries, because Bertie's good arm was strong, and his kiss was like old times. He whispered, 'Why in hell haven't you been to see me?'

'Why in hell haven't you written to me?'

'My right arm was broken.'

'You could have telephoned.'

His arm about her waist persuaded her into his room. 'I've been wanting to come home, but how could I when you didn't want me?'

She laughed at him. 'We'll just have to get used to the idea of not wanting each other, won't we?'

He shook his head slowly. 'I needed that dip in the dock. To cool my insanity.'

For a long while they stared at each other, each thinking things it seemed unnecessary to say.

'I can't stop loving Elsie, Kit.'

She shrugged, turning slightly from him. 'I might have a yen for Henderson-Hobbs for all you know.'

He smiled fleetingly. 'Sauce for the goose.'

They continued to stand for what seemed a long while, just looking at nothing, but each aware of the nearness of the other, each understanding a little more of what life can do.

Kit asked, 'Have they said anything about you coming home?'

'Nice word, isn't it? Home.'

'Have they?'

She turned to him then and looked into his eyes; they were clear, no longer surrounded by blue shadows. 'It looks as if the rest has done you good.'

'They think I need another week.'

'Then a week you shall have.'

He came to her and held her, then kissed the tip of her nose. 'Where's the money come from for all this. A private room – '

'You have a damn good wife, Albert Hemsworthy. She took on half a dozen canvassers and they are doing well. At the moment we owe her parents, but all will be repaid.'

'Lorraine? Head Office?' He was his old self, bristling indignation.

'Head Office has been to inspect, and Head Office approves.'

She coaxed him gently to the bed and he sat on it, then she pressed him back. For a moment he looked as if he was going to resist, but then he sighed and patted the narrow space beside him. 'I need a cuddle.'

'So do I,' Kit laughed softly, 'so move up a bit.' They lay together and Kit said quietly, 'Things are going to be different, Bertie. It's no longer YOUR house and YOUR job. It's our house and our job. We are partners; not possessor and possessed.'

'Good lor!' he sat up quickly, staring back at her. 'It has never been like that!'

Kit laughed indulgently. 'If you come home, you come home to me – '

And as she watched him nod, his face puzzled, she hoped the lesson she had learned from Henderson-Hobbs had been the right one: a man will oblige all the niceties before he takes a woman to bed.

THE END

THE PRICE OF LOVING

BY EDITH COURTNEY

She was young – too young for respectable Bertie Hemsworthy – and cheap, and brave, a 1930s Swansea slum kid desperately trying to make good.

She crashed into Bertie's life, with a vibrant gutter cheekiness, winning first a job, then a place in his heart, creating havoc in his arid middle-class marriage.

It was a love-affair that wouldn't go away, that ended in drama and tenderness and a caring passion that taught both Bertie and his wife what the meaning of love really was.

0 552 12719 1

SUSAN SALLIS

A SCATTERING OF DAISIES

THE DAFFODILS OF NEWENT

BLUEBELL WINDOWS

ROSEMARY FOR REMEMBRANCE

Will Rising had dragged himself from humble beginnings to his own small tailoring business in Gloucester – and on the way he'd fallen violently in love with Florence, refined, delicate, and wanting something better for her children.

March was the eldest girl, the least loved, the plain, unattractive one who, as the family grew, became more and more the household drudge. But March, a strange, intelligent, unhappy child, had inherited some of her mother's dreams. March Rising was determined to break out of the round of poverty and hard work, to find wealth, and love, and happiness.

The story of the Rising girls continues in The Daffodils of Newent and Bluebell Windows, finally reaching it's conclusion in Rosemary for Remembrance.

A Scattering of Daisies	0 552 12375 7
The Daffodils of Newent	0 552 12579 2
Bluebell Windows	0 552 12880 5
Rosemary for Remembrance	0 552 13136 9

CORGI BOOKS

DIANE PEARSON
THE SUMMER OF THE BARSHINSKEYS

'Although the story of the Barshinskeys, which became our story too, stretched over many summers and winters, that golden time of 1902 was when our strange involved relationship began, when our youthful longing for the exotic took a solid and restless hold upon us . . .'

It is at this enchanted moment that *The Summer of the Barshinskeys* begins. A beautifully told, compelling story that moves from a small Kentish village to London, and from war-torn St Petersburg to a Quaker relief unit in the Volga provinces. It is the unforgettable story of two families, one English, the other Russian, who form a lifetime pattern of friendship, passion, hatred, and love.

'An engrossing saga . . . she evokes rural England at the turn of the century with her sure and skilful touch'
Barbara Taylor Bradford

'The Russian section is reminiscent of Pasternak's *Doctor Zhivago*, horrifying yet hauntingly beautiful'
New York Tribune

0 552 12641 1

CORGI BOOKS

JILLY COOPER
RIDERS

'Sex and horses: who could ask for more?'
Sunday Telegraph

If you thought you knew what to expect of Jilly Cooper – bursts of restless romance, strings of domestic disasters, flip fun with the class system – RIDERS will come as a pleasurable surprise.

A multi-stranded love story, it tells of the lives of a tight circle of star riders who move from show to show, united by raging ambition, bitter rivalry and the terror of failure. The superheroes are Jake Lovell, a half-gipsy orphan who wears gold earrings, handles a horse – or a woman – with effortless skill, and is consumed with hatred for the promiscuous upper-class cad, Rupert Campbell-Black, who has no intention of being faithful to his wife, Helen, but is outraged when she runs away with another rider.

Set in the tense, heroic world of show-jumping, Jilly Cooper's novel moves from home-country gymkhanas through a riot of horsey events all over the world, culminating in the high drama of the Los Angeles Olympics.

'Blockbusting fiction at its best'
David Hughes, The Mail On Sunday

'I defy anyone not to enjoy her book. It is a delight from start to finish'
Auberon Waugh, Daily Mail

0 552 12486 9

CORGI BOOKS

THE LIVING SLEEP

BY KATE ROBERTS

When her husband suddenly deserts her, Lora Ffennig is forced to abandon her simple, peaceful existence and work to support herself and her two young children, Rhys and Derith. But Lora's problems are only beginning . . .

The Living Sleep is the story of how one woman's courage and fortitude enable her to overcome the problems of enforced independence and, finally, to discover a more genuine happiness.

0 552 11685 8

FEET IN CHAINS

BY KATE ROBERTS

Feet in Chains is the story of Jane and Ifan Gruffydd and their children. They live in a smallholding in the hills near Caernarfon. Ifan, like Kate Robert's father, is a 'quarryman-crofter'; their lives are dominated by the struggle to feed and clothe their family. The story begins in 1880 and ends during the First World War.

This book is the opposite of *How Green Was My Valley*. It is about slate, not coal. There is no sentiment, no garrulousness, and little of the warmth of the South Wales valley community. There is instead a strong sense of convention, a guardedness in social relations and an integrity born out of the struggle to survive.

0 552 11596 7

OPAL BY ELVI RHODES

Edgar Carson has returned from the trenches to find that the land fit for heroes didn't exist. The only nice thing that happened to him was OPAL, the small, tough, Yorkshire beauty who married him. But by the time the 20's came, Edgar was on the dole, and Opal was pregnant for the second time. Bitterness began to corrode Edgar's spirit.

But Opal was a fighter – she wasn't going to let the times, the drudgery, the poverty destroy her, or her family. She started with a 'house shop', just sweets and cotton reels sold from the top of her sideboard, and from then on she didn't stop – for Opal's dream was her own department store and a grand life for all of them . . .

0 552 12367 6

DOCTOR ROSE BY ELVI RHODES

To be a woman doctor in the 1920's was tough, especially if you worked in the Welfare Centre of an industrial Yorkshire town. Rose – who had the added disadvantage of being young and pretty – found she had to cope with elderly male prejudice from those above her, and apathetic ignorance and poverty from those she was trying to help.

DOCTOR ROSE, a new novel of Yorkshire from Elvi Rhodes.

0 552 12607 1

COPPER KINGDOM

BY IRIS GOWER

The Llewelyns lived in Copperman's Row – a small backstreet where the women fought a constant battle against the copper dust from the smelting works. When Mali's mam died there were just two of them left, Malia and her father, sacked from the works for taking time off to nurse his wife. Mali felt she would never hate anyone as much as she hated Sterling Richardson, the young master of the Welsh copper town.

But Sterling had his own problems – bad ones – and not least was the memory of the young green-eyed girl who has spat hatred at him on the day of her mother's death.

COPPER KINGDOM is the first in a sequence of novels set in the South Wales copper industry at the turn of the century.

0 552 12387 0

PROUD MARY

BY IRIS GOWER

Mary Jenkins had dragged herself up from humble beginnings – first to be overseer in the Canal St laundry, then to running her own market stall in Sweyn's Eye. But constantly fate – and the Sutton brothers – knocked her down again.

Dean Sutton was prepared to set her up in a shop of her own – but only at his price – while Brandon Sutton threatened to destroy her with a love neither of them could control.

But Mary – Proud Mary – was a fighter, determined to win whatever the odds, however great the sacrifice.

PROUD MARY is the second of Iris Gower's sequence of novels set in the Welsh town of Sweyn's Eye at the turn of century.

0 552 12637 3

A SELECTED LIST OF NOVELS AVAILABLE FROM CORGI BOOKS

THE PRICES SHOWN BELOW WERE CORRECT AT THE TIME OF GOING TO PRESS. HOWEVER TRANSWORLD PUBLISHERS RESERVE THE RIGHT TO SHOW NEW RETAIL PRICES ON COVERS WHICH MAY DIFFER FROM THOSE PREVIOUSLY ADVERTISED IN THE TEXT OR ELSEWHERE.

☐ 12719 1	The Price of Loving	Edith Courtney	£2.50
☐ 12638 1	Spinners' Wharf	Iris Gower	£2.95
☐ 12637 3	Proud Mary	Iris Gower	£2.95
☐ 12387 0	Copper Kingdom	Iris Gower	£2.50
☐ 12565 2	Last Year's Nightingale	Claire Lorrimer	£3.50
☐ 10584 8	Mavreen	Claire Lorrimer	£3.95
☐ 11207 0	Tamarisk	Claire Lorrimer	£2.95
☐ 11726 9	Chantal	Claire Lorrimer	£2.95
☐ 12182 7	The Wilderling	Claire Lorrimer	£3.50
☐ 11959 8	The Chatelaine	Claire Lorrimer	£3.50
☐ 10249 0	Bride of Tancred	Diane Pearson	£1.95
☐ 10375 6	Csardas	Diane Pearson	£3.95
☐ 10271 7	The Marigold Field	Diane Pearson	£2.50
☐ 09140 5	Sarah Whitman	Diane Pearson	£2.95
☐ 12641 1	The Summer of the Barshinskeys	Diane Pearson	£2.95
☐ 12607 1	Doctor Rose	Elvi Rhodes	£1.95
☐ 12803 1	Ruth Appleby	Elvi Rhodes	£2.95
☐ 12367 6	Opal	Elvi Rhodes	£2.50
☐ 11596 7	Feet in Chains	Kate Roberts	£1.95
☐ 11685 8	The Living Sleep	Kate Roberts	£2.50
☐ 12579 2	The Daffodils of Newent	Susan Sallis	£2.50
☐ 12375 7	A Scattering of Daisies	Susan Sallis	£2.75
☐ 12880 5	Bluebell Windows	Susan Sallis	£2.50
☐ 13136 9	Rosemary For Remembrance	Susan Sallis	£2.95

All Corgi/Bantam Books are available at your bookshop or newsagent, or can be ordered from the following address:
Corgi/Bantam Books,
Cash Sales Department,
P.O. Box 11, Falmouth, Cornwall TR10 9EN

Please send a cheque or postal order (no currency) and allow 60p for postage and packing for the first book plus 25p for the second book and 15p for each additional book ordered up to a maximum charge of £1.90 in UK.

B.F.P.O. customers please allow 60p for the first book, 25p for the second book plus 15p per copy for the next 7 books, thereafter 9p per book.

Overseas customers, including Eire, please allow £1.25 for postage and packing for the first book, 75p for the second book, and 28p for each subsequent title ordered.

NAME (Block Letters) ....

ADDRESS ....

....